Murder at the Theatre Royal

An Inspector Warren Mystery

By Albert Clack

Copyright © 2015 by Albert Clack

ACKNOWLEDGMENTS

Heartfelt thanks for reading the first draft and providing constructive criticism to my former Reuters colleague Chris Peterson and my actress friend Samantha Powell. Thanks also to my solicitor friend Barbara Hecht for her advice on legal procedures; to retired Metropolitan Police officer Edward Deans for help with police procedure; to the charity DogLost for information about dognapping; and to theatre director Scott Ellis for casting me as Polonius in Hamlet. Above all, big hugs to my wonderful wife Fazilet for encouraging me to keep going whenever I felt like giving up.

SATURDAY 14 JUNE 2014

1

Sir Roger Nutley stood in front of the full-length mirror in the Number One dressing-room of the Theatre Royal, North London, reflecting on how wonderful it felt to be working again. Even though he had not been convicted, his trial two years earlier for alleged rape and sexual assault had resulted in ostracism and unemployment. The tabloid newspapers had made his life hell because of something that was alleged to have happened almost half-a-century ago.

Meticulously he checked his costume, as he always did. To be honest, there was not much that could go wrong with this particular outfit; but he was an old-school professional, and he knew that attention to detail before stepping out in front of the public was important.

While he was examining himself in the mirror, the backstage tannoy high on the dressing-room wall spoke in the crisp, well-articulated Yorkshire tones of Fiona Holland, the visiting touring company's Stage Manager: "Ladies and gentlemen, this is your fifteen-minute call."

Sir Roger locked his dressing-room door, sat down opposite the mirror, took out a blue-and-white j-cloth from his make-up bag, and carefully wiped a small area of the surface in front of him. Then he returned the cloth to the bag and took out a clean, white handkerchief, a playing card, a cardboard packet of plastic drinking straws, and a small plastic grip-seal baggy.

He removed a straw from the box, unsealed the top edge of the baggy and poured a small quantity of fine, white powder on to the cleaned area. Using the playing-card, he deftly rearranged the powder into two neat little lines.

Holding his right nostril closed with his index-finger, he picked up the straw, leaned forward and inserted one end into his left nostril. Then he lowered the other end to one of the lines, sniffed and slid the straw along, snorting until the whole line was up his nose. He repeated the operation with his right nostril.

Within seconds, a rush of energy swept through his brain. He felt completely energised, as if he could sprint a mile while singing at the top of his voice. Along with the euphoria came a sense of incredible mental clarity. He packed away his cocaine paraphernalia, leaned back, and relaxed.

"Ladies and gentlemen, this is your beginners' call. Sir Roger Nutley, Mr Dean and Ms Comerford to the stage please."

Jason Dean was playing the much younger lead role of Hamlet, Sir Roger was Polonius, and Claire Comerford was Queen Gertrude.

Sir Roger walked along the corridor and opened the door marked Stage Left. He was always early; another old-hand practice.

Claire Comerford came into the darkened wing a moment later and whispered to him: "Here we go for another flaming row with my bloody son, then."

"You should have brought him up better," Sir Roger whispered back with a playful grin.

There was an enthusiastic hubbub from the auditorium as the audience settled into their seats for the second half. The passionate cadences of Rachmaninov's Prelude No 2 in B Flat Major were warming the public up over the theatre's sound system for the continuation of Shakespeare's Danish tragedy.

"They're a good lot this afternoon," whispered Claire.

"I always like matinee audiences," said Sir Roger. "They know how to enjoy themselves."

The music ended, the house lights were extinguished, the stage was flooded with light, and the curtains parted.

Just a few seconds before striding purposefully on to the stage, Claire totally took on her character of Queen Gertrude. She was followed immediately by Sir Roger as the courtier Polonius, delivering the opening lines with compelling urgency. "He will come straight. Look you lay home to him." To which Gertrude, hearing Hamlet approaching, replied, "I'll warrant you, fear me not. Withdraw, I hear him coming." Polonius walked upstage and slipped behind a heavy curtain to eavesdrop unseen on the conversation between the Queen and her son, Prince Hamlet.

Jason stepped on from the opposite wing, asking: "Now mother, what's the matter?" The argument between Hamlet and Gertrude swiftly escalated to the point where Gertrude protested: "Thou wilt not murder me? Help, ho!" This so alarmed the concealed Polonius that he cried out: "What, ho, help!"

Hamlet, thinking that the hidden eavesdropper was his uncle, Claudius, against whom he had vowed revenge, stabbed the curtain with his sword. He knew that Sir Roger would be standing well back. Polonius, still out of sight, gasped: "Oh, I am slain!" Gertrude, shocked, turned on her son: "Oh, me, what hast thou done?"

From behind the curtain, Sir Roger uttered a further, muted cry and an unpleasant gurgling sound, and there was an audible thud as the dying Polonius fell to the floor out of sight. 'The old goat made rather a noisy meal of that tonight,' thought Claire, uncharitably.

Hamlet pulled the curtain aside and began dragging the inert Polonius out on to the stage. Then he realised to his horror that Sir Roger's head was hanging limply at a bizarre angle from his neck. Jason dropped the body and cried out, "Oh, my God! He's been murdered."

Claire Comerford, who was facing the audience and thus could not see the lolling head, thought Jason had dried, and stepped in with an improvisation: "Of course he has, my prince, and that by thee."

But by now the audience, too, were gasping with horror.

"No," shouted Jason, "I mean he's really dead. His neck's broken." He turned to Fiona at the control board, offstage left, and called: "For Christ's sake - curtain!"

2

A black Audi Q7 with 2014 number plates and heavily tinted windows cruised along Norton Broadway at a sedate 25mph, passing some of the most expensive luxury goods shops in north London. There were four men on board, all wearing plain, black overalls and black industrial boots. They were powerfully built and had shaven heads. One was in the seat beside the driver, two in the rear.

If they had been walking along the pavement, the group of burly, t-shirted men would have stood out like a triple-decker bacon and pork sandwich at a Bar Mitzvah, because Norton Broadway was the focus of retail therapy among the well-off, well-dressed Jewish ladies of Norton Green.

As it was, the status symbol large SUV went entirely unremarked as it cruised past the reinforced plate-glass display window of a boutique called Bags of Fun. The driver kept his gaze straight ahead to avoid any hint of suspicion.

The boutique was located 150 yards south of a minor road junction, where a quiet, residential street of terraced houses emerged on to the Broadway at right-angles. The driver noted that the double yellow line was being dutifully respected by the law-abiding citizenry, so the kerbside was clear in front of Bags on Fun and on either side. His passengers scoured the street for any sign of a police presence, either on foot or in parked vehicles. They confirmed to each other that the coast was clear.

A quarter of a mile further south, the car turned right into another street of terraced houses, then took two more right turns to bring the Q7 back round to the Broadway. The driver paused momentarily until there were gaps in the traffic both ways, then turned right again and pulled up outside Bags of Fun. The four men donned matching motorcycle helmets and pulled down the heavily tinted visors.

The gang burst out of the car and rushed in through the shop's open door; the driver first, holding an axe, while the man who had been sitting beside him brandished a sawn-off double-barrelled shotgun. The two men who leapt out of the rear of the car were unarmed.

Inside the shop, a woman in her mid-fifties, with blonde hair in its mid-twenties, had been examining a pink, padded handbag bearing the back-to-back linked letter Cs of Chanel. She cowered against a side wall, dangling the bag loosely by her side. A slim female assistant in her early twenties, smartly turned out in navy-blue suit and white blouse, stood motionless behind the counter. None of the gang said a word. Neither of the women screamed, for their throats had dried from fear. Behind a rear door with a small two-way mirror set into it, the shop's owner, Zev Mendelsohn, dialled 999.

The man with the gun remained menacingly inside the doorway. The one with the axe smashed open ten locked glass cabinets. The two others moved rapidly around picking up handbags and skilfully looping the handles over their forearms until they each had six bulging on either side. The axe-man grabbed another half-dozen.

The assistant, Zoe Mendelsohn, who was the owner's daughter, mentally noted that they had obviously done their homework. They were grabbing the most expensive bags without having to look twice: limited editions by designers such as Chanel, Hermes, Birkin, Kelly, Christian Louboutin, and Alexander McQueen.

Zoe recovered her senses, decided enough was enough, and pressed a button under the counter. Acrid smoke billowed into the shop from both sides and the alarm began shrieking. The man with the gun fired a warning shot high into a wall, away from the women. The report was deafening in the confined space.

Still without a word, the gang strode back out into the street, piled into the Q7, and the huge car streaked away. Twenty-seven minutes passed before the police armed response team arrived on the scene.

3

Fiona Holland had witnessed countless murders during her 22 years as a stage manager, but on all previous occasions the victim had stood up as soon as the curtain came down, and walked back to his or her dressing-room unharmed.

Now she was quick to perceive that something had gone so seriously wrong that the performance would not be able to continue. From her seat in darkness at the control panel in the wings left of downstage she began issuing authoritative instructions via the microphone in front of her.

"Lighting to blackout," she ordered, and the stage was plunged into darkness.

There was a mounting hubbub among the public in the auditorium.

The tannoy was inaudible on the stage, so Fiona turned to her right and shouted across: "Jason and Claire, stand well back, I'm going to show them the iron. Do you hear?"

The actor and actress who had been playing Hamlet and Gertrude both called back, "Yes."

Fiona again spoke into the microphone: "Lower the iron, I repeat, lower the iron."

Amid a grinding of gear-wheels above the proscenium arch, the safety curtain descended until it touched the front of the stage. Nowadays it was made of thick fibreglass, but by tradition it was still referred to as the iron.

The door from the backstage corridor swung open and shut, and Ivan Strange, the Manager of the Theatre Royal, strode across the dark wing space to confront Fiona. At 70, he ought normally perhaps to have retired; but he and his wife didn't fancy downsizing their lifestyle for so long as he could hang on to the job, and Norton Borough Council, which owned the venue, had been content with his management over the past thirty-odd years and saw no reason to rock the boat for the time being.

"What the hell's going on?" he demanded.

Without turning away from the control panel, Fiona replied, "Roger Nutley's dead. I think he's been murdered."

"You mean really dead?"

"As the proverbial doornail. Call the police. I'm going to make an announcement."

Strange stood rooted to the spot.

"Well, go on, man, get on with it," said Fiona.

"Right, I'll call the police."

Strange swept back out to the corridor.

Fiona flicked a switch to make her microphone audible everywhere, including to the public in the auditorium, which had become a cauldron of noise and alarm.

"Ladies and gentlemen, your attention please." She

waited a few seconds, and the hubbub subsided. "As you are aware, a very serious accident has occurred on the stage. Unfortunately this means that we shall not be able to continue with this afternoon's performance." Using her initiative, she jumped ahead of reality and went on, "The police are on their way to the theatre, and they have asked for your cooperation. There is no danger, but nobody should leave the theatre until the police have advised us that it is all right to do so." Fiona flicked off the public address switch and the hubbub roared back into life on the other side of the safety curtain.

There were now raised voices from the corridor behind the stage, where most of the cast had gathered. They had been dissuaded by Ivan Strange from venturing into the wings. Fiona flicked another switch to activate the backstage tannoy.

"Full cast to dressing-rooms or green room, please, and remain there until further notice. I repeat, all cast to return to their dressing-rooms immediately." Then she added: "This is an instruction from Mr Spiller." It wasn't, but Daniel Spiller was not the sort of man whose instructions actors disobeyed, at least if they ever wanted to work again in one of his prestigious productions. He usually paid better than the Equity minimum; and who was to know she hadn't already made a quick phone call to him?

Claire Comerford called from somewhere on the stage: "Fiona, darling, could we have a bit of light, please? We're a bit sort of stuck here and we don't want to trip over anything."

Good grief, Fiona realised, those two are still out there in the dark with the corpse. Flicking the switch for crew instructions, she said, "Stage lights back on, please." Nothing happened. "Hello, lighting, is anybody there?"

More silence, then an apologetic male voice in her headphones: "Sorry, love, here now. What was it you wanted?"

"Stage lights, please."

"Okay, here you go."

The stage became illuminated, revealing two distressed-looking actors standing a few feet apart, and the corpse of Sir Roger Nutley lying near them.

"Thanks," called Jason. "We'll head off to our

dressing-rooms, then."

"Hang on," said Fiona, thinking on the hop. "I think it might be better if you two stayed up here. You're the only witnesses."

"Didn't see a thing until I'd dragged him into view," said Jason.

"I'm not staying here with a dead body," said Claire, heading for the stage-right wing.

"I think it's what the police would expect."

"Fiona's probably right," said Jason.

Claire stopped in the corner downstage right, as far away from the corpse as she could be, and sat cross-legged on the floor. She might be 53, but she practised yoga regularly and was suppler than plenty of women half her age. "Then I hope they arrive soon," she said.

Jason went and sat next to her. He considered venturing a consoling arm around her shoulders, but thought better of it.

Ivan Strange reappeared in the wing behind Fiona. "The police are on their way," he said.

"Have you had the stage door locked?" she asked.

"Do you think I should?"

"If the murderer's still here we don't want him slipping out, do we?"

"I'll see to it." He rushed off again.

Fiona now called Daniel Spiller on his mobile phone. She knew he was working at his costume warehouse near Lewes in Sussex this afternoon. She told him in three concise sentences what had happened.

"I'm on my way," he snapped. "Tell the cast to stay in their dressing-rooms unless the police say otherwise. Tell them that's a direct order from me."

Fiona Holland had not been Daniel Spiller's closest lieutenant for the past 22 years for nothing.

4

Bob Brannigan washed out his tea mug and turned to see whether Archie had eaten up his mid-afternoon meal. The handsome two-year-old Golden Retriever had become Bob's best friend since he had retired from the force three years ago and his wife, June, had died of cancer four months later. The dog was licking around the remaining crumbs in his bowl. He looked up at Bob expectantly. They had a routine for this time of day.

Bob picked up his Daily Telegraph from the kitchen table, went into the hallway and took Archie's leash down from a coat-hook on the wall. The dog came bounding towards him. Bob clipped the leash on to Archie's collar, opened the front door, and led the dog down the four steps on to the pavement, where he turned right towards the little park at the end of the street.

He took Archie for daily, longer walks across Norton Common first thing in the morning, and mid-evening. These afternoon outings were for socialising, both human and canine.

A few moments later, he was opening a gate. It led into an enclosed rectangle of grass, trees, flower-beds, and a central, raised, gritted, circular area with four wooden benches facing inwards. A sign on the gate said: 'London Borough of Norton. Welcome to Fernhill Road Gardens. Opening hours 8am to dusk daily.' Archie's arrival was greeted with a chorus of excited barking, with which the Retriever joined in. Bob walked him on the leash to the raised area, where another man in his fifties, sitting on the northeast-facing bench, looked up from the Times crossword.

"Afternoon, Bob. Turned out nice again."

"Looks set fair, so they said."

Before sitting down next to his casual friend Grant Sturman, Bob unclipped Archie's leash, and the dog bounded joyfully away to play. Bob glanced around the little park to see what other regulars were there. On the grassy area to the rear of the bench a middle-aged woman, Anne Golding, was throwing a tennis ball for two border collies, Max and Sasha, who repeatedly raced to reach it first and bring it back to her. Beyond her, in the southwestern corner, a tall, skinny youth in a dark blue baseball cap, plain grey tee-shirt, jeans and trainers, sat reading a paperback book on a bench in the shade of the low-hanging branches of a mature sugar maple tree. The youth was partly masked from view by a concrete war memorial. A woman whom Bob immediately clocked as a nanny or au pair came in through the gate pushing a toddler in a small, folding McLaren buggy. She began walking along the concrete path that led all around the outer edge of the rectangle. Bob sat down next to Grant and placed his Telegraph on the bench between them, and Grant did the same with his folded Times, in a tacit mutual signal that conversation would be in order before crossword-doing and reading resumed. On the other grassy area covering most of the northern half of the square, they watched Archie playing chase with Grant's grey Staffy bitch, Milly, and two little Yorkies. The Yorkies belonged to an older woman, in her seventies, Grace Milford, who was at this moment walking back towards the benches in the middle from the northeastern corner. She had just placed one of her dog's poops in the bin provided.

As she approached, she called out in an accent so posh that it resembled the Queen's, "Good afternoon, Bob. It's quite a beautiful day, isn't it?"

"Just right for doing nothing."

"I think you've got the right idea there."

Grace sat down on the bench to the right of Bob and Grant, the one facing northwest, where she had left a hardcover book lying. For the time being she, too, preferred to watch Archie, Milly and her Yorkies, Coco and Lily, as the dogs gave a lesson in how to enjoy the carefree life. The two south-facing benches were unoccupied, although some more regulars would no doubt be arriving soon.

"What do you think of England's chances?" asked Grant.

"You mean tonight against the Italians or getting through to the knockout stage?" replied Bob.

"Well, both."

"Could go either way against Italy. It's a tough one to

start with. But I reckon we should see off Uruguay easy enough, and definitely Costa Rica, so we'll go through all right."

"Wish I was as optimistic as you. Have you had a bet on who'll win the cup?"

"Twenty quid on Brazil. How about you?"

"Same on the Germans. They're like a machine."

"People always say that. I wouldn't bet on it. Oh, but you already have."

"Brazil have got all their eggs in one striker, if you'll forgive the mixed metaphor."

"I know, but Brazil are on their home territory. Gotta be the favourites, mate."

The Yorkies began running around Milly in circles, and Archie, tired of this, trotted past Bob's bench to join in the fun with the border collies in the other half of the park.

Anne Golding sat down next to Grace, holding a soggy tennis ball.

"They're happy running around with Archie now," she said in her working-class London accent, "so I think I deserve a rest."

They picked up their newspapers, Bob to read the sports pages first, Grant to continue with the crossword. With the day growing warmer, and the birdsong and happy dog noises around him, Bob felt as content as was possible while he was still missing June and trying to adjust to retirement from the job which had given the other half of meaning to his life. Alone and having failed to find an alternative occupation that would satisfy his fidgetiness, he felt sorry that their marriage had not been blessed with children; a regret that had not affected him while he had still been working and June had still been alive. He looked up and noticed that the collies were now running around with Milly and the Yorkies on the grass in front of him. He twisted around to look behind him to see what Archie was up to, but there was no sign of the Golden Retriever, so he stood up to look around. He couldn't see him anywhere.

"Anybody seen Archie?" he asked Grant, Grace and Anne. They all looked around them.

"He was with Max and Sasha," said Anne.

"I know, but I can't see him anywhere."

"He'll be in among the trees," said Grant.

"I hope so," said Bob, anxiety creeping into his voice.

The only other people in the park now were the young woman and the toddler. She was sitting on a bench in the southeastern corner, and the child was trotting about in front of her. Bob strode rapidly over to her.

"Excuse me," he said, "but did you see where my dog went?"

"Which dog is yours?" she replied in what sounded to Bob like an east European accent.

"The Golden Retriever."

"It is the big one with the light colour hair? The beautiful one?"

"That's it. His name's Archie."

"He is yours? I thought he was with the other man."

"What other man?" Panic creeping in now.

"The one who was sitting over there." She pointed towards the bench behind the war memorial, now vacant. "He go out with him."

"What, you mean my dog followed this man out into the street?"

"No follow. The man stroke him, and put, how you say, like string on collar to take him."

"He put a lead on him?"

"Yes, lead."

"Oh, my God. Thank you."

He shouted across to the others, "Archie's been stolen," and ran out through the gate. The quiet, residential street was deserted, and there was no sign of Archie or the man in the baseball cap.

Retired Detective Chief Inspector Bob Brannigan, who had toughed out a lot of very nasty situations during his thirty years in the Metropolitan Police, felt tears welling up as he pulled out his mobile phone and called his old boss, Superintendent James Astbury, at Norton Hill Police Station.

5

At his warehouse in a converted farm outbuilding about ten miles northeast of Brighton, Daniel Spiller told his costumière, Monika Rybczynski, that an urgent crisis had arisen in the production of Hamlet which was currently playing in the Theatre Royal North London. He said he needed to go and attend to it in person immediately, and that they would have to postpone until Monday their preliminary discussion of costumes for next year's touring Shakespeare production, Twelfth Night. He grabbed the jacket of his lightweight linen suit, which had seen better days, and carried it over his shoulder, climbed swiftly into his battered old black Range Rover, and manoeuvred it across the cracked tarmac of the farm quadrangle, down the dusty approach track, and on to the narrow B-road which would take him to the A27. Much as he felt guilty for doing so, he was already wondering how the hell he was going to salvage the rest of the Hamlet tour, on which the survival of his business and the lovely old theatre he owned in Brighton depended. He tried to remember whether anything in his insurance policies covered him against his big-name star being murdered. He thumbed through his vast mental card-index of experienced older actors who might have played Polonius relatively recently. He needed someone who would be able to recall the lines quickly and be flexible enough to step into Roger Nutley's shoes after just a few days of rehearsal. One thing was certain: he was going to lose all next week's performances at the Festival Theatre in Malvern, which was almost fully booked - dammit.

On the M23 he used his hands-free phone to call his regular freelance casting director and occasional drinking chum, Sebastian Pickles. Without mentioning the murder, he asked him if he could suggest a Polonius who could be slotted in at short notice; preferably one with a name that audiences would recognise.

"Don't tell me the soap star's flounced out. I did warn you."

"Not exactly. I'll fill you in later; but what do you think?"

"A couple of possibles spring to mind. I'll get back to you."

"Tomorrow, please; or even tonight, if you can. I need to take some tough decisions, fast."

"Leave it with me."

He was making good time, and if he swung all the way around the M25 rather than driving through central London, he ought to be in Norton Hill in about an hour and twenty minutes. He thought about phoning the theatre in Malvern with the bad news, but decided to wait until he'd got the full story from the police on the spot. No doubt someone down there in Worcestershire would see the news on the telly, anyway. They wouldn't be pleased; but he could hardly be expected to have foreseen that his star would be murdered in mid-tour.

*

Ivan Strange made his way down two long, steep, narrow flights of stairs to the pentagonal rear hallway where the stage doorkeeper, Paula Gregory, was sitting in her booth behind a sliding glass panel above a counter with two clipboards on it. She was reading the World Cup football coverage in the Daily Mail. Yesterday, Holland had provided the first shock result of the tournament in Brazil, by thrashing Spain, the reigning champions, 5-1, in what the paper described as revenge for the 2010 final. She looked up, saw Strange, and slid the panel open.

"Is the stage door open?" asked Strange.

"Well, it's not locked."

"Lock it, please. Nobody's allowed to leave the building until the police say so."

Paula propelled her wheelchair, using her hands to push the tops of the big side-wheels, out of the doorkeeper's cabin and around Ivan Strange to the outer door. She was a big woman, amply filling her custom-built tall-backed chair. But she kept up her femininity in defiance of her disability by wearing good make-up, dying her hair auburn, and wearing a voluminous, sea-green kaftan-type dress which tastefully concealed any lumpiness beneath it. The only concession to practicality over style was a pair of trainers, and even they had a matching green designer tick over their white background.

"Just a matter of slipping the latch," she said.

There was a ramp outside the door for her to get in and out in her chair. The rest of the rambling backstage part of the theatre was inaccessible for a wheelchair user, with too many stairs.

"I need you to lock the deadlock as well, otherwise you're just stopping people from coming in, not getting out."

"Oh, yes, sorry," she said, and propelled herself back to the little cabin, plucked the appropriate key off a hook on a board, re-emerged and locked the outer door properly. "If there's no show tonight, do you want me to stay here?" she asked.

"I'm afraid so. Everybody has to wait for the police."

"No problem." She went back to reading her newspaper.

Ivan Strange set off towards the dressing-rooms, then had an afterthought and turned to ask her: "Has anybody come in or gone out since the interval?"

"Not a soul."

"Sure? Nobody at all?"

"Definitely. What shall I do if anybody rings the bell wanting to come in?"

Strange thought for a moment: "Send them round the outside to front-of-house."

*

November Foxtrot 23 raced into Castle Street, Norton Hill, and halted on the double yellow line outside the main entrance to the Theatre Royal. Three uniformed policemen, Sergeant Neville Quigley and Constables Neil Caborn and Andy Jasper, leapt out of the car, ran up the four broad steps, pushed open the heavy glass double doors and swept into the foyer.

The facade of the theatre would have been an unprepossessing brick wall studded by tall sash windows, were it not for the imposing Roman-style arch above the main entrance, formed of alternate blue and maroon stones. Its appearance betrayed its original purpose, the building having opened in 1865 as the Norton Hill Corn Exchange. In 1913 it was refitted and renamed The Norton Variety House, functioning as both a music hall and a cinema, the latter usage becoming prevalent as time passed. In 1940 it suffered damage to a rear corner during a German air raid. In 1947 the town council began refitting it as a theatre. The damaged corner, which was at the lowest level of the slope where the building had been constructed, was expanded to accommodate the Green Room and part of the workshop above it. It was formally opened in 1948 by a member of the Royal Family, and thus gained its present name. The auditorium had been refurbished with larger, more comfortable seats, paid for largely out of a National Lottery grant, in 2007.

The only person in the foyer was a young woman, Rebecca Bunting. She had been stowing away the unsold refreshments behind the bar when she heard an uproar from the audience. She walked across to the nearest entrance to the back stalls, saw the safety curtain being lowered and heard Fiona Holland's announcement. She had not seen the corpse of Sir Roger Nutley being dragged from behind the curtain. She was now back behind the bar, looking anxious.

"What's going on?" she asked the three policemen.

"We were called to an incident on the stage," said Sergeant Quigley. "How do we get there?"

"Well," began Rebecca, "you really need to go back out and around to the stage door."

"There must be a way through," said Quigley, impatiently. "Show me."

"I can't leave the till," protested Rebecca.

"We'll take care of that." He turned to Andy Jasper: "Stay here and make sure nobody comes in or goes out."

Jasper took up a position in the centre of the foyer half-way between the outer doors, the doors at the back of the stalls, and the foot of the stairs that led up to the Circle.

Rebecca led Quigley and Caborn to a door marked 'Private – Staff Only' leading off the side of the foyer. She punched a six-figure code into a combination lock and pushed the door open. She led them along a plain, grey-painted corridor with three downward flights of five steps spaced along it, then punched in the code on another door at the far end. This brought them backstage. To Quigley, into whose private life, dominated by kids, telly and Tottenham Hotspur, thespian activities had never intruded, this immediately felt like menacing and unfamiliar territory. It was a situation guaranteed to bring out the aggressive attitude that had prevented him, for the past eighteen years, from rising any higher in rank. They emerged into the rear hallway inside the stage door, where Paula Gregory looked up from her newspaper.

"How do we get to the stage?" demanded Quigley.

"Up there," said Paula, pointing to the steep, narrow staircase down which Ivan Strange had come from the stage a few moments ago. The three policemen bounded upstairs, followed by Rebecca Bunting. They found themselves in a large, workshop-like area containing gantries, a variety of period items of furniture, bits of costume on hangers for quick changes, and a lot of other mechanical-looking gear. The only person in sight was a middle-aged man wearing black overalls, headphones, and with a tiny radio microphone in front of his cheek.

"Who are you?" asked Quigley, unceremoniously.

"Mike Moore," answered the overalled man. "Stage Manager. I'll show you where you need to go." He sounded brisk and efficient.

"I need to get back to front-of-house," said Rebecca. "The ushers have all gone in with the audience to calm people down." She sped off downstairs.

"Walk this way," said Mike Moore. Quigley and Caborn followed him to the far end of the big workshop, where they turned right, crossed a corridor and found themselves facing a large, heavy black door marked in big, plain white lettering, 'Stage Left'. Mike Moore led Quigley and Caborn through it into the wing. The stage was now lit up behind the safety curtain, while the wings were in semi-darkness. Quigley took in the scene on the stage at a glance. Caborn hung back behind him.

On the stage, Claire was still sitting on the floor, facing away from the corpse. Her gaze was fixed on a props table in the other wing. On it she could see some of the paraphernalia of Hamlet – swords, ornate goblets, a bouquet of plastic flowers, grotesquely in the present situation the skull of Yorick, and beside the table, Ophelia's coffin.

Jason, meanwhile, was pacing back and forth downstage just behind the safety curtain. Unlike Claire, he could not resist casting glances at the body.

"Who are you?" Quigley asked Jason.

"My name's Jason Dean. Hamlet."

"I know what the play is, laddie. What's your part?"

"I just told you. Hamlet."

"Oh, right." He looked down at Claire. "And you are?"

"Claire Comerford. Playing Gertrude." She could see Quigley looked none the wiser. "The Queen. Hamlet's mother."

"Have I seen you on the telly?"

"Quite possibly. I was in Mansfield Park."

"That's somewhere up north, isn't it?"

"It's a novel by Jane Austen."

"Oh, right." Quigley looked round at Caborn. "Right, I want the whole of this stage taped off, plus these side bits."

"The wings," Claire explained helpfully.

"Like you say, the wings, and that corridor behind, okay, nobody goes along that from now on. Where's that manager bloke gone?"

"I'm here," said Mike Moore from behind him.

"Have you got stage hands coming and going?"

"The technical crew are in the store room."

"Right, go and tell them to stay there until I say. Have you got that?"

Mike Moore was not used to being patronised.

"Yes, I think I can just about remember that," he said, and headed off away from the stage area.

6

Detective Inspector Keith 'Bunny' Warren was weighing up the relative merits of a chicken and prawn paella and a Thai green curry in the ready meals section of Sainsbury's when his phone rang in his jeans pocket. The caller ident showing on it was 'CMU', standing for Crime Management Unit, and he groaned inwardly. It was his day off, he had tickets to go to see Hamlet with Yolanda this evening, and they had both been looking forward eagerly to the play. Even though his wife, who was Argentine, struggled a little to understand the Elizabethan English, she fully appreciated the stories and the acting, having seen most of the major plays of Shakespeare performed in Spanish back home in Buenos Aires in her youth. Indeed, she was sufficiently intelligent that she probably got more out of it than some English people did. Grudgingly he took the call. He turned and saw a woman with a trolley and a boy aged about ten standing close behind him. He reversed away from the chill cabinet with his loaded trolley, to give her access.

"Warren."

"Sorry to interrupt your day off, sir," said the voice of Sergeant Kevin Foster, on duty in the Crime Management Unit, taking and referring incoming calls.

"What's up?"

"Sudden death at the Theatre Royal, sir. Looks like a murder. On the stage, would you believe?"

Warren let out his breath in exasperation, sensing a joke by some fool at the station at Foster's expense.

"Do you know what play they're doing there this week, Sergeant?"

"No, sir. I never go to plays myself. The wife prefers a good film."

"Hamlet, laddie. Nearly everybody gets murdered, except if they commit suicide. Bodies all over the stage. Blood and gore and guts everywhere. Somebody's pulling your leg. By the way, I'm going to see it tonight."

The female shopper beside the chill cabinet was now looking askance at Warren, apparently not liking her delicate offspring being exposed to his description of the bloodbath in

Elsinore. However, the kid was looking as if he might ask his mum if he could go and see it.

Warren moved away towards the pizzas.

"No, sir, we had a call from the manager, a Mr Strange. Seems like one of the actors was actually killed during the play. Sergeant Quigley's attending."

"So why are you calling me?"

"It's the Super, sir. It's already got on the local radio somehow, and he called in, wants you on the case personally; you being a bit of a theatre buff yourself, so to speak, sir."

"It's my rest day."

"Sorry, sir, I'm aware of that."

"Jesus wept. All right, give me, say, half-an-hour. Who else has gone?"

"Constables Caborn and Jasper, sir."

"Well, call up Quigley and tell him I'm coming and that nobody, and I mean nobody, not even Sir Roger Nutley himself, is to be allowed to leave the building until I say so."

"How did you know it was Sir Roger Nutley, sir?"

"He's the star, even though he's not playing the leading role. He's been in all sorts of TV series, and back in the sixties he was a very big star in a cop series called The Filth; but these days he's better known as a first-class classical actor. Having a TV star in a play puts a lot of bums on seats."

"Well, you needn't worry about him leaving the building, sir. It's him that's been murdered."

Warren was momentarily lost for words.

"Sir?"

"Now I know why the Super wants me on it. Thank you, Kevin, I'm on my way."

Warren knew full well that Sergeant Neville Quigley, a uniformed officer with a querulous attitude, was not going to take kindly to being supplanted on what was certain to be a very high-profile case. He also knew that Quigley's opinion of anything to do with the arts was that it was 'poncey stuff for poofters', and that he was probably putting thespian backs up already. This was undoubtedly what had been in the mind of Superintendent Astbury. He would just have to smooth over ruffled feathers as best he could, but it wouldn't be pretty.

He had an almost full trolley, and began unloading it on to the conveyer belt at the checkout with the shortest queue, consisting of one woman in her forties with a big pile of purchases. She was irritatingly packing only two or three items into each of numerous plastic bags. While she was on about the seventh, the screeching voice of what Warren took to be some X-Factor singer began issuing from her handbag. She rummaged around for her mobile phone, pulled it out, answered it, and ceased packing. A conversation about whether or not she had agreed to drive somebody – Warren suspected teenage offspring – to somewhere – degenerated into a futile argument. Her purchases were piling up at the bagging end of the checkout to the extent that the cashier was forced to suspend operations. Warren glanced behind him. There were now two more customers queuing with fully-laden trolleys. He looked at his wristwatch ostentatiously. He reckoned the woman had now been talking on her phone, apparently oblivious to all around her, for more than three minutes.

"Excuse me," he said.

"D'you mind?" said the woman. "I'm on the phone."

"Yes, I can see that. You're being rude to this lady who's trying to serve you, you're being rude to me, and you're being rude to those people waiting behind us."

"I am talking to my daughter, if you don't mind."

"Well as a matter of fact I do mind, so would you please finish packing your groceries so that we can all get on with it."

Into the phone the woman snarled petulantly, "Sorry, dear, I've got to go, there's a very nasty man being rude to me here."

She shot Warren a filthy look, continued packing in silence, slamming her groceries angrily into the bags, then flounced off, pushing her trolley. Warren stepped forward to be served. The cashier tried not to look up at him any more than necessary.

His shopping having at last been packed and paid for, Warren propelled his trolley to the exit as fast as he dared without risking collisions.

He phoned Yolanda to make sure she was at home, and told her the bad news about their planned evening at the theatre. He knew that although she would be disappointed she would not be angry, because she was accustomed to the antisocial demands of his job. Then he navigated his Mystic Blue BMW 525i out of the crowded car park on to the main road and headed for their detached 1930s house in Oakwood. At the front door he handed the groceries over to Yolanda, saying: "This could take all night. Don't wait up."

"I had already realised that, *mi amor,*" then added in a joke that was to turn out to be prophetic, "but I shall stay up until one o'clock watching England lose against Italy." Warren shot straight off to attend the crime scene.

*

Warren pulled up his BMW behind the patrol car, bounded up the steps, and pushed through the glass doors into the foyer.

"Where's Sergeant Quigley, laddie?" he asked Constable Jasper.

"He went along that way, sir," replied Jasper. "They were going on to the stage."

"They?"

"Him and PC Caborn, sir. This lady took him," said Jasper, indicating Rebecca Bunting, who was back behind the bar.

Warren turned to Rebecca: "Show me the way, would you, please?"

Rebecca stood up and again pressed in the combination.

"How many people know those numbers?" asked Warren.

"Management, front-of-house staff and backstage technical crew."

"Don't let anybody leave," Warren said to Jasper. "If anyone gets stroppy, ask for their ID and whether they feel like being a suspect in a murder case."

"Yes, sir," said Jasper, hoping he wouldn't shortly be taking on the enraged hordes of the north London middle class single-handed. He had a feeling it would be more difficult to cope with than a pub brawl on the Hollingdown estate.

Warren followed Rebecca through to the stage door hallway.

Paula Gregory looked at his civilian clothes and said, "I'm sorry, sir, you can't come in here, in fact you shouldn't be backstage at all."

"Quite right," said Warren, "you have to keep the riff-raff away from what goes on behind the scenes. However, as I happen to be a policeman, perhaps you could make an exception just this once."

"The police are already here, sir."

Warren humoured her by flashing his warrant card.

"I'm the kind that don't wear pointy helmets," he said. There was no opprobrium in his voice. "Detective Inspector Warren, Metropolitan Police. And you are?"

"Paula Gregory, stage doorkeeper." Paula pointed at the stairs again. "Up there."

At the top of the stairs he encountered Mike Moore, and behind him in the big room lined with equipment and costumes stood Sergeant Quigley.

Warren gave a nod to Quigley and showed Mike Moore his warrant card, saying, "DI Warren. And you are?"

"Mike Moore, Stage Manager."

"Does that mean you're the big boss man round the back here?"

"It does indeed."

"Then I'd be grateful if you would tell your staff I'll be needing to talk to them all, so nobody's to think about going home or round the pub." Warren spoke politely and in an even, unintimidating tone, in total contrast to Quigley's manner, which had succeeded in putting the stage manager's back up within minutes.

"No problem. In normal circumstances we'd have had another performance tonight starting only a couple of hours after the matinee finished, so nobody would have been going anywhere."

"Good. Now lead on, Macduff."

"For God's sake don't mention the name of that play

while you're in the theatre."

"I'd say you've already had your share of bad luck for today, wouldn't you?"

Quigley moved across to Warren: "What's going on?"

"Super's orders. I'm taking over as SIO."

"No way," said Quigley. "I was the senior officer present in the station when the call came in."

"I know how you feel, but that's the way it is. Call in and check it out."

"Too bloody right I will."

Quigley went into a corner beside a gantry to make his angry but pointless phone call, and Warren asked Mike Moore to show him where the body was.

PC Caborn was standing guard a few feet downstage from the body of Roger Nutley. He was staring intently at the featureless rear surface of the safety curtain, seemingly oblivious to the people nearby, almost to the point of looking daft. But Warren knew the lad well enough to be aware that he would have been listening very carefully to any conversations that took place, and would remember them with total recall if he needed to ask him later.

Jason Dean was now sprawled on a brown chaise-longue in the stage-left wing, a few feet from where Fiona Holland remained perched at her control-board. The young actor's eyes were closed and his arms were drooping by his sides. Claire Comerford was sitting on a red-upholstered upright chair with gold-painted legs, leaning slightly forward with her hands on her knees.

"All right, Constable, you can relax a bit now," said Warren.

"Sir," said Caborn, not feeling at all relaxed.

"How many uniforms have we got here?"

"Just me and Sergeant Quigley and Constable Jasper, sir."

Warren asked Quigley, who was hovering indecisively, "Did it not occur to you that in a packed theatre with a celebrity murdered in full view, and goodness knows how many people wandering around backstage, you might need a few more bods on the ground than two?"

"I was about to call for backup when you arrived, sir." The lie was transparent.

"I'm sure you were. In any case, we obviously need more. There are hundreds of people out there, and I'm going to need all their names and addresses before they go home. By the way, when did Soco say they'd be getting here?"

"I was just going to ask for them, sir."

There was no point in exploding. It would go in his report, and hopefully Quigley would never get within ten miles of a murder investigation again in his stunted career.

Warren pulled out his phone, called the CMU, and got Kevin Foster again. "Get Soco down here fast," he said. "This is going to be very high profile; and I need uniforms, as many as you can spare."

"Can't manage more than four at the moment, sir. Saturday afternoon and all that. Plus there's been an armed robbery in The Broadway, and I've got nobody above constable to send to that."

"Call in manpower from all over north London, it's top priority, get the Super's authorisation to override other shouts, if you need to. I could do with thirty or forty bodies here, it's going to be a huge job."

"I'll do my best, sir. You know how it is."

"Oh," Warren said, "tell you what, I'll send you a sergeant to take charge of the robbery. Where was it?"

"Bags of Fun, sir."

"This is no time for jokes, Foster."

"No sir, that's the name of the shop. Up-market handbags. The gang fired a sawn-off."

"What, for a few bloody handbags?"

"Apparently they're worth a fortune, sir."

"Country's gone stark raving mad. All right," he threw a glance at Quigley, who nodded, "Sergeant Quigley's on his way now."

Warren sympathised with Kevin Foster. He did indeed know how it was at any time, let alone on a Saturday afternoon, after the latest round of budget and manpower cuts. He turned to the people sitting in the wings.

"Right, who's who? Everybody come out here, please."

Fiona, Jason and Claire stood up and came out on to the stage. Fiona had kept a disciplined grip on her emotions during the initial minutes of crisis, but she looked visibly shaken now as the delayed shock cut in.

"I'm Fiona Holland, Company Stage Manager."

Warren pointed to Mike Moore.

"He said he was Stage Manager."

"I'm the Stage Manager for the theatre," explained Mike. "This lady's the stage manager for Daniel Spiller Productions, the visiting company."

"I run the touring show, he runs the people who make it happen here," added Fiona.

"I see." Turning to the actors: "And you are Miss Claire Comerford and Mr Jason Dean."

"How come you know our names?" asked Jason Dean.

"In case you've forgotten, you're quite well-known; and in any case, I've got tickets to come and see you this evening."

"Sorry about that," said Jason, lamely.

The door into the stage-right wing opened and closed. Warren turned as Ivan Strange stepped on to that side of the stage. Looking him swiftly up and down, he saw a man in good shape for a man in his seventies, but no Charles Atlas; small, probably no taller than five-foot-five; not much excess weight, suggesting some exercise such as walking, swimming, gardening, or perhaps all of these, but certainly none of the bulging muscles of a regular enthusiast for workouts in a gym.

"Good afternoon sir, and what do you do here?" asked Warren.

"I'm Ivan Strange, the Manager."

"Good grief, not another one. What do you manage?"

"This theatre. And you are?"

"DI Warren, Metropolitan Police."

Beyond the safety curtain the sound level was rising. It was obvious the audience were becoming restive. Warren realised it was going to be a long job checking their IDs and taking their names and addresses.

"How many people are there out there?" he asked Ivan Strange.

"Nearly a full house. Getting on for six hundred."

"Is there any way anybody at all could have left the audience, got round backstage during the performance, and then got back to their seat without anybody noticing?"

Strange thought for a moment. "Well," he replied, "on the one hand, they wouldn't have needed to leave their seat in the auditorium, because it happened a couple of minutes after the interval. So they could have simply gone outside at the end of Act One and then not returned to their seat, and snuck around the back, if they knew the way. Then with all the hullaballoo going on after the murder was discovered, they might have slipped back into their seat."

"Wonderful; that's just what I didn't want to hear. So what you're telling me is, we've got six-hundred-odd suspects."

"What I was going to say was, they couldn't have gone through the interconnecting corridor without knowing the combination for the locks, and I change that every week; and I've already asked the stage doorkeeper whether anybody came in from outside, and they didn't."

"So are you saying it would have been possible for someone in the audience to slip backstage, or impossible?"

"I shouldn't like to commit myself to impossible; but it seems highly unlikely."

"I suppose somebody could have just walked in off the street and come through the foyer, if they had the nerve, and then walked out again," said Fiona Holland.

"I was really hoping nobody was going to suggest that," said Warren.

Mike Moore stepped forward and chipped in: "D'you mind if I express an opinion in my professional capacity?"

"Go ahead," said Warren. "Nothing I like better than a professional opinion."

"Well, the killer would have had to have a very clear idea of the way the set was devised for Polonius to get behind the arras – I mean the curtain. Sir Roger needed to be able to stand far enough back to avoid getting stabbed by Hamlet's sword, and then be able to lie down ready for Hamlet to drag him out. The killer would have needed to know what the access to that space was from behind. It's pitch dark in the gap

Sir Roger was hiding in, he couldn't see the curtain in front of his face. I know, I've been in there testing the set. You'd have to know exactly which narrow gap to walk through from the back of the wings to get there, and that you could only get into it from stage right without the certainty of being seen. I'm not saying it's impossible, but the odds against a member of the public pulling all that off are pretty stacked against. I mean, finding out the door codes, getting into that space in the dark, then getting out again without being seen, and getting clear of backstage again before the body was discovered. I don't really think so. But I'm no detective, I'm just saying."

"If you ever want a job as one, just give us a ring. Thank you very much Mr Moore. I'm inclined to go along with that," said Warren. "Well, we can't keep them all cooped up much longer, and I don't have the manpower to take all their names and addresses without causing a riot. How many ushers and whatnot have you got?"

From beyond the safety curtain an angry male voice rang out: "How much longer have we got to stay here?"

"Ay-ay," said Warren, "this is going to kick off any time now. Is there a little bit of stage on the other side of that curtain I can get on to so as I can tell 'em they can all go home if they leave their names and addresses?"

"Walk this way," said Mike Moore.

Mike Moore led Warren offstage into the stage-right wing, where they turned left. Mike punched a code into a black door leading to a small flight of steps down into the front corner of the auditorium. They went down it with 600 pairs of eyes boring into them, and Mike led Warren across the front of the stage through the gap in front of the stalls to the foot of another small flight of steps leading up on to the narrow strip of stage in front of the safety curtain. A very posh female voice from further back shouted, "What's going on? At least give us some information, won't you?"

"Shall I stay down here and wait?" asked Mike.

"No, come up and hold my hand, I might need to ask you something."

When Warren walked to the centre of the stage and turned to face the audience, his unassuming charisma was sufficient for them to fall silent at once. He was tall, at five-foot-eleven, and broad-shouldered; but that wasn't it. He wasn't one of those muscly-looking middle-aged types who look as if they only stopped playing rugby a couple of years ago and would prefer to settle an argument with a punch rather than reasoning. Neither overweight nor skinny, he could still take part comfortably in a 10-kilometre charity run, and did so twice a year for various causes. He had a full head of wavy brown hair, which he combed back without a parting. His eyebrows seemed a lighter brown, but that was because the light smearing of gel, that he used to hold his hair back, also darkened it a shade. But that wasn't it, either. It was from the mouth and eyes that the charisma radiated. His warm smile was usually quick to appear for friends, colleagues, and the decent folk of this world, but could conceal a razor-sharp ability to spot a lie or evasion by a suspect; and the twinkle in his penetrating mid-blue eyes could fool a gullible criminal into believing that it would be easy to pull the wool over them; which was always a big mistake.

He turned to Mike and asked, "Is there a microphone anywhere?"

"No. Actors don't need them. Just talk normally and they'll listen."

"Ladies and gentlemen," Warren began. "My name is Detective Inspector Warren. As you are all aware, the death has occurred during this afternoon's performance of the actor, Sir Roger Nutley. I can now tell you that his death was no accident." A collective murmur began. Warren held up the palm of his right hand to silence it. "We are treating this incident as murder. Now I want to thank you all for the patience which you have already shown at being asked not to leave the theatre, but I am going to have to ask you to be patient for just a little longer because we shall need to take all your names and addresses before you go." Another murmur, and Warren saw PC Jasper hurrying down the centre aisle.

"Reinforcements have started arriving, sir; they're in the foyer."

Warren squatted down to whisper to Jasper: "Right, then we can start letting these people go home. Go back out the front and tell them to be ready to take an awful lot of names and addresses."

"Yes, sir."

"Oh, and they're to ask to see everybody's tickets, and note the seat numbers against their names; plus obviously check IDs. The slightest thing iffy, bring them to me."

Warren stood up and spoke to the audience: "Ladies and gentlemen, some more of my colleagues have now arrived and they will shortly be ready to start taking your names and addresses. Please also have your tickets and some form of identification ready to show them, so that we can let you go home as quickly as possible. This is purely routine and you'll probably never hear from us again. Thank you again for being so patient."

He was surprised to hear a ripple of applause.

7

Warren found Fiona Holland, Jason Dean and Claire Comerford sitting in the wing as before, with Neil Caborn still standing in the middle of the stage.

"You stay here and hold the fort," he told Caborn. "Don't take your eyes off the crime scene. Mrs Holland, take me to where the dressing-rooms are. Miss Comerford, Mr Dean, you can come too."

"Thank God," breathed the actress.

"I'm sorry you've been left here with your colleague's body for so long."

Fiona Holland led Warren out to the corridor behind the stage and down two steep flights of stairs to a similar corridor directly underneath, off which gave the dressing-rooms and a laundry-room.

Turning to Fiona, Warren asked her, "How many actors in the cast?"

"Thirteen," she said.

He wasn't superstitious but it crossed his mind that this was an inauspicious number.

"I thought there were more people than that in Hamlet."

"If you cast every role that Shakespeare wrote," she said, "there would be 26 named characters and umpteen non-speaking courtiers, sailors and suchlike, which in the commercial theatre would be totally unviable financially. The National Theatre or the Royal Shakespeare Company might do it, but nobody could put on a touring show like this with that kind of numbers. Besides, quite apart from the cost, if you'd ever had any contact with actors you'd know it would be like herding cats. Plus there wouldn't be anything like enough dressing-rooms to go round. So we have people doubling, you know, playing two roles in different costumes and with different voices, or even tripling or quadrupling in some of the smaller roles. And of course we do without all those extra courtiers and soldiers hanging around the stage saying nothing, which is a depressing job for an actor anyway. Thirteen's a big cast these days. You need good houses to cover that many actors' wages, even though they mostly don't get paid much. Where do you want to start?"

They had entered a cosy room with well-worn sofas, chairs, a kitchenette and a small bookshelf stocked with paperbacks left behind by legions of previous touring actors. Nobody else was in there.

"What's this?" asked Warren.

"The Green Room. Normally they'd be relaxing in here and maybe microwaving some ready meals between shows."

"Perfect. I'll see people in here." He sat down in the comfiest looking armchair. "But with thirteen actors and I don't know how many technical staff back here, I'm going to need some help. Hold on a minute."

Warren took out his mobile and pressed a contact. When it was answered, he asked, "What are you doing right now?"

Detective Sergeant Philippa Myers was in fact less than half-a-mile away, enjoying a retail therapy expedition with her friend Hazel Graham, a teacher, who was going through a divorce. When Philippa's phone rang, she was waiting outside the changing rooms in Debenhams for Hazel to emerge and show her the black crepe dress by Den de Lisi that she was trying on to cheer herself up. Seeing Warren's name displayed on her phone brought on an inward groan as she foresaw her weekend evaporating.

"Hello, guv," she said, resignedly.

"Duty calls," said Warren. "Murder investigation. I need you here, pronto."

"Oh, no," said Philippa, "We were just going to..."

"Sorry, I know it's your rest day. It was mine, too."

"What's up?"

"Celebrity murder, no less. All hands to the pump."

"Blimey. Which celeb?"

"Not now. Just get down here, will you?"

"Oh, well," said Philippa, "if I really must. But where's here?"

"The Theatre Royal. Main entrance. A uniform will let you in and show you where to come. I'll fill you in when you get here."

"Twenty minutes, sir."

"Good."

Warren turned back to Fiona Holland. "You first," he said. "Where were you and what were you doing when Sir Roger Nutley was killed?"

"At the control panel," said Fiona, "where you saw me when you came in."

"Should we go and wait in our dressing-rooms?" asked Claire.

"No, you can stay here for the moment. Take a seat."

Claire and Jason sat together at opposite ends of a sofa, Fiona on another.

"You didn't move from the control panel at all?"

"No," said Fiona. "I can't leave it while the show's under way."

"Would anybody have noticed if you'd moved away for, say, a minute?"

She thought for a moment.

"Act Three Scene Four is a very long one with only Hamlet and Gertrude on stage once Polonius has gone behind the arras."

"Nobody waiting in the wings to make an entrance?"

"Claudius, Rosencrantz and Guilderstern come on for Act Four Scene One, but that's some while after it happened, and they hadn't come up from their dressing-rooms yet. So in a sense, perhaps I could have got round the back, killed Roger and got back in time, if you like. Except that I didn't. I think the actors on stage might notice out of the corners of their eyes if I moved, because it would be so unusual."

Warren turned to Claire and Jason. "Can you be absolutely certain that Mrs Holland remained at her control panel all the time?"

"Of course, she always does, she has to," said Claire.

"I understand that," said Warren, "but I'm not asking whether she always does or she has to; I'm asking whether you are certain, with your own eyes, that she actually did on this occasion."

"Well," said Claire, "I suppose I couldn't swear to it. I had my back to that side for most of the time, but in any case, you don't spend your time looking at what's going on in the wings. In fact, you can't see what's going on there, because it's dark and you're standing in the light."

"What about you, Mr Dean?"

"I'm thinking," said Jason. "The trouble is, Hamlet's a deeply involving part. As an actor, you have to really feel you're in mediaeval Denmark trying to cope with the fact that your father's ghost has told you to avenge his murder by your uncle. At this point I'm having a blazing row with my mother whom I'm sure was complicit in that murder, and she's married my uncle. Then I think I've stabbed him through the arras with my sword, only it turns out to be Polonius, my girl-friend's father. So it's all a tiny bit fraught."

"I know the play, Mr Dean," said Warren.

"Then you'll understand that I wasn't exactly keeping an eye on what the stage manager might have been doing at the time."

"I see. Are you absolutely sure you wouldn't have noticed if she'd gone away and come back again?"

"I told you, I'm thinking. It's something that would never happen, so there's no way of saying if I would notice if she did. Except that I was facing that way for most of that scene up till then, and there's a very faint glow from the control panel all the time that obviously you just ignore. But if she did move away during a show, I don't know, perhaps I would have noticed, but honestly, I don't know, I couldn't swear either way. To be honest, the only way to be sure would be to do a test run under actual lighting conditions."

"Might have been possible in Poirot's day," said Warren. "Not any longer. Everything has to stay as it is until the scene of crime officers have done their stuff. I'll talk to the rest of the actors in their dressing-rooms until Soco arrive. What's at the other end of this corridor?"

"Through the doors at the end leads to the stage door," said Fiona.

"Maybe I'll just have a word there first." Warren went out and along past the line of dressing-rooms. Each door had a pair of visiting actors' names stuck on the outside. He pushed open the double-doors at the other end which led down three steps into the small entrance hall inside the stage door; and realised it was the one he had passed through when he arrived. Paula Gregory was now watching a small television set mounted on the wall in the booth.

"Aha, I seem to have come round in a circle," Warren said.

"Can I help you?"

"What exactly is it you do here?"

"Stage Doorkeeper."

"Of course. You're aware of what's happened?"

"Sort of."

"Have you been here all the time?"

"Since half-past-twelve."

"Anyone come in or go out during the interval, or afterwards?"

"No. Not since the half."

"The half?"

"Thirty-five minutes before the start of the play. The actors all have to be in by then. They were. They tick themselves in on that sheet." She pointed to a printed list on a clipboard on her ledge.

"Why 'the half'?"

"Half-an-hour before the five-minute call."

"Every industry has its jargon, I suppose."

"Plenty of it in this one, I can tell you."

"Been in it long?"

"Not at all. I'm a volunteer, same as all the front-of-house staff. I've fancied working here for years, but there's too many steps and narrow doorways for me to do front-of-house. Plus it gets very crowded in the foyer, so my chair would be a nuisance. Then this job came vacant last March, and Mr Strange said he'd have a ramp put outside this door, and he's made the downstairs loo accessible." She indicated the toilet opposite. "Wider door, grip-bars, you know. Suits me nicely; I can do my bit to keep the theatre going, and I get to meet the actors."

Warren noticed that Paula had a delightful, almost bell-like soprano voice that enhanced her femininity despite the wheelchair, and wondered idly for a moment whether she could sing.

"That was extraordinarily kind of him," he said. "Why did he go to all that trouble? Is he a friend of yours?"

"No. I'd mentioned it to the others when I came to plays. He was quite honest about it. He did it because it looks good on applications to arts funding bodies to have somebody disabled on the staff, even if it's unpaid."

"You have been in the front of the theatre, then?"

"Oh, yes, I go to plays sometimes, but it's a heck of a palaver in this old theatre, I have to be carried in the chair up the front steps, and then they park me in an aisle when everybody else is in, and take me out after the rush is over. When you've been immobile as long as I have, you take what you can get and thank God you're alive at all."

"Do you mind me asking ... why the wheelchair?"

"Car accident. My fiancé was driving. He was drunk. He was killed. It was a long time ago."

"I'm sorry."

"So am I."

"Can you think of anything that could help our enquiries?"

"Wish I could. Not really, though. Quiet as the grave

down here. Sorry, not the most sensitive turn of phrase."

"Don't worry, we're used to it. I may or may not need another word with you later. You've been told not to go home, I take it?"

"No problem, Inspector. Just send for me when you're ready."

"We'll need your address – is it Mrs Gregory or Miss?"

"Miss. Mr Strange has got it."

"That's fine, then."

Just then Andy Jasper appeared through the door from the corridor from front-of-house. "How long d'you reckon till the public are all out?" Warren asked.

"Not long. Plenty of reinforcements in now. Stage hands are asking if we can't cover the body up with a sheet or something."

"Not till the surgeon's done his stuff, as you well know. Talk of the devil."

A tall, slim, fit-looking man wearing jeans and an England football shirt appeared from the corridor.

"I got here as soon as I could," he said to Warren.

"Mike Moore, this is Ian Fairbanks, our Divisional Surgeon, even if he does look more like something the wind's blown in from Wembley Stadium."

"Thought I was having the day off. There's a slightly important match in Brazil tonight, in case you hadn't noticed. Where's the stiff?"

"On the stage. I'll show you."

After examining the body of Sir Roger Nutley, Ian Fairbanks stood up and said, "He's dead." To a layman, in the circumstances, this might have sounded like a sick joke; but it was a legal requirement that the surgeon formally declare life extinct before going into any details.

"Windpipe bashed in, neck broken," he said to Warren. "The killer wasn't taking any chances on the victim waking up."

"Could a woman have done it?"

"Not in a million years. Not even the vast majority of men. The killer was very tall and very strong. This is a professional job. Sort of thing that would probably require military training. Commando training."

"Jesus. I shouldn't have thought there would be much of that sort of skill around among our thespian friends. But would it necessarily have needed a lot of strength if somebody had the know-how?"

"Oh, yes, especially as they needed to be sure of doing it silently. Holding on to the victim while you do it, that would require a powerful grip, plus height and weight. Yes, I should say it would almost certainly have to be a man; and a very strong one. Especially as the victim was quite a big man himself. He was pretty old, but he looks in good shape."

"He was 76. That would make it easier, surely."

"Probably, but still, I wouldn't have said it was a method somebody would choose with any confidence unless they had the training. By the way, you can get the body taken away now."

"Thank God for that," said Mike Moore.

"I don't suppose he's the first act to have died on this stage," said Fairbanks.

"I was wondering who'd be the first tactless bastard to say that," said Moore.

"Sorry," said Warren, "but you can rely on a police surgeon for graveyard humour."

"Stops us going insane," said Fairbanks.

"I've yet to see proof of that."

*

Returning to the Green Room, Warren ordered Jason Dean and Claire Comerford back to their dressing rooms, to leave him alone with Fiona Holland. Settling on to the sofa opposite her after they had gone, he said, "As you'll appreciate, Mrs Holland, we have a problem. Now I'm not accusing you, but you could have left your position for long enough to reach Mr Nutley and got back again in the time, without anyone noticing."

"I realise that. To be honest, I'd be astonished if they would have seen me go away and come back. Of course, I didn't. But I don't know what I can do to prove it."

"How tall are you, Mrs Holland?"

"Five-foot-three."

"And how much do you weigh?"

"About eleven stone."

"Would you describe yourself as fit?"

She glanced down at her considerable girth.

"Unfortunately not."

"Do you think you would be physically capable of taking a man as tall as Roger Nutley by surprise and breaking his neck without any resistance?"

"No. I couldn't even reach. And my tummy would get in the way."

"Exactly; which is why I'm not considering you as a suspect; but on the other hand, I'd rather you didn't disappear on any sudden trips abroad for the time being. Does that sound fair enough?"

"Perfectly."

"I'm glad you see it that way; but please stay in this area until either I or one of my officers gives you the all-clear to go home. Do you live locally?"

"No, I live in Portugal, on the Algarve, and just come over to do tours. I'm staying with friends in Barnet this week. Actually I have to wait here for Mr Spiller. He's on his way up from Sussex."

"Good. As soon as he arrives I want to see him. Have you got a list of all the actors' names I can borrow?"

"In my dressing-room."

"Stage managers have a dressing room? What for?"

"I use it as an office. And it's somewhere people can come and see me if they've got a problem."

"Did Roger Nutley ever come to you with any problems?"

"He'd have been the last one. Mr self-sufficient. Even sewed his own buttons back on his costume. If they were all like that, life would be a breeze."

Warren and Fiona made their way back to the deserted Green Room via Fiona's dressing room, where she picked up the cast list.

"Right," said Warren, "how many have we got?"

"Ten, not counting poor Roger, and Jason and Claire whom you've already met."

"Who are the others?"

Fiona read aloud from her sheet: "John Montgomery who plays Claudius. He shares a dressing-room with Julian Rainford who doubles as the Ghost and the Gravedigger. Paul Grant who plays Rozencrantz shares with Theo Chapman who plays Guildenstern. Tessa Verrall, she's Ophelia, is in with Emily Grady, she doubles as the Player Queen and Osric; and Nick Velliadis and Tim McGarry are in a dressing-room together, they're Laertes and Horatio."

"What about the Player King?"

Fiona looked up, surprised: "Well spotted. Our Player King is an amazing puppet operated by three of the cast. The audiences love him."

"Never play opposite children, animals or puppets."

"Quite. Do you want me to call them in one by one, or all together, or what?"

"I think it's time I made some house calls. I'll go to them in their rooms. I'd like you to show me in and introduce me, then wait outside, please."

"Fair enough. Walk this way."

The first dressing-room was immediately beside the Green Room, occupied by Nicholas Velliadis and Timothy McGarry. Fiona knocked and opened the door. The two actors looked up from books they were reading, sitting up at the dressing-tables. Warren could immediately see that they were both too short and lacking in muscular development to have committed the murder.

"This is Inspector Warren of Scotland Yard," said Fiona.

"Not exactly Scotland Yard," he corrected, "Norton Hill Division of the Metropolitan Police." Tim McGarry stood up. "No, stay where you are, that's all right," said Warren.

Fiona left the room and closed the door behind her.

"You're aware of what's happened?" asked Warren, remaining standing; not that he had any choice, for there were no other chairs in the small room.

"Roger's dead," said Nick, "and I think we can assume

from your presence that it's being treated as murder, although that's pretty hard to take in."

"He was behind a curtain at the rear of the stage, to be precise," said Warren.

"Behind the arras he conveyed himself," paraphrased Tim.

"Exactly," said Warren, "where he was supposed to be run through by Hamlet; only somebody else got there."

"He wasn't stabbed with the sword by accident, then?"

"No. Now what I need to ask you first of all is where you were at that time."

"Here," said Tim. "We both were."

"You didn't leave this dressing-room for any reason after the interval?"

"No," said Tim. "We chatted with some of the others in the Green Room until beginners was called, then came back in here to read and listen out for our cues. Same as we do in every performance. You get into a fixed routine after weeks and weeks of the same play on tour. We don't talk much, we tend to read for a short while and then sit and think about what's about to happen to our characters when we go back on. We're neither of us back on until Act Four Scene Five, so there's quite a while after the interval."

"You didn't perhaps pop out to the toilet, either of you?"

"No. You even get into a regular routine with that. I always go in the interval, whether I need to or not," said Tim.

"And I go towards the end of the first half," said Nick. "I'm not on stage for ages after Act I."

"Taking your fair hour in France," said Warren.

"Exactly. Well done. You seem to know Hamlet rather well, Inspector."

"Did it at school, and I was coming tonight. So you were both in here together. I don't suppose you heard anything untoward?"

The two young actors glanced at each other, then back towards Warren.

"All you can hear is the squawk-box."

"The what?"

Nick pointed up at the small, old-fashioned, wooden loudspeaker on the wall.

"The intercom, relaying what's being said on the stage, so that we know when to go up to the wings and get ready to make our entrances."

"Right. What about during the interval? See or hear anything unusual then? Or before?"

The actors looked at each other again.

"Sorry," said Tim.

"Did you at any time, either today or previously, overhear Sir Roger having an argument with anybody?"

Both shook their heads. "No," said Tim.

"How was he killed?" asked Nick.

They would find out soon enough. "Somebody broke his neck," said Warren. Both actors winced. "I'd be grateful if you'd remain here until you're told to go through and sit in the auditorium, and then don't take anything with you. Your things will be returned to you when the scene of crime team finish; probably tomorrow. When I'm through with questioning all the cast, you'll be told if you can go home."

Soco in fact arrived as Warren went back out into the corridor. In their protective clothing of white plastic suits, hoods and footwear protectors, pale blue plastic gloves, goggles, and masks covering noses and mouths, they resembled something between astronauts and polar explorers. PC Jasper also arrived to report that the public had all gone home.

"Right," said Warren. "Everybody out of backstage and into the auditorium. No bags, no clothes, leave it all here; they'll get it all back as soon as the search is over."

He turned to the Soco team leader, Jameel Kazemi: "All yours, Jim. You can seal off everything behind the safety curtain. Andy'll show you where the body is."

There was an orderly departure from backstage to front-of-house, during which Jim Kazemi came back to Warren and pointed out that the stage doorkeeper was a woman in a wheelchair who was physically incapable of getting up the stairs to go through to the auditorium with the others.

"I could take her round the outside and get somebody

to help me carry her up and through the front door," said Philippa.

Warren paused to think for a moment, then said: "I've already questioned her. She saw nothing unusual and there's no way she's a suspect. Tell her she can go home. Then put one of the uniforms to mind the stage door."

8

Daniel Spiller turned his ancient Range Rover into the car park at the rear of the Theatre Royal, switched off, locked it, strode across to the stage door, yanked at the handle, found it to be locked, and rang the bell. After a delay which irritated him, Paula Gregory's wheelchair hove into view through the glass panel.

"Sorry, sir, nobody's allowed in," Paula called through the closed door.

"I'm Daniel Spiller," he said; a statement which was normally sufficient on its own to make actors, technicians and ancillary staff stand mentally to attention; but Paula was a relatively new volunteer and knew little of the hierarchy of authority in the theatrical world.

"Who did you say, sir?"

"Spiller. Daniel Spiller. It's my show you've been putting on here."

"I'll have to ask the police, sir. If you'd just wait there."

Spiller was not used to being kept waiting outside stage doors but he was no fool and realised that the police having taken charge, the woman had no option. Paula returned to her cabin to phone upstairs and try to locate that police inspector who'd spoken to her. While she was waiting, PC Mark Greenwood appeared through the internal door to tell her she'd been cleared to go home and he was taking over on the door.

Daniel Spiller tapped on one of the glass panels of the door and made an arms-spread-wide 'what's going on?' gesture. PC Greenwood tried unsuccessfully to open the door, got the key from Paula Gregory, and opened up.

"Can I help you, sir?" asked Greenwood.

"I'm Daniel Spiller. Take me to the man in charge, please."

"I'm sorry sir, nobody's allowed in or out of the building at the moment."

"I've just told you, I'm Daniel Spiller, it's my production."

"How's that, sir?"

"It says on the posters for Hamlet, 'Daniel Spiller Productions'. That's me. The actor who's been murdered was working for me."

"I see. You'd better come in, sir."

Greenwood opened the door and stood back for Spiller to enter, then went back to Paula Gregory.

"Will you be all right getting away on your own?" he asked.

"Been doing it since before you were born. You'd better lock up behind me."

Greenwood turned to Spiller: "Sorry, sir, if you wouldn't mind waiting while I see to this."

"I can find my own way," said Spiller, "I know this place like the back of my hand. Where are they, on the stage?" He made a move to go upstairs alone but Greenwood stepped in front of him.

"No sir, you can't go without me, the whole backstage area's a crime scene. I'll be with you in a tick."

Spiller looked at Paula in her wheelchair, interested. He was always ready and willing to learn.

"You're new here, aren't you?" he asked her.

"Started just under three months ago," she said. "I'm a volunteer."

"Good for you. We wouldn't have any theatres in this day and age if it wasn't for the support of people like you. How do you manage getting around an old building like this in the wheelchair, though?"

"Well, I don't, I only do stage door. Mr Strange had the downstairs toilet made accessible and put a concrete ramp out there."

PC Greenwood opened the double doors for Paula, who propelled herself out and down the ramp and into the car park. Daniel Spiller followed her, for it crossed his mind that there might be lessons to learn here about how he could perhaps improve disabled access at his own home base. He rehearsed all his touring productions at the Victorian-era Grand Theatre in Brighton, which he had bought to save it from closure and sold his own house to refurbish. It was a lovely old building but had been built during an age when people with disabilities were expected to stay at home out of sight.

"How many volunteers are there?" he asked when they reached her car.

"There's four ushers out the front and me," she said.

"Anyway, well done."

Paula pointed the remote and unlocked her car, a bronze coloured Kia; a two-door model because the doors open wider than on four-door cars and allow more room for a disabled person to manoeuvre when transferring from a wheelchair into the driving seat, and vice versa. With the driver's door open as wide as it would go, she pointed her knees into the angle of the hinge, dropped her right foot to the ground while keeping the left one in the chair. She made a fist with her left hand, pushed it down on to the driving seat while dropping her head as far forward as possible to bring her bottom up high, leaned her weight on to her left arm, swung her body over into the seat, slipped her left arm under her knees and lifted her legs into the car as well. Then she spun the lightweight chair using her right hand to bring its back towards her, and folded it forwards. Turned the chair on to one side, snapped open the clip holding the right wheel on, lifted that over and stood it in front of the car's passenger seat. Did the same with the left wheel, then hefted the rest of the chair across her lap on to the front passenger seat, which she had protected with a towel. Closed the door, opened the window and saw Daniel Spiller standing beside the car watching.

"Hope you don't mind," he said. "I was wondering how it was done. That's pretty impressive."

"Needs must," said Paula.

"Tell me something," said Spiller. "I own my own

theatre in Brighton. Is there anything I could do to make things easier in the car park for people like you?"

"Extra-wide disabled bays," Paula replied without hesitation. "If somebody comes and parks right next to me, I can't bring the chair into the gap or open the door wide enough, and I'm stuck."

"I'll do it," said Spiller.

"But you have to crack down on people parking in them who don't need them," she added. "Otherwise they just take the piss – if you'll excuse my French."

"I see what you mean. Okay, I must get on, nice talking to you. And keep up the volunteering."

Paula drove off and Spiller went back in through the stage door.

"If you'll just follow me, sir," said PC Greenwood. "They're all in the auditorium."

At the top of the stairs they ran into one of the Socos who indicated it was all right to pass through the stage-right wing and through the door leading to the front of the auditorium, but not to touch anything and not to stray.

The actors sat up straighter in their seats when Spiller came down the steps. Warren came forward down the aisle, having been forewarned by Paula Gregory's phone call which had been taken by Ivan Strange. He stood up and offered his hand. Spiller shook it firmly.

"Inspector Warren, Metropolitan Police. I understand you're the producer of the play."

"Daniel Spiller. Yes, Inspector, it's my show. This is terrible. Any way I can help, just say."

"Well, at the moment I'm in the process of interviewing the members of your cast, as you can see."

Spiller glanced at the actors. "Hello everybody," he said. "This must be dreadful for you all. Well, obviously you know to cooperate with the Inspector here, so I'm not going to interfere." Then he turned back to Warren. "I wonder if I could have a word with you alone at some point, Inspector?"

"I need to talk to you, anyway, but it's going to take a while to get through with interviewing everybody on the scene. You're under no obligation to wait in the theatre."

"Is there a pub with decent food nearby?"

"Out the front door, turn left, 150 yards down the other side of the road, The Standing Order," said Warren. "Looks like a bank because that's what it used to be."

"I'll go there and get something to eat. Perhaps you'd call me when you're ready for me. Fiona's got my number."

"That'll be fine," said Warren. "If I'm lucky I might even get down there later on for a quick one myself."

*

Ivan Strange's tiny office contained a desk with an upright rotating chair behind it and two slightly shabby armchairs in the corners facing it diagonally. The walls were cream and in need of a new coat of paint. The mottled brown carpet was showing signs of wear. Half a dozen framed posters of plays the theatre had hosted in the past featured the names of famous actors. None of them seemed more recent than the 1980s, suggesting that the venue had long since ceased to attract the top shows. This Hamlet with a television name in it must have seemed quite a coup to Ivan Strange, thought Warren. Perhaps a new poster had been heading for his office wall trumpeting the name of Sir Roger Nutley.

The theatre manager was seated behind his desk talking on the phone when Warren knocked and entered with Philippa and Constable Jasper, who was no longer needed to guard the foyer now that the reinforcements had arrived.

"Sorry, dear, I'll have to go, the police want to talk to me," he said, and hung up.

"Anything I need to know about?" asked Warren.

"My wife. She heard it on the radio."

Warren said: "We'll need your office to interview people." Strange started to stand up. "Sit down, Mr Strange, you're first." Strange sank back down on to his chair. Warren sat on one of the armchairs, Philippa on the other. Andy Jasper stood inside the door and took out his notebook.

The way Ivan Strange peered across at the trio of police officers was neither defensive nor aggressive, these being the two most common attitudes of interviewees, but rather thoughtful; squinting a little as if he were weighing them up rather than the other way around. It was certainly not the posture of a man with anything to hide. His grey, straight hair still contained a few traces of the original black threads, and was cut neatly, but by no means stylishly, and short above the ears as if by a barber who had learned his trade in the 1950s and never moved on. His creased forehead was high but his hair had scarcely receded except where a parting began on the left. Thin, colourless lips pressed tightly together on a wide mouth that pushed apart heavy creases running downwards from the lower edges of a rather bulbous, slightly pink nose which suggested regular if not excessive consumption of wine. His neat pale-grey shirt was made of some sort of synthetic non-iron material, the cuffs held together with simple gold-plated links. He wore a narrow, plain, fawn-coloured woven tie, and an unbuttoned, sleeveless waistcoat with a dull beige and brown diagonal pattern. Overall, he came over as a beige man; unremarkable almost to the point of invisibility.

"Fire away," said Strange.

"Where were you at the time Sir Roger was being murdered?" asked Warren.

"In the foyer, checking with Miss Bunting how we were placed for drinks for the evening performance. We had a full house for the matinee, and it's been a hot day, so I thought stocks might have been run down quite a bit."

"Did you hear Jason Dean call out that Mr Nutley was dead?"

"We both heard that there was a disturbance, but it wasn't clear what was going on. I hurried backstage to find out. By the time I got there, the safety curtain had been lowered."

"I see. And Miss Bunting's job is?"

"Front-of-House Manager. She's also in charge of the ushers."

"Have you ever met Sir Roger Nutley before this week?"

"No. He's never worked in this theatre before, and I've been here most of my working life."

Philippa took over: "Have you had much personal

contact with him this week? Been out for a drink, that sort of thing?"

"No. I gather he tends to keep himself to himself, not one for late-night drinking sessions after the show like some actors; and I've got a wife to go home to."

"Children?"

"Two sons; grown-up, living away from home."

"How far away?"

"Alan's in Edinburgh working for the British Geological Survey. Lawrence is a major in the army."

"Where's he based?"

"He's in Afghanistan at the moment."

Philippa looked across to Warren in case he had any more questions.

"All right, Mr Strange," said Warren, "that will be all for now, but I'd be grateful if you'd stay on the premises and help my officers coordinate these interviews."

"I'll be glad to. Who would you like me to send up now?"

"Miss Bunting, please."

While he was out of the room, Warren said to Philippa: "To be honest, we're just going through the motions here. I haven't seen a soul who looks physically capable of strangling a chicken, let alone a six-foot man, even if he was old."

"None of the actors look up to it, sir," said Philippa, "though I'm not so sure about some of the stage-hands. That's a physical job."

"Nothing like how it used to be in the old days," said Warren. "It's mostly pushing buttons now. Not much pulling on heavy ropes."

Rebecca Bunting knocked gingerly on the door and was told to come in. She confirmed that she had been in the foyer counting bottles with Ivan Strange at the time of the murder.

"Did anyone go through the corridor leading to backstage in either direction around that time?"

She thought about it. "No. Definitely not."

"Would you necessarily have noticed if it was

somebody authorised, somebody on the staff."

"Yes; at least I think so."

Warren told her she could go home, but asked her to tell Ivan Strange to start sending the actors up to see him one by one, other than Jason Dean, Claire Comerford, Nick Velliadis and Tim McGarry, with whom he had already spoken.

The interviews with the remaining actors yielded nothing except to eliminate the entire cast from suspicion. John Montgomery, Julian Rainford, Paul Grant and Theo Chapman had all spent the first ten minutes of the interval chatting in the green room, then returned to their dressing-rooms to prepare for the second half. They had all remained there in the company of the person they were sharing with throughout the rest of the interval and until after the murder had been committed. Besides, although Montgomery was fairly tall at around five-foot-ten, he was weak and skinny; nor did any of the others come anywhere near the physique required to have broken Nutley's neck.

The two young actresses, Tessa Verrall and Emily Grady, both said they had spent the entire interval shut in their dressing-room together and remained there until after the murder.

They were all asked whether they had seen where any of the stage-hands were during the critical period. Given that they had all been downstairs, whereas the production crew tended to remain upstairs on the stage and workshop level, the answer was unanimously no.

When they had all been questioned, they were told to go back and wait in the auditorium.

"Just as we expected," said Warren.

"Let's see what the stage-hands have to say for themselves," said Philippa.

"Tell you what, though," said Warren, "see if you can get someone to send us up a cup of tea first."

"I was going to, sir. How about you, Andy?"

"Milk and two sugars, please."

Jameel Kazemi passed Philippa descending the stairs as he was ascending.

"Warren up here somewhere?" he asked.

"In the manager's office, straight ahead."

Kazemi knocked, entered, and said, "You need to see this straight away, sir."

He placed a clear plastic evidence bag on the desk.

"What is it?"

"The victim's toilet bag; containing four recreational doses of cocaine and the paraphernalia for inhaling it."

"Well, well."

"There were also two empty baggies and a used straw. At a guess I'd say he snorted a line before the performance and another during the interval."

"Or he and a friend had one each."

"There was only one cleaned-up patch of surface in the dressing-room, directly in front of his mirror. No signs of social use. Almost certainly a solitary pick-me-up."

"Right, I'll buy that. Still, four extra baggies unused."

"Two for tonight's show and two just-in-case?"

"Or two extra in case any pretty girls fancied a line?"

"Anyway, that's it, sir," said Kazemi. "I'll leave the deductions to you."

"Thanks for bringing this straight up, Jim. Trouble is, I'm going to have to see all the actors again and ask them if they were aware of Nutley's habit."

Warren filled Philippa in on the cocaine when she arrived back with the teas on a tray for all three of them.

They agreed to split the actors between them to speed up asking them if they knew anything about Nutley's cocaine snorting, Philippa seeing the women plus Jason Dean and John Montgomery in the foyer, Warren the rest. None of them admitted to knowing anything, although Claire Comerford said there had been gossip in the business for decades that Nutley sometimes went to wild parties attended by some pretty dodgy underworld types.

"But before we do that," said Warren, "I think it would be a good idea to see what I can get out of this Spiller fellow, especially about Nutley's carryings-on. Keep things under control while I'm out, will you?"

"Yes, sir." Warren got up to go. "And, sir?"

"Yes, Sergeant?"

"Have one for me while you're down there."

"Cheeky hussy."

9

Daniel Spiller had long since finished his steak-and-ale pie in The Standing Order when Warren appeared and sat opposite him in one of the booths along the far wall, separated by polished wooden partitions. The pub was getting busy, early on the Saturday evening, with England's first World Cup match in Brazil due to kick off an hour before midnight. The big television screens on the walls were muted at the moment, but the general noise of drinkers discussing England's chances would shield their conversation from prying ears. Spiller had drunk a quarter of the pint of Doombar on the table in front of him, his second, and Warren arrived carrying a pint of the latest guest beer. He always liked to try as many real ales as possible. Although some turned out to be less appetising than others, anything was better than lager. Spiller wasn't a suspect, having been more than 50 miles away at the time of the murder, but he should be able to fill in some important background about Nutley.

Warren observed that Daniel Spiller had obviously been a handsome man for most of his life. Even now, in his early sixties, he retained much of the charismatic appearance that had helped propel his successful career as an entrepreneur and occasional actor, despite the puffiness that had invaded his cheeks and neck over the past decade, and the evident but not excessive belly of a habitual *bon viveur*. His hair had turned silver, but he retained a full head of it, and it seemed to be bursting outwards in all directions from a central point above the middle of his forehead, defying any attempt to control it. Even his bushy grey eyebrows gave the impression that they were almost visibly growing. His lightweight pale-grey summer suit looked off-the-peg rather than made-to-measure, but it had been a fairly expensive peg, at the John Lewis end of the range. His white shirt with narrow, pale blue stripes was of pure cotton, and although it was open at the neck on this hot day, Warren guessed there would be a tie in the jacket pocket just in case.

"We're both busy men, so I'll come straight to the point," said Warren. "I'm looking for motives. Why would anybody want to murder Roger Nutley, in your opinion?"

"Well, I suppose we have to assume it's got something to do with his trial," replied Spiller.

"I'd got that far; but I need to know whether there might have been any other dark corners in his life. How well did you know him?"

"We go back a long way. Not best mates or anything like that, but we kept in touch now and then."

"How far back? How did you first meet him?"

"When he was in The Filth. I got my first telly job on it while I was still at stage school."

"So you're an actor yourself?"

"Used to be. Anyhow, as you can imagine, I was as nervous as hell. It was the big break, as I saw it, and I didn't want to screw up. Actually it was only a couple of scenes as a teenage tearaway caught burgling. Roger Nutley, the big star you'd have expected to be a bit stand-offish, took me under his wing, gave me some good, common-sense tips about how to behave on set and how not to piss people off, and I can tell you it's a lot different from the stage."

"When was this?"

"That would have been, let's see, 1968. It was my first telly job, a terrific break. Roger left The Filth soon after my episode and went on to other things. I was only 16, very wet behind the ears, as you can imagine, but the experience stood me in good stead for other screen work later on."

Although he was too young to have seen it at the time, Warren had watched a few old episodes of The Filth on the satellite and cable channels, so he knew why Roger Nutley had become rich and famous back in the 1960s. He had been known to the nation as Geoff Harkness, the much-loved friendly neighbourhood copper in the hugely popular twice-weekly police drama. The tough, rugged, but fair-minded detective-constable was irresistibly attractive to women on-screen, and Geoff Harkness had various girl-friends during his nine years of fictitious existence. But in his private life off-screen, Roger Nutley was reputed to be very much a loner, was never seen around night-clubs and discos, and despite diligent stalking by paparazzi, the gossip magazines had never been able to link him to anyone romantically.

"Did you see anything of him at the time of his trial?" Warren asked.

"Of course I did. That's what friends are for. And, for the record, I never believed he was guilty. The trouble is, mud sticks, and that old saying about sticks and stones is a load of rubbish. It damaged him psychologically, emotionally, and financially. Those women have got a lot to answer for, but they won't have to, the law gave them anonymity. It's a bloody disgrace."

It never ceased to amaze Warren how passionately people could take sides without being in possession of all the facts.

Roger Nutley had eventually gained his knighthood thanks to a long and acclaimed career as a classical stage actor rather than his earlier contribution to popular television crime drama. Then he had been accused, nearly half-a-century after the crimes were alleged to have been committed, of sexually abusing three women, and in one case of raping her.

"When you were acting in The Filth yourself, did you notice any signs of him sexually harassing women? Or hear any gossip?"

"No; but then I was only at the studio for a week, and I was totally obsessed with getting my bits right, so I didn't have the time or the inclination for gossip; not that the regulars exactly took newcomers like me into their circle, anyhow; that's what was so nice about Roger; he had no side, and talked to me in the canteen as if I was an equal."

In the end the jury had been unable to reach a verdict. The Crown Prosecution Service had decided against going for a retrial. They apparently calculated that it would probably amount to nothing more than a re-run of Nutley's words against his accusers', and lead to a similar outcome or even an acquittal. But that had not been good enough for the witch-hunters among the press and public who would never believe him innocent, whatever the evidence and the verdict. So life after the trial had continued to be very difficult. Until this tour came up, his agent had been unable to find him any work, despite the fact that, although he was now in his mid-seventies, his talent remained undiminished.

"So how does he come to be working for you playing Shakespeare after all this time? Bit of a turnaround, isn't it?"

"He was having a tough time after the trial. You don't retire when you're an actor, it's in the blood, you go on until you drop because you love it, and if the work dries up, you're miserable, you don't want to spend your time doing the garden and redecorating your house. He walked out of that court an innocent man, but nobody would give him a part in anything because of that nasty old saying there's no smoke without fire. No telly, no films, no theatre, he couldn't even get a corporate role-play. Then I needed a Polonius. Most people only knew Roger as the heart-throb copper on The Filth, or popping up as guest leads in various drama series on the telly when he was older, but I'd seen him do Shakespeare on the stage quite a few times over the years and I knew why he got the knighthood. You should have seen his Lear; it was breathtaking; plus he was the sort of name that puts bums on seats, and you need that these days, it's pretty hard to get the public into live theatre unless there's at least one name they recognise off the telly."

"You took a risk, didn't you? The tabloids could have hounded you for trying to get publicity from employing a man accused of rape."

"Accused but not convicted, Inspector. Yes, well, I've spent my life taking risks. Sending out plays on tour isn't exactly like working nine-to-five in an insurance office. Sometimes your life savings are riding on your next production. Yes, the pack of wolves might have gone for us, but I have lawyers as well. Anyway, as it turns out we've spent the last five months playing to packed houses in Number One theatres the length and breadth of the land, including in places where a Shakespeare play might normally be expected to attract less than a hundred people and the theatre managements normally book stand-up comedians, hypnotists, psychics and failed politicians, just so as to be able to pay the electricity bills."

"How did he get on with the other actors?"

"People liked him in a quiet sort of way."

"That sounds a bit like one hand clapping. Should I be getting the impression that he wasn't exactly the life and soul of the party?"

"And that's no bad thing. Actors who try too hard to get everybody to like them can be a pain in the arse on a long tour. Roger was never one for late-night drinking parties, but he was no snob, he got on with the job, and he was always quick with a save if somebody else dried."

"I'm sorry, I don't quite follow you. What's a save?"

"All actors forget a line sometimes. We call that a dry. To avoid an embarrassing silence, a real pro will step in and make something up that moves things along, so that the audience don't notice. That's what we call a save."

"I can see how that would make people like him."

"Better than buying rounds of drinks every night."

"But the fact is he's apparently been murdered by somebody in the cast or the theatre staff."

"If you're asking me whether anybody in the cast had a motive to kill him, I'd have to say I find it very hard to imagine; and it's not very likely to have been one of the local theatre staff, is it? He'd only been here less than six days, you'd have to work hard to get somebody to hate you enough to kill you in that time, wouldn't you?"

"You'd be surprised; but okay, leaving aside for the moment the fact that nobody except cast and crew seems to have had access, did anybody else have a grudge against him?"

"Not that I can think of. Why don't you ask his agent?"

"Who's that?"

"Simon Edler Associates."

"Have you got the number?"

"Not on me. It'll be quicker if you google his website."

"Okay, but where's the office?"

"Charing Cross Road."

"Just one other thing," said Warren. "Were you aware

that Sir Roger Nutley was a regular cocaine user?"

"It's not uncommon in the entertainment world, Inspector."

"Would it surprise you that he took a line in his dressing-room before going on stage?"

Spiller drained his glass: "Nothing surprises me in this business. One for the road, Inspector?"

"No, thank you, I need to get back."

"I'll come with you. Can I talk to my actors yet?"

"Yes, they're waiting for you."

Warren finished his drink, and he and Spiller walked back together through the warm summer air.

*

Philippa came back to the manager's office to rejoin Warren for the interviews with the technical crew. This comprised stage manager Mike Moore, sound and lighting engineer Peter Gunn, and stage hands Tony Earnshaw, Ugochukwu Okadigbo and Krzysztof Budziszewski. Mike Moore was first in and said he, Tony and Ugo had been sitting in the store room drinking tea and coffee and quietly talking about the World Cup. Peter worked his electronic magic from the rear of the auditorium and came nowhere near backstage throughout the entire performance.

"What about the fourth chap?" Warren asked.

"Chris? He would have been in the workshop. He's dead keen on a project he's working on by himself, and I don't need him in the wings till later on."

"Anybody with him?"

"I doubt it. He gets very absorbed."

Earnshaw and Okadigbo confirmed they had been in the store-room with Mike Moore at the time of the murder; which just left the man with the east European looking name.

Krzysztof Budziszewski was a handsome man by any measure. When he walked into the office, he radiated assurance without arrogance. He was not smiling, but Warren sensed that if he did it would knock most women off their feet. In his mid-twenties, his black hair was turning prematurely white and thus streaked in an effect which a rich person might pay a hairdresser a lot of money to produce artificially, parted on the left, touching his ears and trimmed tidily in a style which somehow seemed more American than European. His eyes managed to be piercingly bright despite being dark brown. None of these, however, were what struck Warren as his most significant features in the circumstances. What did were his height and strength. He looked to be about six-foot-three, with none of the stoop which very tall men sometimes slide into. He was broad-shouldered and powerfully built, without an ounce of excess fat in sight, and the musculature of his arms suggested regular workouts with weights. He halted in front of the desk, standing almost at attention. Andy Jasper stood behind him, beside the door, and at six-foot-one, it wasn't often he felt shorter than somebody else.

"Sit down, please, Mr ..." began Warren.

"Budziszewski. I am Polish. My first name is Krzysztof. English people call me Chris, it is easier for you."

Warren looked down at the list on the desk in front of him. "That's all right. I'm quite happy to call you by your proper name, Mr Boodzeeshefski," he said, pronouncing it correctly.

The stage hand looked momentarily astonished, but recovered quickly. "So how can I help you, Inspector?" he asked with very little foreign accent.

Speaks better English than a lot of the locals, thought Warren: "You can start by telling me where you were and what you were doing at the time Sir Roger Nutley was murdered."

"I was in the workshop."

"Doing what?"

"Trying out some ideas for my beanstalk."

"I'm sorry?"

"We are producing our pantomime in-house this Christmas. It will be Jack and the Beanstalk. I am designing the beanstalk."

"I thought you were employed as a stage-hand."

"That is correct; for the time being, at least; but in Poland I have a degree from the University of Fine Arts in

Poznan, and I specialised in modern sculpture; so I asked Mr Strange if he would allow me to design a very exciting and unusual structure for our beanstalk, a sort of space-age beanstalk, something to give to the production what you call the wow factor; and he agreed."

"I suppose that's a lot more interesting for you than carrying sofas on and off the stage."

"Yes, exactly. Actually I should like to become a set designer full-time; not only in theatres but also at bigger events, both indoors and outdoors."

"But how come you were working on your project while the play was going on? What about your duties on the stage?"

"I was working on it during the interval, it's not a problem, and actually I have nothing else to do for quite a long time after the start of the second half, because the set does not change at all until the Gravedigger comes on at the beginning of Act Five, when we have to quickly change everything to an outdoor scene. So I have been using this time all this week to work on my beanstalk. It's okay, Mr Moore knows what I am doing, and I am never late, I return immediately to my position in the wings as soon as I hear the Queen telling Laertes that his sister Ophelia has drowned."

"Was anybody with you in the workshop?" asked Warren.

Budziszewski hesitated and glanced briefly down at the desk before answering: "No, they were all too busy with the play."

"So you were alone in there. What, all through the interval, and afterwards?"

Another hesitation: "Yes."

"You didn't see anybody else there?"

"No. Not until I heard all the noise and I came out."

"What noise?"

"The safety curtain coming down, and then people talking loudly, right behind the stage, the actors, I mean, and also a lot of noise from the audience."

"And then?"

"Mr Strange came out from the wings and told us that

Mr Nutley was dead, on the stage."

"What did you do when you heard that?"

"I went to find Mr Moore and Tony and Ugo and we sat down in the store-room, which is also like our room for drinking tea and coffee."

"This is a different room from the green room downstairs?"

"Yes, that is for the actors."

Warren leaned back and looked into the calm face of the stage-hand. He seemed to be unaware of the seriousness of his situation. Either that or he was such a good actor himself that he ought to have been drinking his tea or coffee in the green room instead of the store-room.

"Mr Budziszewski, let me get this clear. At the time when Sir Roger Nutley was being killed, you were completely alone?"

"Yes. In the workshop. I did not see anything, if that's what you mean. Nobody came past me."

"Is there anybody who can confirm that is where you were?"

"Mr Moore. He knows I always go there at that time. So do the others."

"You're missing my point. Could anybody actually see that that is where you were, that you were in the workshop, and not anywhere else, at the exact time of the murder?"

Budziszewski's features tightened: "What are you implying?"

"Can anyone vouch for the fact that you were where you say you were when Roger Nutley was killed?"

A long hesitation before answering.

"Well, no, not really."

"You do see that this places you in a rather compromising situation?"

Anger came into the expression of the hitherto calm interviewee: "Why? Because I am from Poland, from eastern Europe, and of course we are all gangsters and murderers, I suppose?"

"That has nothing to do with it. The workshop is immediately behind the backstage corridor. The dark space in which Roger Nutley was killed runs along the back of the stage behind a heavy blackout curtain. There was nobody in the area of the corridor or in the stage-right wing at the time. You could have walked into that dark space, broken Sir Roger's neck, and got back to the workshop without anyone seeing you, in less than a minute. Nobody else had that opportunity."

Budziszewski looked genuinely shocked. He opened his mouth to speak but closed it again without uttering a sound. Warren leaned forward across the desk and fixed his gaze.

"Did you kill Roger Nutley?"

"Nie!" shouted the Pole. *"Jak śmiesz oskarżać mnie o to?"* He banged his fist on the desk so that a stapler, a pocket calculator and various other bits and pieces of office clutter jumped.

Warren sat back in his chair: "I'd be grateful if you would stick to speaking English."

"I said how you dare accuse me of that."

"You are a big, strong man, Krzysztof. In fact, you seem to be the only person in this theatre who is physically capable of murdering a man as tall as Sir Roger Nutley in the way it was done. You are also the only person who has nobody to witness where you were at the time. What am I supposed to think?

The colour drained from Budziszewski's tanned face. He started to speak: "I suppose I..." then stopped.

"You suppose what?"

"Nothing. I suppose I understand what you are saying, but you are wrong. In any case, why should I want to kill the Englishman? I did not know him. He was nothing to me."

There had been something there for a moment, Warren thought; something that the Pole had been going to tell him, then thought better of. A confession? Or something else? This conversation was going to have to continue for as long as it took to tease out the truth behind all those hesitations. That was probably not going to be possible here at the theatre.

"Did you talk to him at all while he was working here this week?"

"No. He never spoke a word to me; not even hello. Some actors are like that with the crew, you know..."

"Stand-offish? Snooty?"

"Snooty, yes, it is a good word. But most of them are friendly."

"Did you resent the fact that Sir Roger was snooty towards you?"

"Of course not. I would not expect anything from such a famous man. It doesn't matter."

Warren thought, a little common courtesy doesn't cost anything, however famous you might be, but he let it pass.

"Had you heard of Sir Roger Nutley before he came here?"

"Actually, no. Tony told me last week we had a television star coming; a celeb, as you English call it. That is a ridiculous word, in my opinion. Anyway, naturally I believed it would be the actor playing the part of Hamlet. I was surprised when Mr Moore told me on Monday it was this old man who plays the foolish Polonius."

An off-the-wall idea popped into Warren's head: "Do you know the play, then?"

"Of course. The works of William Shakespeare are very popular in my country; especially Hamlet; usually translated into Polish, of course. It is still good, but it loses much in translation. You cannot keep the language from the time of Queen Elizabeth, and the poetic brilliance."

So much for the UK being swamped with uneducated Polish benefit scroungers, thought Warren. This chap would be a real asset to Britain; except that he was beginning to look like the prime suspect for having murdered a celebrity.

"Then you probably know that the name Polonius is thought to suggest that the character is of Polish origin."

"Of course."

"Do you resent the fact that the Polish character is an old fool?"

"Don't be ridiculous, Inspector. You are surely not suggesting that I killed an actor because I consider William Shakespeare to be anti-Polish?"

It had, indeed, been an absurd suggestion. It was

difficult to imagine what motive this urbane Polish arts graduate could have had for murdering Nutley, unless you resorted to the extremely unlikely possibility of a sudden bad-tempered flare-up between the two virtual strangers immediately beforehand. Over what? A perceived insult? A woman? Some remark about the Second World War? It just wasn't on, when you thought about it. Yet the fact remained that the handsome Pole was, in practice, the only viable suspect. Warren decided there was no point in trying to take the interview any further at the theatre, stood up and said, "I must ask you to accompany me to Norton Hill Police Station to answer some more questions. You are not under arrest, you will be assisting us with our enquiries. Do you understand?"

"Can I phone my wife?"

"We can sort that out at the station."

"You are making a mistake," said the Pole. "I did not kill your television celebrity; but somebody did. Be careful not to allow that man to escape."

Warren wished he had a quid for every time he had heard that one. He felt reasonably sure he had his man. The only problem was going to be finding some evidence a bit less circumstantial than the fact that he was physically capable of committing the murder and had the opportunity. The CPS would want more than that, dammit.

SUNDAY 15 JUNE

1

Between half-past-eight and nine o'clock on Sunday morning, the initial core members of the Murder Inquiry Team gathered in the Norton Hill Police Station incident room. Before the briefing got under way, most of the chat was about England's disastrous opening World Cup football match against Italy the night before. Blame was being apportioned between the vulnerability of the England team's defence, and the steamy tropical heat of the rain-forest city of Manaus. At five to nine, Superintendent James Astbury entered the room, took up his seat beside DI Warren facing outwards from behind a table, and shared a few murmured thoughts with him; whether about the case or the football was inaudible to anyone else. At this early stage, no flip charts, whiteboards or other accoutrements had been set up. Facing Astbury and Warren was a small team for a murder investigation, which could be considerably enlarged if and when necessary. The initial, core team consisted of DI Warren, DS Philippa Myers and four DCs; plus the scientific officer, exhibits officers, the head of the Soco team, the heads of the HOLMES computer team, the disclosure team and the admin team, and a statement reader.

The Super stood up and spoke first, after throwing a meaningful look around the room: "This investigation is going to be very high profile, whether we like it or not, so we can't assume we've got our man, however unlikely or even, frankly, impossible it may seem that it could have been anybody else. Any one of you is likely to be badgered by the press, and they might well be pretending to be just an interested member of the public, so now more than ever you'll need to remember your training about keeping your ears and eyes open and your mouths shut. All formal press enquiries must be referred to me. Now then, how much do any of you know about Nutley?"

"He was in The Filth," said Jim McGregor, the statement reader, who was the only person in the room old enough to remember the 1960s television cops series.

"I've seen him in something on telly since then, can't remember what though," said DC Matt Rayner.

"He was more of a stage actor, though, wasn't he?" said DC Sammy Cohen.

"That's exactly right," put in Warren, "and not just any old stage actor, but one of this country's finest interpreters of Shakespeare and other classics; and yes, he was in 'The Filth' in the sixties, and since then he's appeared on television in all sorts of supporting roles."

Superintendent Astbury took over again: "Now, what about his trial for sexual offences, anybody?"

"Couple of years ago, sir, but he got away with it," said DC Rayner.

"He didn't 'get away with it', as you put it, the jury was unable to reach a verdict, and the CPS didn't see any mileage in a retrial. However you're involved in this investigation, you all need to be fully cognizant of the background. You can look up the details as soon as you get the chance, they'll be on the system, but the basic facts are these. On February the 26th, 2012, after a two-and-a-half week trial, the jury failed to convict Sir Roger Nutley of raping one woman and sexually abusing two others. He was 74 years of age at the time of his trial, but the offences were alleged to have taken place between 1964 and 1966, when he was in his late twenties, and the three women who accused him were all in their early twenties and studying to become actresses. All the offences were alleged to have taken place at the prestigious Rosemary Madison Acting School, of which, thanks to his TV stardom, he was a Patron despite his youth, and where he gave guest classes in screen acting. The prosecution barrister told the court that Nutley exploited his position to elicit sexual favours from female students in return for promises of career advancement after they graduated, and that in these three cases he refused to take no for an answer."

"Typical man," muttered DC Georgina Stanbridge.

"Yes, thank you," said Astbury, irritated, "just remember that we're talking about a human being who, so far as we're concerned, may never actually have committed any of those offences, and was brutally murdered yesterday." He paused to allow an uncomfortable silence to produce the desired chastening effect. "Nutley told the court he could not remember ever having met any of the women who accused him. He denied ever holding meetings with any young women alone in his office at the college or anywhere else, saying it would have been far too dangerous for him, as it would have exposed a man in his position to precisely this kind of accusations which, even if unsubstantiated, might well have ended up as his word against the woman's; and knowing the insatiable appetite of the tabloid newspapers for salacious gossip, he would have risked having his career blighted if not finished by a lie. Eventually that appears to be exactly what happened."

"Appears to be," repeated DC Stanbridge. "He still might have done it and just been a good liar in court. Hard to prove anything 50 years later, I should have thought."

"Yes, I'll come back to that in a moment," said Astbury. "Anyhow, a whole string of other famous actors were called as character witnesses during the trial, describing him variously as 'delightful,' 'a jolly good chap,' and 'a perfect gentleman who never told a dirty joke, let alone touched anybody up.' Nutley's lawyers also called defence witnesses who worked at the college at the time and asked them if they had ever seen Nutley alone in the company of young, female students, and they all said no. In the end, it came down to their word against his, and you have to wonder why his alleged victims didn't report him at the time. Enough members of the jury were not convinced."

"So are you saying you don't think the murder had anything to do with the trial, sir?" asked Rayner.

"If we leave the Polish man out for a moment, then that's going to be a central question of this investigation," said Astbury. "But that's enough from me. DI Warren is going to continue as SIO, and I'll hand you over to his tender mercies now."

The Superintendent sat down and Warren stood up. "We're holding a Polish stage-hand named Krzysztof Budziszewski in custody," said Warren. "He's the only person backstage with the physique and the height to have broken the victim's neck in the swift, silent way it was done; the only person backstage with nobody else to vouch for where he was at the time; and from where he was working, alone in the workshop, he was the only person who could have reached the narrow space behind the curtain at the back of the stage without being seen."

"Job done then, sir," piped up DC Tom Pleasance. "Open and shut case."

"The only problem is, why would a fine arts graduate from Poznan in Poland with absolutely no connection to the victim have wanted to kill him?" asked DS Philippa Myers.

"Heat of the moment," said Pleasance. "Maybe they'd just had a row."

"If they did, nobody heard it," said Warren. "In the meantime, I'll need checks with Europol and the local police in Poznan on whether he's got form, and a HOLMES national computer check on whether he had in fact got some kind of connection with Nutley that he's lying about. DC Rayner, get on with that today, please."

"Yes, sir."

"Now, returning to the Nutley trial, if he was really guilty, somebody might have killed him as an act of revenge; but if he was innocent, there's no such motive, and we have to look elsewhere for our murderer. I'm keeping an open mind on that for the moment, and so should all of you. All possibilities have to be taken seriously. We know he took cocaine. So do an awful lot of people, especially in the world of entertainment. That alone isn't usually enough to get them murdered, least of all in such a bizarre and public fashion."

"Yes, sir, I was wondering that, why was he killed in such a ridiculous way?" asked DC Stanbridge. "I mean, if you wanted to bump off an old bloke in his seventies, you wouldn't hang about at the back of a stage with hundreds of people watching, would you? There must be a lot of easier ways of getting away with it."

"You'd think so, wouldn't you?" said Warren.

"It must be the Pole," said Rayner. "Otherwise the killer would have had to be capable of vanishing into thin air."

"Like the ghost of Hamlet's father," said Cohen.

"Well done," said Warren. "Somebody was listening at school."

"I'm in my local Am Dram group, sir."

This was an unwise admission, for an amused "whooo" went around the room as junior officers looked at each other, sensing an opportunity for endless leg-pulling about tights and forsooths.

"Right," said Warren, "maybe forensics will be able to tell us a bit more today. They've been going over every inch of all the backstage areas all night, so something might turn up to give us another angle. We'll be searching Nutley's flat and I'll be interviewing his agent as soon as possible to see what else I can find out about his private life. The actors weren't much use in that respect, he doesn't seem to have talked about himself down the pub at all. In the meantime, DS Myers..."

"Sir?" said Philippa.

"Your immediate job is to track down the three women who accused Nutley of assaulting them. I don't want them brought in, I want you to go and see them in their own homes, no advance warning, use your instincts, obviously find out if they and their husbands or whatever have alibis for yesterday afternoon, and try to get a sense of whether they have anything bottled up inside them that would make it seem worth going as far as killing him."

"They were granted anonymity, sir," said Philippa.

"Not from us, only from the public," said Warren. "They'll be in the national computer; or if you can't find them, let me know and I'll get the names and addresses out of the CPS, even if I have to phone somebody on their Sunday round of golf."

"Or in church," quipped Pleasance.

"Well, we could do with a few prayers being said for us on this one," said Warren.

"Couldn't somebody have snuck in unseen from the auditorium and out again?" asked Rayner. "Or slipped in and out of the stage door?"

"Getting backstage from the auditorium's impossible without being seen, and nobody came in and out of the stage door."

"Who says?"

"The stage doorkeeper."

"And what about him?"

"Her, actually. You mean as a candidate for our murderer? Not unless an overweight, middle-aged, paraplegic woman in a wheelchair could get up and down two steep flights of stairs in under two minutes, meanwhile immobilising a six-foot man and snapping his neck; and like I say, she didn't see anybody go in and out of the stage door anywhere near that time."

"She could be lying to protect somebody who came in, sir."

"I thought of that, but she wasn't. There's a CCTV camera on the outside, and it was recording. It's been checked already. The last person to go in through that door was one of the actors arriving for work forty minutes before the play started; and nobody went out in the whole of that time."

"Then, with respect sir, either it's the Pole, or two or more people who are giving each other alibis have got to be lying; actors or stage hands. Maybe they all hated him."

"You mean they all killed him, like in 'Murder on the Orient Express'? Get a grip, laddie! This is north London, not the Balkans."

*

When Warren went downstairs after the briefing he heard a noisy argument coming from the front hall and went through to investigate. He found a uniformed constable confronting an angry man who was shouting that it was bloody scandalous and demanding to speak to a senior officer.

"I'm a senior officer, what's the problem, sir?" said Warren.

"It's not a problem, it's a bloody disgrace," shouted the man.

Warren turned to the Sergeant and raised a quizzical eyebrow.

"Robbery yesterday at the gentleman's handbag shop, sir."

"Took you lot half an hour to get there," said the man.

"And your name is?"

"Mendelsohn. Zev Mendelsohn."

"Is it true we took half an hour to attend, Sergeant?"

"The phone call reported a shot fired, sir, so we had to wait for armed response."

"I see. Would you like to come through, Mr Mendelsohn?"

Warren led Zev Mendelsohn to a soft interview room and invited him to sit on one of the sofas. He was in his forties, short, slim and moderately fit. Even though he was angry there was something about the directions of the lines which just were beginning to form around the edges of his eyes and mouth that suggested that on a better day he would be a jolly man with a ready smile. Despite his small stature, he was good-looking in a way which probably helped no end in selling designer handbags to ladies. He had a dark brown, full beard which matched his well-coiffed hair. He was wearing a smart Lyle & Scott crew neck t-shirt in broad stripes of tangerine, black and white, lightweight beige cargo trousers, and pale grey and white Nike trainers, all of which looked as if they had come brand-new out of the box that morning. The clothes, though casual, made a statement of wealth.

"Now then, sir, I'm Detective Inspector Warren. If you could just tell me exactly what happened..."

"It was bloody terrifying. They were waving axes and one of them had a gun."

"You saw the gun yourself, did you, sir?"

"Saw it? He fired it at my daughter."

Warren raised his eyebrows. No-one had been reported wounded in the incident.

"He missed, I take it."

"Yes, *barux hashem!* Well, to be honest, it was a warning shot at the wall."

"What sort of a gun was it?"

"A shotgun. Double barrels."

"Sawn-off?"

"Yes, that's it."

"Who else was in the shop at the time?"

"My precious daughter, Zoe, she was serving a customer."

"I see. And have they given statements?"

"Your people in uniform took statements from all of us at the shop yesterday afternoon. This morning I woke up still bloody furious at the slowness, so here I am."

"Yes, I can see that you're angry, Mr Mendelsohn. If you'll just give me a chance to explain."

"Go ahead. I'm all ears."

"When we get a report of a robbery with violence, we get there fast."

Mendelsohn tried to interrupt, but Warren held up a hand to stop him.

"However, if it becomes clear that firearms are involved, we're under an obligation to call in an armed response team, and that obviously takes a little longer. The trouble is, if unarmed police cars arrived with flashing lights and sirens, the robbers might panic and start shooting, or quite likely take hostages; and we wouldn't have wanted you and your daughter and your customers being held at gunpoint. What actually happened when the police arrived, Mr Mendelsohn?"

"The gang were long gone."

"Did they get away with much?"

"Three hundred and sixty grand's worth, if you call that much, I certainly do."

Warren was astonished.

"I thought you said you sold handbags. How many did they take to be worth that much? Sounds like a truckload to me."

"No, Inspector, the bags I sell are from top designers. Nothing under, what, I suppose the cheapest would be seven and a half grand, without any discount."

"Seven thousand five hundred pounds – for a handbag?

"The ones they got away with retail at up to seventeen thousand. They took thirty bags. It's enough, wouldn't you say?"

"I have to confess I'm almost speechless," said

Warren. "I had no idea you could spend that much on a handbag. Who buys them?"

For some reason he didn't understand himself, Zev Mendelsohn had warmed to Warren. He not only calmed down, but actually managed a faint smile. He was, after all, insured, and the explanation about the firearms made a lot of sense.

"You're not Jewish, are you, Inspector?"

"No. Church of England. I go to church once in a blue moon."

"So ... Jewish princesses, we call them. Ever been to a Jewish wedding?"

"Unfortunately not."

"I'll get you an invite to one. Then you'll see where a Jewish husband's money goes." He actually managed a laugh at his own joke.

"I'd like that, thank you."

"Don't bring your wife. She might learn some tricks about using your credit card." Mendelsohn was getting into his stride on what seemed to be his favourite subject, the spendthrift nature of women.

"Fortunately my wife's not a big spender."

"Oh, you're a wise man, like Solomon!"

"I thought he had seven hundred wives."

"A policeman who knows his Old Testament! Well, true, so the Bible says, although personally I don't know where he would have got the energy from; but still, they hadn't invented credit cards then, so I daresay he could afford it."

Satisfied that Mr Mendelsohn's ire had been dampened, at least for the time being, Warren felt that he could safely leave him alone for a few moments without risk of a further outburst.

"Would you mind waiting here a few minutes, while I just go and check on the reports?"

"Be my guest. It's a home from home here," Mendelsohn gestured expansively at his surroundings.

Warren went to find out if anybody knew the details.

"A decision was taken to try to intercept, sir, as we understood they'd left the scene," said Sergeant Brian Sturgess.

"No luck, I take it."

"No, sir."

"Any descriptions?"

"Apparently not."

"What about the vehicle?"

"An Audi Q7, no less. Reported stolen last night and found abandoned in the early hours."

"Where?"

"Potters Bar."

Warren returned to the interview room.

"Were any of you able to describe any of the assailants, Mr Mendelsohn?"

"They were all in black overalls. And they had black motorbike helmets on with the visors down. Look, I'm sorry I lost my temper."

"Perfectly natural, sir. I'd probably be the same. But to be honest, I can't really promise you anything."

"I'll get the insurance, and it'll be in all the papers. You know what they say: all publicity is good publicity. They'll be queuing all the way back to Brent Cross next week."

"Sometimes people remember little details later on, after the shock passes. So if you do, let me know."

"Inspector Warren, wasn't it?"

"That's me."

Mendelsohn held out his hand: "A pleasure doing business with you, Inspector. And if you ever want a handbag for your wife..."

"I'll buy it in Primark."

Mendelsohn roared with laughter as Warren showed him out, feeling rather glad he would never have to pay for a Jewish wedding.

2

Carol Baxter and her husband Peter owned a boarding kennels and cattery north of London, outside Biggleswade. After a courtesy phone call to Cambridgeshire Constabulary, who had no wish to become involved, Philippa headed up the A1 in her unmarked silver Skoda Octavia, accompanied by DC Wayne

Hollier. As a woman herself, she did not want any of the three wronged women from Nutley's trial to turn out to be a murderess. Like most of her gender, she preferred to think of violent crime as being an almost exclusively male province. But as a professional policewoman, she reminded herself that bitter and disillusioning experience had taught her that was far from being the case. In addition to which, the crime figures hid the unpalatable fact that a lot of women had a habit of using their sexual allure to persuade men to do the actual violent deeds on their behalf. Come to think of it, what was she thinking about, mentally referring to the plaintiffs in the court case as 'wronged women'? A jury of seven women and five men had failed to convict Nutley, hadn't it? So in the eyes of the law, they had not been wronged. Yet many in the press had wanted Nutley to be guilty, and had gone on implying, just within the bounds of the law of libel, that the jury had been fooled, because that was more salacious and titillating than the idea of his being innocent. Philippa knew that she must conduct these interviews without showing prejudice either way.

The kennels were reached via a labyrinth of B-roads. On the rare occasions in her life that she ventured out into what she and her family still referred to as 'the sticks', Philippa wondered how she had managed before the invention of the satnav, and recalled frustrating halts in lay-bys to consult a map.

At 32, DS Philippa Myers was still single and saw herself as a dedicated career woman. She had been born in Hackney in 1981 when her father, Colin, was working on lousy wages for a local building company. Her mother, Angela, gave up work for the first few years of her life to devote herself, in a way that was by then going out of fashion, to being a full-time mum. However, she studied book-keeping at home while Philippa was asleep, and later while she was at nursery and primary school. Struggling to get by on just Colin's miserly wages and child allowance, they lived in an unattractive rented two-bedroom terraced house in Stoke Newington. Then in 1987 Colin and a mate at work called Dave decided to ride the Thatcherite wave and go it alone by setting up their own central heating maintenance firm. Dave had contacts along the outer reaches of the Central Line, so they set up shop in Woodford. It was a longish early-morning and evening commute for Colin, but within three years they were prospering and he put down a deposit on a substantial three-bedroom semi with a garden in Buckhurst Hill. With Philippa now at school, Angie did the books for the firm, and soon branched out into book-keeping for other local tradesmen as well. Since the 2008 global economic crash, the business had been struggling, but Colin refused to blame the crooked international bankers who had caused it, cursing instead the Labour government, especially Gordon Brown. Philippa had long shared her parents' view, reinforced by regular reading of the Daily Mail, that anyone who was prepared to work hard need not be poor, especially if taxes were kept low. This was an outlook which brought her into subdued ideological conflict with Warren. She had been buying her modern one-bedroom flat in Burnt Oak, overlooking a stylish landscaped courtyard, since her promotion to Sergeant in 2007, but the mortgage interest constantly gobbled up a high proportion of her salary, inhibiting her ability to spend money on socialising or holidays. The tabloid press gave her the impression that others, less deserving and hard-working than she, were living lives of luxury, with foreign holidays being paid for by benefits that came out of her taxes. However, her day-to-day experience of the grinding poverty and suffering that she witnessed while policing the sink estates of London flew in the face of that prejudice. Although she did not yet realise it, this contradiction between belief and evidence was building up emotional stress inside her.

Eventually, after passing through a village called Hemlington, on a long, straight stretch of narrow road with lush fields of ripening wheat on both sides, a board on a post on the verge announced, "Blue Shingles Boarding Kennels and Cattery – 400 yards'. Then at a cluster of low buildings a larger sign showed cartoon images of a smiling white dog and cat on a blue background. Philippa turned on to the drive and stopped in a small car park. Two other vehicles were parked there: a grey Skoda Superb Estate with a 2012 registration, and a plain blue Ford Transit van with two long parallel scratches along the side facing her. It was old, X-registered. She routinely noted down their numbers. A chorus of barking greeted Philippa and Wayne, coming from four dogs running around in a fenced, grass exercise area: an Airedale, a Schnauzer, and two of what her dad called Heinz Varieties.

Straight ahead, the end of the drive gave on to the front of a neat, red-brick two-storey house with wooden shingles painted pale blue. To the right, across the paved area, was the entrance to the kennels and cattery, with extensive single-storey buildings behind it to accommodate the four-legged guests. A wood cabin entrance with windows bore a sign reading, 'Reception – Ring Bell and Wait – Open 9am to 11.30am & 3.30pm to 6pm". Philippa instinctively glanced at her watch, even though she had no intention of waiting for opening hours. Anyway, it was twenty past ten, so the question didn't arise. She rang the bell. After a short wait, a man opened a door at the back of the reception cabin, closed it behind him, walked through and opened the front door to Philippa.

"Come in," he said amicably, "Sorry I kept you waiting, I'm cleaning out the cats' litter trays."

"Nice job," said Philippa.

"You get used to it. What can I do for you?"

The man had stepped behind a counter, on which were blank booking forms and a telephone. He was big, over six foot tall, in his seventies judging by the lines on his tanned and weathered face, but with a lean, muscular body that would otherwise have put him closer to a well-preserved sixty. He had striking white, wavy hair that hung well below his shoulders, like an ageing rock star. He was wearing a black t-shirt with the words 'Royal Marines Commando – It's a State of Mind' in a big circle around a grinning skull that wore a black beret above two crossed daggers. His black jeans were held up by a broad, black leather belt with a large brass buckle in the shape of an eagle's head, and he had on heavy black boots.

"Mr Baxter?"

"That's me. Canine or feline?"

"I'm sorry?"

"Is it a dog or a cat you'd like us to board? You're a new customer, so would you like me to show you around?"

"Actually it was Mrs Baxter I was hoping to have a word with."

Baxter stiffened.

"She's in the house baking cakes. I can tell you whatever you need to know."

"Actually it's not about dogs or cats, it's a personal matter."

"What are you, reporters? Because you can shove off now if you are. We don't want nothing to do with the bloody papers."

"I can quite understand that," said Philippa, showing him her warrant card. "I'm DS Myers, this is DC Hollier."

"What's this about?"

"If I could just speak with Mrs Baxter, sir."

"I told you, she's busy. I don't want her bothered. I can answer any questions you got."

"I shall be wanting to ask you a few questions as well, sir, but I do need to talk to your wife first. It's just routine. Now, if you wouldn't mind telling her I'm here."

Baxter thought for a moment.

"All I'm asking is what it's about. Carol's had a lot of hassle. Any stress is bad for her."

"It's a murder investigation, Mr Baxter."

"You what?"

"So if we could go and see your wife now..."

Baxter hesitated before making up his mind.

"You'd better come round to the house. She's baking fairy cakes for the WI fete on an industrial scale, and if I interrupt and they spoil I'll be in the dog-house for the rest of the week."

Philippa cast a glance in the direction of the kennels and couldn't resist the obvious quip: "I thought you already were."

Peter Baxter managed a reluctant chuckle: "The old ones are the best. Follow me."

He led her out through the rear door of the entrance cabin into a wide courtyard leading to the kennels on the right and to a small door into the cattery straight ahead. To the left a gate in a six-foot high wooden fence gave into the private garden of the house. Glancing to the right after entering, Philippa observed a beautifully maintained lawn edged by generous beds of tall, well-cultivated perennials, leading to a vegetable garden and fruit trees at the far end, beyond which were a large shed and a greenhouse. All the fencing and the shed looked as if they had been recently treated with preservative in natural wood colour, and the overall impression was of an immaculate haven of tranquillity. She felt a brief twinge of envy for a lifestyle that had never appealed to her before, being a city girl through and through. She wondered in passing if this was the sort of change that comes over you in your thirties.

"Who's the gardener?" she asked.

"Both of us," he replied. "It's our passion."

"It's lovely."

"We'll go in through the conservatory so as not to open the kitchen door and make a draught. If Carol's cakes go flat I'll be..."

"...in the dog-house," finished Philippa.

She reckoned the interview would be more likely to yield results if both of them were disarmed and relaxed than if they had their backs up. Good grief, she thought, now I'm thinking in cat metaphors. I know I'm single but I'm nowhere near forty yet. Mercifully Baxter allowed himself another slight chuckle.

"You're getting the idea," he said. "Take a seat. I'll go and see if I can drag my wife away from her baking."

He passed through an open French window into the main part of the house, leaving Philippa alone in the big, semi-circular conservatory, which had been built on as an extension. It was a sun-trap and very warm. She sat down on an armchair which formed part of a cane-framed three-piece suite upholstered with pale-green-and-cream striped cushions, matching two high, pale-green cane display shelves on either side and a similar glass-topped round table in the middle. The furniture all looked new and of very good quality. The shelves held a full set of crystal glassware which in London would have been kept in a more secure indoor room, various porcelain dogs and cats that Philippa guessed were antiques rather than seaside knick-knacks, several dozen large, hard-cover gardening books, and a stack of magazines on a bottom shelf which seemed to consist mostly of Country Life, Homes & Gardens, and suchlike. She could hear a subdued conversation taking place between the Baxters somewhere within, presumably in the kitchen, but was unable to make out what was being said. Looking in through the French window into a large dining-room, she noticed that everything there looked expensive, including a highly-polished oak dining-table long enough to accommodate ten chairs around it and still leave plenty of leg-room. So much for the yokels living in rustic squalor, she thought. This beat any of her friends' pads in town.

Peter Baxter returned through the dining-room, followed by Carol Baxter. She was a short, slim woman who Philippa already knew from the files on the Roger Nutley trial to be seventy years old. She was certainly no yokel: she had highlighted, dyed light-brown hair in a simple, bobbed style that didn't come cheaply, and subtly applied make-up which combined to make her appear under sixty in a good light.

"Thank you for interrupting your baking," said Philippa. "I know how important timing is."

"That's all right, dear," said Carol, "I've just put another batch in the oven." She had a cultivated, prim voice.

She was wearing a plain, pale-blue apron over a smart, long-sleeved, plain grey jumper, with a deceptively simple, pleated, grey skirt to just below the knee. The image suggested Middle England conservatism, sobriety and righteousness; the Church of England, the Women's Institute and the Conservative Party incarnate.

Carol Baxter accommodated herself elegantly on the cane armchair facing Philippa. Peter Baxter half-sat, half sprawled on the two-seater cane sofa, leaning sideways on the end cushion furthest from Philippa, his long legs stretched out towards her, still wearing his heavy boots. He stared at her in a pose of passively aggressive affected nonchalance. DC Hollier remained standing at the rear of the conservatory, taking notes.

"You said this was about a murder inquiry," Baxter said. "What murder inquiry would that be?"

"You must have heard," said Philippa, glancing from husband to wife.

"Heard what?" asked Carol. "We don't listen to village gossip."

"About Sir Roger Nutley."

The demure country lady's expression twisted into a mask of hatred: "Don't tell me that bastard's gone and murdered some poor cow now." The cultured accent had degenerated instantly into estuary. "Not that it would surprise me. As if rape wasn't enough for him."

"No, Mrs Baxter, you don't seem to understand. He hasn't murdered anyone; he's been murdered."

"Serves the bugger right," said Peter Baxter. The reaction did not entirely surprise Philippa. People who felt they had been wronged often over-reacted verbally.

"Is that how you feel, Mrs Baxter?"

"Well, I shan't exactly be sending flowers to his funeral, if you know what I mean. Who killed him?"

"That's what we're trying to establish; but what I don't understand is how you didn't know. It's been all over the television news and on the radio and on the front pages of all the national newspapers."

"We don't buy the Sunday papers and haven't had the radio or telly on today," said Peter Baxter.

"Hasn't anybody mentioned it to you, though, considering your connection to Mr Nutley?"

"D'you think I've gone around telling everybody in the village I was one of the women in the Roger Nutley trial? We were given anonymity, in case you've forgotten; but enough people knew about it where I used to live so that I didn't feel comfortable, which is why we both gave up our jobs and bought this place. The villagers and customers have no idea, and I'd like to keep it that way, thank you very much."

"Why don't you want people to know? And by the way, where did you used to live?"

"Beckenham in south-east London; and because we'd have the press and all sorts of nutters on our doorstep nonstop; not that you can tell the difference some of the time. So I'd like to remind you that my anonymity was granted by the judge, and that's legally binding, even on the police."

"Just a minute," said Peter Baxter, sitting up angrily and eyeballing Philippa more directly. "Are you here because you think one of us murdered Nutley?"

"We have to visit everybody involved in the trial, if only to eliminate them. It's routine."

"I know all about police routine," snapped Carol Baxter. "It was police routine that let him get off the hook. Well, police incompetence more like."

Philippa was growing anxious in case Peter Baxter's anger should explode, but instead he became affable again and, turning his head towards his wife, resumed his relaxed, sideways slouch on the sofa.

"The young lady's right, though," he said. "I can see how they'd have to come here; and it's not as if we've got anything to hide." He threw his wife a meaningful look.

"Come on then," said Carol. "Ask your questions."

"Thank you, Mrs Baxter. Where were you between three and five o'clock yesterday afternoon?"

"That's easy. I was here. We're open from half-past-three to six o'clock every afternoon except Sundays for customers to bring their pets in and take them out."

"Did you have any customers yesterday afternoon?"

"I should say so. It's summer, people go on holiday."

"Anyone who could corroborate that you were here between those times?"

"A whole list of them. I can give you a photocopy if you like," said Peter Baxter.

"That would be perfect. And what about you, Mr Baxter?"

"I was here, too, though I was out the back with the dogs most of the time."

"Can anybody corroborate that, apart from you, Mrs Baxter?"

"Well, they wouldn't have seen Peter unless they came through the back with me to see which pen their pet was being put in and give it a goodbye stroke. Some people do."

"John Blagden came through, I remember that," said Peter Baxter.

"Yes, he did," said Carol.

"And he waved at me and we both called out good afternoon."

"Who's John Blagden?" asked Philippa.

"He runs a car repair business in Royston," said Peter Baxter. "He's a regular customer twice a year when he takes his family on their summer and winter holidays. German Shepherd."

"Bella," said Carol.

"I beg your pardon?" said Philippa.

"The dog's called Bella."

"Would you mind giving me his address?"

"It'll be on the list I give you," said Peter, "but you won't catch him at home in the daytime, he'll be at the business, even on a Sunday, knowing him. It's called Blagden Motor Repairs. It's on the internet."

"I can look it up," said Philippa, standing up. "Well, thank you both for your cooperation. I'll speak to Mr Blagden, but I don't suppose we'll need to bother you again. Oh, and I'll take that list of yesterday's callers on my way out, just as a matter of routine."

"Aren't you going to tell us what happened, then?" said Carol Baxter.

"How do you mean?"

"You said Nutley was murdered. You didn't say how or where."

"I'm sorry, I forgot you don't read the papers. He was killed during a performance of a play he was in. Round the back of the stage. In London. The murderer broke his neck from behind." She looked at Peter Baxter's t-shirt again. "Were you actually in the Commandos, Mr Baxter?"

"Eighteen years". He grinned. "You can call me Sergeant, if you want, Sergeant. I know what you're thinking, but it wasn't me that broke that bastard's neck."

3

As Senior Investigating Officer, Warren's role could be, if he chose to treat it as such, largely managerial. There was no need for him constantly to get his hands dirty at the coal-face. Nonetheless, he preferred to go out and involve himself at first hand whenever possible. That urge did not spring from a refusal to delegate, but because he understood that the human brain was still the best and most intuitive computer in existence; able to process immense quantities of information subconsciously, then unexpectedly produce answers to seemingly insoluble problems. Reading other people's statements and reports might never achieve this. So he needed as much random information as possible, visual, aural or even olfactory, to enter his brain at the scene of the crime and as many other relevant locations as possible.

That was why he attended in person the search of Sir Roger Nutley's apartment. It was at Swiss Cottage, a stone's throw from the Hampstead Theatre and the Royal Central School of Speech and Drama. They could tell on sight that it must be worth a few million quid. It was in a modern block built of cream-coloured stone on a leafy corner. Looking upwards he could see that the penthouse apartments on the sixth floor had a great deal of glass on both sides. A uniformed concierge at a reception desk had been warned by the block's management that the police were likely to be coming, but he'd figured that out for himself having heard the news on the radio. He took Warren and DC Cohen up in the lift with him to the sixth floor and used his pass key to unlock the door of Nutley's flat, which was the one on the front corner. "Best apartment in the block, sir; the view's rather good." The concierge then went back down to bring up DCs Rayner and Pleasance. His remark about the view proved to be an understatement. From the floor-to-ceiling windows on the south side of the huge living-room, the eye was drawn across Regent's Park to the skyline of central London and, in the distance, the Shard on the south side of the river. Not for the first time Warren surmised that the Shard must have the best view in London because it would be only place you couldn't see the Shard from. The whole flat enjoyed bright sunlight thanks to huge windows in every room, white-painted walls throughout, and honey oak solid wood flooring which by itself would probably cost enough to buy a small house in a more modest area. The living-room furnishings were sparse; this was no cosy, lived-in family home. At one end a low, pale-grey leather four-piece suite surrounded a huge glass-topped coffee-table strewn with showbiz magazines and copies of The Stage. At the other, a stylish wooden dining table accommodated half-a-dozen simple but expensive dining chairs. There was nothing on the table, and there were no signs of leftovers. Presumably Sir Roger had eaten out yesterday lunchtime, and at some time in the day a cleaning-lady had come in and made everything spick and span before the news of his death was broadcast.

The living-room walls were hung with frames containing posters of past productions in which Nutley had appeared. Some had been with Britain's most prestigious publicly subsidised theatrical companies, some in the West End and major provincial theatres, some in New York. More than half were plays by Shakespeare. As Warren allowed his gaze to dart around the walls, he noticed Macbeth, Titus Andronicus, Richard III, Julius Caesar and King Lear. A lot of darkness there, he silently mused; a lot of death, mental suffering, torture, tragedy, leavened with some cruelly misogynistic male domination and humiliation of women. There were also posters for 'Tis Pity She's a Whore by Thomas Dekker from the same period, Women Beware Women by Thomas Middleton, which Warren knew to be one of the bloodiest of the Jacobean tragedies but had never seen performed, and The Duchess of Malfi by John Webster, another Jacobean feast of horror and nastiness, showing what happens when a woman has the temerity to refuse to conform to the norm of meekness and submissiveness to men. None of these plays seemed likely to lift the spirits of those performing them into joviality. If, as seemed likely, Sir Roger Nutley had enjoyed the privileged position of being able to choose his roles, these might be viewed by a psychiatrist as disturbing in the consistency of their attitudes. Warren's musings on the relevance or otherwise of Nutley's thespian choices were interrupted by DC Cohen's voice calling from the kitchen.

"Sir, there's something here you need to see."

Warren stepped through the hallway to the kitchen: a visually striking oversized galley with shiny black granite worktops and floor tiles and shiny white walls and cupboards, showing no signs of regular use.

"What is it?"

"Looks like drugs, sir."

"Hardly surprising, as he was using cocaine at the theatre. Let's have a shufty."

DC Cohen was an enthusiastic 24-year-old from Barnet who had come into CID from uniform the previous October and showed initiative and a willingness to go the extra mile that ought to take him far. He had lifted the lid of a cube-shaped porcelain jar, decorated to look like a liquorice allsort, that was standing in a rear corner of a worktop between one of those wooden box digital radios and a cordless telephone unit. Without touching, Warren leaned over, peered inside and saw a clear, polythene bag full of white powder.

"If that's the Devil's Dandruff, it's an awful lot of it, and worth a small fortune," he said. "You haven't touched the bag, have you?"

"No, sir, just the knob on the top of the pot to lift the lid off."

"Fine. Bag up the whole pot and we'll have it gone over for dabs. A hundred to one there'll be nobody's except Nutley's own, but you never know your luck until the ball stops rolling."

"No, sir," said Cohen, wondering where Warren got his archaic turns of phrase from.

"And keep on searching," said Warren to all three of them; but an hour later, nothing else of note had been turned up.

*

Retired DCI Bob Brannigan and Superintendent James Astbury were friends as well as former colleagues, which is why Brannigan's phone-call about Archie had prompted Astbury into doing a little homework on the subject of dognapping gangs. In consequence, a circular was going to be sent around Norton Hill Police Station ordering all officers to treat reports of dog thefts more seriously and issue crime numbers. It was why Warren was now standing in the Super's office on a Sunday, being told to find somebody to coordinate whatever reports came in and initiate some kind of action.

"With respect sir, people's pooches going walkabout are hardly our top priority at the moment," said Warren. "Quite apart from the Nutley murder, there's enough proper crime out there to keep us more than busy; especially after these cuts in manpower."

"I know we're stretched," said Astbury, "but I'm not talking about missing pooches; you may not realise it, but dognapping has become big business."

"Somebody nicks a pedigree poodle from a garden and flogs it down the road for a couple of hundred quid; it's not exactly the Mafia, is it, sir?"

"You'd be surprised. It's organised crime."

Warren was unable to suppress a chuckle.

"It's no laughing matter, Bunny. Do you know how many dog thefts are reported? Around five thousand last year; and that's the tip of the iceberg. Precisely because we don't take it seriously, the animal charities reckon the number of unreported crimes is a multiple of that."

"But still..."

"We've got an epidemic of it in north London, especially the outer suburbs where there's more money. A lot of people round here think nothing of spending a couple of grand on a pedigree animal."

"More money than sense, if you ask me. There's plenty of dogs in rescue centres looking for a good home. That's where I'd get one if I wanted one."

"Look, I'm not asking you to divert resources from serious crime. What I am telling you to do is to make sure every officer in this station takes reports of stolen pedigree dogs seriously and issues a crime number. We haven't been doing that. All officers are being sent this."

The Superintendent handed Warren an A4 page of Metropolitan Police headed paper. He glanced at one. It was headed: 'Why We Must Take Dog Theft Seriously."

"Read it. And keep your own eyes and ears open. In my opinion a lot of the thefts around here are the work of a single gang. But we've got nothing on them. I want that changed. Okay?"

"Yes, sir," said Warren, wondering where you started on something as random as dogs being stolen.

"How's the Nutley investigation coming along?"

"Prime suspect in detention, sir. A Polish stage-hand, built like a brick outhouse. He's the only person who could have done it. He had the opportunity and the ability."

"What about motive?"

"That's the only problem, sir. There's nothing to connect him to the victim."

"You sure he's the only realistic suspect?"

"Everybody backstage is accounted for at the time of the murder, and the stage doorkeeper swears nobody came in or went out. It's just conceivable that somebody who was in the audience could have got backstage just before the curtain went up for the second half, but they would have also needed to have not only a detailed knowledge of the layout of that part of the theatre, but also of the way the set was arranged for Polonius to hide behind the curtain, and the exact timing of that scene; and where everybody else was going to be backstage at that time so as not to be seen sneaking on to the back of the stage and off again; which means we've got over 600 suspects for pulling off a feat that looks virtually impossible anyway."

"Well, keep at it. I don't need to tell you we're in the spotlight on this one, and I really don't want to start reading headlines of the Police Are Baffled variety."

"No, sir."

*

It wouldn't be much of a detour to visit the car repair business, so Philippa decided to swing by on the off-chance Mr Blagden might be working on a Sunday, as Baxter had suggested he would. The workshop turned out to be not quite in Royston but a couple of miles outside the town on the A10 London Road heading south. On the right-hand side of the road was a cluster of small businesses, all related to motor vehicles. The words 'Blagden Motor Repairs' stood out in red on white on a long, low signboard attached to a metal barrier, with a long black arrow pointing along a narrow access road. A sixty-yard walk brought them to wide-open double gates in a high metal fence, leading into a yard with three cars parked along the right-hand side, none of them exactly in their prime. There was a portacabin office on the left, and an enclosed workshop at the far end. There appeared to be nobody in the office, although a German Shepherd dog had put its front feet up on the windowsill at their approach and let out a single, deep-throated warning bark to its owner, who now emerged from behind a grey Nissan Primera in the workshop.

John Blagden was of medium height, medium build, had medium-length brown hair and was wearing an oily grey overall. His appearance, Philippa thought, was immediately forgettable.

"Can I help you?" he asked.

"Police," said Philippa.

"Really? No dodgy motors here, love, you'll have to go to Arthur Daley for those." He laughed at his own joke, and his smile was amiable enough, so Philippa ignored the "love".

"Nothing like that, sir. I just need some corroboration from you relating to an ongoing enquiry. Actually it has nothing to do with the motor trade. You are John Blagden, I presume?"

"Well, if I can help the boys in blue in any way; or should I say the girls in blue." His voice wasn't quite London; it had a touch of East Anglian elongated vowels, but not enough to sound rural. "You'd better come into the office. Fancy a cuppa? Any excuse, eh?"

"That's very kind of you, Mr Blagden, but I shouldn't think we'll need more than a few moments of your time."

He led them up two small wooden steps, pushed open the door of the portacabin, and stroked the dog's head. It looked up at DC Hollier, who confidently showed it the back of his hand, drooping, which it correctly interpreted as a sign of friendship and proceeded to lick his hand and wrist. "Friendly dog," said Wayne.

"She loves people, but if you'd come in here uninvited you wouldn't have got far. I can't keep an eye on the office when I've got my head buried under the bonnet of some old banger, but she lets me know when there's anybody about. Her name's Bella. Take a seat."

"Good girl, Bella," said Philippa, sitting on a battered, beige two-seater sofa with bits of foam rubber poking out through rips. The dog trotted over to her and she tickled its neck and ears. Blagden sat on an upright chair behind a desk. Wayne found an old leather armchair at the far end of the office.

"So, what can I do for you?"

"If you could just tell me where you were between three and five o'clock yesterday afternoon, sir."

"Landed at Luton from Prague lunchtime, drove home, collected Bella from the kennels at half-past three. We'd just come back from one of those City Breaks, the wife and I, beautiful place Prague, never been before."

Philippa stopped tickling Bella and the dog walked to a corner and lay down on her blanket.

"What's the name of the kennels?"

"Blue Shingles. They look after the dogs very well."

"Do you know the owners?"

"I wouldn't say know, but I've put Bella there a few times, so I've chatted with Pete and Carol a bit."

"Did you see them both there yesterday?"

"I saw Carol, she checked Bella out. Nothing wrong is there? Not an infectious canine disease or anything?" He cast an anxious glance towards Bella.

"Not at all. It's nothing to do with the dogs, don't worry. And did you see Mr Baxter?"

"Yes, but he only waved and said hello, he was working down the other end."

"But you were close enough to be sure it was him?"

"Absolutely."

"Thank you, Mr Blagden, that's all I needed to know. We shan't need to trouble you anymore."

"Mind if I ask what it's about?"

"Routine enquiries, sir."

Philippa and Wayne stood up to leave and Blagden came around his desk to see her out. They looked up from outside and saw Bella's face at the window watching them go. Philippa momentarily fancied she might quite like a dog, then dismissed the thought as totally impracticable in her job.

*

"What I want to know," asked Warren, "is how a man could be murdered on the stage of a theatre in the space of a few seconds, without any noise, without apparently a weapon being used, and without leaving any blood."

The canteen was quiet before lunch. DI Warren and Police Surgeon Ian Fairbanks had popped in for a caffeine blast. The only others in there were a couple of PCs in uniform. The rush for grub would start in an hour or so.

"Killing a person with one's bare hands is not so difficult as most people assume," said Fairbanks, "although it helps to be stronger than your victim and have the element of surprise, especially if you need to do it with a minimum of noise. This is what commandos are trained to do quickly and efficiently, typically to neutralise guards around an installation that's about to be attacked."

"So how's it done?"

"The commando killer needs to know the vulnerable points of the body that allow death to be inflicted quickly by causing the maximum damage in the minimum space of time," explained Fairbanks. "Of course, he could do it by cutting the victim's throat from behind with a knife, but that's messy, so our killer used his bare hands. Let me tell you the murderer's options; although I warn you none of it's pretty."

"I'm sure I can take it."

"Right, well, don't say I didn't warn you. To kill with

your bare hands, you have to focus on the head and throat. The skin in the hollow of the neck is very thin and can be pierced much like one would a plastic bag with the fingers and nails, and ripped open to allow access to the windpipe directly. But that would also be messy, with blood spurting everywhere."

"There wasn't any," said Warren.

"Exactly. Our man needed a clean kill that would leave no blood on his clothes or skin. He could have done it by constricting the throat with his forearm in a rear armlock. That requires terrific strength to be sure of causing death without a struggle. A strong man with commando expertise could have the victim under control in five seconds and unconscious within twenty. Ideally he then needs to maintain the grip for three minutes, until the body has stopped convulsing and all the tremors have ceased."

"He didn't have time for that," said Warren. "The actor was going to be dragged back into the view of the audience in less than a minute, pretending to be dead."

"Exactly," said Fairbanks, "when Hamlet pulls aside the curtain. Anyhow, the way to do it fast is with hard, well-aimed blows against the windpipe and the voice-box at the front of the neck, so as to completely crush and flatten the windpipe. Once the windpipe is squashed, the mucous in the throat seals it and the victim can't breathe. You can do it with a fist, but it's more common in the army and the marines to use a karate chop with the edge of a hand."

"So is that what our man did?" asked Warren.

"Yes. He used the karate chop method first, then broke Nutley's neck with a twisting wrench to make sure, or possibly for dramatic effect. The body being dragged on to the stage with the head hanging loosely to one side was probably intended to cause maximum horror. Your murderer wanted to put on a show, Inspector."

"Pour encourager les autres."

"How's that?"

"It's a quote in a story by Voltaire: 'In England it is good, from time to time, to kill an admiral, to encourage the others.'"

"Oh. Right. Well, I'll take your word for it."

"Sorry, I just mean, perhaps he intended to issue some kind of warning; but to whom is a puzzle. People who don't pay their debts for recreational drugs, maybe?"

"Look, I only tell you the how. The why, I leave that up to you."

4

The lanky, skinny young man in a dirty white t-shirt, black running shorts and grubby trainers seemed friendly as he smiled down at Joanna Wenham's tiny white, fluffy puppy.

"What's your dog's name?"

"Louis."

"That's French, innit?"

"Yes. He's a French breed."

"What, foreign dog is it?"

"He's a Bichon Frisé."

The youth recognised the name as an expensive breed. "Right, I'm havin' that," he snarled, grabbing the lead and jerking it away.

"Get off, get off," yelled Joanna, holding on with grim determination to the puppy.

The youth punched her in the face. Blood streamed from her nose. She held on to the lead and screamed.

A big, black man in his thirties came out of a convenience store a hundred yards along the street on the other side. He saw what was happening and began running towards Joanna and her attacker.

Seeing him coming and judging him to be a dangerous opponent, the youth let go of the lead and legged it in the opposite direction. Spitefully he kicked the puppy before he went.

The puppy howled pitifully from the pain and fell on to its side. Joanne's rescuer decided there was no point in pursuit.

"What was that about?" he asked.

"He tried to steal my dog."

Joanna had difficulty talking through the pain in her

face and the blood running over her mouth.

"My name's Dumle. We'd better get you to A&E. I'll drive you there."

"Please, can we take Louis to the vet first? He looks bad."

Dumle Nwoko squatted beside the whimpering puppy and tentatively examined it.

"Okay. They can probably staunch your bleeding too."

Dumle's white Citroen C5 was parked outside the shop. He gently scooped up the puppy and carried it, leading Joanna to the car, and drove them both to Norton Vale Veterinary Centre.

A veterinary nurse patched up Joanna's nose, which was cut but not broken. A vet said the puppy's leg wasn't broken and he had only suffered soft tissue damage and bruising, but he would limp for a few weeks. They decided to keep him in overnight for observation.

*

Warren was growing impatient to find out whether there was anything on Nutley's computer that might point towards who his killer was, so when he arrived back at the station he made a bee-line for the cyber boffins.

"Nothing unusual in his browsing," said Johnny Chen. "What you'd expect, really: a lot of scripts of plays and films, the record of YouTube videos watched, mainly drama and feature film excerpts; plus he liked steam trains."

"No insights into his sexual predilections, then?" asked Warren.

"No porn at all, which is actually rather unusual, although he has visited some extremely expensive escort sites."

"That could be helpful. Let me have a list of them."

"Already in my report; but the thing is, I think it's some emails that you're really going to be interested in."

"What about?"

"Well, the polite expression would be professional jealousy, but I'd say it goes further than that, there's some pretty nasty stuff."

"Written by Nutley?"

"No, the other fellow. Another actor by the look of it. Name of Noel Wharton."

"Thanks, I'll take a look. Anything else?"

"Sorry. That's about the whole of it so far. Though we could go deeper into the hard disk looking for deleted material that's still lurking around in the shadows."

"Do it. We're all under pressure on this one. Anything at all, however unlikely or bizarre, come straight to me with it."

*

It was the start of DC Marion Everitt's third week in CID. She was hoping something a little more interesting than the routine tasks she had been given so far might turn up soon; taking part in this celebrity murder investigation, for example. She had grown up in the small west Dorset town of Bridport and joined Dorset Police when she was 18, learning the job on the streets of Bournemouth and Poole, which turned out to be a tougher place than most people might think. When a chance to move to the Met had come up unexpectedly, she had jumped at it to gain experience, although she was not one of those who saw London as their ultimate goal, and could easily imagine moving back out to the provinces if the right opportunity arose. Her West Country accent sometimes fooled suspects into thinking of her as a country bumpkin; an arrogant error which could lead to fatal indiscretions. What she had not expected was that her potential as a detective would be spotted swiftly by DI Warren, and that he would request her transfer to CID within 18 months of her arrival in Norton Hill. So far, however, it had been a matter of observe, help with paperwork, watch and learn. Her spirits lifted when Warren asked her to pop into his office.

"I've got a special assignment for you," he began.

"Is it to do with the murder, sir?"

"No, you'll be on your own on this, at least to begin with. There's been a spate of dognappings in our area."

Marion's heart sank. This sounded very low priority.

"The Super's been on to me to get it stopped. He actually had me in his office about it on a Sunday, so I reckon he must have some personal interest. See what you can find out. If you get anywhere with it, it'll be a feather in your cap."

Okay, she thought, the priority level just went up a notch or three, unless this was bullshit.

"Yes, sir. On my own, you say?"

"Absolutely. Use your initiative."

"Yes, sir."

"Well, off you go then, get on with it."

*

In an interview room, the recorder was running. Krzysztof Budziszewski sat calm and erect, beside duty solicitor Barbara Pike and across the plain metal table from Warren. PC Paul Duddigan was standing beside the door. The Pole had not lost his self-assurance. Well, that would soon break down under pressure.

"So tell me about this beanstalk," said Warren.

"Why? Do you think I hit him with a beanstalk?"

"You're not helping yourself with that attitude."

"And you are not helping yourselves by wasting your time on me. There is a killer out there somewhere."

"I think I've got my murderer in this interview room. Why did you do it?"

"Inspector, when I talked with you yesterday in the theatre you seemed to be an intelligent man, but now I am starting to think you are a fool."

Warren refused to take the bait: "You walked from the workshop to the back of the stage in your black overalls at exactly the time when you knew that Sir Roger Nutley would be alone in the dark behind the curtain. You smashed his throat with a karate chop and you broke his neck with your arms. Then you walked back to your beanstalk as if nothing had happened."

"Nothing had happened. I never left the workshop. It would have been very stupid to do what you have just described. Somebody could have seen me; an actor, a member

98

of the crew, Mr Moore might have come by."

"It was Saturday. There had already been six performances of this particular play, every evening from Monday to Friday and on Wednesday afternoon. You had used those performances to test the timing and the walk, to memorise exactly the lines that were being said by the actors on the stage. Six times you tested your walk both ways and by yesterday afternoon you were certain that you would not be seen, and you carried out your plan."

Barbara Pike cut in: "Do you have a question to ask my client, Inspector, or do you plan to waste everyone's time making baseless accusations?"

Budziszewski ignored the interruption: "For God's sake, Inspector, that is rubbish. In any case, why would I want to murder an English actor who nobody in my country has ever heard of?"

That was the million-pound question, but Warren didn't allow the doubt to show on his face.

"Maybe somebody English paid you."

"You are fantasising. I do not think that even in this crazy country a professional assassin would resort to such an exotic method of killing."

"You do not need to say so much, Mr..." Ms Pike looked down at her notes, "Budziszewski. Just answer reasonable questions."

But the Pole had made another valid point. A hit-man could have taken Nutley out almost anywhere else with less difficulty and risk; and professional killers are notoriously risk-averse. Move on.

"Have you ever served in the Polish or any other armed forces?"

"The Polish government abolished compulsory military service in 2008, inspector. As a matter of fact I was lucky; my year was the first to be excused; although it would have been delayed until after I had completed my university studies."

"I think you received commando training somewhere and that you exploited that knowledge to kill Sir Roger."

"Is that a question, Inspector?" asked Ms Pike.

Warren could feel the thin ice cracking, but Budziszewski was the only possible suspect and he must have learned to do that chopping and choking somewhere; perhaps in a terrorist training camp? Get a grip man, this has nothing to do with terrorism, how could it have?

"Inspector," volunteered Budziszewski, "I am a pacifist and a vegetarian. I do not know karate or judo. I do not know how to break another man's neck. Now I have had enough of this helping with your enquiries when you do nothing but accuse me."

"If you have no evidence with which to charge my client, I must ask that you release him," said Ms Pike.

"You killed him, admit it."

Budziszewski held up the palm of his right hand in front of Warren. "Enough. You are bullying me in a language which is not my own. I am therefore at a disadvantage. All right. *Odmawiam dalszej współpracy, aż podasz tłumacza.*"

"What?"

"I said, I refuse to continue to cooperate until you provide me with an interpreter."

"Come off it, Krzysztof. You speak better English than most of the English riff-raff we get in here."

"I will continue to help you, but not until the interpreter is here."

"It's Sunday. That probably won't be possible until tomorrow."

"He's within his rights," said the solicitor.

"Yes, thank you Ms Pike, and I have no doubt that you are aware that, by the time I've found a Polish interpreter, the time I can hold the prisoner without charging him will be running out."

"Well, I'm sorry, but you should have thought of that before you started bullying my client."

"Of course," said Warren, "if your client is innocent he could help himself by giving a sample of his DNA."

Ms Pike turned to Budziszewski: "You are under no obligation."

"That's fine," said the Pole. "The sooner they do it, the sooner I can go home."

5

Sylvia Thorbinson lived in a red-brick terraced house with bay windows. The doors and windows were in need of repainting. There was a 2006 grey Vauxhall Astra parked on the drive, next to a tidy rectangular garden of low-maintenance small shrubs and weeds. Philippa rang the doorbell. The tiny woman who opened the door was about 70, her grey hair tightly permed in a short, conservative style which was no longer fashionable. She wore a plain beige blouse above a calf-length, beige, pleated skirt, and despite the hot weather, a beige lambswool cardigan. Her brown eyes seemed small and sunken as if retreating from a hostile world, and the lines of her face seemed etched into a permanent pattern of anxiety, or disappointment, or both. Her thin lips were tightly closed whenever she was not speaking, and the ends of her mouth curved steeply downwards, conveying an impression of permanent offence. She pointed at a sticker on the glass of the door intended to repel cold callers: "Can't you read?"

Philippa showed her warrant card: "DS Myers, Metropolitan Police, this is my colleague, DC Hollier. Would you be Mrs Sylvia Thorbinson?"

"Yes, I would. What's this about?"

"I'm here in pursuance of a murder investigation, Mrs Thorbinson. I need to talk to you. Could we come in for a few moments, please?"

Sylvia Thorbinson looked Philippa and Hollier up and down, took a step back and opened the door wide: "I don't see why not."

They followed her into a living room that even a teenager would have described as a tip. The dining-room table was covered in dirty dishes from what appeared to be last night's dinner and this morning's breakfast. The floor was strewn with celebrity and TV listings magazines. The room reeked of cat food. Sylvia Thorbinson sat herself down in the far corner of the sofa. A huge flat-screen television occupied much of the long wall facing her, showing a dinner party in progress.

"Sit yourselves down, you can move one of the cats,

they won't mind," said Mrs Thorbinson. A grey cat lay half-curled like a chocolate-box illustration on the armchair beyond the sofa, achieving a degree of elegance that none of the human occupants of the room could manage, and a tortoiseshell-and-white moggie was grooming itself assiduously on the nearer chair. Philippa deftly scooped up the latter feline and deposited it on the carpet, where it paused to throw her a swift look of disgust before continuing unruffled with its ablutions. DC Hollier remained standing and took out his notebook.

"What's this about a murder? Nothing to do with me."

"The murder of Sir Roger Nutley."

"Oh, yeah. Somebody cut his bloody throat, didn't they? Serves the bastard right, if you ask me."

"Broke his neck, actually. I have to ask you about your whereabouts at the time, Mrs Thorbinson."

"What, you think I killed him?" Her bitter laughter dissolved into coughing. "Yeah, all right, I can see where you're coming from, cos he got off from raping me you think I wanted me revenge, fair enough. But I didn't. He's ain't worth it, love."

"Where were you yesterday afternoon?"

"Down the Railway Inn, same as always."

"Did anybody see you there?"

"About twenty of 'em, I should think. Go and ask the manager, Geoff, he'll tell you. Is that all?"

"For now," said Philippa. She stood up to leave and picked up a family photograph on the mantelpiece. The woman in the middle was clearly Sylvia Thorbinson, younger, wearing a smart dress and a broad-brimmed hat on a sunny day. On her left stood a younger woman; beyond her a tall man in a suit; and in between those two, a little blonde girl in a summer dress.

"Your family?"

"My daughter Helen, my ex-son-in-law, and my grand-daughter Elizabeth," said Mrs Thorbinson. "Well, not exactly grand-daughter, she's adopted, the poor bugger was firing blanks," she added with unnecessary candour.

"See much of them?"

"Helen pops round sometimes to see if I'm all right. Dunno where he is."

"They're separated?"

"Divorced."

"Name?"

"Gavin. Gavin Burridge. He was in the army when they first met, pensioned off with a leg wound, couldn't walk for six months, recovered physically in the end, but after Iraq he was never quite right in the head if you ask me."

"Where is he now?"

"No idea. Haven't seen him since he buggered off up north."

"What about maintenance?"

"Elizabeth's over eighteen. But anyway, they made a clean break, he gave Helen a lump sum, good luck and goodbye; wham, bam, thank you, ma'am. Helen's got a nice little business, so she's all right."

"Elizabeth?"

"Their adopted daughter."

"Where does she live?"

"Somewhere south of the river, sharing a house with some friends."

"And you've no idea where Mr Burridge lives?"

"He might as well be on the planet Mars as far as I'm concerned."

"I'll need to talk to your daughter," said Philippa. "She might know where he is."

"I doubt it, but you're welcome to go and see her. She lives in Chingford. Number 14 Lordship Way." She looked up at Hollier, who was taking notes: "Have you got that, dear?"

*

Helen Burridge's home was a large 1930s semi with garage, glistening with well-maintained exterior paintwork. Philippa and DC Hollier were admitted with polite professionalism, and offered seats in the spacious modern kitchen-diner around a pine breakfast table gleaming with freedom from all known germs. Tea or coffee was offered and declined. Like the house,

Mrs Burridge was spotless and tidy, even though it was Sunday, wearing a smart but cool and comfortable-looking pale-beige linen trouser suit.

"You live alone here, Mrs Burridge?"

"Yes, I'm divorced and my daughter's grown up and flown the nest."

"This is just a formality. Can you tell me where you were yesterday afternoon, please?"

"At work. I run a local estate agency, Thorbinson's. I took it over after dad died."

"So you were, what, in the office, or out showing people around houses?"

"In the office. We don't do accompanied viewings on Saturdays."

"So you were on your own."

"Yes, well a few people came in to ask for particulars, that sort of thing. Pretty quiet, though."

"Is there anybody who can confirm you were actually in your office between, say, half-past-three and half-past-four?"

Helen Burridge had to think.

"It is rather important, to eliminate you from our enquiries."

"It's all right. Mr and Mrs Godsalve popped in. We've got their detached house on the market. A very desirable property in a sought-after neighbourhood. They were out shopping and came in to ask if we'd got any more viewings in prospect. We hadn't, unfortunately. They say the mortgage market's loosened up since the government brought in their help-to-buy scheme, but you don't exactly get a lot of first-time buyers above the million-pound mark."

"What time would that have been?"

"Oh, four-ish I suppose."

"I'll need Mr and Mrs Godsalve's phone number."

"Now? I haven't got it here. I can call you tomorrow first thing from the office if that's all right."

"That'll be fine. Now, the other thing is, your ex-husband."

"Gavin? What about him?"

"I need to contact him."

"Sorry, can't help you. We went our separate ways, and agreed there would be no contact. He was never interested in Elizabeth, it was me that wanted to adopt, so he hasn't bothered to stay in touch."

"Surely you must have some idea of where he lives."

"Nope. Not the foggiest. Look, when we split up he said he was going to stay with some mates up north. Bradford? Blackburn? Somewhere beginning with B with a lot of Asians. He could still be there, but to be honest, he could be in Australia for all I know."

"Okay," said Philippa. "If he makes contact, let me know."

"I will," said Helen, "but don't hold your breath. I haven't had so much as a phone call since he buggered off."

*

When Philippa rang the bell of Abigail Taverner's Georgian house in Highgate, it was not the 69-year-old actress who came to the door, but a tall woman in her early thirties. She was wearing jeans, trainers and a white t-shirt, and holding a yellow duster. She looked infuriatingly slim and elegant despite being discovered in the midst of domestic chores.

Given the similarity in their ages, Philippa felt a frisson of discomfort at the difference between this woman's effortless attractiveness and her own appearance. The minimum height requirement for police officers having been abolished in 1990, Philippa had been able to join despite being only five-foot-three. However, anyone who thought this would make her a pushover when matters kicked off in the street or a pub had soon learned their mistake, as she had been doing martial arts from the age of eight. The real problem was that her height made it harder for her to ignore her broadening beam, a consequence of meals grabbed on the hoof and consisting too often of English breakfasts, burgers and chips, and pizzas. Yet again, she mentally promised herself she would start eating more healthily.

"Can I help you?" asked the woman.

Philippa showed her warrant card and said, "I'm looking for Abigail Taverner."

"She's away, working. Can I help?"

"And you are?"

"Tracey Costick. I lodge with her. I'm a bit busy, having a bit of a clean-up around the house."

"I really need to talk to Mrs Taverner herself. Can she be contacted at work?"

"Well, she's filming in Venezuela, so not really."

"Filming?"

"Yes, it's one of those celebrities in the jungle reality programmes."

"I didn't realise she was still an actress."

"I take it you don't watch much television. She's one of the stars of Docklanders. She plays Dolly Spivey, the pub landlady."

"Oh, right, I know who you mean, now," said Philippa. "I don't watch it myself, but I've caught the odd few minutes. When did she fly out to South America?"

"Beginning of the month."

Well, thought Philippa, that's that. She wasn't too sure exactly how far away Venezuela was, but a good few thousand miles.

"Do you know when she'll be back?"

"Look, do you mind telling me what this is about?"

"It's a murder inquiry."

"I see." Realisation dawned. "Sir Roger Nutley?"

"Yes."

"Couldn't have happened to a nicer bloke," she said sarcastically.

"Yes, well, thank you for your opinion, but we have to talk to everybody involved in the trial."

"I suppose you do. But Abigail's not back till Thursday."

"Well, she's hardly under suspicion now I know she's in South America, but I'd still like to ask her a few questions. Does she phone home at all?"

"From what I hear there aren't any phones where she's gone. They might use carrier pigeons for all I know."

"Or carrier parrots," chimed in Hollier.

"Yes, thank you, Constable," chided Philippa. She handed Tracey Costick her card: "Tell her to give me a call the moment she gets back."

Driving home, Philippa reflected that she had little to show for a day's driving around the home counties and north London; but perhaps tomorrow Warren would nail the Polish stagehand.

MONDAY 16 JUNE

1

In 1991 the young, bright Keith Warren, burning with passion for the arts and the wide world, had stunned his liberal, academic family when, at the age of 23, he told them he had applied to join the police. It was less than a year after he had graduated from Manchester University with a degree in Spanish and French, and he was living in the parental home in Oxford, the city where he had been born. His father, Ralph, was at the time a Professor of Philosophy, and his mother, Pamela, taught English and Drama in an independent girls' school. Initially they were incredulous, but Keith explained to them how, after witnessing the senseless stabbing of a friend one evening in Manchester by three muggers wearing balaclavas, he had been gripped by frustration and rage at his own helplessness. The attack had happened shortly before finals were due to begin. The friend, a male fellow-student who had looked a certainty for a first-class degree in mathematics, had died in an ambulance. The muggers had never been caught, and the police had seemed more interested in making snide remarks about the supposed homosexuality of Keith's two other mates than in pursuing the perpetrators. A lot of people would have reacted by nursing a lifetime's grudge against the police, and that was certainly how Keith felt for several months. However, back at home in Oxford, as summer dissolved into autumn and he needed to think hard about what to do with his degree, his intelligence and the rest of his life, he became determined to use whatever talents he could muster to make Britain a safer place for decent people to walk the streets in, and if possible, to change some of the prehistoric attitudes of the police from within. First, however, he would have to learn his trade, like any other copper, at the sharp end. For a while after joining the police, Keith had wondered about perhaps seeking a way of using his language skills in some international section of the force, or perhaps even transferring to Europol or Interpol. But the more he became embroiled in the day-to-day job of policing first Oxford and later London, the more he realised that he was already pursuing his true vocation, and was happy in it. Now, at the age of 46, he had no regrets about his choice of career, and in any case found plenty of ways to use his languages and their associated studies for his private satisfaction while on leave. There was, for example, a lot of deeply satisfying cultural travel with Yolanda and, once he was old enough, their son Oscar, especially in France, Spain, and of course visiting Yolanda's family in Argentina.

When Warren logged on to his computer at ten past eight on Monday morning, the replies from Europol in The Hague and the local Polish Police in Poznan were already in, attached to emails. "Sod it," he muttered to himself; for Krzysztof Budziszewski was as clean as a whistle, or at least had never been caught out at anything. No international file existed, and he had never been so much as cautioned for swearing at a traffic cop. Indeed, the local Poles had gone the extra mile and searched their own national computer system to see if anything turned up. Nothing had.

Half-an-hour later, he was addressing the team in the incident room: "I'm still convinced we've got our man downstairs, simply because he's the only person who could have done it, but he seems to have no form either here or back home in Poland or anywhere else in Europe. There's no trace of him on HOLMES, and the replies are in this morning from Europol and Poland. There's nothing, they've never heard of him, he seems to be a model citizen. Of course that doesn't mean that he and Nutley had no connection, it's my belief they had, although goodness knows what, and I want you to see what you can turn up on that, DS Myers. You can start with his agent, one Simon Edler, get everything he knows about Nutley out of him, see if Sir Roger ever went to Poland as an actor, maybe to shoot some scenes for a film or a TV series, or for any other reason, holiday, historical visit to Auschwitz, skiing in the Tatra mountains, whatever; and get the low-down on his friends and family, if he had any. So far he comes over as a loner."

"Yes, sir," said Philippa.

"We found a substantial stash of cocaine in Nutley's

flat, far more than what he had on him in the dressing-room, maybe he was dealing as well as using. If he was and it was only among other theatricals they're unlikely to tell us, but DC Cohen, I want you to ask around the trade whether there's ever been a whisper. I'm not holding my breath on that but it's a stone we've got to turn over."

"Yes, sir."

"There were some nasty emails on Nutley's laptop from another actor who seems to resent the fact that Nutley apparently nicked the Hamlet part off him. It all sounds a bit luvvie to me, but who knows how far thespian jealousy can go. DS Myers, check it out with the agent, and also see if you can find out the names of any other actors or whoever might know anything about this feud, if it was one; and now tell us all how you got on yesterday with the women from the trial."

"Yes, sir. Well, two out of three. Carol Baxter's moved out of town to get away from all the fuss and now runs a boarding kennels and cattery in Cambridgeshire with her other half, Peter Baxter. He's a big enough bloke to be our man, and he's got Royal Marines commando training to boot, but it was a busy Saturday afternoon with people bringing in their pets to go on holiday and picking them up afterwards and he's got plenty of clients to confirm his alibi. He was definitely at the kennels all day. Sylvia Thorbinson, the one who claimed she was raped, lives on her own, no sign of any male company. I also went to see her daughter, a Mrs Helen Burridge, who's an estate agent, also living alone, divorced, hasn't had any contact with her ex for more than six years. He had been in the army years ago, but was badly wounded in Iraq and pensioned off. Couldn't even walk for a while. The third one, Abigail Taverner…"

"What, the one who's Dolly Spivey in Docklanders?" interjected Georgina Stanbridge.

"The very same, I'm glad somebody's in touch with popular culture," said Warren.

"Anyway," Philippa went on, "she's away doing some celebrity programme in the South American jungle, uncontactable up the Orinoco, not back till Thursday. The only person living with her is a lodger called Tracey. I left a message for her to get in touch as soon as she gets back. None of it much help, I'm afraid."

"Thank you Philippa," said Warren. "In the unlikely event of our Polish friend somehow turning out not to be our murderer, that's a road we'll have to travel back down, but you can leave it for now. As for today, I'm going to re-interview Mr Budziszewski and try to catch him out or extract a confession. If I can't, we're going to have to go back to basics, including the horrendous prospect of interviewing six hundred people from the audience. So we'd better hope he either trips up or sees the error of his ways and coughs."

*

"I need to speak to the officer in charge of the Roger Nutley case," said the female caller. She sounded edgy, breathless, as if she had needed to psych herself up to make the 999 call, which the Operator Assistance Centre had put through to the Crime Management Unit at Norton Hill.

"What's it regarding, Miss Verrall?" asked Kevin Foster, having already been told the caller's name and location by the OAC.

"Is Chris still under arrest for the murder?" asked Tessa.

"I'm sorry, I don't know who you mean. Chris who?"

"Chris the stage hand from the Theatre Royal. He's Polish. I've just heard he's been arrested for killing Roger Nutley. He didn't do it."

"I see. Well, I'm afraid I can't disclose information about the investigation, Miss Verrall. Why do you think he didn't do it?"

"I don't think, I know. Look, I need to talk to the Inspector, the one who was at the theatre. I can prove Chris is innocent."

"I see," said Kevin. "Just hold the line please while I find out where he is."

Warren was back at his desk from the briefing catching up on emails when his phone rang and he took the call from Tessa Verrall. "Miss Verrall? This is DI Warren. I interviewed you at the Theatre Royal on Saturday. I understand you have some information for me."

"Yes, but I don't want to say it over the phone. I can prove to you that Chris didn't kill Roger Nutley."

"I take it you mean Krzysztof Budziszewski."

"Yes. Is it true he's been charged with the murder?"

"He's helping us with our enquiries."

"Please, I need to talk you. In person."

"Where are you now?"

"At home, in Wimbledon."

Warren thought for a moment. Time was running out on holding the suspect any longer. He ought to interview this young woman as soon as possible, but it would take her more than an hour to cross London on the tube, plus walking distances at either end.

"Miss Verrall, what's your address, where you are now?"

"142 Kenilworth Avenue, Wimbledon Park."

"I need you here quickly. Stay where you are, don't go out, I'm getting Wimbledon Police Station to send a car to pick you up, it should be there in less than ten minutes, and they'll bring you up here to Norton Hill."

Eighteen minutes later, Tessa Verrall was zooming northwards over Wandsworth Bridge in a police car with its siren wailing and blue lights flashing.

2

DC Marion Everitt ordered a Diet Coke with ice and slice at the bar of the Three Tuns in the Hertfordshire village of Potters Crouch, and carried it out to a vacant table in the huge garden. She was early for her half-past-ten appointment, having unnecessarily allowed herself an hour for the drive just in case the country roads proved tricky. More to the point, it was a warm, sunny day and she got few enough opportunities to sit in the garden of a country pub as opposed to frequenting the less salubrious parts of Norton Hill. This was, indeed, like another planet, even though it was only twelve miles away from her north London manor. Inside the timber-framed 17th century pub, Marion had stepped into a world of exposed beams, antique dressers, varnished tables, and a fireplace where there would obviously be an open fire in winter. At this time of day there were few other customers in the garden, which made it ideal for the little chat she was planning with a representative of the anti dog theft charity K9 Recovery, which she had found on the internet. Having phoned them at 9.15 this morning and been told they were a nationwide network of volunteers, she had been given the choice of either talking to somebody in Hounslow or Sidcup, both of which would have fallen within the Metropolitan Police area but would have entailed a long, slow, irritating drive across much of London. Alternatively, they said, she could meet a man called Nick Boyd who lived in Hatfield, an easy nine-mile drive north into Hertfordshire. It was he who had suggested they meet at the Three Tuns. Marion leaned back to enjoy the sunshine, sipped her Diet Coke, and congratulated herself on having taken on a task that might not be a surefire stepping-stone to promotion but had put her in the garden of a country pub on a summer's morning, and getting paid for it. She had worn a simple, beige summer dress for Hertfordshire, and felt it allowed her to feel at home in rural Middle England.

Nick Boyd arrived ten minutes later, emerging from the rear door and looking around the garden, seeing Marion, and looking around again. He was dressed unconventionally in an orange, purple and white Hawaiian-style short-sleeved shirt depicting surfers on huge waves; pale green surfing-shorts reaching below the knees; and deep blue trainers; and carrying a black leather document case. He had not been expecting a well-dressed, slim, attractive woman in her mid-twenties, so she waved, and he came over carrying a cup of coffee.

"Are you the lady from the police?" he asked.

"That's me. DC Marion Everitt."

"Of course. It was the detective bit I forgot. I was looking for someone in uniform."

He sat down opposite her.

"This is lovely," she said, taking in with a sweep of her right arm the garden, the pub, and possibly half of Hertfordshire.

"Isn't it, though? That's why I suggested it. Hatfield's okay, but what's outside is better, at least in summer. I noticed you're based in Norton Hill. Do you have anything to do with the Roger Nutley murder?"

"No, it's sort of passed me by so far. What do you do when you're not volunteering for this dogs charity?"

"Nothing exciting. I'm a lecturer at Hertfordshire University. It's just up the road."

"Sounds pretty interesting to me. What subject?"

"Music technology, actually."

"Good grief, I had no idea there was such a thing. What does it involve?"

"Oh, you know, digital audio hardware and software, sampling, sequencing, sound editing, recording, digital signal processing, internet audio, all that sort of thing."

She became aware that she had slipped into conversation with this man so easily and comfortably that she felt as if she might almost be flirting with him, although she certainly wasn't intending to. In his late twenties, he was not bad looking in the conventional way but, she thought, his presence was supercharged by an indefinable aura of high intelligence. He was of medium height, and his straight, blonde hair, reaching his shoulders, was too long for a stodgy job. "Right," said Marion, "so where do the dogs come into it?"

"Oh, I've always liked animals, and I can't keep one myself with nobody at home to look after it while I'm at work, so this is just a way of doing something, you know."

She caught herself wondering whether there was nobody at home because his wife was also out at work or because he was single. She decided it would be a good idea to steer the conversation on to business.

"So," she said, "tell me all there is to know about dognapping."

"Well, the first thing you need to know is that we're not usually talking about opportunist individuals grabbing a dog from down the road and giving it to a relative. It's done by organised gangs for serious money. They scout for targets, and once a dog's been kidnapped it's taken a long way from its home to minimise the chances of its being recognised; unless it's been kidnapped for ransom, there is a bit of that."

"When you say serious money, what kind of sums are we looking at?"

"You want some prices? Okay, for a good example of a popular breed, it can go to over two grand; but more commonly it'll be between five hundred and fifteen hundred. Bear in mind they're doing this on an industrial scale."

"Upsetting for the owners."

"Devastating would be a better word. People who don't keep pets often don't realise that for people who do they're a member of the family. When a pet dies, people cry real tears. When it's kidnapped, they're wracked with anxiety about what might be happening to it."

"You mean like being used as laboratory animals?"

"That's a common fear. At least if it's a pedigree dog we can assure the victims their pet's almost certainly going to a new home; but it's still a painful loss."

"I don't get how they can sell them."

"Sometimes a dog is stolen to order; especially among the criminal fraternity, it seems to be a matter of principle to get something illegally."

"Yes, I'm well aware of that."

"But mostly it's done over the internet. Take a look on any of the main selling websites and you'll find pedigree dogs on offer cheaper than from reputable breeders; which is mainly what's driving the increase. Dogs from proper breeders have gone up in price a lot over the past few years. So people look for a bargain. There's no regulation of who can sell a dog over the internet. The criminals set up multiple accounts, and they sell completely innocent items on them, so that it looks like they're just normal people. The buyer gets a sob story to explain why they're selling the family pet. One of their tricks is to insist they'll only sell the dog to a loving and caring person who'll give it a good home, so you end up spending all your time trying to prove that's you when you ought to be trying to find out whether they're genuine. People just don't think of that. By now they've fallen in love with this dog they're getting at a knock-down price because of somebody else's misfortune, and the last thing they want to do is create obstacles."

"You'd have thought dogs like that would be microchipped."

"They usually are; but people are greedy, so they ignore that. Of course they may run into problems when they have to take the animal to a vet, if the microchip gets scanned; but a lot of people don't think of that until it's too late."

"So what does your organisation do?"

"We have an online register of missing dogs, and we help people search for their dogs, we produce posters for them to put up in the local area."

"That's not much use if the dog's been kidnapped in Penzance and sold in Manchester."

"To be honest it's mostly only useful if the dog's got lost rather than been kidnapped. So we concentrate a lot on prevention. You'd be amazed how careless people are. I've brought you a leaflet."

He unzipped the document case, pulled out an A4 sheet, and handed it to her.

"It covers microchipping, don't leave your dog loose in the garden while you go out, if you think you're being watched by the same person more than once when you take it for a walk, report it, that sort of thing. Dogs get stolen from gardens, kennels and outhouses, sometimes a gang member actually burgles the house and takes nothing but the dog, and they even get snatched when they're being taken for a walk by their owners."

"Report it to whom?"

"The police. The trouble is, to be brutally frank, you lot just don't seem to take it seriously. People usually get told their dog's probably wandered off, and you won't even issue a crime number. So to be honest I'm a bit surprised you're here talking to me now."

"Orders from my Inspector."

Marion had no idea it was the gang making the mistake of stealing a recently retired senior police officer's pet that had sent her off on this unlikely course as her first semi-independent assignment since her move out of uniform.

"Okay. Well, d'you want to take it any further?"

"Try and stop me."

"What do you think you can do?"

"Well, my idea is we could pretend to be intending to buy a dog we're pretty sure has been stolen, and I could arrest the sellers on the spot."

"All right. I'm up for that."

"I'll have to run it by my boss, though."

She rose to leave. Standing up, Marion looked every inch a country lass. With her fresh-looking complexion on which she seldom inflicted make-up, and a natural stride which sometimes had male officers struggling to keep up, she often stood out from the crowd as hearty and healthy among the pasty faces and slack bodies of the metropolis.

"Got time for another coke?" he asked. "Talk about, life, the universe and everything for a bit?"

"I'd love to. Better get back now, though. I'll give you a ring when I've talked to my boss."

As soon as she got back to the station, Marion emailed Nick details and photos of the latest stolen dogs.

3

In the soft interview room, Tessa Verrall was perched on the edge of a sofa, Warren on an armchair at 90 degrees to her so that the conversation would not seem confrontational, a uniformed female constable in an armchair on the other side, taking notes.

"So how are you going to prove to me that Mr Budziszewski is innocent?"

"I was with him."

"When? At the exact moment when Sir Roger Nutley was being murdered?"

"Yes."

"Where were you with him?"

"In the workshop."

"He says he was alone in the workshop." Warren looked down at the notes taken of his interview with Tessa Verrall at the theatre. "And you told me you were in your dressing-room with Miss Grady."

"I lied. I was with Chris."

"And did Miss Grady lie as well?"

"Yes; but only because I asked her to; well, begged her, actually."

"I see." At least, he thought he might be beginning to. "And if you were in the workshop with Mr Budziszewski rather than in your dressing-room with Miss Grady, what exactly were you doing there? It's not where actors normally hang around waiting for their turn to go on the stage, is it?"

Tessa Verrall looked down at the floor, embarrassed. Warren waited patiently for her to come out with it, as if it were not obvious by now.

"Having sex."

"In the workshop? During the play?"

"I'm not proud of myself."

"Must have been a quickie?"

"Not really. I'd been off since Act Three, Scene Two, then there was the interval, then I wasn't due back on until Act Four, Scene Five. Ages, actually."

"Anybody could've come in."

"They never did. We knew that from the previous performances."

"Still, a bit risky."

"I got carried away. You've seen him. He's amazing. And nice. And very clever."

Warren pictured the handsome Pole in his mind's eye. Yes, he could imagine him sweeping women off their feet. He wondered how many other actresses had been taken round the back to see his beanstalk, as it were.

"He insists he was on his own," said Warren. "He's never mentioned being with you. The man's probably facing a murder charge. Wouldn't you think he'd have told us if he had an alibi?"

"I suppose he must be protecting me."

"Why would he be doing that? Rather excessively noble, wouldn't you say?"

"I'm getting married in August. It's been planned since January. My fiancé and I have been together five years. If Steve found out about this, it would finish it. It was just a fling. A stupid, final fling."

"And how long has this fling been going on?"

"Since Wednesday. I'd never met Chris till I came to this theatre. I was never going to see him again afterwards."

This was all sounding horribly true, which was all very well in the interests of justice, but was going to leave Warren up the creek without a suspect if it was confirmed.

"Why have you waited until now to come forward? Why not yesterday?"

"I didn't know Chris was under arrest yesterday, did I? You sent me home, remember? I only found out when Mr Spiller phoned this morning. He was calling around everybody to see if we were all right and tell us he plans to get the play back on the road as he's already found another actor to play Polonius, and to report for rehearsals in Brighton tomorrow. He mentioned that a Polish stage hand had been arrested for the murder, and I knew it must be Chris. That was the first I heard of it. I didn't say anything to Mr Spiller, but I rang you straight away, and here I am, as soon as I knew, honestly."

"I shall need a statement."

"Is that really necessary? If Steve finds out about me and Chris, it'll be a disaster."

"If it's not needed for a prosecution, I'll make sure it vanishes into a black hole where not even Captain Kirk could find it. Now if you'll just wait here, I'll send somebody to take it down."

In the CID room, Warren set DC Georgina Stanbridge the task of contacting Emily Grady to see if she confirmed Tessa Verrall's new story, as well as asking as many of the other actors whether they had been aware of any hanky-panky in the workshop.

*

The waiting-room of Simon Edler Associates was expensively designed to convey modernity, space, and coolness. It was a large, uncluttered, high-ceilinged room on the tenth floor of a steel-and-glass tower on the east side of Charing Cross Road. Floor-to-ceiling windows gave a view out across Covent Garden towards Drury Lane and its cluster of major West End

Theatres. An actor waiting here in the hope of being signed up for representation would feel they were at the gateway to fame and fortune. But if they failed to deliver the goods at auditions within their first eighteen months on the books, they would find there was also a door marked exit. Not that the stage was by any means what the agency had to offer. The pale green wall at the far end was hung with three rows of six large, framed posters showing images of clients, some of whom were instantly recognisable to Philippa, in leading roles in major feature films. In two corners stood a couple of those big, shiny-leaved pot-plants that specialist horticultural firms supply and maintain in up-market offices. Two lines of pale-grey sofas faced each other along the long sides of a rug striped from side to side in gentle shades of blue, grey and cream. Two large, rectangular, glass-topped coffee-tables supported a couple of scary-looking potted cacti and a scattering of showbiz magazines. At the far end of one of the sofas, a young woman with long, wavy, chestnut hair, wearing a white t-shirt with an orange, yellow and blue cartoon leopard face on the front, and lightweight desert camouflage chinos, was quietly practising a monologue.

A middle-aged woman with short, blonde-highlighted hair and the figure of a fit 25-year-old bustled out from a door in the far corner and headed straight for the two police officers. "You must be Detective Sergeant Myers, and..."

"DC Hollier," supplied Wayne.

"Penny Foulkes, Simon Edler's PA. Well, you're certainly punctual, if you'd like to come through, Mr Edler will see you now. Tea or coffee?"

Figuring the coffee might taste a tad better than the mysterious dark liquid that got served up in the Norton Hill canteen, they both opted for it.

Simon Edler's private office was the antithesis of the reception room. It was small, cosy, and not intended for business visitors or actors. The former he would see in a more luxurious room along the corridor, the latter in a plain audition room with a piano, a table, and a few upright chairs. Here in his personal workspace there was a plain wooden desk with an iMac and a phone, one wall completely lined with shelving filled with neatly labelled red, green, mauve, blue and black box-files, another hung with framed posters of stage shows from yesteryear. He stood up and came around his desk to shake their hands as Penny showed them in and departed.

"Simon Edler. Thank you for coming all this way to interview me. Sorry to be meeting you in such terrible circumstances. Have a seat at the desk. I'm afraid I don't have any comfy chairs in here, but I thought it would be more discreet in my personal den. How can I help you?"

Philippa and Hollier did as suggested, and Hollier deployed his notebook on the surface of the desk.

"How long were you Sir Roger Nutley's agent?" asked Philippa.

"Since 1988."

"Any idea why somebody would have wanted to murder him?"

"No. Everybody who worked with him liked him."

"Could somebody have been jealous?"

"Professionally, you mean?"

"Professionally or any other way."

"Look, there are always people who think they should have got a part when somebody else did; especially on the telly. There's an old joke: How many actors does it take to change a light-bulb? A hundred. One to stand on a chair and do it and ninety-nine saying 'That ought to be me up there.' But thinking back, I can't remember Roger putting anybody's nose out of joint in that way. What he got, he was right for. Unless..." Another pause.

"If there is something, however small, you need to tell me."

Penny floated in almost imperceptibly with the coffees and floated out again.

"Roger read about the Hamlet tour in The Stage. He thought it might be his chance to make a comeback after that disgraceful trial, so he phoned me and asked me to suggest him for it. The only role he could play was Polonius, and I'd seen the breakdown a couple of months earlier and hadn't mentioned it to Roger because he was keeping a low profile after the trial and hadn't told me he wanted to emerge from the shadows, so to speak. So I told him it was probably too late, but he asked me to call Daniel Spiller and see what I could do. So I did, and of course the auditions had finished two weeks earlier and he was about to give his chosen cast the good news. But when I mentioned Roger, he said he hadn't got anybody with a TV profile in the cast and it was worrying him a bit in box office terms, and he knew Roger of old and had never believed the allegations, but as he hadn't done anything for a couple of years he'd have to audition. As it happened, Spiller was coming up to London from Brighton a couple of days later to talk about a possible one-week West End slot for another show of his, so I sent Roger to see him there and do a party piece. Apparently Roger produced a fantastic rendition of a Shakespeare monologue, John of Gaunt in Richard the Second, the 'this England' speech, and Spiller offered him the part on the spot. He knows a money-spinner when he sees one, although he was taking a chance that some mud from the trial might have stuck and put audiences off. As we now know, his judgment was right, which it nearly always is, and Hamlet was playing to packed houses all around the country, which I can tell you is pretty remarkable in this day and age."

"I'm not sure where this is getting us, Mr Edler," Philippa interjected.

"Well, the point is this: I did hear a few weeks later that the other actor who was to have got the part of Polonius found out through the grapevine that he'd been zapped by Roger at the last minute, and got into a right paddy about it, threatening all kinds of fire and brimstone against the effing superannuated old twat who'd only got the part because he'd been on the telly, and he was a bloody pervert who should never have got off, and he'd got it coming to him, blah, blah, blah, you know the sort of thing."

"When you say, 'he'd got it coming to him', what do you suppose he meant?

"Bear in mind this was in a pub very late at night with some other actors and so far as I can make out a considerable amount of alcoholic libations had been consumed, so I can't believe it was really anything more than bluster. Actors get emotional, inspector; it's what they're paid for."

"He also sent threatening emails. You can't blame those on drink and the heat of the moment."

"I can't account for that."

"And the name of this emotional actor?"

"Noel Wharton. But I honestly can't believe…"

"What does Mr Wharton look like?"

"Handsome, distinguished, dyed black hair."

"How tall?"

"Over six foot."

"Strong, would you say?"

"I should imagine so. Last time I saw him, he looked remarkably fit for his age."

Well, well, thought Philippa; at last a thespian who might fit the part of our murderer physically.

"We'll just have a quiet word with him, Mr Spiller. How do I find him?"

"He's with Hayes & Clifton. I'll get their website up and give you their phone number. I'll give you their email address as well."

Hollier took down the details of Noel Wharton's agent and Philippa returned to the subject of the victim.

"Is there anybody else you can suggest who might be able to give me some more background about Mr Nutley?"

"Well, I don't think he had any close family. I know his parents are dead, he never married or had any children, and so far as I know there aren't any brothers or sisters."

"Bit of a loner then."

"Not at all. He was married to the theatre and the studio, and the people he worked with were his family; but outside work; well, there was nobody much I know of. The last two years away from the beehive must have been sheer hell for him. Mind you, he had his dodgy mates. Well, I probably shouldn't have said that."

"You certainly should. When you say dodgy, this wouldn't be connected with his cocaine habit, I suppose?"

"Oh, you know about that, do you? I didn't like it, but with a star like that, it's outside my control. How did you find out?"

"It was in his make-up bag, in his dressing-room. Now, you were saying about dodgy mates."

"You remember how the Kray twins used to enjoy being seen around with celebrities, and vice versa?"

"I've read about it."

"Same thing with Roger."

"So who's in place of the Kray twins?"

"Have you heard of a man called Ralph Tennyson de Clare?"

"I'm a police officer. How could I not have? Are you telling me he knew Nutley?"

"Bosom pals, Sergeant. Roger goes to all the Big Ralph parties – used to go, I should say."

"Everybody knows Tennyson's the north London cocaine boss, but the Drugs Squad have never been able to pin so much as sharing a joint on him. Was he Nutley's supplier?"

"Haven't the faintest. I don't go anywhere near that territory. I'm a family man with a wife, two kids at school and a ten hours a day business to run. I want nothing to do with drugs."

"One more thing," said Philippa. "Did Sir Roger ever work in Poland, or go there for any other reason? Please cast your mind back as far as you can."

"No, he didn't. I'm sure."

"What about holidays?"

"He liked the sunshine. Spain, Greece and so forth in summer, Thailand or South Africa in winter, when he could get away, which wasn't all that often. He wouldn't have fancied eastern Europe. In any case, I would have known. Why?"

"Oh, just a loose end we needed tidying up." Philippa thanked Simon Edler and told him he might need to be interviewed again later on, and Penny Foulkes showed her and Hollier out of the rarefied atmosphere of the shining tower, back into the thunderous traffic and swirling exhaust fumes of Charing Cross Road.

4

Warren was contemplating the accumulated information pinned to the board in the incident room when Georgina Stanbridge walked in.

"Any luck with the actors?" he asked.

"Depends on what you call luck, sir. Emily Grady admitted lying to protect Tessa's private life and said she knew Tessa was having it away with the Pole in the workshop during the intervals and the first scenes of the second half. She said she didn't like lying and thought Tessa was behaving like a stupid tart but she didn't want to be the one to drop her in it with her fiancé. I got through on the phone to a couple of the others, Mr Chapman and Mr Rainford, and they both said everybody knew about it, gave them a wide berth while they were at it, and hoped for her sake Fiona Holland didn't find out because she'd have been for the high jump. It's going to take me a bit longer to track down the rest of the actors, sir."

"Forget it," said Warren, "I don't think there's any doubt, do you? I'll tell you what."

"What, sir?"

"There's a lot of truth in the old song."

"What song's that, sir?"

"Don't Put Your Daughter on the Stage, Mrs Worthington."

"Sorry, sir, don't know it. Before my time, probably."

Warren groaned inwardly at the ignorance of the young, and at that moment Tristan Hadaway, head of Technical Services, came in to put the cherry on the cake.

"It's not what you want to hear, sir," said Hadaway.

"So tell me."

"Your Polish man with the difficult name isn't your murderer."

"What are you telling me?"

"There's no DNA match. Absolutely no way."

"Can you be that sure?"

"You know how we work. We've looked on every conceivable area of the victim's skin and clothing where the murderer would have left traces, obviously concentrating on the neck, face, head, collar and the shoulders of the costume. Nothing to show that the Pole ever touched him. He couldn't have done it."

"Maybe he didn't leave any traces big enough for you to find."

"You've got to trust me on this. If he was the killer, he would have done, and he didn't."

"Look, I've got a fair knowledge of how this DNA evidence works, but just run this one by me in a bit more detail, if you don't mind."

"Sure. Human beings shed tens of thousands of skin cells each day, and those cells are transferred to every surface our skin comes into contact with. When a violent crime is committed, if the perpetrator deposits enough skin cells, DNA analysis may be able to link him to the crime scene. In this case I used two methods called scraping and tape lift, which are what they sound like, scraping the soft clothing with a blade and lifting the surface of the skin with a sticky tape. It's tried and tested. Earlier this year a man was convicted in Scotland of murdering a teenage girl in 1986, that's 28 years ago. He'd strangled her, and got away with it. Then the Scottish scientists re-examined the tapings from the girl's body, and found identical male DNA profiles from her back and her face. It was a one-in-a-billion match with the suspect, and he's inside where he belongs now, serving life. In the case of your Pole, we've got his voluntary DNA sample, and there's nothing remotely like it on the tapes we lifted from the body."

"I'm going to have to let him go."

"Then who the hell else was it?" asked Georgina.

"We're back to square one. There was nobody backstage who could have done it; nobody in the auditorium could have got through unnoticed; and nobody came in from outside."

"Sorry," said Hadaway. "Sounds like a three-pipe problem."

"Thank you, Dr Watson. Perhaps you'd have me playing the violin as well."

Warren went down to the custody suite in person and told Krzysztof Budziszewski he was free to go. What had promised to be a quickly solved case had just been blown wide open.

Philippa came into the room, back from her sortie into the world of razamattaz.

"What are you looking so cheerful about?" asked Warren.

"You'll never guess who Nutley was best mates with."

"Go on."

"Ralph Tennyson de Clare."

"What, Big Ralph? He of the industrial-scale white powder imports?"

"The very same."

"Who told you that?"

"His agent. Didn't seem to be part of the drugs world himself, hard-working family man and all that, but he knew about Nutley's habit. He put up with it because he wanted to keep a big earner on his books."

"Well, well. That puts a whole new complexion on things, does it not? Nice one, Philippa my girl. We shall have to have a chat with Mr Tennyson; but we'll need to tread carefully or we'll have the Drugs Squad telling us we're queering their pitch."

*

DC Marion Everitt's phone rang.

"Got one for you," said Kevin Foster. "Missing dog."

"Missing or stolen?"

"I'd say probably stolen. Thought you'd like a big-time crime to celebrate joining CID."

"Don't knock it, it's big business."

"What is?"

"Dognapping."

"Yeah, right, if you say so. Anyway, I think you'd better shoot over and talk to the lady, she sounded in a bit of a state."

"I'm not surprised. What's the name and address?"

"It's a Mrs Constance Prestwich, 41 Roedale Avenue, Norton Vale."

"Down the posh end. I'm on my way."

"I'll ring her back and tell her to expect you. Fifteen minutes?"

"Say twenty, while I finish this cuppa."

Norton Vale was very much the up-market side of the coin from Norton Hill. It was well-endowed with green spaces, health food shops and the kind of coffee shops where yummy-mummies gathered to discuss pilates and the difficulty of finding reliable cleaning women. Roedale Avenue was a haven of middle-class tranquillity, the 1930s detached houses built in the Arts and Crafts style, which made the district look like an isolated northern outpost of Hampstead Garden Suburb. Number 41 was painted white on the outside, very recently by the look of it. Its front-door was in the middle, like the way you draw houses at primary school, thought Marion, even if the one you live in is poky and has the door round the side. She rang the doorbell. A woman in her forties looked out of the window to her right; Marion held up her warrant card for the woman to see, and she came around to the front hall and opened the door. She looked as if she were on the verge of tears.

"Mrs Constance Prestwich?"

"Yes, that's me. Would you like to come in?"

She was a slim, tidy woman of medium height, her shortish hair an unobtrusive shade of light brown, wearing a simple but stylish pale blue Hobbs dress. The hall was painted magnolia, and led into a living-room furnished in keeping with the style of the house. An original fireplace with dark green tile surround had been retained, and a dark green floral chintz three-piece suite, obviously fairly new, blended in tastefully, as did the paler floral curtains; all set off by an oval, oak coffee-table. There was money here, but spent in moderation. Nothing was flashy and nothing was tatty. Everything was just right; typical Norton Vale, in fact. Marion accepted Mrs Prestwich's invitation to sit down.

"Now, I understand your dog's gone missing and you believe it to have been stolen."

"I don't believe her to have been stolen; they broke into our house and took her."

"So, you've been burgled?"

"They forced open the kitchen door."

"Couldn't the dog have simply been frightened and run away?"

"No. There's nothing else missing. The only thing they took was Molly."

"I see. Who else lives here?"

"My husband, Christopher, but he's not home from work yet; and our daughter, Penelope. She's fifteen. She'll be devastated."

"And what sort of dog is Molly, Mrs Prestwich?"

"A Welsh Springer. She's quite valuable, we paid £500 for her from a good breeder. But that's not the point, she's our Molly and we love her."

"How old is Molly?"

"She'll be five in September."

"Have you got any photographs of her?"

Mrs Prestwich fetched a photograph in a silver frame from the mantelpiece.

"Do you have any that aren't framed so that I can take one away and make copies?"

"There are digital ones in my laptop."

"That's perfect. Can you email me some please?"

Marion handed Mrs Prestwich a business card.

"I'll do it as soon as you go." She replaced the framed photo on the mantelpiece.

"You were out when the burglary happened, were you?"

"I'd just gone for a manicure. I was only out for less than an hour. They must have been watching the house."

"You're probably right. At least you can feel reasonably confident they won't come back while you're at home. May I see where they forced their way in?"

"It's the kitchen door. I've called a repair man, he's coming as soon as he can."

They went through to the kitchen, which was pine throughout with beige stone flooring; nothing to offend the eye, nothing exciting. The outer door was an expensive PVC replacement jobbie, but had been jemmied open and was damaged in two places where the lever or levers had been inserted.

"You're quite sure they took nothing else?" asked Marion.

"They don't seem to have touched anything." She looked up at a line of coat-hooks on the kitchen wall near the outer door. "Oh ... Molly's lead's gone."

"I saw that the dvd player and so on were still in place. Do you have any jewellery?"

"It's upstairs. I've checked. It's still there. To be honest, I don't think they went up there, or even beyond the kitchen."

"Would Molly go with a stranger?"

"I'm afraid so. She thinks everybody's her friend. When I tie her up outside a shop there's often somebody stroking her when I come back out."

"Right. So she wouldn't have barked or made a fuss."

"Probably not."

"Is she microchipped?"

"Yes."

"Good. If she turns up at a vet's they should notice."

"Why should she?"

"I'm guessing she's been stolen to be sold. At some point the people who buy her will have to take her to a vet. They'll probably be completely innocent, by the way. But I wouldn't get your hopes up too much, at least not in the short term."

"I realise that."

"But I do want to reassure you that the police take this kind of crime seriously, and every effort will be made to recover Molly. I'll have a word with your neighbours in case anybody saw anything."

"Oh, please do, we're all friends along here."

Marion rang the doorbells of the next-door neighbours on both sides, the next-door-but-one neighbours, and the five nearest houses on the opposite side of Roedale Avenue. Of those that answered, none had seen anything. Walking back to her car, which she had parked on the Prestwich family's drive, she encountered a man in his seventies. He was walking with the aid of a stick, wearing a brown and white short-sleeved shirt, cream slacks and polished tan leather shoes.

"Excuse me, sir," she asked, "I'm a police officer. Do you happen to live nearby?"

"Number 22," he said in a surprisingly cockney accent for such a street. "What's up?"

Marion was struck by the briskness of his response.

"There's been a burglary sir. I was just wondering if you saw anything suspicious earlier this afternoon."

"Afraid not, sweetheart. Been down the Three Horseshoes since two o'clock."

"I'm sorry to have bothered you, sir."

"That's perfectly all right, my love. Sorry to hear about the burglary. Whose house was it?"

Marion ignored the question, thanked him, and resumed walking towards her car. The man called her back.

"Hang on a minute," he said. "I said I never saw anything this afternoon. That don't mean I never saw anything any other time."

She turned back to him.

"And did you?"

"Yeah. There's been a geezer hanging about this week. Well, not hanging about so much as walking up and down. He'd go down my side in the morning then back up this side. Then do it the opposite way a bit later. Maybe eight, nine, ten times a day. I thought he was just exercising at first, you know, taking a brisk walk like they tell you to for your heart, but he wasn't going fast enough. Dawdling, in fact, having a good look around. I was beginning to think about calling you lot to tell you, but you don't want to seem a fool, do you?"

Marion realised this septuagenarian witness was a brighter spark than many half his age.

"I wish you had. Did you happen to notice whether he had a vehicle somewhere?"

"If he did, he didn't bring it down here."

"What did he look like?"

"Big geezer. Fortyish. Tough guy. Suntanned. Tattoos on his neck and arms. One big gold earring."

"What was he wearing?"

"Oh, t-shirt, jeans, nothing unusual."

"Any design on the t-shirt?"

"I think so. Can't remember what, though. Some heavy metal band? I couldn't say for sure."

"Would you be able to identify him from a photograph?"

"I doubt it. Sorry."

"Not at all, sir, you've been very helpful. Do you think you'd recognise him if you saw him again?"

"Oh, yeah, I reckon so, there was something about him."

"What sort of something?"

"I can't put it into words, a sort of craftiness, the way he walked, a creepy type, dodgy, like. Yeah, I reckon I'd know him if I saw him again."

Marion took the man's name, Dennis Griffiths, and address, and gave him her card. She asked him to phone if he saw the visitor again; but more in hope than in expectation. If it was the dog thief, he wouldn't be showing his face in Norton Vale again in a hurry.

5

When the young Keith Warren announced to his family that he had applied to join the police, it was not the first shock he had given them that year. A beautiful young woman called Yolanda Carrasco Lindstrom had flown in from Argentina in February so that the pair of them could announce that they were getting married. They had met and fallen in love during Keith's compulsory study year abroad, which had formed the third of the four years of his BA course, and which he had chosen to spend at a university in Buenos Aires. Yolanda was almost exactly the same age as Keith, and from a similar academic background, although she also had an uncle who owned a vast ranch out on the pampas. Her appearance had come as a surprise to Keith's solidly Anglo-Saxon family, who had assumed that South Americans were all short, black-haired and dark-skinned. Yolanda, however, was five-foot-eleven tall, slim, and a natural blonde, with skin which might have passed for Scandinavian had she not flown in with a splendid tan acquired during the southern hemisphere summer. As with appearance, so with personality; the myth of the fiery Latin could hardly apply less to Yolanda. She was cool, even-tempered and tolerant. The clue, of course, was in her maternal surname and her mother's Swedish ancestry. Keith's father had had a quiet word with him about the risk that marrying so young out of infatuation with an exotic beauty would lead to disaster. The wedding had taken place in November of the same year in St Saviour's Anglican Church in Belgrano, a middle-class northern suburb of Buenos Aires. The Warren family flew out to attend and meet Yolanda's family, most of whom spoke English as well as Spanish. Keith's parents stayed on for a fortnight's holiday to enjoy the warm springtime in the southern cone while England was descending into winter. Keith and Yolanda honeymooned way down south in Patagonia, based in a gorgeous hotel that looked like a giant Swiss chalet.

Right now, the idyllic mountains and lakes of southern Argentina seemed like another planet. Warren needed to talk to Ralph Tennyson de Clare. The gangster had not murdered Roger Nutley; of that Warren was certain. If he had wanted him killed, he would have had underlings or freelancers do the job for him. That would still make him guilty of conspiracy to murder; but there was a decades-old trail of bodies that ought to lead back to Tennyson, and not one ever had. Besides, if Nutley owed Tennyson serious money, having him topped was the one way of making certain he would never get paid. He might have him frightened, or even hurt, but definitely not bumped off. On the other hand, if the debt had in reality got out of hand, if Nutley had ignored one warning too many, and above all if he had started bragging about not paying, he would have had to be made an example of, old pals or not. That was the way all gangsters maintained what they called respect and what decent people called a reign of terror. It was, indeed, the way all monarchies and dictatorships had always worked, from Ancient Rome through the Plantagenets to Stalin. However, if Tennyson indeed had a motive for killing Nutley, it was hardly the style of his hired assassins to creep around the back corridors of crowded theatres in order to produce an unexpectedly early climax to the Saturday matinee. If Ralph Tennyson de Clare had wanted Roger Nutley dead, the actor would probably have come to a sticky end at night in a deserted alleyway. Nonetheless, Nutley had been involved with Tennyson, which placed him for part of his life outside the glamorous limelight and in a very murky underworld where very nasty things happened to people who got on to the wrong side of any Mr Big. Yes, indeed; Warren needed to talk to Mr Tennyson de Clare.

He knew there was no way he was just going to drive up to Tennyson's house unannounced and walk in. For that, he would need reasonable suspicion and the intention of making an arrest. There would be a top-flight lawyer on the scene before he had time to finish saying, "I'm feeling your collar, Ralph". In any case, he had no intention of nicking him. In addition to which, God only knew who else's operations he might be barging in on: the Drugs Directorate; the Specialist, Organised and Economic Crime Command; HMRC. Tread on any of those toes and you were on a fast track back to directing traffic. Still, he needed a meeting with the bad guy. He didn't personally know where he lived, even though he'd heard of him; but he knew a man who would, so he called him. He was in luck, because he caught him at his desk at Scotland Yard.

"Rowbottom," came the terse reply.

"Gerry, it's Keith Warren."

"Watcha, Bunny. Long time no see. Where are you now?"

Gerald Rowbottom and Keith Warren had been DCs together and mates immediately after Warren's transfer to the Met from Thames Valley. Rowbottom had gone for a specialist career. He was now working in the Metropolitan Police's Middle Market Drugs Partnership, a joint operation between the Specialist, Organised and Economic Crime Command and the government's National Crime Agency, dealing with Class A drug supply throughout London above half a kilogramme of heroin or a kilo of cocaine.

"Still at Norton. Centre of the universe, mate."

"So what can I do you for? Love to chat but the shit's about to hit the fan in one of our little operations so I'm a bit rushed."

"Ralph Tennyson de Clare."

"Big Ralph as he likes to be known. What about him?"

"I need to talk to him. Not bust him; I need his advice."

"With respect to...?"

"The Roger Nutley murder."

"The TV copper that got topped while he was on stage. Almost one of our own in a way, I suppose you could say. You've never got Tennyson in the frame for that? Not in a million years."

"No, but I think he could help, if he had a mind to. Nutley knew him, and I've no doubt he was indirectly supplied by him. I'm hoping he might have actually liked him and might give me some ideas if I make it clear I'm not interested in his own activities. Only I don't want to step on any toes."

"They like being seen around with the stars, his sort. Some of the stars get a buzz out of hanging around with people who are dangerous; not to mention the tasty wenches that go with it. Anyway, I can tell you now he won't talk to you without somebody giving you a recommendation. Give us your mobile and I'll call you back."

Warren told Rowbottom the number of his mobile phone and hung up.

*

DC Marion Everitt had cycled eleven-point-three kilometres up hill and down dale and was bracing herself for the taxing, steeply uphill stretch before the glide down the final kilometre, when her mobile rang.

She stopped the machine, took the phone out of her bag on the floor beside it, and looked resignedly to see who was calling. She smiled when she saw the name Nick Boyd.

"Hi, Nick. What's up?"

"I think I've got a live one. Are you all right? You sound breathless."

"I'm in the gym at the station, grabbing a quick half-hour work-out. What exactly do you mean?"

"You know those photographs of stolen dogs you emailed me? I've found a really good match. I'd like you to see it, go over it with you, decide what to do."

"You're a fast worker. I only sent you them two hours ago. Can you come into the station?"

"Norton Hill did you say?"

"That's the one. Do you want me to text you the post-code?"

"That would be helpful."

"What time can you get here?"

"Say in an hour?"

"Okay."

No point in finishing the cycle-ride now, so Marion headed for the showers. She felt energised. Of course, the exercise always had that effect, but this lunchtime it felt moreso. That was presumably because it now looked as if there was going to be something pro-active she could do to try and catch the dognappers; unless, of course, it had more to do with the possibility she was going to see Nick again so soon. Dismiss that thought, Marion; you're a copper, act like a professional.

Mercifully, when he arrived, he had changed into more conventional clothing; a beige-and-white short-sleeved check shirt and cream slacks.

They brought the online advert up on a computer screen in the CID open-plan office: "For sale - £599: our 2 years old Golden Retriever, Buster. Heartbreaking to let him go but we must. He has a pedigree, he has champions in his line and very good breeding, although unfortunately I have lost the paperwork. He is a lovely boy and could produce some lovely offspring. He is great with other animals and kids. He is very loyal and needs a lot of attention. He loves being with other dogs and is excellent to walk and in every other way. He needs plenty of exercise, he is currently walked twice a day for a minimum of 30 minutes and is taken for long walks at the weekend over the hills behind our house. He will come with dog bed, bowl and lead. He listens to your commands like; Sit, heel, stay, fetch, lay down, etc. Only to a good home and genuine people. For sale through no fault of his own. No time wasters, please. Watford."

"What makes you think this is the one?" asked Marion.

"The advert's got quite a few clues in it," said Nick. "Firstly the price: ordinary people selling their pet don't knock a pound off to make it look cheaper, that's a commercial trick; secondly, the dog's name doesn't sound right. Buster's the sort of name you might give a Staffy or a Pit Bull, but not a Golden Retriever, people give them names like Jasper or Marley. As for that rubbish about the pedigree with champions in the line, that is really over-egging the pudding; I mean, would you seriously expect somebody to have lost the paperwork for a first-class pedigree dog? But the big giveaway's that bit at the end about no time wasters. That's something dodgy car dealers put. I'm pretty sure this isn't coming from the happy little family it's made out to be."

"Well, you've convinced me."

"Besides, it matches up with one of the police files you sent me. Look at the photos."

Nick opened up another window on his laptop and brought up a photo of Bob Brannigan's Golden Retriever, Archie, beside the picture of Buster.

"Well, it's hard to be sure from such a different angle," said Marion, "and to be honest all Golden Retrievers look the same to me. Could be the one in Downton Abbey for all I know."

"Worth a go, though, don't you think?"

"I suppose so. I don't imagine we'll get a closer match. Watford's not so far away. If it was up north or somewhere there's no way my boss would let me take the time to go there."

"Shall I call them or will you?"

"Hold on. We'll need a cover story first. And I'll need the okay from Inspector Warren. I'll call him now."

Marion got voicemail on Warren's phone, left a message saying she needed to talk to him urgently as she had a lead on the dog thieves, realised that sounded like a bad pun, and saw Nick closing down his laptop and smiling at her.

"Got time to go outside for a coffee?" he asked.

"I wish. Love to, but a policewoman's work is never done." She pointed at a pile of paperwork on her desk. "I'll give you a call as soon as I get the green light. Are you up for tomorrow if I do?"

"Sure. I'm working on research, what I don't do tomorrow I'll do the day after." He stood up. "See you then."

Marion looked around the office. There was only DC Matt Rayner working on his computer in the opposite corner. She said quietly: "And I'll take you up on that coffee as soon as I can, all right?"

"Excellent."

When Nick had gone, Rayner looked up from his screen. "Looks like you've pulled, Marion love. Who's the unlucky fella?"

"He's a man who likes dogs."

"Well, he'd have to wouldn't he?"

"Do you want a smack in the mouth?"

But Matt had such an infectious grin that she couldn't be angry at him for a sexist joke, and with a sigh of resignation she drew the paperwork towards her.

*

"You're not going out on this with a civilian," Warren told Marion. "These are nasty people. By all means this man from the dog charity can fill you in on background, brief you on what's likely to happen, whatever, but he is not going with you. Is that absolutely clear?"

"Yes, sir. So should I go on my own?"

"Out of the question. If it gets rough, you'll need a male officer with you. And CID are in the middle of a high profile murder investigation. I just can't spare anybody at the moment."

"I thought we were under pressure to clear this up, sir."

"Yes, I know. I just can't spirit men out of nowhere."

"May I make a suggestion, sir?"

"Go ahead, try me."

"PC Robin Merryweather's very keen to show he's good enough for CID, sir. Could we borrow him from uniform for half a day?"

Warren thought for a moment. He was well aware that Constable Merryweather and Marion had got on well before she left uniform.

"Not trying to get a job for your boyfriend, I hope?" he asked.

"No, sir. Robin's not interested in the ladies, actually."

Whoops, she thought, maybe I shouldn't have said that.

"You mean he's gay?"

"Yes, sir. That's not a problem, is it?"

On the contrary, Warren was well aware that having gay men and, come to that, lesbian women on the force had been making an important contribution to relations with those communities in recent years. He was also aware that, at the moment, he didn't have a single gay officer in CID.

"Do you happen to know whether he's a member of the Gay Police Association?"

"Yes, sir. I believe he plays quite an active part. Attends all their meetings."

Warren thought, I should have known about that. He liked to keep close tabs on who was who in uniform, with a view to poaching the talent. He'd been getting slack in that department, he thought.

"I'll have a word with the Super," he said.

6

A phone call to Noel Wharton's agent, Emmeline Clifton of Hayes & Clifton, told Warren the actor was rehearsing in a play by George Bernard Shaw. It was to be performed in the open air in the garden of the writer's house, Shaw's Corner, in the Hertfordshire village of Ayot St Lawrence. He could have asked Hertfordshire Constabulary to bring the actor into Welwyn Garden City police station for questioning, but instead he succumbed to the temptation of a trip into the countryside on a summer's day, just as DC Everitt had done when she had first gone to meet Nick Boyd.

After turning off the A1(M) at Junction 6, he found himself in a labyrinth of narrow B-roads, and three times had to pull over into bumpy recesses to allow vehicles heading in the opposite direction to pass, on one occasion needing to reverse nearly 100 yards. However, the rolling countryside, a patchwork of wheat fields, coppices and hedgerows rising and falling around him, shimmering in a haze of heat even though it was only late morning, felt a million miles from the stifling pollution of the streets of north London. At a little T-junction at the top of a hill he turned right into the deep shade of a tunnel of overlapping tall trees, emerging into the village and passing a semi-ruined church that looked a good eight hundred years old. A few yards further on, signposts indicated that the main entrance to Shaw's Corner, now a National Trust property open to the public, lay down a lane to the right. He swung his car in through the gate on to the car park, where an attendant in his sixties stepped out in front of him, held up his hand for him to halt, and spoke through his driver's side window.

"I'm sorry sir, there's no parking for visitors, you'll have to go and leave your car in the village."

"Police," said Warren. "I believe you have some actors working here."

"Is there a problem, officer?"

"I just need to talk to one of them. It won't take long."

"In that case you can park over there." He indicated a space which would block in a red Toyota Yaris. "It's one of the volunteers' cars. She won't need to move it till half past five."

"Where do I go then?"

"I'll take you through to the house."

"I'd like to avoid barging in on the rehearsal and starting tongues wagging. Is there any way you can prise him away discreetly to somewhere I can talk to him?"

"I'll have a word with the director, officer. My name's Doug Turton, by the way. I'm a volunteer, too."

Warren parked up and walked back over to the obliging attendant outside a cabin which served as the box office for admission to the house, gardens, and outdoor plays, as well as doing service as a shop selling souvenirs and small garden tools.

"I'll just take you in through the main entrance to the house, where if you don't mind waiting in the entrance hall, I'll go and sort something out. What's the name of the actor you want to talk to?"

"Noel Wharton."

"Oh, yes, the tall, very well-spoken one; in his seventies but still has the bearing of a military man, which I believe he was in his younger days. Royal Navy, I believe."

Was he, indeed, thought Warren.

Warren followed Doug Turton along a scrunching gravel pathway past a long, neat lawn on the left and a high hedge on the right, to the house of Bernard Shaw. It was a massive yet well proportioned Edwardian structure from the Arts and Crafts school, its multiple window-frames and drainpipes tastefully picked out in an olive green that somehow both contrasted and blended with the terracotta brickwork of the walls. They entered through the main door, into a large entrance hall. A lady volunteer rose from a chair to the left, beside the foot of the stairs, to greet them; but was pre-empted by Doug, who sensed that his temporary role as Warren's assistant gave him 15 minutes of authority.

"This gentleman's a policeman," he almost whispered. "I've asked him to wait here while I just pop and sort things out for him." He added conspiratorially, "Mum's the word."

Doug disappeared through a door to the right, beyond which could be heard a buzz of conversation.

"It's the old kitchen," explained the female volunteer, in her sixties, with a smart, short, hairstyle dyed to a tone which somehow seemed more straw-coloured than blonde, thick-lensed rimless glasses, a dark brown blouse and an infectious smile. "That's where they have their breaks and change in and out of their costumes." She asked Warren if he would like a cup of tea, and he politely declined.

"You can sit down on that modern chair," she said, indicating a plain, wooden chair near the foot of the stairs, "but you're not allowed to sit on anything with a thistle on it."

"I beg your pardon?"

"We put a thistle head on all the original furniture, you know, the chairs that GBS himself had in the house, so that visitors know not to sit down on them. You still get people doing it sometimes, and then we have to tell them off."

"Quite right," said Warren. "That would be doing GBH to GBS's chairs, wouldn't it?"

"GBH?" the lady enquired, until the penny dropped, at which point she hooted alarmingly with girlish laughter. "Oh, I get it, GBH, grievous bodily harm."

Warren accommodated himself on the wooden chair, and an elderly, handsome tabby cat materialised from somewhere and brushed against his legs. He leaned forward and rubbed its forehead and ears. The cat jumped nimbly on to his lap.

"Not a bad jumper for an old 'un, is she?" said the volunteer.

"How old is she?"

"Fourteen. She's a bit of an actress herself. Always appears in the open-air plays, walks across the set, jumps on to a table. The audiences love her, so do the actors."

"What's her name?"

"Socks."

Warren looked at the cat's white forelegs and paws and said, "Yes, I can see why you call her that."

He continued stroking the purring Socks, and surveyed the room while he was waiting. The walls of the entrance hall were painted cream. It had a high ceiling. Facing Warren in front of a large fireplace was a small, black, coal-burning stove. The mantelpiece above supported a plaster cast of an ancient Egyptian head, he couldn't tell whether it was male or female; and above that a convex circular mirror was surmounted by a mythical plaster bird. All around on the walls were paintings and prints, many of them of birds, some of which looked to be of Japanese origin. To the right of the front door was Shaw's Bechstein piano, a simple design made of light-coloured oak, and with something he had never seen before: tall, slender, wooden posts forming part of the fabric of the instrument at either end of the keyboard, each supporting a candle-holder.

What must it have been like, reading music and playing by candlelight? Immediately inside the door, a tall hat-stand held a collection of the writer's favourite hats, including a strange-looking green leather helmet.

Socks decided she had had enough fuss, jumped down and strode elegantly towards her outdoor kingdom, so Warren stood up and walked across to the hat-stand for a closer look. "What's that?" he asked the volunteer, pointing.

"It's a Cornish miner's helmet," she explained. "You see the broad peak? He wore that at the back when he was chopping wood, to protect his neck from flying wood-chips."

Doug reappeared from the kitchen area and said, "I'll take you up to the kitchen. You can talk to him there. I'll make sure you're not disturbed."

"I thought that was the kitchen," said Warren, pointing at the door Doug had just emerged through.

"That's Shaw's original kitchen. It's still got the old range in it, and some other museum pieces. Upstairs is a modern one, it's really part of the curator's flat, but that'll be all right today."

Upstairs, Warren sat down at a round kitchen table. Doug disappeared and a moment later Noel Wharton entered; at least six feet tall, fit and lean, wearing jeans and a plain white t-shirt; a man with the tanned, weathered face of a retired farmer rather than the indoor stereotype of an actor; thick black hair slicked back with a lick of gel to collar length at the back; but the most striking feature was his luxuriant, fluffy sideburns, largely obscuring his ears from the front; a deep, strong chin with a couple of days' growth of stubble emphasised the appearance of a son of the soil, yet the overall impression still somehow suggested upper-class origins. Therefore it seemed perfectly natural that, when Wharton opened his mouth, his exasperation came out in a West Country burr: "I hope this isn't going to take long. I'm in the middle of an important rehearsal."

"Please sit down, Mr Wharton," said Warren, not smiling.

Given the man's confrontational attitude, Warren omitted any polite preamble. "Where were you last Saturday afternoon between four and five o'clock?"

"Why, what's this about?"

"Just answer the question, please, sir."

"Well, if you must know, I went to the theatre."

"What did you see?"

"Hamlet; or rather, half of it."

Warren stifled a gasp of astonishment: "Are you telling me you were in the audience at the Theatre Royal North London when Sir Roger Nutley was murdered?"

"I should have thought you'd already know that. Your people took everybody's name and address."

Warren was kicking himself for not having checked the list; but he said, "Well, that puts you in a rather awkward situation, doesn't it?"

"I don't see why."

"Because you'd previously threatened Sir Roger."

"Well, yes, I was pissed off at him at the time for nicking my part. Some people would say it's all part of the game. In my opinion it was pretty damned underhanded."

"You threatened violence in front of a group of people in a pub."

"Oh, for God's sake, I'd had a few drinks and I told my friends that if he walked in now they'd have to hold me down or I'd probably give him a smack in the mouth. Not exactly a mafia death threat, is it?"

"It's threatening behaviour. I could arrest you for that alone."

"You'd look pretty foolish if you did."

"Not as foolish as you'd look if your play couldn't open because you're in a police cell. You also sent threatening emails."

"My word, you have been busy. Look, that was months ago, in the heat of the moment; in any case, I don't remember threatening any violence in those emails."

Warren produced a printout from his inside jacket pocket and read aloud:

"I will make you regret this, you see if I don't. You won't finish this tour, I guarantee you that. In fact, by the time I've finished with you, you'll never be seen in public again."

He looked up at Wharton and raised his eyebrows for a response.

"Where does it say anything about killing him in that?"

"It's the clear implication, in the light of what's happened."

"No, it's you twisting my meaning in the light of the facts."

"So what was your meaning?"

"Do you really think Sylvia Thorbinson, Carol Baxter and Abigail Taverner were the only girls who ever came in for that dirty bastard's unwanted attentions?"

"What are you saying?"

"I know where plenty more bodies are buried, Inspector. I know names and places; and some of them were a lot younger than those three. They just prefer not to expose themselves to the publicity after all these years. But I'm sure I could have persuaded at least some of them to come forward. Another trial would have finished off that bloody pervert's career once and for all."

"So why didn't you?"

"Life's too short. I let off my steam when he nicked my part, then I got over it. It's what you do, isn't it? Those emails were childish, petulant, unworthy, I admit it. Why do you think I went to the show last Saturday?"

"At the moment I'm assuming it was to carry out a murder. You look tall enough and strong enough to break a man's neck from behind. Did you?"

"No, I damn well didn't."

"Have you ever had any military training?"

"A very long time ago I was in the Royal Navy. It was a teenage mistake. I hated it and I got out as soon as I could."

"Are you a member of a gym? You look very fit for your age."

"Yes, an actor has to keep in shape. I do the cycling machines, treadmill, rowing, that sort of thing, three or four times a week in the mornings. I don't go in for weights and punchbags and suchlike."

"Why exactly did you go to the play?"

"I live in Barnet. It's been on tour in the provinces. If

you've checked the tour itinerary, you'll know this is the first time it's come to London, unless you count Richmond, which is right on the opposite side. I wanted to see what sort of a job Nutley would make of Polonius."

"And?"

"He was infuriatingly good. Bumbling, scheming, fatherly, controlling and amusing all at the same time. He had the audience in fits with his timing of the "Yet here Laertes," scene, although I don't suppose a policeman would know what I'm talking about."

"The wind sits in the shoulder of your sail," responded Warren.

"Bloody hell. Well done, Inspector. I take that back. Anyway, I have to admit, he had the character nailed."

This all seemed credible, but Warren wasn't forgetting that Wharton was an experienced and accomplished actor himself, and could easily be putting on the performance of his life in this interview. "Did you go backstage during the interval?" he asked.

"No."

"Can you prove you didn't go backstage at any time?"

"I don't see how I could have done without anybody noticing."

"How well do you know the Theatre Royal? Have you ever worked there?"

"Oddly enough, no. Always seems to be the way with the theatre that's nearest where you live. It would be nice to walk to work, or at least go on a short bus-ride, but I always seem to end up in places hundreds of miles away. Sod's Law. But I've been in quite a few times to watch touring productions. It saves the hassle of going in to the West End, and it's a lot cheaper."

"Did anybody go with you this time?"

"No. I like going to matinees by myself sometimes, and my wife likes going shopping on Saturday afternoons with her friend Sandra."

"That's a pity."

"I don't see why. There were people sitting either side of me. You must have their names and addresses and you can cross reference them with their ticket numbers, can't you, the theatre must have a record. You can check with them whether I was in my seat for the start of the second half."

"You didn't leave your seat during the interval?"

"Yes, I shot straight out to the loo at the side of the foyer, it can get rather urgent at my age, then I bought a coffee and a Kit-Kat in the bar, had them in the foyer, and returned to my seat, I suppose five minutes or so before the bell; sat down and read one of the articles in the programme before the show got started again; the interview with Jason Dean about playing Hamlet being an actor's dream."

This was beginning to look like another blind alley. He certainly would get somebody to find the audience members who had been sitting beside and behind Wharton in the auditorium. But he had little doubt they would turn out to be people completely unconnected with him, and that they would confirm he had been in his seat at the time of the murder. It was annoying; he fitted the bill so perfectly: motive, physical ability, impetuously nasty nature. The trouble was, total lack of opportunity, apparently, despite his having been right there in the theatre at the time. On the one hand, it seemed too much of a coincidence; on the other, he had to admit, it was impossible. Or was he missing something?

"All right, Mr Wharton, thank you for your time. I'll let you get back to your rehearsal. What's the play, by the way?"

"Heartbreak House."

"Shaw's great satire of the end of Edwardian complacency," said Warren. "For the centenary of the outbreak of the First World War, I presume."

"Well done again, Inspector. I had no idea the police were so literary."

"We're not all Plods. I had tickets for Hamlet on Saturday evening."

"Oh. Bad luck. I can get you a couple of comps for this if you'd like."

"Nice of you to offer, but obviously in the circumstances..."

"Yes, I see, I'm a suspect."

"Which character are you playing?"

"Captain Shotover."

"It is not my house; it is only my kennel."

"My God, you know Shaw as well?"

"My mother taught English and Drama. Break a leg, but just a couple of things before I go, Mr Wharton."

"What are they?"

"Don't go off anywhere for the time being, watch your mouth in pubs in future, and the next time you feel like sending a nasty email, shut down your computer and go and make a cup of tea. It's not only juvenile, as you yourself admitted, but it could constitute a criminal offence and get you into trouble."

"Point taken."

Warren gave the chastened actor a few moments to return to his colleagues before going back downstairs himself. He had no desire to cause consternation among the cast of Heartbreak House. Doug Turton was standing waiting for him in the entrance hall.

"If you've got time, Inspector, I could show you around the house and grounds," he said. "There's a shed hidden among the shrubbery at the bottom where GBS used to write for hours so as not to be disturbed."

I could do with one of those on the other side of the car park at the nick, thought Warren. "Much as I'd like to, duty calls," he said. "There's a grindstone awaiting the attention of my nose."

While Warren was walking back to his car, his mobile rang.

"Warren."

"Watcha Bunny, it's me Gerry. You're on, mate."

"What, you mean Tennyson?"

"That's it. Tomorrow, ten in the morning, don't be early or late. I spoke to him, he's fine about it, anything he can do to help catch the bastard were his exact words. Just you in your own unmarked car. Describe it to me now and tell me the reg number."

Warren told him, wrote down the private address of one of the most notorious gangsters in London, and said thank you.

7

Yolanda was on the sofa in the living-room reading a novel called *El Verdugo de Dios* by a Spanish authoress called Toti Martínez de Lezea when she heard Warren's key turn in the front door. He came into the room and kissed her on the cheek.

"What are you reading?" he asked.

"It's a historical novel. A very good one, based on real events in the thirteenth century."

He spotted the glass of white wine and open bottle on the coffee table: "I'll get myself a glass. Dinner under way?"

"Claro que sí, mi amor."

"So tell me more about the thirteenth century."

She turned to the back of the book and read him some of the blurb in Spanish: "In the spring of 1239, in the north of France, 183 Cathars were burned alive by the inquisitor Robert Lepetit. One of the victims was the wife of the master builder Geoffroi Bisol, and he fled to Navarre in search of a new life. But his tranquillity was destroyed when Lepetit reappeared there sowing fear and death."

"Sounds bloodthirsty."

"Of course it is. It's about the Catholic Church."

Yolanda's passionate anti-clericalism sometimes shocked Warren, but never surprised him. He knew it was rooted in hatred of the Church hierarchy in Argentina who had supported the murderous right-wing dictatorship that had ruled her country between 1976 and 1983.

"If I ever get time I'll read it. Unusual for you to drink white. What's for dinner?"

"You will have to ask the cook."

"We don't have a cook."

"We do now. Take a look in the kitchen."

Warren put his glass down on the coffee table and walked through the hall to the kitchen, where Oscar was busy at a work-top beside the stove.

"Hi Dad."

"Bloody hell," exclaimed Warren. "Have you been taken over by an alien or something?"

"No, Dad. You have to learn to look after yourself at uni."

"Things have changed since my day, then." Warren remembered eating in the university and halls of residence refectories and going out for fish-and-chips and curries most of the time. "So what are you regaling us with, if I dare ask?"

"No need to be like that. It's smoked haddock baked in garlic-and-herb sauce, boiled new potatoes and sweetcorn. Nothing complicated."

"Where did you learn to make garlic-and-herb sauce?"

Oscar laughed. His laugh sounded very grown-up to Warren; the mature laughter of a young man, nothing like the teenager who had gone off to Lincoln. ""I didn't. They put it in the pack at the fishmonger's counter in Morrisons if you ask them, and you just stick the whole thing in the oven."

"That's a relief. I'd have started feeling seriously inadequate if I thought you were turning into a Jamie Oliver."

"Better that than a Gordon Ramsay, wouldn't you say?"

"Want me to lay the table?"

"It's already done, Dad. Go and talk to Mum and I'll call you when it's ready."

"Can't say fairer than that."

Warren returned to the living-room, picked up his glass, sat down beside Yolanda and put his arm lightly around her shoulders.

She stopped reading and looked at him: "We need to talk about Christmas."

Warren almost spluttered over his wine: "You're joking. It's only June. Christmas is, what, more than six months away."

"But we have to plan. Are we going away or staying here? If we want to go to see Mummy and Daddy we need to book our flights soon, or they'll be too expensive."

"Won't make any difference. They cost a fortune over Christmas and New Year. If you want to go home when it's winter here, that's fine with me, but we're not tied to the school holidays anymore and the prices go down a lot in January."

"So you want to have Christmas at home and go to Argentina in January?"

"Could do. Or February. We can have my Mum and Dad over at Christmas. Or more likely get invited down to Bournemouth. Walks along the beach to Poole and Boscombe if it's fine, roast turkey with all the trimmings back at the house, out for a Chinese on Boxing Day. And still have the southern hemisphere summer to look forward to."

"It's a deal."

"Hold on a bit though. I'll need to check on when I can take leave. What about you?"

"I've already booked out the first two weeks in February."

"So ... what was all that about, then?"

"I needed you to think it was your idea."

Oscar called from the dining-room: "Mum, Dad, come on, it's ready."

"I could get used to this," said Warren.

"Don't," said Yolanda. "It's your turn next, and I'll want a big, juicy *bife de chorizo, jugoso, con papas fritas y ensalada de tomate y cebolla.*"

Sirloin steak, bloody on the inside, with chips, and tomato and onion salad. You can take the girl out of Argentina, thought Warren, but you can't take Argentina out of the girl. Thank God.

"And a bottle of Malbec from Mendoza," he added, giving her another peck on the cheek and standing up. They went through to the dining-room to enjoy being pampered by their suddenly oh-so-mature son. He had even set candles, and was lighting them as they entered. They both felt proud.

TUESDAY 17 JUNE

1

At three o'clock in the morning the last stragglers from late night pub drinking had staggered home from the shopping district. The man in the driver's seat pushed the stick into the reverse position on the manual gearbox of the bronze-coloured Volvo XC70. He had stolen the big, heavy car from a Waitrose car park in Orpington two days earlier. He held the clutch pedal down for a few moments more while he took three deep breaths.

"Ready?" he asked.

They were all in black overalls and boots, all wearing black crash helmets with dark visors. The man in the front passenger seat, who had his window wound down, listened to make sure the engine of the silver Peugeot 508 parked a short distance away was running. He exchanged nods with its driver, pressed the button to close his window, and said, "Go for it." The man in the rear seat said, "Ready."

The driver released the clutch and pressed his right foot down hard on the accelerator pedal. The massive car leaped backwards across the deserted square and crashed through the metal security grille and toughened glass of Sacs-à-Porter as if they were made of icing-sugar. The shop was less than half-a-mile away from Bags of Fun, but this area was home to so many rich women, they could both survive.

The three men sprang out of the all-wheel drive crossover wagon, climbed into the shop through the debris, their industrial boots protecting their feet from injury. They swiftly looped five designer handbags on to each of their arms, making thirty in total. In less than two minutes they were jumping into the Peugeot 508, which zoomed away down Norton Vale's deserted Cavendish Avenue.

Less than three minutes after the huge Volvo had shot across Cavendish Square in reverse, the only sound was the shrill ringing of the shop's alarm. It was another four minutes before the first police siren added to the clangour, by which time the gang were already changing cars in Barnet.

*

Seven hours later, DC Marion Everitt dialled the mobile number on the website and it was answered on the second ring by a man with a working-class London accent.

"Hello," said Marion, "I'm calling about the Golden Retriever."

"Oh, yeah, yeah, great. You wanna buy him, then?"

"Yes, that's the breed I'm looking for," said Marion. "We had one until last summer, but he died, and we decided we didn't want another one straight away, but we're ready now. Is he still available?"

"Yeah, definitely, when d'you wanna have a look him?"

"Well, I've got a day off tomorrow, so I could come up then. It's not far to Watford, I live in Kingsbury, in northwest London."

"Well, the only thing is, I've had to move up to me mum's in Peterborough this week, see, the landlord chucked me out in Watford cos I lost me job and got behind with the rent, only the trouble is my mum's got these two Siamese cats and the dog don't get on with them, like, to be honest if we didn't keep 'em apart it'd be fur all over the place, and I don't really want to be parted from Buster but what can I do, so I need to find somebody who'll give the poor little sod a good home and look after him properly."

"Peterborough's a bit far," said Marion.

"Tell you what, what about if I meet you half-way?"

"Well, where do you suggest?"

"I could show you Buster at a motorway services area, if that's any good, but I'd be doing you a big favour, so are you really serious about buying? I mean, I don't want to waste my time driving all the way down the A1 if you're just window shopping."

"No," said Marion, "I really appreciate it, if he's all it says he is in the advert I'll definitely be wanting to take him."

"How do I know he's going to a good home? He's got to be treated right, he's a nice boy, and I don't really wanna lose him, only I've got to."

"Well, I said, we had a retriever before, and we really loved him."

"What sort of a house have you got?"

"It's a three-bedroom semi, and it's really near Fryent Country Park, so he'd get walks there every day."

"Okay. Look, how about eleven o'clock tomorrow morning?"

"That's okay. I'll be coming with my partner, because we both need to like him."

"That's all right, gives me a chance to check out whether I reckon both of you would be good owners. I'll tell you what, I'll come down as far as Baldock Services, that's more than half-way for me, make it easier for you, okay?"

"That's great. How will I know you?"

"I'll wait for you by the Starbucks. I'll have Buster with me, so you'll know who I am."

He's got that bit about Starbucks a bit too off-pat, thought Marion; probably uses the same place every time.

"That's great," she said. "Oh, what's your name?"

"Steve. What's yours?"

"Diana. And my husband's Jeremy."

"Okay, Diana. Oh, by the way, you don't mind paying cash, do you? Only if I pay in a cheque to the bank my ex'll get it."

And if I believed that I'd believe anything, Marion thought; but what she said was: "No problem, cash is fine."

*

Although she was going to be 18 in November, Faith Goodwin's parents were adamant she could not have a boyfriend.

"You're still a child," her mother admonished her whenever she plucked up the courage to ask for permission to go out with friends for an evening. "Until you come of age, you'll do as your father and I tell you."

Joshua and Ruth Goodwin belonged to a strict, some would say fanatical, Christian sect which still regarded the age of majority as being 21, not 18. They considered the legal age of consent, 16, to have no significance whatsoever for their daughter. The fact that she was their only child was a source of sadness and consternation to them, for it was the doctrine of their sect that the women should bear as many children as possible. The purpose was to populate the world with future generations who would eventually vote fundamentalist Christians like themselves into power and establish a theocracy which would usher in the Kingdom of God. But for some reason, the divinity had denied Ruth the fertility required to play her full part in carrying out the plan. Faith Goodwin, however, had no intention of living for another three years and five months under a domestic curfew that she considered more appropriate to a village in Afghanistan than to a north London suburb. Besides, the teenage daughters of repressive parents tend to develop ingenious strategies to circumvent their restrictions.

On this warm, sunny Tuesday afternoon, Faith arrived home from school at a quarter past four as usual, let herself in with her key, and called out, "Hi, mum."

"Don't say hi, how many times do I have to tell you?" came the peevish response from upstairs. "Honour thy father and thy mother: that thy days may be long upon the land which the Lord thy God giveth thee."

Faith paid little attention to this, as Toby had, as usual, come rushing out of the living-room wagging his tail to greet his favourite human. He was now scampering back and forth energetically between Faith, the kitchen and the front door.

"Has Toby been out for a walk?" Faith called up the stairs in a friendly tone of voice, knowing perfectly well what the answer would be.

"When do you think I have time to go dog-walking? I've got the housework to do and the shopping to get and your dinners to cook. I can't be in two places at once."

Faith had always failed to comprehend her mother's need to vacuum, dust and polish the entire house every day. She assumed, since one of her mother's favourite sayings was, "Cleanliness is next to godliness," that she believed her obsessive domesticity would eventually help her get into heaven.

"I'll take him down the common," said Faith. "He needs some exercise."

"Thank you darling," called Ruth. "You're a good girl to look after that animal like you do." This had become an almost verbatim routine nearly every day over the past seven months.

If she had been allowed to dress, wear make-up, and have her hair done like most of her school friends, Faith would have looked a stunner. As it was, even with her glowing chestnut hair cut untidily by her mother in an unprepossessing short bob, and with her well-developed figure always hidden under dull clothes a size too large, boys turned their heads. She fetched the poop scoop and a couple of plastic bags from the cupboard under the sink in the utility room, and took Toby's leash down from its hook on the coat-rack in the hall. Toby bounded up to her and offered his head for the leash to be attached to his collar. "C'mon boy," said the teenager, "Let's go walkabout."

Leading the faithful two-year-old pedigree Doberman Pinscher, Faith Goodwin set off, as she did nearly every day at this time, to meet her 21-year-old boyfriend Matt for their usual half-hour walk across Norton Common. They would throw sticks for the dog to chase and fetch and converse earnestly about the state of the world. The walk would be followed by half-an-hour in Matt's bedroom before his mother came home from work, while Toby rested in Matt's kitchen after his exercise. Allowing the pet into the Goodwin home had been a rare concession by Faith's parents. There had been arguments between her mother and father, with her mother contending that a dog would leave hair all over the house and make her housework more difficult, and was un-Christian, although for once she had been unable to produce a biblical quote to support her argument. Her father argued that caring for a dog would teach the girl to take responsibility for another of God's creatures, and was thus in fact very Christian. Faith strongly suspected that her father had concocted this theological argument, because although he would never admit it, he really wanted a dog himself. It was indeed Joshua Goodwin who always took Toby out for his early morning walk at seven o'clock. He had cost nearly £800, because the snob in Mr Goodwin would not allow him to be seen to own anything cheap, and that included a pet.

When Faith reached the edge of the common with Toby, she unclipped the leash and the dog went bounding off diagonally across the grass to the right of the narrow asphalt footpath. Up the gentle hill ahead there was a coppice of ash, oak and sycamore, mostly made impenetrable by thorn and elder bushes growing in between, with occasional narrow pathways cut through the undergrowth. Faith walked up the path to where Matt Sym was waiting for her as usual on the first bench on the left of the path, in the shade of a towering horse chestnut tree. A moderately handsome, dark-haired young man, of medium height and with the physique of the boxer which he had been since his early teens, he stood up as she approached. They embraced and kissed, then walked on up the path holding hands.

"Did you see Brazil beat Cameroon four-one last night?" asked Matt.

"You don't seriously think we're allowed to watch football in our house," said Faith. "The telly's stuck on the God Channel most of the time, and gets changed at ten o'clock to the News so that Dad can shout at the screen."

"You should come to a match," said Matt. "Lots of girls do."

"Chance would be a fine thing."

Toby had run on ahead and was approaching the coppice. Faith called him back. The Doberman stopped and turned his head to see what his favourite human wanted. "Here," called Faith. Obediently the dog came loping back along the path, went to Matt and sniffed his knee, and was rewarded with having his ear tickled. They walked on until they were enclosed by the woodland.

About a quarter of a mile further on, two big, powerful men appeared from beyond the trees, where Copse Way passed through the Common. One had a shaven head, gold ear-ring, and tattoos on his neck and arms. He was wearing dirty blue jeans and a black t-shirt with an AC/DC 'Lock Up Your Daughters' design on the front. The other had long, greasy, straight brown hair and several days' scruffy growth of beard. He was wearing a white t-shirt with 'All This and a Huge Dick' on the front, and khaki lightweight cargo trousers with side pockets. He was carrying a large pet-carrier. The first man held out a chunk of bloody meat towards Toby, then tossed it into the back of the box. Toby went as far in as his shoulders after the meat, and in a flash the two men had shoved the big dog fully inside, slammed and locked the carrier's gate. The box had been fitted with dual handles. The dognappers ran with it between them, even with the weight of the Doberman.

"Hey," shouted Faith, running after them, "that's my dog."

A lanky youth aged about 19 stepped out in front of her and blocked the way.

"I wouldn't do that if I were you," he sneered in her face.

Matt now came hurtling up the path behind Faith, shoved the skinny man aside and ran after the pair carrying Toby. The younger man caught him, grabbed him by his left arm and pulled him round, ready to punch him. But Matt, a member of Norton Hill Boxing Club who regularly competed in London-wide contests, feinted and got his punch in first, a powerful right to the man's eye. The teenage thug staggered backwards into the undergrowth on the left side of the path, a cut above his eye bleeding. Matt turned to look along the path after the men stealing Toby, but by now they were out of sight. They heard a van pull away on Copse Way. Faith ran from behind Matt with the hopeless intention of pursuing the thief who had her dog. Matt heard the wiry man stand up, caught a glimpse of him coming at him again and feinted to his left; which is why the knife slashed Faith instead. She screamed in pain, clutched her right side below the ribs, went down on one knee, then lay on her side, crying. Matt landed another punch on the attacker's temple then, as he reeled half-senseless, chopped down on to his right wrist with a karate blow that made him drop the knife, and finally kneed him in the groin. It was the wiry man's turn to scream as he doubled up feeling as if his testicles were exploding. Matt scooped up the knife, closed it, pushed it into his jeans pocket and looked down at Faith. He could see blood spreading on the side of her white blouse.

"I'll call for an ambulance," he said.

At that moment, cowardice gave the assailant wings, and he ran off up the path. Prioritising Faith's well-being, Matt let him go and dialled 999.

It rang and rang. Matt kneeled beside Faith and tugged her blouse out of her jeans and up so that he could see the wound.

"What are you doing?" Faith asked weakly.

"Checking to see how bad the cut is. You'll be okay. He caught you a side-swipe, it's not deep."

Matt pulled off his t-shirt, rolled it into a ball, and pressed it on to the wound to staunch the bleeding.

"Emergency. Which service do you require?"

"Ambulance, please. And police. My girlfriend's been stabbed. Please, hurry."

The emergency services operator took the details swiftly and efficiently.

"I'm sorry, Matt," whispered Faith.

"What for? I love you."

Three minutes later, they heard a siren.

2

As it turned out, Ralph Tennyson de Clare was almost a neighbour, living in the exclusive neighbourhood of Hadley Wood, so far out on the northern fringe of Greater London that it felt more like Hertfordshire. Yet its postal district was London enough to give you a Freedom Pass on the tubes and buses when you retired; not that many of its residents were ever likely to get out of their Ferraris and Rollers to make use of the capital's public transport system.

The house was the only dwelling at the end of a tree-lined cul-de-sac, with a couple of hundred yards between the turn-off from the main road and the high wrought-iron gates. Approaching in his car, Warren was pretty sure there would be constantly monitored CCTV, which was confirmed by the gates automatically swinging open as he slowed down.

Warren's car scrunched across a huge, square gravel drive. The house had been built in Georgian style, and although it was relatively new, the architecture looked faithful, at least to Warren's unprofessional eye. A deep-blue front door in the centre of the main section of the building was protected by a simple portico of plain, round, stone columns, with two tall windows on either side divided into small rectangles typical of the Georgian period. There was a line of five windows on the first floor, and two dormer windows protruded from the front of the roof. To the right, a smaller, joined-on section, set a few feet back, might in a lesser house have been added at a later stage as an extension but in this case was clearly an integral part of the structure. It comprised a double garage with two more Georgian-style windows above it. This was money, but by no means flashy; more like the home of a stockbroker or a QC. However, what the house lacked in vulgarity, one of Tennyson's cars more than compensated for; a yellow Lamborghini parked to the left. There was also a more conservative, silver Mercedes E220 CDI on the right. Both bore 2013 registration numbers, which made them a little over a year old at most. They also indicated that Tennyson preferred discretion to personalisation, since neither number was in any way related to his name or his initials. Were it not for the flashy Lamborghini, you could almost believe at this first glance that the man was sensible in the way he spent his money. That was not a trait that Warren would normally expect to find in a man whose income was known, but had never been proven, to derive from the importation and distribution of cocaine.

Warren rang the doorbell. It was opened in seconds by a very big shaven-headed white man in his mid-thirties with expressionless eyes and mouth. He was wearing a black t-shirt, black slacks and black Doc Martins, and had snake tattoos on his massive arms. "Come in, Inspector," he invited with a broad arm gesture. His voice was calm, neutral, London-accented but not heavily cockney. "Mr Tennyson's expecting you."

Warren stepped into a small ante-foyer and was

astonished to be confronted, in the inner arch leading into the main foyer, by a metal-detector archway like those passengers have to pass through at airports for security. The bodyguard picked up a plastic tray from a low table on the right and held it out.

"Please place any metal objects in here, Inspector."

Warren emptied his pockets of keys, coins and his phone.

"Are you wearing a belt?"

Dutifully he removed his trouser-belt with its metal buckle and placed it in the tray.

"Please go through now."

Warren walked through the gate; no beep. The Incredible Hulk flicked a switch to turn off the gate's electronics, followed him through, and held the tray out to him. He put his belt back on and recovered his possessions.

"Very modern security," he ventured.

"Safer for everybody," replied The Hulk, a very slight smile cracking the lower half of his face but nothing in the eyes. "Follow me, please."

They were in a large, stunningly bright entrance hall. It seemed unnaturally light, considering the narrow windows up the sides of the front door. But then Warren glanced up and over his shoulder and realised that the sun was streaming in through a huge triple window on the upstairs landing that ran sideways across the front of the house, allowing the maximum of light to penetrate downstairs.

A tiny middle-aged south-east Asian woman wearing a white t-shirt with a large, black-and-white image of Ho Chi-Minh on the front, loose black pyjama-type trousers, flat grey mules, and a white-toothed smile entered from a room at the rear.

"Mai will look after you from here on," said The Hulk, and headed off upstairs.

The floor of the entrance hall was of cream-coloured marble squares with small dark-grey diamond-shapes set into the corners. The walls were painted pale grey. All the woodwork was gleaming white gloss. There was virtually no clutter; just a two-seater white leather sofa to one side for waiting guests, a couple of cream-painted simple upright chairs, and an occasional table of the same colour with a big vase of mixed flowers, chosen to scent the room, perhaps with south-east Asian skill. She led him into a similarly bright room which he guessed an estate agent might describe as a family room, only its present use looked more likely to be as a meeting-room. It was furnished with a light-coloured rectangular wooden table big enough for ten matching chairs around it, a desk and chair against a side wall, an occasional table similar to that in the entrance-hall with another big vase of flowers, and three framed posters on the walls. Two simply read, 'Keep Calm and Carry On," and "Don't let the Bastards Grind You Down." The third showed two smiling men and a woman harvesting coffee beans along a path leading from a lush, green mountainside into a giant coffee cup under the slogan, "Colombia is Magical Realism."

The rear of the room consisted entirely of sliding glass doors giving on to a broad area of wooden decking outside. On the decking stood a picnic table and chairs. The raised area led to a flight of broad wooden stairs down into a garden big enough to build a fair-sized council estate in. On the left was the obligatory swimming pool which, if not quite Olympic size, was certainly big enough for some serious exercise; on the right an area of lawn edged by colourful perennials, with a summer-house half-way along the hedge behind the flower-beds. Of Tennyson, there was no sign.

"Please, follow me, Mr Tennyson waiting you," said the woman, indicating that they should descend into the garden.

He followed her across the lawn past the summer-house, which showed no sign of occupation, to a concealed gate in the hedge beyond, which she swung open into a vegetable garden on an ambitious scale. The only person in sight was a gardener wearing a worn-looking beige polo shirt, similarly ancient brown corduroy trousers shoved inside grey wellington boots, and a Panama hat. He had his back towards them and was busy with a garden fork.

"Where's Mr Tennyson?" Warren asked the Asian woman.

The gardener straightened up and turned around.

"Good morning, Inspector," he said in a hybrid accent combining Yorkshire and cut-glass posh. Warren knew from his file which famous northern public school had given Tennyson his superficial polish. Glancing at his gold wristwatch, which should have been a giveaway if Warren had been sharp enough to spot it, Tennyson added: "Bang on time. I like a man who's punctual. Just lifting some of my early spuds. There's nothing like eating produce you've grown yourself; and new potatoes lifted straight from the soil possess a superior flavour. Mai, we'll take elevenses in the summer-house. Home-made fruit-cake and elderflower cordial do you, Inspector?"

"That would be lovely," said Warren.

Tennyson led the way back to the summer-house. It was big enough to have its own verandah with a wicker table and two chairs, which is where Tennyson invited Warren to sit. The cocaine firm boss took off his hat to reveal the shaven head that he had been protecting from sunburn, the revelation making his appearance suddenly less benign. Warren knew his age to be 59, but he was fit enough to look ten years younger.

"Nice garden," said Warren.

"Nothing too ostentatious. A lawn for the kids to play on, my wife enjoys taking care of the flower-beds, and as you can see I get a kick out of growing my own veg."

Warren realised it was ridiculous, but he had a stereotypical notion of what a London gangster should be like: expensive, showy clothes, a tough-guy London accent, and the dead-behind-the-eyes look of a seasoned killer. Tennyson only lived up to the third.

"I don't have much contact with the police, apart from when we've had the crime prevention lads round to advise on security for the house," said Tennyson.

"Did they suggest the metal detector gate?"

Tennyson laughed, and there was no harsh edge to it. The man had decided to be charming.

"No, that was my idea. Came to me at an airport, not surprisingly. Bogota, I think it was."

That was a cheeky touch; casually throwing into the

conversation that he was in the habit of visiting the capital of the world's biggest cocaine-exporting country. He was telling Warren that he was untouchable. Well, whatever games he wanted to play, that was fine. All Warren cared about right now was finding out who murdered Roger Nutley.

The maid arrived with a tray bearing slices of fresh-looking fruit-cake and the clear, bubbly cordial, and silently and skilfully set them out on the table. The drink was in a large, crystal jug, from which she poured into crystal tumblers.

"Will there be anything else, sir?"

"No, thanks, Mai, that's all for now."

"Yes, sir." She headed back towards the house.

"Vietnamese," explained Tennyson. "Been with us, what, fourteen years now. Top-notch. A proud, hard-working people. Ever been to Vietnam?"

"Unfortunately not."

"Do the trip. You'll love it. It's the most capitalist country in the world despite having a communist government."

"I might, if I can ever get enough leave."

"You policemen, always with your noses to the grindstone." Tennyson took a sip of cordial and Warren followed suit. "Help yourself to cake, there's plenty of it."

Warren didn't need asking twice where fruit-cake was concerned, though the whole encounter felt surreal.

"Now," said Tennyson, "how do you think I can help you find the son of a bitch who topped Roger Nutley?"

"I understand you knew him quite well."

"Who told you that?"

"It came up in the course of our investigations."

"Somebody in that play, I suppose. It's no secret, anyway. Roger came to a few of my parties, sometimes he brought a few other celebs with him. People like to meet faces off the telly."

"Is there anybody in your circle of acquaintances, Mr Tennyson, who might have had a motive for killing Roger Nutley?"

"Not so far as I know; and that's God's honest truth. Don't think I haven't thought about it. Roger was a really good bloke. If I thought I knew somebody who killed him, I'd be down on them like a ton of bricks; which, believe me, would not be a pleasant experience for them. But I'm at a loss to know who it could have been. As are the police, apparently, since you're desperate enough to come calling on the likes of Ralph Tennyson for favours."

"Mr Tennyson..."

"Call me Ralph. And come to the point. You want to know whether I supplied Roger Nutley with cocaine. Well, the answer's no comment."

"But he did have a cocaine habit?"

"We all have our weaknesses. But why would you think that has anything to do with his murder?"

"Perhaps he owed somebody a lot of money."

"Look. I know you're not wired so anything we say's off the record, right? We both want this killer found and arrested, and at this precise moment we are not discussing matters pertaining to the trade. So if I'm straight with you it's just what the newspapers call deep background. Now is that acceptable to you?"

"Perfectly. I'm not the drugs squad."

"Roger Nutley fell on hard times after that iniquitous witch-hunt of a trial. What with the stress of it, he needed to escape a bit from the stresses and strains of his life a bit more often than he used to; but he wasn't pulling down big bucks any more as a star, so he couldn't afford to pay for it. I indulged him for a couple of years, as a friend. This play he was in was supposed to relaunch his career, and when he got back on the telly he was going to be able to clear his debt. But it was no big deal."

"How much did he owe you?"

"A little under forty grand."

"I'd say forty grand's a pretty strong motive."

"It's peanuts. In any case, I'm not going to get it now he's dead, am I? I can hardly go round to his solicitor and say by the way your client's estate owes me for copious quantities of the Devil's Dandruff, can I? Inspector, I mourn Roger Nutley as a good friend; but I'm also mourning the loss of that money, which I'm absolutely sure he'd have paid off when his fortunes were restored. But the money doesn't matter at all compared with the loss of a friend."

"What about setting an example for others?"

"I'm not a murderer, Inspector, nor do I pay other people to commit murder on my behalf. Things have got a lot more sophisticated than they used to be in the bad old days. We have modern methods of credit control, and they do not involve the use of violence. And like I just said, Roger was a friend. As a matter of fact you could probably have called him my best pal. We go back a long way. So, far from having him topped, if Roger was ever in trouble, I'd have done anything to get him out of it."

Oh, you would, would you, thought Warren, as a new idea popped into his mind about what role Big Ralph might have played in the trial; but he kept a poker face and changed the subject.

"You're quite right in saying the police have got no real leads. To be frank, it seems virtually impossible that anybody could have committed the crime at the time and place they did; and yet somebody got on and off that stage without being seen by anybody backstage or by an audience of six hundred people."

"When you have eliminated the impossible, whatever remains, however improbable, must be the truth."

"Sherlock Holmes in The Sign of Four. Very apposite. Except that, at the moment, nothing remains."

"Somebody who had a right to be backstage did it. That's what remains."

"We've eliminated them all. Anybody who could have got into the right position at that time was with somebody else at the time; and it's inconceivable that two of the actors covered for each other. There are no motives. Apart from anything else, Roger Nutley was the big name that was putting bums on seats and keeping them all in employment on a nice, long tour."

"If you really want my opinion," said Ralph Tennyson de Clare, "it was one of those women. Don't ask me how, but they really had their knives out for him at the trial. I followed every word of it. I don't believe for one moment that he was guilty of any of the things they accused him of; and yet the malice was incredible, and you've got to assume it's even moreso since he got off."

"They had no access. They have no connections with any of the cast or the backstage crew."

"So you're not going to question them?"

"Yes, as a matter of fact we are doing. It's routine; but I can't honestly see it leading anywhere."

"So you've come to me in the hope that I'd confess to putting out a contract on him, is that it?"

"I'm not that stupid."

"I know you're not, otherwise I wouldn't be talking to you like this. And by the way, in this fantasy world where the bad guys send hit-men to eliminate people who owe them money, can you imagine that they'd stage a show like having them killed on the stage of a packed theatre? Damn silly idea."

"Have you any other ideas at all, Mr Tennyson?"

"If I had, I'd have told you at the start; but I can suggest somebody else you might like to have one of these private little chats with, if you've got the stomach for it."

"Really?"

"Have you heard of Tony Cudmore?"

"Who hasn't?"

Tony Cudmore was the biggest pimp in London. He had escort girls from all over the world displayed on the internet and massage parlours scattered all over London. He had never been convicted for so much as having an overdue library book. "He might know whether somebody had it in for Roger, he might not," said Tennyson. "I know Roger enjoyed spending time with some of Tony's girls. He didn't mind paying for it, and Tony guaranteed him discretion. Maybe he might have let something slip. I'm not saying I know he did, because I don't. It's a bit of a long-shot."

"I don't exactly have any odds-on favourites at the moment, so I might as well try a long-shot; but what makes you think he'll talk to me?"

"Because he's a pal of mine. I'll give him a bell right now and tell him to expect you."

As soon as he got back to the station, Warren googled

Tony Cudmore's website and read the introduction on its home page: 'Welcome to Hot London Escorts, a discreet agency featuring fun, flirty and fabulously beautiful female companions. We provide the finest erotic massage service by the most beautiful female escorts in London. Our adult dating service features companions of Oriental, Asian, Latin, East European and Mediterranean origin. We also offer complete VIP services to fulfil any fantasy you may have. Our girls are bursting with excitement and can't wait to meet you. Your every desire is just a phone call away.'

Ignoring the phone number on the website, Warren picked up the phone on his desk and dialled the number Tennyson had given him. It only rang twice before being answered.

"Hello, who's that? I don't recognise your number."

"DI Warren, Mr Cudmore. I believe you've been told I'd be calling."

"Oh, yeah, Big Ralph mentioned it. What can I do for you, Inspector?" The voice was gravelly east London, like somebody who's been smoking forty untipped full-strength cigarettes for the past three centuries or so.

"Not on the phone. Could we meet somewhere?"

"Sure. Hold on a minute."

Silence while Cudmore presumably looked in a diary.

"I could do half-past-ten tonight. D'you know Cloisters in Mile End?"

"The night club?"

"That okay?"

"Fine," said Warren, thinking the time and place were both a pain in the arse but he needed the info. "How will I find you?"

"Just ask a doorman. You'll be expected. No blue lights and sirens, if you don't mind."

"I'll be as discreet as a vicar at a village fete."

"Magic. Leave your dog-collar at home, though. See you there."

The nurse suggested that DC Marion Everitt and Matt should go into the day-room to wait.

"I'll be fine," Faith said to Matt. He leaned forward and kissed her tenderly on the forehead.

The day room was a plain, bright, but institutional space, with a television set on a stand in one corner, switched off, a couple of tables at the far end with leaflets and magazines on them, a drinking water tap, two coffee tables and a variety of chairs. Luckily nobody else was in there, and Marion and Matt sat facing each other.

"So what's the problem with Faith's parents?" Marion asked.

"They belong to a fundamentalist Christian sect. It comes from America," explained Matt. "She's not supposed to have anything to do with boys until her parents choose one for her."

"I thought it was only Muslims did that," said Marion.

"You must be joking. This is much worse. At least they usually give their kids a few to choose from. With this sect it's, like, wham, here's this boy you've never seen before and you're marrying him next week."

"They can't force her," said Marion. "We have laws against that in this country."

"They don't usually need to," said Matt. "They indoctrinate girls from when they're really little. Most of them don't know anything else other than to do as they're told."

"Faith doesn't appear to be very well indoctrinated," said Marion.

"She's managing to get out, but only gradually. Her father's not quite as strict as her mother any more, even though he pretends to be when they're all together. It was him who made her mother let her start going to school when she was thirteen."

"All kids have to go to school."

"Oh, no they don't. That's what most people think; but there's this thing called home education."

"I've heard of it but I don't know anything about it."

"People are allowed to teach their children at home so long as they tell the local council. So this Christian fundamentalist lot use that as a way to keep their kids away from anybody else."

"You got all this from Faith, did you?"

"Of course. My family aren't religious."

"Surely you could tell somebody if she's unhappy about it?"

"Faith doesn't want me to. She says she'd be risking chastisement. No way."

"Chastisement? You mean beating?"

"That sort of thing. And locked in your room. One meal a day."

"That's child abuse. They'd be committing a crime."

"If you could prove it, and if any of the kids would give evidence against their parents, which from what I've heard they won't. It's all supposedly in the Bible; but that's just the twisted way they read it."

"I still think she could have told somebody."

"Look, she's doing it her way, right? She's seventeen, she can leave home if she wants, only she doesn't want to yet."

"Why not? I'd have been out of there on my sixteenth birthday."

"But then you wouldn't have been who you are, would you, so you don't know what you'd have done."

There was a wise head on those shoulders beyond the lad's years, Marion was beginning to realise.

"They give her a nice house to live in and feed her and all that, plus she's not used to going out anywhere except school and church. Meeting up with me took real determination, I can tell you. She doesn't want to make a break from her family until she's good and ready."

"And when will that be?"

"When she's passed her A-levels she's going to uni, whatever they say. She'll get a student loan, they won't be able to stop her."

"And where do you fit in then?"

"Who knows? They usually forget about the bloke back home, don't they?"

The nurse came in and told them they could go and see Faith.

"That was quick," said Marion.

"She was lucky. It's not too deep."

"Will she be okay?" asked Matt.

"She's fine. There's no infection."

"Thank God," said Matt, closing his eyes.

Faith was walking again, fully dressed.

"Are you sure you don't need a wheelchair?" asked Matt.

"She's fine to walk, but slowly," said the nurse. "She'll have to take it gently for a few days while it heals up."

Faith's parents stormed in.

"What is my daughter doing here?" demanded Joshua Goodwin in a voice loud enough to bring down the walls of Norton General Hospital if not Jericho.

Marion intervened between him and Faith. "Mr Goodwin?"

"Yes, and who are you?"

Marion showed him her warrant card. "Detective Constable Everitt, Metropolitan Police. Now, I will thank you to keep your voice down, sir, this is a hospital."

"And this is the boy who attacked her, I suppose."

"No, sir, this is the young man who defended her."

"I see." He turned to Matt. "You just happened to be passing by, did you?"

"Aren't you going to ask me how I am?" Faith asked her father.

"Who is this boy?" demanded Ruth Goodwin.

"For God's sake, they've stolen Toby, tried to beat up Matt and stabbed me. I could have been killed."

""Thou shalt not take the name of the Lord thy God in vain, for the Lord will not hold him guiltless that taketh his name in vain," droned Ruth.

"Yes, thank you, Mrs Goodwin," said Marion, "I'm sure we're all familiar with the Ten Commandments."

"You said Matt," said Joshua Goodwin. "How do you know this boy's name?"

In pain, and under the stress of her parent's reaction,

or rather lack of it, to her injury, Faith snapped.

"Because he's my boyfriend."

Joshua Goodwin made a fist to take a swing at Matt. Marion easily grabbed his arm and restrained him. In violent situations, she knew all the ways to retain the upper hand without over-reacting.

"I wouldn't advise that, if I were you, sir," she said.

"I think you'd better go and wait outside," said the nurse to Faith's parents.

"What do you mean, boyfriend?" demanded Ruth Goodwin.

"You filthy little harlot," hissed Mr Goodwin.

Matt squared up to him. "You mind your mouth," he threatened.

"Of course we're going," said Ruth Goodwin. "And we're taking our daughter with us."

"No, you're not," said Faith. "I'm going to the police station to see if I can recognise any of the men from photographs."

"You'll do as I tell you," shouted her father.

"Right, that's it, out, now," commanded the nurse.

"Not without our daughter. We're her parents."

"Then start acting like it," said the nurse.

"Actually," said Marion, "it's up to Faith to decide. She's over sixteen. Faith?"

"I'm coming with you."

"Fine." Marion turned to the parents. "You can follow us down to the station if you wish or I can have Faith sent home in a police car when she's finished trying to identify the attackers."

Joshua Goodwin looked at his wife. She shook her head.

"I'll take my wife home, then I'll come to the police station for my daughter." He glared at Faith. "You are in very, very serious trouble, young lady. I'll deal with you when you get home."

"What exactly do you mean by that?" demanded Marion.

"Do not withhold discipline from a child; if you punish

172

them with the rod, they will not die," intoned Ruth Goodwin.

"Jesus, you're both mad," said Matt.

"I must warn you," said Marion, "there are very severe penalties for assault and child abuse."

Mr and Mrs Goodwin turned and stalked out, and it struck Marion that not once during their intrusion had they referred to their daughter by her name.

Matt put his arm gently around Faith's shoulders to comfort her. "You okay?" he asked.

"Come on," she said, "Let's go and do what has to be done." Then she burst into tears, and added, "They've got Toby. Poor Toby, I hope they haven't hurt him."

It was only during the ride to the police station that Faith remembered that, if only she had thought fast enough and called out the words "bad man" to the well-trained Doberman before the big men had got him into the cage, the outcome might have been very different; but it had all happened too quickly.

4

A flashing red neon sign announced Cloisters. Warren drove past, parked a little further along Mile End Road, and walked back. A squad of black-suited, black-shirted, black-tied doormen guarded the entrance. One stepped forward to bar Warren's way.

"Sorry sir, it's a private club."

"I'm here to see Tony Cudmore."

"Really? And you are?"

"Don't make me flash my warrant card, it'll only frighten the punters off."

A short, wide-shouldered white man in his mid-thirties emerged from the club. He was wearing a pale grey silk suit, a black shirt, and a cream silk kipper tie with large pink polkadots. His fit body was more than offset by his incredibly unprepossessing face, with a misshapen nose that had obviously been broken more than once, and his appalling taste in retro clothes that didn't quite seem to belong in the fifties, sixties or seventies, but certainly had no place in 2014. His head was shaven in the *de rigeur* fashion of early 21st century thugs.

"You Warren?" he rasped.

"Got it in one."

"Follow me."

A bouncer opened the front door to let Warren and the man who was apparently Cudmore's minder through. Their ears were immediately assailed by thunderous, pounding noise, or music, depending on your taste. It wasn't to Warren's, so to him it was noise. A second set of double doors obviously led straight ahead into the main club area, but they turned immediately right though a smaller door and up a flight of stairs to another door. This one was heavy and padded with soundproofing materials, and opened into a modern office-cum-lounge. It was sparse but reeked of tasteless new money: white leather armchairs, a huge glass-topped coffee table, and a bar topped with rippled white marble. 'All in the best possible taste,' as the TV comedian Kenny Everett would have said. If Ralph Tennyson de Clare had seemed like the antithesis of the popular stereotype of a gangster, Tony Cudmore made up for him. In his late fifties, he was short and stocky with a paunch that belied the image of fitness he would like to exude. He had reddish hair in a menacing crew-cut, and his arms were unnaturally muscular and covered in swirling tattoos. He was wearing a cream silk shirt open at the chest, pale blue cotton trousers, and cream soft leather shoes. He was smiling, but it was the smile of a jungle predator. He was seated in one of the armchairs, with an incongruously proletarian glass of light ale in front of him on a corner of the coffee table, beside an open packet of Marlboro and a large, square, pink glass ash-tray. As the door swung shut, the noise from the club was reduced to a distant, unobtrusive, throbbing buzz.

"Thank you, Cy," said Cudmore in a grating, throaty rattle. "Get Inspector Warren a drink before you go. What'll it be, Inspector?"

This was neither the time nor the place for formalities about being on duty.

"I'll have what you're having, thanks."

Cy went behind the bar and poured the drink.

"Take a seat, Inspector, It's a pleasure to meet you."

"Thank you," said Warren, sinking into white leather opulence and not believing a word of it.

Cy placed the glass in front of Warren and left the room.

"You own this place?" asked Warren.

"I have an interest."

"Did Roger Nutley ever come here?"

Cudmore laughed, a revolting noise which rapidly dissolved into a coughing fit.

"You're having a laugh, ain't you? This place is for kids. I just happened to be spending the evening here for a business meeting."

"You knew him well, though?"

"I knew him. Not as well as Ralph, but I knew him. Nice guy."

"And he was one of your punters."

"A client. If there's any way I can help you find out who killed him, I will. But some of this is going to have to be strictly...

"...off the record," finished Warren. "That goes without saying."

"Just so long as that's understood. How can I be sure you're not wired?"

"Well, Ralph Tennyson had me walk through a metal detector gate."

"Oh, yeah, you gotta laugh, ain't you?" Another repulsive descent into smoker's cough. Cudmore sounded as if he was only a couple of hours away from the lung cancer ward.

"You could have me strip-searched, I suppose."

"Piss off, you wouldn't come here wired asking favours. Fire away with the questions then we can have another drink."

"How long had Roger Nutley been using prostitutes?"

"Horrible word. Anyway, as I understand it, most of his adult life," replied Tony Cudmore. "At least, ever since he started pulling down the big money from being on the telly. Obviously I was still a kid then, but I have it on pretty good authority."

"So as soon as he started playing Geoff Harkness in The Filth?"

"Seems like it. That's when he would have started being able to afford it."

"But he would only have been, what, in his late twenties then, and he was a good-looking lad. As I remember it he was considered the heart-throb of the programme. It's one of the things that kept the ratings up."

"You don't have to be old to pay for sex, Inspector. We even get the odd teenager."

"But why would a man like Nutley have had to pay? The girls must have been queuing up for him."

"You said this is off-the-record, right?"

"I'm just trying to get an idea of the man in the hope of gaining some insight into what might have motivated somebody to murder him; and the most obvious road to go down, although it's not the only one, is whether it had something to do with his relationships with women, which it's becoming increasingly clear were, well, let's say unconventional."

"What you really need to know is whether the women at his trial were telling the truth or lying, isn't that right?"

"Exactly."

"Well, I can't tell you that. But I can tell you that he told quite a few of my girls that he never hurt any of those women; but he thought they rejected him unfairly when he asked them."

"And I suppose it depends on what you mean by asking."

"Yep. In the sixties or seventies that might have involved some preliminary touching, and it was what you did. Nowadays if a man touches a woman on the arm and asks her if she wants to go for a drink he's in danger of being accused of sexual harassment."

"But that wouldn't have been so much of a problem then. Besides, I'd be amazed if there weren't women and girls practically throwing themselves at him."

"Inspector, would it surprise you to learn that I've actually talked this over with him in private?"

"Of course it would."

"Well, I have, and on more than one occasion. He was a good friend of Big Ralph, as you know, and so am I. We've met at a few parties at Ralph's over the years. Not what you're thinking, orgies or something, just civilised get-togethers for dinner, drinks, a bit of swimming in the summer, a game of cards. A couple of times he wanted to talk to me privately. It's not exactly a subject he'd have wanted to discuss with other people."

"So can you tell me why a man like Roger Nutley would pay for sex when he could have had it on a plate?"

"Because it's not like a girlfriend or a wife. You get to choose like from a catalogue. Look, men pay for women because they can have whatever and whoever they want. We're living in the age of instant coffee, instant food. This is instant sex. No strings attached, no bother about buying presents and flowers, it's a one-off financial commitment. You're more in control of everything, you choose all the factors. You don't have to please her, you're paying her to please you. You don't get affection from escort girls, it's just a transaction; but my girls are special, they're so good at their job the punters feel as if some sort of emotional connection's really happening."

"So it's all down to selfishness in the end?"

"Not as simple as that. A lot of men pay for escorts so they can do things real women wouldn't put up with."

Warren noted with distaste the expression 'real women' with its implication that women who sell sex are almost less than human. He promised himself he wasn't going to develop any sort of empathy with this glorified pimp, even if he needed to pretend to in order to get the information he needed.

He pressed the point: "So what do you think drove Nutley to it?"

"I don't think, I know; but how come you're so interested in his shagging preferences?"

"In the first place, to see if there's anything he did to any woman he was involved with more recently that could have motivated her or somebody connected with her to murder him."

"Well for a start I wouldn't use the word 'involved' where poor old Roger was concerned. I honestly don't think he was capable of getting involved with a woman emotionally, otherwise he would have had no trouble finding one to marry, which as you know he never did. You said, 'in the first place.' So what's in the second place?"

"Because it affects our main line of enquiry."

"Which is?"

"The three women who put him on trial for sexual abuse and rape."

"But he got off. He was found not guilty on all counts. He never did it. You gotta have faith in the British jury system, ain't you?"

Try as he might, Warren couldn't penetrate Cudmore's expression to see whether his tongue was firmly stuck in his cheek.

"Not exactly. The jury couldn't reach a verdict and the CPS decided not to go for a retrial. The women still say he was lying in court, and he did it, and he maintained to the last he was innocent. It was his word against theirs, and enough of the jury chose to believe that three people were lying and one was telling the truth."

"Reasonable doubt?"

"Which is not the same as being a hundred percent certain he was innocent; and that could have given one of these women, especially the one who said he raped her, a motive for murder. "

"I see where you're coming from, Inspector; but I'll tell you this. Like I said, Roger was incapable of striking up an emotional relationship with a woman. But that doesn't mean he didn't want to. He did. Desperately. So what did he do? With all the money he had at his disposal, he pretended that he could; by paying my ladies for what we call in the trade a girlfriend experience. Which is exactly what it says on the tin. For most of the punters there's never any thought of having any kind of relationship with the girl as a person; she's just available and at their disposal and there's no real motivation to try to go any deeper."

"But it wasn't that way with Nutley?"

"Let me just say I wouldn't be talking about him like this if some bastard hadn't done him in. Roger was capable of totally switching off his sense of reality when he was with an escort girl; and switching it back on again immediately afterwards. I mean, a lot of punters like to think the girl's enjoying it too, or even likes them, but I can tell you for a fact, that's a load of old bollocks. One hundred percent pretend. If you want a brilliant actress, hire an escort. The point being, if a punter pays for the girlfriend experience, where the girl does a role-play that they're actually in a relationship, it's just an act. But Roger really believed it. It gave the poor sod the illusion of a real emotional connection that he couldn't achieve with normal women."

The nasty implication behind the words 'normal women'; slightly better than 'real women', Warren supposed; by now feeling extremely glad he hadn't sent Philippa out on this one.

"Where did he see them? I mean, the newspapers never got hold of it. They'd have had a field day."

"Mostly at the flats where they work. My girls don't work in crappy little doss-houses, they're luxury apartments in good areas."

"But still, if he wanted this fantasy of a relationship, wouldn't he have had to book them for a date, you know, going out to dinner, maybe away for a weekend?"

"He was too famous. The tabloids would have been on to that in a flash."

"All right. With all your knowledge and practice, what's your opinion of the Nutley trial? Friendship aside, did he do it to those women, or not?"

"Again, I don't need to venture an opinion, because he told me often enough. Up to you whether you believe me, or more to the point whether you believe I ought to have believed him."

"And?"

"Number One, and lots of people have been saying this, in the sixties and seventies the rules of the game were different. If a young guy fancied a woman at work, he could ask her for a drink, and if she didn't fancy him, she could just say no. End of story. Plus there was always horseplay, doesn't matter whether you worked in a television studio or a supermarket, and so long as it didn't go too far, nobody minded, women had put-downs up their sleeves and knew how to use them. You know, 'The only thing you use it for is stirring your tea,' that sort of thing. Then along came the eighties and nineties and if you told a colleague she was wearing a nice dress you could find yourself up in front of a tribunal for sexual harassment; which is why we've got people like Nutley being accused of crimes today for things that were just a bit of harmless fun fifty years ago."

"What would you call horseplay? Would you call rape a bit of harmless fun?"

"I'd call rape a hanging offence if you must know."

Warren didn't feel like even trying to resolve the contradiction between that statement and how Cudmore earned his millions.

"As for horseplay," Cudmore went on, "look, if a guy puts his hand on a colleague's shoulder or waist and tells her he finds her attractive, that's called flirtation. If he comes up behind her and puts his arms round her and his hands on her tits, that's called a bloody liberty and he deserves a smack, which is exactly what he would have got back then, end of story."

"Nutley?"

"He was gauche; didn't know how to flirt. He admitted it himself, but only to me. You wouldn't believe it, if you saw him on screen in The Filth, he came over as Mr Charming, but only because he had a script. So in his real life he made some clumsy mistakes; but rape, no way."

"Which if what you're telling me is right, leaves me with three women who might have been bitter and resentful enough to take him to court, but hardly with a motive for murdering him after he got off."

"I'd say that's right. They'll have had lawyers telling them they could get their own back, and tabloid journos offering nice fat cheques for their stories. Only it didn't work out because juries aren't that stupid."

Or, thought Warren, his mind flitting briefly back to

something Ralph Tennyson de Clare had said, because a few jurors have been leaned on by heavies and paid off in cash.

"That's how it sounds, but it leaves me up a gum-tree. If it wasn't one of them, who was it?"

"Search me. Not one of my ladies. He was the goose that laid the golden eggs."

"Did he have a favourite?"

"Well, down the years, various, you know, they move on after they're about thirty or so, but the last few years, yeah, Jasmine."

"Is she one of the exotic ones?"

"Not unless you call Dagenham exotic. It's in the east, innit?"

"Can I talk to her?"

"I don't want her upset."

"I'll be nice. But there might be something."

"All right. I'm doing this for my old mate Roger, mind. I'll give you a bell. Got a mobile number?"

Warren handed him a business card, and Cudmore phoned down to Cy, who appeared in twenty seconds.

On the steps outside, Cy said, "I'll walk you to your car, sir."

"No need."

"Mr Cudmore's orders. More than my job's worth not to. This is a well dodgy area at night."

"So be it."

Driving homewards though the lights of the London night, he thought about the bizarre lifestyle of a man like Nutley, and counted his blessings. He switched on Classic FM and allowed the gentle voices singing Gabriel Faure's Cantique de Jean Racine to massage away some of his tension. Was Nutley's lifelong sexual behaviour really the key to his murder, or was this entire line of inquiry a dead end?

WEDNESDAY 18 JUNE

1

In a cafeteria at the University of Hertfordshire on the southern outskirts of Hatfield, Nick Boyd reached into his jacket's right-hand side pocket and showed a small object to DC Marion Everitt and PC Robin Merryweather, who was temporarily working in plain clothes comprising jeans, trainers and a plain white t-shirt. It was a black plastic device about five inches in diameter with the word 'Halo' in yellow and orange sunburst printed on the lower side and a small digital display window above that. It looked a bit like a tiny steering wheel.

"What's that?" asked Marion.

"Microchip scanner. Anybody with any sense who keeps a pet gets a chip embedded under the loose skin on the back of its neck. Incontrovertible ID. Every pet has a unique fifteen-digit number."

"Still their word against ours that it belongs to them or not," said Merryweather.

"If you lose your pet you call the microchip company and tell them; but this isn't just any scanner. If the microchip belongs to a dog that's been reported missing, it flags that up on this little screen. Every time I plug it into my computer, the database in here gets updated. So if this dog's the one we're looking for, we'll know straight away."

"If this dog's the one we're looking for, they're hardly going to let us scan it," said Marion.

"Which would in itself be practically an admission of guilt," said Nick.

"Not enough for an arrest," said Merryweather.

"So at that point you admit that you're the fuzz and insist," said Nick.

"The fuzz?" exclaimed Marion, smiling. "I think you've been watching too many 1930s movies."

Hello, thought Robin, not failing to pick up on the note of familiarity, but instead of commenting he said, "Obviously that's when it could get nasty."

"We'll play it by ear," said Marion.

"Before we get to that stage," said Merryweather, "we'll be finding out everything we can about the sellers, noting any vehicle registration numbers and makes and types of vehicles, and if we can possibly take any photographs, we will."

"If they make a run for it, try to get the dog," said Nick. "Then we can scan it and get proof."

"As I said, we'll play it by ear," said Marion.

*

Marion pulled off the A1(M) at Junction 10 down the slip road and around the roundabout on to the rump of the A507 leading to Baldock Motorway Services. She drove to the far end of the car park, then back along past the front of the buildings, while Merryweather discreetly looked out of the front passenger window.

"There they are," said Merryweather, without pointing. "Two men and the dog. A big man and a scrawny teenager."

"Sounds like two of the ones who attacked Faith Goodwin and Matthew Sym," said Marion.

"Could be."

"That means there could be a knife."

Marion drove back to the car park entrance then back along the way they had originally entered and parked in a bay on the back row. Then they walked to where the two men were standing outside the low front wall separating the outdoor terrace of Starbucks from the car park. Marion pinned on what she hoped was a convincingly sincere-looking smile as they approached the dog and the men.

"Steve, is it?" asked Marion, extending her arm for a handshake to the older man, who was wearing a black t-shirt with a Black Sabbath design on the front.

"That's me, and this is my son Dave."

Steve and Dave. Yeah, right, thought Merryweather.

"I'm Diana, and this is my husband, Jeremy."

"You all right, mate?" said the big man.

"And this must be Buster," said Merryweather.

The retriever gave no response to the name; a sign that Nick had warned them to expect if it was stolen, and which they ignored. It was standing, not sitting, and occasionally whimpering.

"Shall we go and sit in Starbucks?" Merryweather suggested.

"Yeah, all right," said the big man.

Marion led the way on to the Starbucks terrace and pulled out one of the dark blue chairs at a table for four. They all sat down and the dog finally settled down beside the big man.

"Shall I get coffees?" suggested Merryweather.

"Nah, don't worry, mate, can't stop for too long," said the big man.

Marion had learned the drill from Nick about how to check whether a dog is genuine: ask to see paperwork such as vet's bills, insurance, micro-chipping and a kennel club certificate; ask to see photographs of the dog with the family; ask the seller to agree to the sale subject to a vet's examination; ask the seller for a written bill of sale stating they are the owner. She knew that a thief would be full of excuses for not having paperwork or photographs.

However, the last thing she wanted to do in this case was make them nervous, in case they pulled out and walked off before she got the chance to run the scanner over the dog's neck. So she simply held out the back of her hand limply in front of the retriever's snout. He duly sat up, wagged his tail, sniffed the proffered hand then licked it, thereby giving her permission to tickle his ears and neck, which she did.

"He's a lovely boy," said Marion, "isn't he, Jeremy?"

"Seems very friendly," said Merryweather. "How old did you say he was?"

"Two," said the big man.

The teenager stood up. "I'm going for a fag," he said.

"No, you're not," said the big man, his tone of voice and facial expression momentarily betraying the thug beneath the salesman. "Sit down and wait here."

"Well, he seems lovely," said Marion. "Can we have him, Jeremy?"

"If you like him." Merryweather put on his bargaining expression. "Five hundred pounds, wasn't it?"

"Five ninety-nine, actually, mate."

Jeremy let his face drop slightly.

"Tell you what, though, don't wanna disappoint the little lady, do we?" He grinned at Marion, who smiled back. "I can do you five-fifty for a quick cash sale. Them bloody cats at my mum's are driving young Buster up the wall."

"That'll be fine," said Merryweather.

It was now or never.

"Can I just walk him up and down a bit before we pay? Just to make sure he likes me?" asked Marion.

"Course you can, darlin'. Don't go out of sight, though."

"Just down that way a bit," she said, indicating towards where the car park extended past a Day's Inn.

The big man handed Marion the lead. The dog stood up and trotted along beside her enthusiastically. They went past on the other side of the low wall. As Marion carried on walking, the big man stood up. "I think I'll go and keep her company," he said. Merryweather decided to follow him, and the teenager followed him.

Marion reached a grassy play area with a colourful climbing frame beyond the far end of the motel. She pulled the scanner out of her pocket, squatted beside the docile dog, and ran it over his neck.

The big man started running towards her and yelled, "Oy, what's going on?"

"Checking for a microchip, I think," said Merryweather. "Just in case there's any mistake."

Marion peered at the little window on the scanner. Nothing, dammit. The big man had now given up any pretence, and shouted, "Gimme that dog!"

Then, ping, a reading came up in the window: a long number followed by the words, "Reported stolen."

Marion stood up, replaced the scanner in her pocket, and called out to Merryweather: "It's stolen."

The big man had now almost reached Marion. She held up her warrant card towards him in her left hand while holding on to the dog's lead with her right, and snapped, "Police, stay where you are."

The big man ignored her and made a grab for the lead, which slipped out of her hand. The dog panicked and ran back the way they had come, across the front of the Day's Inn. The man took a swing at Marion with his right fist, missed, thought better of it, and ran for it across the car park. A stream of cars crossed behind him and in front of Marion, preventing her from giving chase.

The teenager was running after the big man, but Merryweather grabbed him from behind saying, "Police, you're under arrest."

The tall, skinny man picked up instantly on Robin's slightly camp voice. He spun around, whipped a flick-knife out from his jeans pocket, and thrust it towards the policeman, who was forced to let go and step back.

"I didn't know they let poofters in the police," he snarled, his face twisting into a contemptuous leer. He stabbed forwards with the knife. Robin stepped back skilfully out of range, refusing to be fazed by the homophobic jibe. He jinked ahead and sideways to grab the thug's knife arm. But the youth was even quicker and slashed the blade across the back of Robin's left hand, drawing a three-inch long line of blood. Instinctively Robin screamed from the shock. The teenager was away in a flash, legging it across the car park. Robin turned to pursue him, trying to ignore the pain from the gash across his hand. He tripped over the fleeing dog and fell spread-eagled on to the road, grazing the palms of both hands.

Marion gave up hope of catching the big man and detaining him on her own, and went to help Robin stand up.

"Sorry, I lost the kid," said Merryweather.

"Sorry, I lost the dog," said Marion. "Jesus, look at the state of you." PC Merryweather was holding his hands up in front of him, the left one bleeding from the knife wound across the back and from the grazes on the palm, the right also bleeding from the palm. "We'll get you cleaned up with the first aid box and then I'd better get you to the nearest A&E."

"I'll be fine," said Merryweather. "I just wish I hadn't screwed up."

"You didn't," said Marion.

She was looking across to the far corner of the car park, where a blue transit van was burning rubber as it hurtled on to the loop around the Shell station and towards the exit.

"Bloody criminals watch too much Top Gear," she said. "I'll call in the local cavalry, but we don't have the number and there's three fast ways out of here, north, south and west."

She made the call as they were walking back across the car park, and they both spotted Nick Boyd, crouching beside his own pale blue Volkswagen Golf estate, which had a dog grill separating the rear compartment from the seats, petting the Golden Retriever.

Marion walked over to him: "In the first place, what the hell are you doing here? And in the second place, how on Earth did you manage that?"

"In the first place," Nick replied, "you don't seriously think I wanted to miss out on this, do you? You told me the time and place, so I made my own way here before you arrived; and in the second place: easy, I just called the little fellow by his real name. He's the one we thought he was."

"Well done, that man," said Robin.

"What do you want to do with him?" asked Nick. "And what happened to your hand?"

"The teenage loony had a knife," said Robin.

"Look, Nick, we need to get the dog back to the station," said Marion, "plus you'll need to come and make a witness statement, but more urgently, I need to get Constable Merryweather to an A&E, and I'm wondering where the nearest one is."

"Lister Hospital, Stevenage," said Nick.

"I'm taking Robin there as the number one priority," said Marion. "Would you mind taking Fido to Norton Hill Police Station and we'll meet you there as soon as we can?"

"His name's Archie," said Nick.

The dog gave a bark of pleasure at hearing his real name, and Nick tickled his ear.

"Turn off at Junction 8 and the hospital's signposted," said Nick.

Marion stuck her blue light on the roof, started her siren wailing, and accelerated off the roundabout up the slip-road to the southbound carriageway of the A1(M).

"Get yourself a dressing out of the first aid kit and press it on the wound," she told Robin.

Robin managed a mischievous grin at Marion and said, "Nick, eh?" Marion tried unsuccessfully not to blush. Before they even passed the Letchworth exit at Junction 9 she was doing the ton down the fast lane. In under four minutes she peeled off down the slope at Junction 8 for Stevenage, squealed the tyres into the A&E approach road, and accompanied Robin to the reception desk.

2

Back on the Hot London Escorts website, Warren looked up Jasmine. There was a small image of her, wearing a black lacy bra and with a hand on her hip, on the top line of a page showing a gallery of women to choose from. The caption described her as 'Your Supermodel Girl Next Door'. Well, the last bit fitted in with what Cudmore had said Nutley looked for. Warren clicked on the picture, opening a page entirely about Jasmine, with half-a-dozen more photos of her in alluring poses in various stages of undress. The description wasn't exactly understated, either.

'Extraordinarily sexy and elegant, Jasmine is an absolutely gorgeous English escort. She really has the wow! factor. With her warm and affectionate nature, Jasmine is a young lady to enchant and delight you in every way. She can provide a genuine girlfriend experience so that you feel totally relaxed and at ease. Take her out to dine, and be the envy of every man in the restaurant; or maybe you would prefer to keep her charms all to yourself and spend a cosy night in.' Jasmine wasn't cheap: one hour £500, two hours £850, three hours £1,100, overnight £3,000. That would put a strain on the financial resources of any actor except a top TV star, thought Warren; and Nutley hadn't been pulling down the big money for at least two years; plus he had a cocaine habit. It was beginning to look as if he might have been heavily in debt to other unsavoury people as well as Tennyson.

Cudmore had phoned him and given him an address for Jasmine and a time to be there, eleven in the morning, pointing out that she was potentially giving up income by keeping half-an-hour clear for him so he'd need to be on time. The address was in Bloomsbury, a mews flat. That would be handy for businessmen arriving and departing through King's Cross, St Pancras and Euston railway stations, thought Warren. He rang the bell, heard footsteps coming down a staircase inside, and a middle-aged woman opened the door to him.

"Come in dearie. You're the policeman, are you?" she said as he followed her up a brightly-lit staircase with fresh-looking white-painted walls and a newish beige carpet.

"DI Warren."

"Well, Inspector, Jasmine's expecting you, only she's just having her breakfast, I hope you don't mind, only she's got an appointment at twelve o'clock and she needs to get ready."

The woman pushed open a door at the top of the stairs and Warren followed her into a small but comfortable living-room. Jasmine was sitting up at a round, glass-topped table spooning Coco Pops into her mouth. She was not, at this moment, the sex-charged vision of irresistible temptation that had been depicted on the website. She was dressed in a loose-fitting, long-sleeved, dark-blue jumper, similarly comfortable-looking black trousers, and a pair of beige, fluffy carpet slippers that wouldn't have disgraced her granny.

"Jasmine?" asked Warren.

She put down the spoon, stood up and came over to shake hands.

"It's Liz, actually. Jasmine's just my working name."

The maid or whatever she was disappeared into the kitchen.

Jasmine-Liz had one of those telephone voices that cockney women cultivate because it sounds posher.

"Carry on with your breakfast, Liz, this isn't an official visit," said Warren.

"I know. Tony's put me in the picture." She sat down

and scooped another spoonful past her rosebud lips. "You want to know about poor old Rog. Well, if I can help you catch the bastard what killed him, I will; but I dunno how."

"This is a little embarrassing, but I need to establish how he, well..."

"How he behaved with women. I know. In case you think one of those ones in court did it. Tea or coffee?"

"If the tea's made, that would be very nice."

"Well, siddown then, we don't stand on ceremony. Cup or mug? Sugar?"

"Er, mug please. No sugar."

Liz turned in her chair and called out: "Carol, mug of tea for the Inspector, no shoog," and turning back to him, "I'm having toast and marmalade, d'you want some?"

"That's very kind, but I had breakfast in the canteen."

"In the canteen, eh," she said, looking him up and down. "No Mrs Inspector to get your breakfast for you before you go out, then?"

"She starts work early herself."

"Well, I've shown you mine, so d'you wanna show me yours?"

"I beg your pardon?"

"Your name. I can't keep calling you Inspector if it's unofficial, can I?"

Carol appeared with tea and toast, placed it on the table and disappeared back to the kitchen.

"It's Keith, actually."

"Well, Keith, ask away while I take in some fuel." She began eating the toast, and Warren explained the situation.

"Roger Nutley was accused of sexually abusing three young women under his supervision at a drama school in the sixties. In two cases the allegation was of repeated groping, but one of the women accused him of raping her. The jury at his trial couldn't make up their mind whether he was guilty or not, so he walked. Since he was murdered, my female Detective Sergeant on this case has interviewed two of the three women who accused him. The other one's abroad."

"What's all this got to do with him being killed?"

"If he really did attack these women — especially the

rape – well, that could constitute a motive for the victim to go out and take the law into her own hands after he got off scot-free."

"Or one of their husbands or friends."

"Exactly."

"So where do I come in?"

"Mr Cudmore tells me you got very close to Roger Nutley."

"Roger's been coming to see me for, what, eight years. I was only 20 the first time. And yes, he confided in me. But to be honest I don't think I ought to be telling all his bedroom secrets to the police."

"Miss .... Liz. This is entirely off the record. If there was anything about his behaviour, or anything he told you in confidence, that might help me decide whether to either eliminate the women in the trial as suspects, or continue to investigate them, I'd be grateful."

"Well, I shouldn't think any woman would kill a feller for trying to grope her, however famous he was. So basically you need to know whether he might have done the rape, is what it comes down to." She looked at a tiny, delicate, gold wristwatch. "D'you mind waiting here a few minutes?"

"Sure, that's okay."

She went out through a door which Warren assumed must lead to the bedroom. Carol came in and asked if he'd like more tea. He said no thanks and she shut herself back in the kitchen.

It was Liz who had gone out but it was Jasmine, a while later, who came back in. Jasmine, the sex goddess, her face made up, her expensively dyed blonde hair in place, wearing a low-cut, slinky black mini-dress and shiny, black leather shoes with incredibly high stiletto heels that showed off her tanned legs to perfection.

"This is the girl Roger came to see," said Jasmine, walking with cat-like sinuosity to a sofa where she sat down looking like temptation incarnate. "Now, in normal circumstances, if I was dressed like this and started chatting you up, say at an office party, what would you do?"

"I suppose I might come over and sit down and put an

arm around you to see if you minded."

"Exactly. But not Rog. He absolutely could not make the first move. Even with a girl he was paying five hundred quid a pop for. I'd have to touch him first. Don't ask me why, but Roger Nutley was scared witless of sexual rejection. Now I'm no psychologist, but I think I know a bit about men, and if you ask me, it would have been amazing for Roger to touch a woman without being invited; but if she touched him, even say a little stroke on the arm, he was likely to start going off the deep end."

"If you're saying he didn't seem like a rapist, I'm stuck for a motive and a suspect."

"I'm only saying I don't think he was capable of initiating things. A girl's entitled to change her mind and say no at any stage. If the feller won't stop, it's still rape, even if she did start it."

"But you don't think he'd be the one to start trying it on physically?"

"Look, Keith, let me put it to you this way. He might have been a slow starter, but once I lit the blue touch paper there was no stopping him, even if I'd wanted to. I had to pretend I didn't want him to, so that he could hold me down and push me around, and roll me over and force me."

"He was acting out rape?"

"Something like that. Then he'd apologise afterwards and I'd have to say it was all right."

"So now you're saying the jury might have got it wrong?"

"What I'm saying is this, and it's only my opinion. Never in a million years would he have tried it on with any of those women if they hadn't given him a bit of encouragement. But if one of them sent out the wrong kind of signals by touching him, then she might have had a problem stopping him before he'd had his wicked way."

"I see what you mean."

"I can only tell you what he was like with me, Inspector. Doesn't necessarily mean anything, but Tony asked me to tell you what I could, so that's it."

"All right. It does help. I'm very grateful to you."

"My pleasure, Keith." She gave him a smile that made him wish momentarily she wasn't a working girl; but that, of course, was part of her job.

On his way out, Warren spotted a very distinctive leather handbag lying on a small shelf near the door; featuring vertical stripes in burgundy and two shades of blue, and a silvery rope strap. He turned back into the room.

"Unusual bag," he said.

"It was a present," said Liz. "Can't say I like it. Not my style at all. I haven't used it. Probably never will. Take it for your wife if you want."

"I couldn't possibly."

"Oh, go on. It's going to a charity shop otherwise. I can't stand the bastard who left it here."

"Oh, really? And why would that be?"

"He's one of Tony's strong-arm boys. Piece of shit. Comes round here once a week for a freebie. Taking the piss. And he likes it rough, if you know what I mean."

"Has this creep got a name?"

"Cy. That's all I know him by."

Well, well. The minder who had seen Warren in and out of Cloisters night-club.

"Thanks," said Warren. "I will give it to my wife, if that's all right."

"She's a lucky woman," said Liz.

Warren looked down at the bag again.

"I wasn't talking about the bag," said Jasmine, smiling.

*

Yolanda's office wasn't too far away and Warren hoped she might be able to snatch a break and have a coffee with him. He texted her and they agreed to meet in the Cappadocia Cafe, which although too near the noisy King's Cross road junction, was mutually handy.

With both of them committed to demanding jobs, Warren working unpredictable hours at all times of the day and night, and Yolanda frequently abroad, some couples might have drifted apart. They had learned that one small way of holding on to the togetherness was to grab the odd twenty minutes for a chat wherever and whenever a brief opportunity became available.

As a senior analyst in a company called World Wide Monitor, Yolanda specialised in producing up-to-date political risk assessments for companies planning to set up operations in the Spanish-speaking countries of the western hemisphere. This involved four or five field trips every year, typically for ten days to a fortnight; but at the moment she was working in the firm's headquarters just off Gray's Inn Road. She had been able to step up to the more senior position she now held, necessitating the travel to anywhere from Mexico in the north to Chile and her own country in the south, since Oscar had become old enough to fend for himself at home.

"So what have you been up to this morning, *mi amor?*" Yolanda asked Warren over her cappuccino and his americano.

"Visiting an expensive prostitute."

Yolanda's expression flitted through horror to realisation: "So now you are working in the *brigada antivicio?*"

"No, I haven't joined the vice squad. I wanted information."

"And was she beautiful?"

"Very; and surprisingly intelligent."

Yolanda's eyes twinkled: "Did she give you what you wanted?"

Warren was not stupid: "Only you can do that, *mi alma.*"

"That is the correct answer. But seriously?"

"It was part of the investigation of the murder of Sir Roger Nutley. He was one of her clients."

"Dirty old man."

"Rich old man without a gorgeous Argentine wife. Be fair."

"De acuerdo. Fair enough. So did she, let me be more careful how I say it, tell you what you wanted?"

"I think so. It's complicated."

"If it is about sex, it is always complicated."

"She gave me something for you."

"Oh my God. I hope it is not a vibrator."

"You Latins have such filthy minds. No, it's this."
Warren produced from his lap an orange Sainsbury's plastic bag that had been sloshing around the back seat of his car and in which he had secreted the handbag. Yolanda unwrapped it.

"Puta madre!" she exclaimed.

"Never mind whether anyone's mother was a whore, do you like it?"

"Are you saying this woman gave you this, for nothing?"

"Sure. She didn't like the man who gave it to her. It's only a handbag. If you don't like it, or don't like the fact that it came from a *puta, pues no hay problema.*"

"Do you know what this is?"

Warren did a corny imitation of Lady Bracknell in The Importance of Being Earnest: "A handbag!"

"Not just any handbag, darling. My God, you need more women in your police. This is the latest Christian Louboutin."

"Is that a designer?"

"A big, big designer. And this is worth big, big money."

"How much?"

"I don't know exactly. You know I don't have expensive tastes. But I know a little bit about these things. Any woman does."

"How much, *mi vida?*"

"You will have to ask an expert; but I think, between five thousand and ten thousand pounds."

Warren held out his hand: "Give it back."

"You want to put it on eBay now?"

Warren opened up the bag and peered inside. The shop label was tiny and tasteful but unmistakeable: 'Bags of Fun'.

He showed it to Yolanda: "I'm really sorry, darling. This bag was stolen last Saturday in an armed robbery. Unfortunately I'll have to take it away as evidence."

"You're welcome. I don't want some old tart's cast-offs, anyway."

"She isn't so old."

Yolanda grinned across the table: "I wasn't talking about her."

But Warren was already thinking: "Gotcha, Cy."

3

Warren spent a couple of hours closeted in his office. His first job was to check out Cyrus Gordon on the national police computer system. It told him Gordon had form, but nothing as serious as armed robbery. A couple of muggings as a teenager, some thefts from filling station shops, and an ABH in a pub brawl. Four years ago it had all stopped; when he started working for Tony Cudmore, probably, and was told to be on his best behaviour. Was Cudmore mixed up in the handbag robberies? It seemed unlikely. He was making millions out of prostitution, why would he risk it? So Gordon had presumably started branching out on his own with some mates. There was an address in Enfield. The problem was, there were four members of the gang. If Warren ordered a raid on Gordon's home and it turned up nothing, the rest of the gang would be alerted and the bags would vanish into thin air. He would have to be watched. With manpower stretched almost to breaking point it was asking a lot. But the losses from two raids totalled more than half-a-million pounds, and luxury retailers all over London were clamouring for action by the police. When Warren phoned the Super to ask permission to set up a round-the-clock obo on Gordon, James Astbury raised no objection. Warren then spent a couple of hours going back over the evidence in the Nutley case, until his head was spinning, so he drove home at three o'clock to recharge the batteries mentally in the empty house. He felt the need to take his conscious mind right away from police work for a couple of hours, so despite the bright, summer's day outside, he drew the living-room curtains and watched a dvd he had bought off Amazon. It was *Le Beau Serge,* the black-and-white film that had launched the *nouvelle vague* career of Claude Chabrol in 1958. It was subtitled in English, but his French was good enough to enjoy the film without referring to them, even though the characters had strong *auvergnat* accents.

Afterwards he set about making himself a gourd of strong *yerba mate*, the Argentine *gauchos'* version of builders' tea.

While the kettle was boiling his mobile rang. It was Yolanda: "Where are you, *mi amor?*"

"At home. I needed to give my brain a rest. You on the way?"

"Have you forgotten? It's Vlad Malikov's retirement dinner. I'll be late."

"Sorry, yes, I forgot. Where are they having it?"

"Ciao Bella in Lamb's Conduit Street."

"Okay. Have fun. I might go back to the station for a few hours. This murder's doing my head in. Any idea where Oscar is, by the way?"

Their son was home for the summer vacation from Lincoln University after completing the first year of his BA in Criminology and Social Policy. His name, Oscar, had been chosen as one that worked equally well in English and Spanish, and also after the jazz pianist Oscar Peterson, whose music both of them liked.

"He was going out with some of his friends from school. Comparing notes from their various universities. He'll probably be home late, too."

"Okay. Only he said he wants to talk to me about his vacation reading, which is going to be a little difficult if our paths never cross. See you later."

"Ciao, mi amor."

Deprived of his anticipated family evening at home, he phoned Philippa: "How busy are you?"

"Planning a quiet evening at home with the laundry and the dishes, unless I get a better offer."

"How about a brainstorming session over a takeaway round at the office?"

"On my evening off?"

"Your brain's never off-duty."

"Actually, sir, I had something vaguely similar planned for myself, alone in my living-room with some stuff I've brought home."

"What sort of stuff?"

"I'll bring it with me."

"I've got all the evidence files here already. What else have you got?"

"I'll show you when I get there. What time shall I come?"

"If you can be at the station before eight we could watch Brazil v. Mexico with some of the others while we're eating."

Three-quarters of an hour later, Philippa was taking foil trays with white cardboard lids out of a plain blue plastic bag and lining them up on a desk in the open-plan CID office. The television was on for the football and half-a-dozen colleagues were sitting watching the warm-up interviews. They hoped the criminal fraternity in Norton Hill were doing the same and the phones wouldn't ring.

"Here you go," Philippa said to Warren, "EFR. Egg fried rice."

"We're back where we started," he said, uncharacteristically disconsolate.

"SPHK?" asked Philippa.

"Sweet and sour pork Hong Kong. That's me."

"Why Hong Kong?"

"It means it's got pineapple in it. Don't ask me why."

"Maybe there's a lot of pineapples in Hong Kong."

"More likely dreamed up by some Chinese restaurant owner in Gerrard Street."

"Anyway, I thought it was Hawaii when you got pineapple."

"That's when it's pizza. What's that you've got there?"

"Chicken with ginger and spring onion."

"I like that, too. I'll swap you half of mine for half of yours."

"It's a deal. I'll put the lid back on the sweet and sour pork Hawaii to keep it warm and we can start with this."

"Hong Kong."

"Hong Kong, Hawaii, it's all pineapple chunks to me."

"I've brought some beers."

"I'm strictly a champagne girl."

"Here's a can of John Smith's bubbly, then."

Warren withdrew two cans of bitter from a supply in a

Sainsbury's plastic bag. Philippa served the rice and chicken on to the plates he had already set on the table.

"Ying-tong ying-tong ying-tong ying-tong diddle I po," sang a male voice from the near the telly.

Warren waved his chopsticks menacingly: "Beware the terror of the tongs."

The murder of Roger Nutley was starting to slide towards becoming an unsolved crime. That would be acutely embarrassing for the Metropolitan Police in general and Norton Hill nick in particular, given the victim's high public profile. Half the public – those who regarded Nutley's accusers as lying opportunists trying to make a small fortune out of the publicity – would excoriate the police for letting his murderer get away scot-free. The other half - aware that the dead cannot be libelled - would be singing the praises of a killer for ridding the world of a man they regarded as a monster. His alleged crimes would be republished with salacious ornamentation as if they were undeniable facts, and there would be tribal rejoicing in the failure of the police to catch his executioner.

The takeaway was all gone before half-time in Fortaleza, but they decided to watch the rest of the match before doing any work. At ten to ten they wondered if it had been worth it as the host country only managed a goalless draw in a match mainly enlivened by a series of outstanding saves by the Mexican goalkeeper. The group of colleagues got up to leave and somebody pressed the remote to turn off the telly.

"I reviewed all the statements in the office this afternoon and can't be arsed to go through it all again this late," Warren confessed, "but you said you'd got something else."

"I don't know if it'll be of any help. It's press reports of Nutley's trial. I printed them out."

"This woman will go far."

"Thank you, kind sir."

"Although I'm not sure in which direction. Come on then, let's have a look at it."

Philippa removed a fat, pink cardboard file from her bag and placed it on the desk.

"Okay," said Warren. "If either of us thinks we've spotted anything, however silly it might seem, speak up and we'll talk it through."

They read in silence at separate desks, each with a pile of print-outs waiting to be read, and a discard pile. When they finished, neither had spoken. The session was becoming dispiriting.

"Is it worth swapping piles, sir?"

Warren sighed. "Let's do it. Then we'll call it a night."

"Sorry, sir," yawned Philippa in the end. "I'm afraid this has been a waste of time."

"No, it wasn't. It was worth a try. Another beer before you go?"

"No, thanks, I need to get some sleep."

In the car park, Philippa paused and turned to him.

"The only thing is," she said, "I've got a sort of funny feeling."

"That'll be the pork Hong Kong."

"No, I'm serious. I feel as if a light bulb did come on in my head, only I can't remember what it was. Just for a nanosecond, so that I didn't even realise till now."

"You're just tired. The mind plays tricks."

"Maybe. I'm not sure. You know when a word or a tune pops in and out of your brain so quick you miss it, then you can't get it back?"

"There was nothing in those press reports we didn't already know. Don't forget I read it all, too."

"Yes, I know; but there's something nagging at me."

"Women's intuition, you mean?"

"Now that is sexist."

"Sorry. Just intuition, then, without the women bit. Ninety-something percent of thinking is subconscious. That's what intuition means. It's real, it's valuable, and it's the same for men as for women."

"Agreed. The trouble is, I just don't seem to be able to get the thing back again, whatever it was."

"The best way to bring something you want to remember forward into the conscious part of the mind is not to try. Think about something else. If you're lucky, it'll come back when you least expect it."

"Maybe after I've had some sleep."

"Sleep that knits up the ravell'd sleeve of care."

"If you say so, sir."

"Not me. Shakespeare."

"Hamlet?"

"Macbeth. Another one full of murder and dead bodies."

THURSDAY 19 JUNE

1

The call came through at a quarter-to-nine while Warren was stuck in traffic at Whetstone on his way in to work. Kevin Foster put it through to Philippa, whom he had seen arrive at half-past-eight.

"CID, DS Myers speaking."

"I wonder if I might have a word with Detective Inspector Warren," said a mature, confident, middle-class voice that sounded vaguely familiar.

"I'm afraid he's not here at the moment. Can I help?"

"Well, it's about the Roger Nutley case. I understood Inspector Warren to be in charge of the inquiry."

"Yes, he is, but I'm working with him on it. Can I ask who's calling?"

"This is Daniel Spiller. I own the company producing the play."

The voice clicked in Philippa's memory. "I remember meeting you at the theatre, Mr Spiller. How can I help?"

"Well, actually I think I might be able to help you; the fact is, some new information's come to light, and I think it might be important."

"In that case could you come into the station and tell us about it, please?"

"Unfortunately not. I've just started rehearsing Hamlet again with a new actor playing Polonius, so I'm down here in Brighton with the cast, but I think you need to know this as soon as possible."

"All right," said Philippa, "you can tell me."

"It's like this. You interviewed all my actors on the evening of the murder, right?"

"That's correct."

"One of them was a young actress called Tessa Verrall, who plays Ophelia; but what it never occurred to her to tell you was that she only came into the production in the second week of the rehearsals after another actress pulled out. I'm sorry, it should have occurred to me to tell you, but as you can imagine my head was spinning with the horrendous events of that night, and to be quite frank, with how I was going to get the show back on the road, and when."

"So you're saying that somebody else had been going to play that part but changed her mind? What happened, was she ill?"

"Some vague excuse about family problems is what she said at the time. I was bloody furious, I can tell you. It's a major role in possibly the greatest play ever written, going on tour with a top company for six months, getting paid above the Equity rate and doing scenes with one of the country's finest actors. It was a huge break for her. She'd done nothing much before, but she had terrific chemistry at the audition so I took a chance. I'm not very often wrong."

"Look, I'm sorry, but I don't really see what this could have to do with the case," said Philippa.

"Bear with me. Last night we all went to a pub and I stood everybody drinks, we had a bit of a party and tongues were running pretty loose. There's another young actress in the cast called Emily Grady, she's an ASM playing Osric and the Player Queen."

"Sorry, ASM?"

"Assistant Stage Manager. It's a job most junior actors do. As well as acting they have to make sure props are in the right place, wash and iron costumes, help with the get-ins and get-outs. It's tough but it's all part of the training."

"So what about this Emily Grady?"

"She was well away on the red wine and blathering away with girlie gossip to anyone on her table who would listen. I was up at the bar having a quiet pint with John Montgomery when I suddenly overheard her talking about Libby Lennox."

"Is that the actress who walked out?"

"Exactly. Anyway, I pretended not to notice but asked John to be quiet while I listened, and what I heard came as a bit of a shock. It turns out that the real reason the poor girl walked out was that bloody Nutley came on to her in his dressing-room and she was terrified."

"You mean, came on to her as in...?

"As in tried to get his leg over, yes. For Christ's sake, he was more than fifty years her senior. Anyway, I had a word with young Emily this morning and she confirmed it. Apparently it was her walking in on them that put a stop to it."

"Was he trying to rape her?"

"From what I can make out, I think he might have done if Emily hadn't turned up when she did. This has really shaken me up, Sergeant. I mean, I believed Roger when he told me those women who accused him at his trial were making it up in the hope of getting money out of the tabloids. I trusted him and put his career back on its feet with this tour, and now I find he was sexually abusing one of the young actresses in my charge during the very first week of rehearsals and I didn't know a damn thing about it."

"Why do you think she didn't report it to you?"

"No idea; well, maybe she thought I was Nutley's old mate so I wouldn't believe her."

"And this other actress, Emily, she's never mentioned the incident before?"

"Libby swore her to secrecy. God knows why. I should imagine her career's taken a nosedive before it had even got off the ground. I do know her agent sacked her straight away."

"We shall need a statement from Emily as soon as possible, Mr Spiller. She can do that at Brighton Police Station, she doesn't need to come up to London, at least not right away, but I do need her statement as fast as possible."

"I'll pick her up and drive her there myself, hold her hand, will that be okay?"

"That would be marvellous. And now I need to talk to this Libby Lennox. I don't suppose you've got a number for her?"

"I'll phone her former agent and have him call you with it."

*

Libby's former agent, a one-man band called Chris Majendie working from home in Swindon, phoned Philippa less than ten minutes later, gave her Libby's mobile number and asked if she was in any trouble. Philippa said no, it was a routine matter in which she might be a witness. Then she called Libby. The actress was rehearsing in a room at the London Academy of Music and Dramatic Art (Lamda) in Baron's Court for an unpaid fringe play. Philippa told Libby she was coming straight there to talk to her. It would be a heck of a drive, but this was a murder investigation and it couldn't wait.

Lamda occupies a long, three-storey building sandwiched between the south side of the six-lane A4 trunk road leading west out of London, and Barons Court tube station on the Piccadilly and District lines. It seemed to have no parking spaces, so Philippa drove on past a huge billboard and pulled on to the forecourt of a BP filling station just beyond. She left her car in a space at the rear, popped into the shop to tell an attendant it was a police vehicle, and walked with DC Hollier back along the main road to the college entrance. The traffic noise was deafening.

Two male students were sitting on the steps, smoking cigarettes and chatting. They swung their legs aside to let Philippa and Hollier pass. Inside, at the reception counter on the right, Philippa told a smiling young woman she was looking for Libby Lennox.

"Do you know what she's doing?" asked the receptionist.

"Rehearsing a play. I think it's called The Shoemaker's Holiday."

"Thomas Dekker, 1599. It's very funny once you get your head around the Elizabethan language. They're in room W4. May I ask what it's about? Directors don't like people interrupting."

Not wanting to advertise her presence to the entire college, Philippa discreetly showed the receptionist her warrant card: "It's nothing to worry about, we just think she might have been a witness to an incident."

"I understand. An accident, was it?" Philippa didn't bother to contradict her. "If you don't mind waiting here, I'll go and see if I can fish her out."

A couple of minutes later the receptionist returned with a petite woman in her early twenties.

"This is the lady," said the receptionist to Libby.

Libby was pretty in an innocent-looking way, slim, devoid of make-up but not really needing any. Her naturally blonde hair was cut to curve in towards her chin in a way that cleverly emphasised her high cheekbones. She was wearing a loose-fitting blue-and-white striped matelot top, blue jeans that had seen better days, and tired white trainers.

"Hello," said Libby in an educated accent which retained a little of east London, "we're rather busy, we open next Tuesday, is this important?"

"Very," said Philippa, and, turning to the receptionist, "Is there anywhere we can talk in private?"

"Everywhere's full. We're bursting at the seams."

"What's it about?" asked Libby.

"An incident you were involved in a theatre in Brighton earlier this year."

"Oh." Libby's face fell.

"Exactly. Where can we talk?"

"There's a park around the corner. That'd be best. It's not far."

"Okay, let's go."

The three of them walked along the pavement back in the direction of central London, not speaking because of the traffic noise. They turned right into Palliser Road and over the slightly hump-backed bridge over the tube lines, right again into Margravine Gardens, and left through a gate into what Libby had called a park.

"This isn't a park, it's Hammersmith Cemetery," said Hollier.

"Sorry," said Libby. "I always think of it as a park. I come here and eat my sandwiches and run my lines at lunchtimes. You'd hardly know you were in London, it's so quiet, and there are squirrels running about."

As indeed there were, as well as birdsong.

"That's what I like about London," said Philippa. "It's really just a lot of villages joined together. By the way, I'm Detective Sergeant Myers." It was too early for lunchtime sandwich-eaters, and the benches at the junction between paths were unoccupied, so they sat on a south-facing one with the warm sunshine on their faces, with Libby in the middle.

"So," said Libby, "who told you?"

"The actress playing the Player Queen."

"Emily. She walked in on it. We agreed not to tell anybody. Does anybody else in the play know?"

Philippa ignored the question, and asked one of her own.

"Why didn't you come forward?"

"When he was killed, you mean?"

"Yes."

"It was months later. Nothing to do with me. I left the show on the weekend after the first week of rehearsals. It's water under the bridge. Hasn't done my career any good, walking out. As you can see, I'm back to working in the fringe for no pay. Hamlet was my big break and that bastard screwed it up for me."

"Why did you feel you had to leave?"

"After the man I'd have to do emotional scenes with eight times a week playing his daughter practically tried to rape me in his dressing-room?"

"What exactly happened?"

"We finished Friday's rehearsal, it was all going well. A few people were going to a pub for a drink but most were rushing off home for the weekend. We were in Brighton at Daniel Spiller's home base, the Grand Theatre, and one of my old school friends lives there, her name's Val, so I was going to stay with her and have a girlie weekend together; so I was in no big hurry to catch a train like most of them. Roger Nutley must have overheard me talking about it with the others. Being who he is, he'd been given a private dressing-room at the Grand even though it was only rehearsals, and he invited me for a drink and a chat. Well, I thought why not, I might even pick up some tips. He opened a bottle of champagne, which I must admit I thought was a bit over the top, but I supposed he was earning a lot more than the rest of us, so why not let him share it around a bit for once."

"So, what did he do?"

"He seemed really awkward. He started off telling me he thought I was a really good Ophelia. There's a scene early on where I have to explain to him, he's my dad in the play, you know, how Hamlet's been behaving really strangely towards me, and I had to look into Roger's eyes quite a lot from close up, and he said my acting in that part was very truthful. I was flattered, you know, he had years and years of experience and he's telling me I'm a good actress. But then he sort of ran out of conversation, awkward, like a schoolboy. So I tried asking him what it had been like working in The Filth for all that time. I'd drunk a couple of glasses of the champers and I must have put my hand on his knee, just in a friendly way. I wasn't thinking, I was tired and maybe a bit emotional from the role I'd been rehearsing, it didn't mean anything; but he sort of went bonkers and put his arms around me and tried to kiss me and said he was crazy about me and wanted to go to bed with me and asked me to come back to his hotel room. Well, I'm used to looking after myself of a Saturday night, you know how it is when the lads get a bit lubricated, but no harm done, and I said not to be silly, but he squeezed me hard and tried to get his tongue in my mouth. Well, I wasn't having that, disgusting old fart, so I was pushing him away but he was too strong. So then he said he'd give me five hundred pounds and I asked him what he thought I was and he pushed me away and back down into the chair, really hard. I was shouting by then and there was a knock on the door and I heard Emily call out and ask if everything was all right. I called back no it bloody isn't, then I just got up and walked out and Emily put me in a taxi to my friend Val's house in Moulsecoomb. I asked Emily not to tell anybody else because I didn't know what to do, I was in a real mess inside my head. As soon as I got there I burst into tears and told Val I was going to have to leave the show, and it was the biggest break I'd ever had, walking out was going to be awful, but she's a singer and knows about these things, and she said I ought to phone my agent and tell him, and I said I'd think about it in the morning. Then I phoned my mum and she reckoned I ought to keep my mouth shut because nobody would believe me, it would be my word against his, and in the end I did as my mum told me, and in the morning I phoned my agent and asked him to tell Daniel Spiller I couldn't go on with the show because I had family problems. Sure enough, a week later I got a letter saying I'd been dropped from the agency, and I still haven't got an agent now."

"Surely you could have reported the incident to Daniel Spiller, or maybe Equity?"

"You don't know much about the theatre business, do you? Roger Nutley was the star. It was his name that pulled in the punters, gave Daniel Spiller full houses week in, week out, up and down the country. Plus him and Spiller were buddies, drinking companions. And me? I was a nobody, and I'm even more of one now."

"Why should that be?"

"I walked out on Daniel Spiller after he'd given me a chance, didn't I? The business doesn't forgive you for that, you get known as unreliable. So a few months ago I was on top of the world, I was going to be playing Ophelia in proper theatres all round the country, and next week I open back where I started in a room over a pub in Kentish Town. To be honest, I feel like giving it all up, which is three years of drama school down the drain. All because of Roger bloody Nutley."

"You don't feel sorry for him that he's been murdered, then?"

"He's ruined my life as far as I'm concerned. What do you think?"

"You do realise that gives you a motive?"

"A motive? For what?" Her face fell as it dawned on her. "You don't mean for murdering him? Oh, for God's sake, don't be ridiculous!"

"Where were you between three o'clock and five o'clock last Saturday?"

"You mean, have I got an alibi?"

"It's just routine."

"I was at my mum's. She was at work in the afternoon and I sat in her garden learning lines, and in the evening I cooked us both dinner and we watched the telly and stayed up for the England match."

"Was your father there?"

"Haven't seen him for years. They're divorced. He went up north somewhere, cut himself off. Good riddance, he was a prat. He wasn't my real dad, anyway, they adopted me, he couldn't have kids."

"So you didn't tell him about this?"

"I couldn't if I wanted to. I've got no idea where he is."

"Okay. Now, are you quite sure you haven't told anybody else about the attack?"

"No, definitely not."

"Why did you agree to be in the play with him, knowing about his background?"

"I didn't. He wasn't going to be in it, originally. We were all gobsmacked when Mr Spiller told us. But then to start with he seemed a really nice guy at rehearsals, absolutely not coming on to the women, no dirty jokes, and I can't remember ever hearing him use the f word; which is pretty amazing, if you've ever heard what actors are usually like. Mind you, he was in his seventies, and they have different standards in front of ladies, don't they?"

"Have you got a boyfriend, or a brother?"

"No regular boyfriend, we split up after five years together, I was broken up, then I got told I'd got the tour and it really gave me a lift. And no brother. To be honest, I still don't see how any of this is going to help you find out who killed Nutley."

"Nonetheless, I shall need you to come back to the station with me and make a formal statement."

"I'm in the middle of a rehearsal."

Philippa's voice hardened: "You've been withholding evidence from a murder investigation. I do need you to accompany me."

"All right, what the heck. Only if I'm doing a written statement, you'd better stop calling me Miss Lennox."

"What do you mean?"

"That's only my stage name."

"So what's your real name?"

"Elizabeth Burridge."

*

Before pulling out of the petrol station, Philippa phoned Warren, who said he would be waiting to sit in on the interview. Elizabeth Burridge silently fretted in the back seat of the police car, beside Hollier, all the way to Norton Hill. In the interview room, Warren made clear that she was making a statement as a witness and was not in any trouble. She would not, therefore, need a solicitor present, unless she especially asked for one. DC Hollier took down her answers to questions in the form of a statement which she read and signed afterwards. To begin with, she reiterated what she had told Philippa in the cemetery. She added the detail that her mother was indeed the Helen Burridge whom Philippa had interviewed on Sunday. When Philippa had arrived at the house, she had just missed Elizabeth, who had left for her flat-share in Streatham after a late breakfast with her mum.

After signing the statement, she said, "I don't actually see what the big deal is."

"Don't you?" asked Warren. "Your own grandmother put Nutley on trial saying he raped her at drama school and ruined her career, and now you're saying he tried the same thing on with you just a few months before he was murdered, and you don't see what the big deal is?"

"It's just a coincidence. He had no idea who I was."

"Really?"

"Definitely. I never told anybody about gran. Ever. I didn't want to be connected with that stuff."

"How did your mother react when you told her he attacked you?"

"She said I should get out of there and keep my mouth shut about it, and there would always be other opportunities; which is what I did, only I knew there wouldn't be other opportunities. I'm going to end up working in an estate agency after this, I know I am."

"You must have hated Roger Nutley after that."

"Of course I did; but I didn't kill him."

"Nobody's suggesting you did; you're too small, and you weren't there; but perhaps somebody you know did; somebody who cares about you."

"I told you, I haven't told anybody else."

"You told your mother."

"You can hardly think she did it."

"No, but what about your father?"

"We don't even know where he is. He could be in Australia for all I know. Or dead. In any case, I can't see him murdering a man for groping me. He never gave a shit about me even when he was around."

Warren looked at Philippa: "Anything else you want to ask, DS Myers?"

Philippa shook her head.

2

After lunch, Philippa appeared in Warren's office carrying the pink cardboard file of press cuttings about the Nutley trial and placed it on his desk.

"What's this?" he asked.

"There's something in the press cuttings. I'm convinced my subconscious is trying to show it to me, but I can't seem to access it."

"I can't quite decide whether that's psychobabble or computer babble. But go on."

"I'd really like to go through it all with you again, sir, right now, before the hidden memory goes away, and bounce any ideas off you."

"And what is it you think you've got buried down there in the unfathomable recesses of your grey matter?"

"I don't know." She patted the file. "But it's in here somewhere."

"Really. So how come we spent half yesterday evening on those and found nothing?"

"I know I saw something, only there was something not quite right about it that made me ignore it. I just can't pin down what."

Warren looked down at his desk trying to suppress his irritation.

"We both need to get out there making enquiries; not poring over paperwork we've already looked at."

"Half-an-hour. Please."

"You'd better be right," said Warren. "All right; I never underestimate hunches."

Philippa was inwardly delighted at Warren's willingness to go along with her hunch, or feeling, or intuition, or whatever it was. After twenty minutes she was close to giving up; and suddenly there it was. She jabbed a finger at a photograph next to a newspaper report on the last day of the Nutley trial.

"Him," she said.

The photo showed Sir Roger Nutley looking relieved outside the Old Bailey. In the background was a group of onlookers.

"Who?"

"The big bloke in the background."

A tall, powerfully-built man was standing between two women whom Philippa recognised as Sylvia Thorbinson and Helen Burridge.

"So that's our murderer, is it?"

"I think so."

"Why?"

"I know him from somewhere. I just can't think where. Damn it."

"No, you saw this last night and it stuck in your memory without you realising it. *Déjà vu*. Doesn't prove a thing."

"I've seen him somewhere else. If only I could remember."

"Not good enough."

"Let me close my eyes and think."

"Go on, then."

Philippa did so. Warren had the sense to keep quiet.

"I've got it," she said. "He was in a framed photo on the mantelpiece at Sylvia Thorbinson's house."

"So what? You saw the photo at the house, now you've seen this one, it's the same man, which is not surprising if he's a relative of Mrs Thorbinson and he went to the court to support her. Sorry, Sergeant, this is a waste of time. You need to get out there and do some real police work."

"No, sir, you're missing the point. He's Sylvia

Thorbinson's son-in-law, Helen Burridge's ex-husband, Elizabeth or Libby's adoptive father, and all three women swear blind they've had no contact with him since the divorce six years ago; but this photo was taken of him outside the trial, only a few yards away from Helen Burridge, only two years ago."

"Bloody hell, I see what you mean. Let me have a look." Warren picked up his mug and slurped a mouthful of tea, peered at the photo, and choked, spluttering tea on to the floor.

"Jesus wept!" he exploded. "Don't you realise who that is?" Then shaking his head, "No, I'm sorry, it can't be; it's impossible."

He slid the cutting back across the desk to Philippa, and she turned it around, held it up, and stared at the face.

"Can you see who it is yet?" he asked her.

"No, sir."

"Think laterally."

There was a long pause, and then Philippa gasped: "Oh ... my ... God."

"So?"

"He must have had it timed to the second."

"We've had the wool pulled over our eyes good and proper," said Warren. "Come on, we should have the address in the computer."

Philippa logged in and within seconds found the address the police had been given at the theatre on Saturday afternoon.

"71 Simmons House. That's on the Hollingdown Estate."

"Let's go. If he's still there we'll be heroes in the national press tomorrow."

*

Simmons House was a run-down 1960s tower block of council flats. The car park was deserted apart from four youths in grey hoodies holding a conspiratorial-looking conversation behind a line of stinking recycling bins. Everything about their demeanour suggested they were up to no good, but they were not a priority. Normally there might also have been a few mangy mongrel dogs scavenging around, but in the heat they had probably curled up in shady spots in the stairwells or dustbin sheds. Faded graffiti on the side of Simmons House had proclaimed for years, 'Jesus loves you,' 'Taylor Jenkins is a slag,' and 'Keep Britain White.' Apparently it was nobody's job at the council to arrange for them to be painted out. However bad the air out here might be, Warren and Philippa breathed in big lungfuls of it, aware that the lifts in the block, if they worked, would reek of stale urine, sniffed solvent and random other olfactory delights. They need not have bothered. As soon as they reached the entrance they saw that the bell-pushes on the rectangular metal plate beside the door numbered from one to sixty-four.

"We've been had again," said Warren, pulling his mobile phone out of his trouser pocket and calling Ivan Strange's number.

Strange was alone at a table in the Café de Paris in Castle Street, a couple of hundred yards west of the Theatre Royal, eating a cream cheese and salmon bagel and sipping an americano, when his mobile rang.

"Ivan Strange."

"Mr Strange, this is DI Warren. I need the home address of one of your staff, urgently."

"I'd have to look."

"Could you do that, now, please?"

"I'm out having lunch. I haven't got it here. It's in my office at the theatre."

"Fine. I'll meet you outside the front door in fifteen minutes."

"Is it really that urgent?"

"Yes, Mr Strange, it is. Be there."

Warren disconnected. Strange wolfed down what was left of his bagel and paid his bill at the desk on the way out.

In his office at the Theatre Royal, he read the address out: "71 Simmons House, Gernon Avenue."

"It doesn't exist," said Warren. "We've just come from there."

"Well, I'm sorry, but that's the only address I've got."

"Didn't you check?"

"Not to the extent of going there in person. I had no reason to."

Warren turned to Philippa. "Where does Helen Burridge work?"

"Chingford."

"Let's go. Blue light and sirens. I'll call for local backup."

Ivan Strange gave it five minutes after they left, then made a phone call.

*

Thorbinson's estate agency was a relatively modest concern. There were four desks in the front office, facing diagonally inwards from the walls. The front two were occupied by male members of staff in their early twenties wearing dark suits and trying to look busy. The desk at the rear on the right was unoccupied. Helen Burridge was sitting at the rear left desk. She recognised Philippa, stood up and came forward to greet her, although her body language was that of a bouncer trying to shepherd an unwanted customer back out through the door: "Can I help you?" she asked in a tone intended to suggest to her staff that the visitors were customers. Warren was having none of that and showed her his warrant card and his you're-in-deep-trouble-sunshine face. There was certainly none of the diffident courtesy in his voice that Philippa had used on her earlier call.

"DI Warren, Metropolitan Police. Is there somewhere private we can talk, Mrs Burridge?"

Across the road a patrol car pulled up. Two uniformed constables from Chingford got out. Philippa waved them over, and they crossed the road and came into the agency, which was beginning to feel rather crowded.

"You'd better come through," said Helen Burridge. She led them into a small back room which was mostly a store room for cardboard boxes containing paper, ink cartridges and suchlike, but also had a small desk with another computer screen and one chair; and was where she worked when she wanted to be outside the public gaze. Philippa told one of the constables to come through with them and take notes, and the other to remain in the front office.

"Nobody's to go out, is that understood?" said Warren.

"I've got to go and do a viewing in ten minutes," said one of the young men.

"Tell them you're double-booked," said Warren.

On Helen Burridge's desk in the front office, Philippa spotted a framed family photograph; the same one she had seen at Sylvia Thorbinson's house. She scooped it up and took it through with her to the back room, closing the front door behind them.

"Sit down, Mrs Burridge," said Warren. "We'll stand."

Philippa handed Warren the picture. He nodded and held it up in front of Mrs Burridge.

Philippa said: "You keep a photograph of your ex-husband on your desk, Mrs Burridge. Isn't that a bit peculiar? A man you divorced six years ago, haven't seen since, and supposedly can't stand?"

"I have it there because my daughter's in it. Happier days."

"Where's your ex-husband now?" demanded Warren.

"How should I know? I told you, I haven't seen him for six years."

"We know that's a lie. You saw him at the trial of Sir Roger Nutley two years ago. Since you lied about that, we have no reason to believe you haven't remained in contact with him all the time. Where is he now?"

There was no mistaking the authority and underlying threat in Warren's voice.

Philippa slipped back out to the front office.

"How should I know? What do you want him for, anyway?"

"Murder," said Warren.

"Are you crazy?"

"Not at all. If you're withholding information about his whereabouts, I suggest you think very carefully about the consequences for yourself."

"Gavin? A murderer? You obviously don't know him."

In the front office, Philippa opened and closed the drawers in Helen Burridge's desk. The same young man protested: "You can't do that, it's private."

Philippa held up her warrant card for him to see across the room: "I can do what I like. Nothing's private in a murder enquiry." She turned her attention to Helen Burridge's large, brown, leather handbag-cum-holdall on the floor, propped against the wall, beside the desk; plucked out an old-fashioned filofax with a pink polkadot cover; flicked through the names and addresses; and smiled when she reached the letter G. Returning to the back office, she held it up for Warren to see: "It's in here sir."

"How dare you…" began Helen Burridge.

"Shut up," said Warren; and to Philippa: "Where is it?"

"Right back in our very own Hollingdown Estate. We were that close. Not quite as far away as Bradford or Blackburn, eh, Mrs Burridge? That's assuming that an address that's only got 'Gavin' written next to it means your ex. Does it?"

Helen Burridge's mask of respectability slipped: "You've got a bloody nerve, bitch. And I've got no idea what you're talking about."

"Watch your language," said Warren; and to the constable: "Now then, I wonder if you and your colleague would be so kind as to convey this lady to Norton Hill nick until such time as I'm ready to deal with her. Sorry to send you off your patch, but under no circumstances must she be allowed to make contact with anybody at all by telephone, and that includes a lawyer, until I come back and say so. We don't want this maniac warned that we're on to him. Is that understood?"

"Absolutely, sir."

"You can't force me to go anywhere," spat Mrs Burridge.

"Helen Burridge, I am arresting you on suspicion of being an accessory to the murder of Sir Roger Nutley," said Warren. "You do not have to say anything, but it may harm your defence if you do not mention, when questioned, something which you later rely on in court. Anything you do say may be given in evidence. Do you understand?"

"What for? I haven't done anything wrong."

"Do you understand?"

"Yes, I bloody well understand, but you're off your bleeding trolley."

"Good, well, if you would be kind enough to allow these officers to accompany you to their car, I'll see you later."

*

In terms of social status, comfort and local facilities, much of the Hollingdown Estate ranked only just above sleeping in shop doorways. It was a decaying local authority sink. One side consisted of tower blocks. The other comprised a zig-zag pattern of low-rise rectangular blocks of hutch-like flats, apparently designed by its 1960s architects to depress its occupants into final surrender. Triangular lawns in the angles of the low-rise blocks had long since been crushed into litter-strewn wastelands of mud and weeds. Occasional tiny islands of brightly coloured flowers showed where some brave individuals struggled to restore a little horticultural cheer in patches underneath their own ground-floor windows.

Warren parked his BMW outside the estate in a resident-permits-only space on the opposite side of Bavaria Way. It was a quiet street forming not only the westernmost boundary of the fully pedestrianised estate, but also the socio-economic frontier between the haves and the have-nots of this part of north London. The other side of the street comprised an elegant, two-storey terrace of recently-gentrified Georgian cottages, all with gleaming paintwork on their doors and windows, hemmed in by a neat line of black, arrow-headed, three-foot-high, spiked railings from an earlier and altogether more dignified era. The car parked immediately in front of Warren's was a spotlessly clean pale blue Audi convertible with 2012 registration plates. Not for the first time, Warren questioned the wisdom of arranging a city so that the poor and the rich could enjoy constant views of each other. As he reasoned, it merely led to the former envying the posh gits in their poncey bijou residences, while the latter despised the feckless proles in their deservedly run-down hovels. He was amazed that the Audi still had wheels.

Warren and Philippa disembarked and walked across the almost-deserted street to a locked gate set into the eight-foot high grey metal fence surrounding the block of unenticing deck-access flats.

"Nice smell," said Philippa.

"Rotting fish," said Warren. "It'll be in one of those bins in there. Some kind person won't have wrapped it up before dumping it."

"I couldn't live in a place like this."

"There but for fortune."

Philippa let that pass. She knew Warren was a soft-hearted liberal under that tough cop exterior. Unlike him, she came from a working-class background, though nothing like as far down the heap as this place. She was a firm believer in the notion that nobody needed to be this poor in England if they were prepared to get off their arse and work.

The only other human being in sight was an old black man with strikingly white hair, hovering on the opposite kerb holding a leash with a brown-and-white Jack Russell Terrier on the other end, apparently unable to decide whether he could be bothered to cross the road. Perhaps the smell of fish was immobilising him. Eventually the dog yapped and he took the plunge, heading in the direction of the Hare and Hounds pub on the opposite corner of the road at the top of this one. Line me up a pint, old buddy, thought Warren.

There was a sign on the gate in red and black lettering: "Warning – These Premises are Protected and Regularly Patrolled by SPQR Security."

Warren chuckled: "They've either got no sense of history or the owner's a school teacher."

"How's that, sir?" asked Philippa.

"SPQR; *Senatus Populusque Romanus:* the Senate and people of Rome. It was on the standards carried by the old Roman legions when they spread out conquering the world."

Philippa, whose comprehensive school had not included Latin on its curriculum, thought this was probably a joke that only public school kids would find amusing, and that there probably weren't very many of those living on the Hollingdown Estate.

At chest level on the gate, above a handle, was a metal box with numbered buttons and an audio grille.

"Are we going in, sir?"

"No way. If he's in, he's a big violent bastard with nothing to lose, and I have no illusions about you and me being able to detain him if he puts up a fight. And if he's out, ten to one in a place like this the neighbours'll tip him off the fuzz have been ringing his doorbell. Let's just see if we can figure which flat it is first."

They walked along the pavement beside the fence, which felt like circumnavigating a concentration camp, "It's number 239 we're looking for," said Philippa, "but I can't see any numbers."

"There's one on the top of the door of the third flat from the left on the middle floor, but I can't quite make it out," said Warren.

Philippa walked back down a few paces and pointed up. "It's 222," she said. "We're in the right area."

"Don't point," said Warren. "Some low-life'll clock you for a cop."

Philippa walked further back down the way they had come, looking up at the decks, then came back. "Four doors along is 226. So they number from left to right; twelve flats on each level."

"But are the bigger numbers on the top level or the ground floor?"

"Can't see, sir."

"Let's go and find out."

He led her mysteriously back to the gate and punched the numbers 2, 4, 1 into the box. The audio grill crackled and a male, Caribbean-accented voice said, "Yes, who is it?"

"Plumber, sir. We have a report of water leaking from your flat into the one below."

"Is that so?" said the deep, fruity voice. "Well, they must be in Australia, then, because I'm on the ground floor." The voice erupted into laughter.

"Sorry, sir," said Warren, "the Council must have given me the wrong address. I'll have to go back and check."

"Bloody typical of those lazy bureaucrats down the town hall," said the voice. "Have a nice day, man." The intercom went off in another burst of crackling.

"Ground floor, then," Warren said to Philippa.

"Twelve flats on each level," said Philippa, "so the last one on the middle deck must be 231, and the bottom ones run from 232, which makes 239 the eighth from the left or the fifth from the right."

"The question is whether he's in," said Warren. "If we go in and he's out, chances are we'll never see him again."

"You could do the plumber thing on his number, sir."

"He might sus it. He's bound to be on his guard. Then he could leg it out the back. No; I'm calling in the cavalry."

Half an hour later two minibuses disgorged half-a-dozen uniforms on to the spot where Warren and Philippa had been standing and another half-dozen behind Flat 239. Warren buzzed the helpful occupant of Flat 241 again: "Police, open the gate, please sir." He obliged at once, Warren and Philippa jogged ahead of the uniforms to the front door of 239, and Warren pressed the doorbell. No reply. He hammered on the door with his fist and shouted, "Police, open up!" Nothing. He turned to the Sergeant in charge of the uniformed squad: "Break it down." The battering ram smashed the flimsy wooden door off its lock at the first attempt. Warren went in. "Mr Burridge?" But the flat felt deserted. He went along the short passageway far enough to peer in through the doors to the kitchen, living-room and bedroom. There was no sign of clothes, bedding, dishes or any personal possessions. He checked the toilet and bathroom; no Gavin Burridge hiding on the loo or in the bathtub.

He turned back to Philippa and stated the obvious: "Our bird has flown."

FRIDAY 20 JUNE

1

Despite the continuing fine weather, Norton Hill Police Station, like the rest of the nation, was pervaded by melancholy on Thursday morning. The reason was not a crime wave, but England's second 2-1 defeat in the World Cup, this time by Uruguay, a tiny South American country with a population of less than three-and-a-half million. With Luis Suarez, who normally played for Liverpool, having scored both goals for Uruguay, and Wayne Rooney, the Manchester United captain, having bagged England's only face-saver, there was a joke doing the rounds that the score was actually Liverpool 2 Manchester United 1. The fact remained, however, that to stay in the competition England now needed not only to beat Costa Rica next Tuesday, but also for Italy to defeat both Uruguay and Costa Rica. The reality was looming of our lads coming home early at the end of the group stage.

Philippa was on her way back from the canteen carrying her elevenses of a mug of tea and a Danish pastry when she noticed DC Marion Everitt watching the CCTV footage from Baldock Motorway Services and decided to offer a bit of friendly moral support.

"Anything helpful in that?" she asked.

"Not a sausage," replied Marion, "I'm just running it by me again more in hope than expectation. They got clean away and we haven't the foggiest who they are."

"Mind if I have a look?" asked Philippa, mainly as a way of bonding with the female newcomer to CID.

"Help yourself," said Marion, standing up and offering Philippa her seat. "It's been edited to start where they arrive about a quarter of an hour before us, then the meeting we have and me going on to check the dog's microchip, and then that skinny bastard goes crazy with the knife and slashes Robin, and while I'm attending to him they run off across the car park and get in their van and race off like bats out of hell."

"You've got CCTV of the van? With the registration?"

"Yep. It belongs to a Volkswagen Beetle scrapped in

Sunderland last year."

"False plates. Quite professional, so long as they don't get stopped anywhere. Maybe they didn't come so far as they said."

During the conversation, Philippa had been watching the video of the run-up to the knife attack, and then followed it through to where it showed the men climbing into the van and driving off. She peered at it more closely and stopped it on a diagonal rear view of the van.

"I need a side view. Do we see it arriving?"

"Right at the beginning. Why?"

Philippa didn't answer, but fast-reversed the video. There were several minutes of the men standing waiting with the dog, then them walking backwards to where they got out of the van, and the van being parked. As it turned into the bay, at the corner of the car park nearest the lorries area, there was a sideways-on view. Philippa froze the frame and zoomed in.

"I've seen it before," she said. "See those two long parallel scratches?"

"Yes, but a lot of vans have scratches."

"Those are very distinctive. They both end in deeper dents at the front end, and they both turn upwards at the back, as if the van went down off a kerb or a step while it was still in contact with whatever was scratching it. It's the same one I saw."

"Can you remember where?"

"Oh, yes," said Philippa, standing up, "and it's a bit too much of a coincidence to be a coincidence; because the place I saw it was a boarding kennels; and that kennels is not a million miles from that service area."

"Bloody hell. Bit of luck you walking by while I was looking at that. I wouldn't have seen that."

Warren had entered behind them and been watching and listening for the last couple of minutes.

"Which just goes to show you can't only rely on computers to match everything up," he said. "Coppers still need to talk to each other, however good the technology gets. Well done, both of you."

"Thank you, sir," said Philippa, smiling at Marion.

"So," said Warren, "I think we have a surprise visit to organise, don't you?"

"We, sir?" asked Marion.

"Yes, 'we', because interestingly enough, that kennels happens to be owned by a certain Mr and Mrs Baxter, and as Sergeant Myers knows, Carol Baxter just happens to be one of the women who accused Sir Roger Nutley of sexual assault."

"You're not suggesting there's a link between stealing dogs and the murder, are you, sir?" asked Philippa.

"Possibly not," said Warren, "but we've got a gang of thugs and a woman with a powerful grudge against Nutley and a van that links them, and that's enough to get me very interested. Remind me what it's called and where it is."

"Blue Shingles Boarding Kennels and Cattery," Philippa remembered. "It's outside a village called Hemlington."

"Herts or Beds?"

"Cambridgeshire, sir."

"Okay. I'll get on to Cambridge and sort some reinforcements out, they're bound to want to be involved. The Super wants this dognapping sorted, and we all want the nasty little scumbag who slashed Robin Merryweather and that girl, Faith Goodwin. He's well chuffed Constable Everitt here got his old mate's doggy pal Archie back, but we need the gang in the bag. I'll round up a couple of our own uniforms to go with you in case it gets nasty again."

Warren turned to leave.

"Just a minute, sir," said Marion, "what was that about the Superintendent's pal?"

"Oh, didn't I mention it?" grinned Warren. "That Golden Retriever you recovered was nicked from a certain retired DCI Bob Brannigan, of whom you may or may not have heard, still very chummy with our own Super, you know, down the lodge and on the golf course, sort of thing. You're already looking at some brownie points for that one, young lady, so get on and finish the job."

Marion went back to her computer. Just in case this trip turned out to be her chance to shine, she wanted to keep as much information as possible about the recent dognappings in and around Norton Hill fresh in her mind. While she was studying the files, her phone rang.

"Young woman calling for you," said the voice of Kevin Foster.

"Has she got a name?"

"Faith Goodwin."

"All right, put her on."

Faith's voice came on the phone: "Is that Constable Everitt?"

"Hello, Faith. How are you feeling?"

"I'm fine. The wound's healing up. It's only a scratch, really."

"How are things with your mum and dad?"

"We had a massive row and I've moved out."

"So where are you staying?"

"With Matt and his mum. They've been brilliant. My parents don't know his address, and I'm over sixteen, so they don't have to be told. I'll contact them when I'm ready. They were horrible. They never once asked me if I was badly hurt. Just shouted stuff at me from the Bible about fornication."

"It's not for me to comment," said Marion, "but look, I'm actually rather busy at this moment, so was there anything I could help you with?"

"I was just wondering if you'd found anything out about Toby."

"I'd have told you if we had; but look, the reason I'm in a hurry is we're just going to a boarding kennels which we think might be involved in the dognapping. So I can't promise anything, but keep your fingers crossed, you never know."

"Where is it?"

"Oh, it's outside London, up in Cambridgeshire."

"What's it called?"

"Blue Shingles. But look, if you want you can give me a ring here this afternoon and I'll tell you if there's any news. All right?"

"Okay, I will if that's okay."

"Don't get your hopes up too much."

"I won't; and thank you."

As soon as she put the phone down, Marion thought,

dammit, that was careless, I shouldn't have told her that. Still, she's only a kid, there's no harm.

2

In the light of the stabbing of Faith Goodwin when her Doberman, Toby, had been stolen, and of the slashing of Robin Merryweather when he and Marion Everitt had attempted to apprehend the two dognappers, Warren was adamant that there should be plentiful backup for the visit to the Blue Shingles Boarding Kennels and Cattery. Strictly speaking it was a job for Cambridgeshire Constabulary, but young Marion had put in some excellent work on the investigation during what was still her first month in CID, and he would like to see her claim a good collar if there was one to be had. So he spoke to Jim Astbury, who in turn gave his old friend Superintendent Stewart Haynes in Cambridge a ring, and they agreed on a joint operation. They were to meet up with a Cambridgeshire dog-handler, although he wouldn't be bringing along any of his own four-legged friends, but rather keeping an eye on the operation while at the same time being on hand to take charge of any canine situation that might develop.

Merryweather was keen to take part in the bust in the hope of getting a crack at nailing the gangly teenage hothead who had wounded him at Baldock Motorway Services, and although he had been confined to tedious paperwork while he convalesced, Warren agreed to his coming. They also took two male uniformed officers for additional muscle in case it should turn out to be required.

They travelled up the A1 in three cars: Warren and Philippa in Warren's unmarked BMW, Marion and Merryweather in a marked car, the two uniforms in their panda. At ten o'clock in the morning the traffic was relatively light and they covered the 35 miles to the rendezvous point east of the Bedfordshire town of Biggleswade, just across the county border in Cambridgeshire, in fifty minutes, without speeding. There was a Cambridgeshire Police Dog Van waiting for them, and Sergeant Colin Waldron stepped out of the cab to greet the posse. A Cambridgeshire uniformed constable was waiting in the passenger seat.

"It's empty," he said, indicating the van, "so if we have to take any dogs away I can deal with it. I've got one of our lads with me for a bit of extra muscle should you need it."

Philippa briefed Waldron on the investigation and the reason they were calling on Blue Shingles Kennels. She pointed out that whether it turned out to be more in the nature of a raid or a visit would depend on what kind of a reception they got. She also mentioned that, purely coincidentally, the female half of the duo running the establishment had been one of the women who had taken Sir Roger Nutley to court a couple of years earlier for alleged sexual abuse.

"He was killed on your patch, wasn't he?" said Waldron.

"Yep," said Warren.

Without further ado the convoy set off eastwards with Waldron leading the way in his van through the B-roads. The village of Hemlington looked as deserted as when Philippa passed through it the first time. She wondered whether anybody actually lived in these rustic backwaters in the daytime. As the three police vehicles swung into the kennels car park, it was immediately apparent that there was no blue van there this time; the only vehicles present were an old maroon Renault and a bronze-coloured two-door Kia. The eight police officers disembarked and Waldron introduced his Cambridge colleague, Constable Dennis Grindey.

"We have to assume that the suspects may be on the premises and may resist arrest," said Warren. "The younger man is known to have used a knife at least twice, so be ready to deploy tasers at the slightest sign that he's reaching for one."

"Yes, sir," all round.

"Constable Grindey, would you be so kind as to stand guard outside the front door of the house in case anyone tries to leave?"

"Yes, sir."

"You two," Warren addressed the hefty uniformed

constables, "stay out here in the car park and make sure nobody tries to drive away in anything."

Peter Baxter emerged from the kennels reception cabin trying unsuccessfully not to look anxious about the arrival of so many coppers.

"What's going on?" he asked.

Philippa stepped in front of him. "You remember me, don't you, Mr Baxter? Detective Sergeant Myers."

"Course I do. I thought we cleared all that up. We had nothing to do with that murder. We were both here, looking after our customers. I gave you a list of witnesses as long as your arm. Didn't you ask any of them?"

"Yes, Mr Baxter, I paid Mr Blagden a visit straight after I left you, and he said he was here and saw you both; and I phoned several of the others."

"So I don't get it. What's the problem?"

"We're not here about the murder of Sir Roger Nutley, sir," said Warren.

Philippa said, "When I came here before, there was a blue van in your car park. Is it yours?"

"No. Must have been a customer's."

"There weren't any customers here. An old blue Transit van with two long scratches on the passenger side. Whose was it? I assume you don't let every Tom, Dick and Harry park here."

"Oh, yeah, the Transit. Belongs to a mate of mine. I let him park it up here while he was on holiday. Used it to get a few slabs and stuff from the garden centre."

Philippa threw Marion a glance to take over.

"What's this mate's name?" asked Marion.

Baxter hesitated before replying. "Ken."

"Ken what?"

More hesitation. "I dunno actually. I just have a drink with him now and then."

"Where does he live?"

"Out St Neots way somewhere, I think."

"What's his address?"

"No idea."

"So, you look after his van for him, and he leaves you

the keys to go shopping for slabs, and you don't know his name or where he lives? You expect us to believe that?" said Philippa.

"It's the truth. Take it or leave it."

Warren stepped up to Baxter, who, judging by his shifting facial expressions, couldn't make up his mind whether to be accommodating or aggressive. "We have evidence that vehicle was used in the commission of a serious crime."

"Not by me. You must have the wrong van."

Warren asked Marion: "Is this the man you met at Baldock Services?"

"No, sir. Nothing like."

Warren stepped up to Baxter: "I'd like my officers to take a look around, sir, if you don't mind."

"What, you want to search my house?"

"I was thinking more of the kennels, actually," said Warren.

"What for?" Baxter looked rattled.

"Stolen dogs."

"Well, you won't find any here." Baxter tried to look scornful, as if it were a ridiculous suggestion. "They're all signed in by their owners. I can show you the paperwork."

"I'm sure you can, but we'd rather take a look at the animals themselves. How many have you got here?"

"Twenty-three. Have you got a warrant for this?"

"Do I need one, sir? I can soon get one sent over, if you insist. We'll just hang around while we're waiting for it, to make sure none of the doggies get taken for walkies in the meantime."

Baxter hesitated, mentally starting to rehearse his story about how people must have brought dogs to board without telling him they were stolen. He had fake paperwork in reception. He would say he must have been lied to. That had always been the fallback explanation. He knew it was pretty thin but he'd never really expected to have to resort to it. What better place to hide a dog than in kennels among dozens of other dogs? So what the hell had those bloody fools been up to that would bring the law all the way out from London to his place in the back of beyond, and mob-handed at that? Come to that, how had they connected the van to him? They were supposed to always use the false plates.

Warren moved towards the kennels entrance, circumnavigating Baxter, who stood momentarily rooted to the spot as if he had been gazing into the eyes of Medusa. He was followed by Philippa, Marion, Merryweather and Waldron. Bowing to the inevitable, Baxter followed the police group through his entrance cabin into the kennels courtyard, where they all halted. By now many of the dogs were barking furiously, unsettled by this intrusion of so many two-legged strangers, in voices ranging from soprano Shih Tzu down to basso profundo Boxer.

"So now what?" asked Baxter.

"This officer," said Warren, indicating Waldron, "is going to read the microchip in every animal you've got here that's got one, and then we'll go through their paperwork. Then we'll have a chat."

"Fine," said Baxter, now trying hard to bluff, "if you want to waste your time. Like I told you, all their papers are in order. And it takes five of you to sort this, does it? No wonder you can't get hold of a copper when you actually want one."

"Eight, actually, sir. I also have a constable posted outside the front door of your house, and two more in your car park, so if any of your accomplices are thinking of slipping out that way..."

"Accomplices? I don't have accomplices, Inspector, I'm not a criminal; only friends and business associates. And the only person in my house at the moment is my wife. Maybe this lady would like to go and annoy her again," he indicated Philippa, "she was only round here bothering Carol the other day, weren't you, love?"

Philippa refused to rise to the provocative "love", but looked at Warren and raised an eyebrow enquiringly.

"Actually you might as well go and have another word with Mrs Baxter," Warren told Philippa. "Go round the front, ring the bell, go inside with Constable Grindey and stick close to him in case Mr Baxter's mistaken and Laurel and Hardy are in there; although I don't honestly think it's very likely. See what you can get out of Mrs Baxter."

"Yes, sir," said Philippa, and went back out the way they had come in.

Warren glanced at a door opposite the entrance leading into a separate, single-storey, enclosed outhouse. "What's in there?" he asked.

"The cattery."

"Is it locked?"

"Not the outside door, no."

Warren turned to Marion: "Go and have a snoop around the pussycats, Constable."

"Anything particular I'm looking for, sir?" asked Marion.

"Anything that looks out of place."

"Like what?" asked Marion.

"I don't know, a grand piano, Hitler's diaries, whatever. Probably nothing, but just in case."

"Yes, sir."

"And don't waste time stroking the moggies."

Marion disappeared into the feline section of Blue Shingles.

Down each side of the slightly sloping courtyard there were eight dog pens, mostly containing a single animal.

"Right, let's start checking the doggies," said Warren.

Baxter opened the first pen on their right, and Waldron stepped in to be greeted enthusiastically by a dark brown and white Cocker Spaniel whose name, according to a card in a slot on the gate, was Poppy. Avoiding direct eye contact, Waldron proffered the back of his hand, drooping limply to indicate that he intended no threat, and the dog obliged by sniffing it, then licking it, all the while wagging her tail happily. He stroked one of her long, floppy ears with his left hand while running the microchip reader over the back of her neck with his right, until it detected the chip and displayed Poppy's registration number in its window. Waldron looked up at Warren: "This one's okay."

Moving along the line of pens, he repeated the procedure on a tiny Shih Tzu, an Airedale Terrier, a Beagle, two black Miniature Poodles sharing a pen, a German Shepherd, two little white West Highland Terriers sharing another pen, and a dauntingly grumpy-looking but mercifully soppy Boxer; none of whom activated the 'stolen' or 'lost' warning on the microchip reader.

It was while this was under way that Faith Goodwin and Matt appeared in the yard.

"What are they doing here? demanded Baxter.

"I might ask the same thing," said Warren. "Get outside, you two, now."

"I'm looking for my dog," snapped Faith, suddenly sounding older than her years.

"Well, you won't find it here," snarled Baxter, the mask of civility slipping.

Faith pulled up the left side of her t-shirt and showed Baxter the dressing over her stab wound.

"And the cowardly pig who did this," she spat.

Baxter's colour drained, and he turned to Warren. "What the hell is that about?"

Looking at Baxter's worried expression, Warren reckoned he didn't know about the stabbing; or, presumably the slashing of Robin Merryweather's hand.

"Didn't you know? One of your so-called business associates did that while he was stealing this young lady's dog; not to mention a similar knife attack on one of my officers at Baldock Motorway Services."

Baxter was definitely shaken: "I don't know what the hell you're talking about."

"Don't you? They used your friend Ken's van. Or maybe it's yours."

"Must have been another one. There's thousands like it."

"Not with those magnificent scratches all down the side. No use changing the number plates if you carry around a trademark like that."

"You've lost me, mate. I dunno what you're on about."

"Two big men in their forties. Is one of them your mate Ken, if that's his real name? And a tall, gangly teenager. We've got them on CCTV of course; and the van. Silly place to choose for a dodgy deal, when you think about it, motorway services, they might just as well have done it on the Jeremy

Kyle Show, the number of cameras there are there."

"The stupid bastards," fumed Baxter.

Faith and Matt were still there, watching and listening. "I don't know how you knew to come here, but I want you to leave," Warren said. "There may be some danger."

"No way," said Faith. "I want to see if Toby's here."

There was no way of forcing them to leave without sending an officer away from the scene with them.

"All right," he said, "but keep well back, over there." He pointed towards the entrance. "If your dog is here, we'll bring him to you."

Baxter was standing at the far end of the yard, arms folded, fuming with irritation and anxiety.

"He knows we're going to find something, all right," Warren murmured to Philippa. However, examination of the nine dogs in the eight pens opposite also failed to yield any results.

"All right, Mr Baxter, that's nineteen dogs we've seen," said Warren. "You said twenty-three. Where are the other four?"

Baxter indicated a paved pathway around behind the far end of the cattery. "There's some more round here," he grunted.

Marion emerged from the cattery: "There's something you ought to see, sir." Warren ordered everybody to wait while he went in with Marion.

"What is it?" asked Warren, quietly.

"Just down here, sir."

Marion led Warren round a right-hand corner that led past cat pens on both sides, quite humanely large he was pleased to see, some of them containing guests who miaowed as they passed, including a pair of beautiful Blue Persians. At the far end was a particularly large pen, presumably intended for multiple boarders from the same home.

In it was parked an unusually large wheelchair with a high back and extra-large wheels. Beside it were three large black refuse sacks, stuffed full and tied at the top with drawstrings.

"Now I wonder what that's doing here," murmured

Warren. "You haven't touched any of it?"

"No, sir."

"All right, I'll get a forensics team to take it away as soon as possible; but before I do we'll just take a tiny peek inside one of those bags, shall we?" He untied one, opened the top and peered inside. "Clothes. Women's clothes. Looks like they're waiting to go to a charity shop. Well, well."

"Yes, sir," said Marion.

"Best you stay in here with the moggies until forensics arrive."

"Yes, sir."

Warren returned to the group. "Just a misunderstanding," he said. "We're not interested in Persian cats."

"They belong to a Cambridge professor," said Baxter. "I've got paperwork for them, too."

Good. No questions about whether he'd seen the wheelchair.

Behind the cattery was a third row of dog pens; only four but considerably bigger. "Used to be quarantine pens," explained Baxter, "back in the days when the poor little sods had to be shut up for six months after they were brought in from abroad, in case they were carrying rabies." Two of the big pens were occupied; one by a family of three tiny Yorkshire Terriers which ran around crazily yapping when the humans appeared, the other by a handsome Doberman Pinscher who disdainfully ignored them until Faith appeared around the corner, when he emitted two deep barks and wagged his tail for joy.

Faith came rushing over, pursued by Matt, and exclaimed, "Toby!" There hardly seemed any need to check the dog's identity further, but Waldron entered the pen and Faith went in behind him. The Cambridgeshire police dog expert ran the microchip reader over his neck, while the teenage girl hugged the Doberman and cried.

Warren glanced towards Baxter. The big man had no bluster left in him. Actually, he looked surprisingly contrite as he watched the heart-warming reunion.

Waldron looked at Warren, holding up the reader.

"Reported stolen."

"He's my Toby," said Faith, weeping with joy.

"I thought they were a dangerous breed," said PC Caborn, sounding a little nervous.

"There are no dangerous breeds, only dangerous owners," corrected Waldron.

"He's not looking very dangerous at the moment," said Warren, observing Faith tickling the animal's ears affectionately.

Baxter was making no attempt to deny responsibility, and stood rooted to the spot, staring at Faith and Toby, finally muttering self-pityingly, "I wish I'd never got into this."

Warren told him: "I'm going to have to ask you to come to the station to answer some questions, Mr Baxter."

Baxter said: "I never stole it. I was just looking after it."

Warren and Philippa were both coming around to the view that this man was more of an idiot than a criminal. Then Baxter suddenly looked Warren square in the eye and said: "There's only one thing I want to say, and that's my wife don't know nothing about this, and that's God's honest truth, d'you understand? But she spends money on stuff for the house like it grows on trees, so we've got debts, but all I do is board the dogs here for a few days, that's all, I swear, I don't get involved in the rest of it."

"Who are the men who steal and sell the dogs?"

"You must be bloody joking. They'd bloody kill me if I told you."

"Suit yourself. Only it'd go better for you if you told us who the maniac is who stabbed this young lady." He indicated Faith. "As it is, I'm only planning to charge you with being in possession of stolen property; but I've got accessory to GBH up my sleeve as well as accessory to assault on a police officer with a deadly weapon, and the judge'll throw away the key for those. Ever been to prison?"

Baxter was looking shaken and pale. "No, course not."

"I thought not. Well, if you help us arrest those men, and if what you say is true about only looking after the dogs, and I must say you seem to take good care of them, I should think you'll be looking at a suspended sentence, or maybe a community service order, which is a lot better than a few years in ... where is it they put them in Cambridgeshire, Sergeant Waldron?"

"HMP Highpoint, sir."

"Fancy that, do you, Baxter?"

"I told you, they'll bloody kill me if I grass 'em up."

Warren looked at Faith, still inside the cage petting her beloved Toby, Waldron having emerged and left her to it. "Where can we get a leash for the girl to take her dog home?" asked Warren.

"There's some in reception in the cupboard," said Baxter.

"Would you mind, Constable Merryweather?"

"I'll go and find one, sir."

"Bring one of the strong ropes," said Baxter, suddenly turning helpful, then, looking at Faith, "I'm sorry, love. I'm glad you've got your friend back. He's a fine animal."

"All right," said Warren, "I'm not going to cuff you in the circumstances, but behave yourself."

Merryweather returned with a leash, Faith attached it to Toby's collar, and he trotted contentedly beside her as the whole group returned to the main yard, where Merryweather turned to Warren with a look of slight anxiety.

"Should I go and see if Sergeant Myers and the Cambridge man are all right in the house, sir?" he asked. "It's been a while."

"They'll be having tea and biscuits with the wife," said Baxter. "I told you, she don't know nothing."

"Nobody else in the house?" asked Warren.

"If you're worried that my so-called accomplices might be there, then no. I never let them anywhere near the house. Handover at reception, end of story."

Then everything suddenly went pear-shaped.

Philippa emerged into the yard at the top end through the wooden gate from the back garden of the house. Behind her, a tall, powerful man was holding her neck in a vice-like left-handed forearm lock, with the right hand outstretched and flattened menacingly, ready to execute a sudden karate chop.

His face, staring wildly over her shoulder, was the face of Paula Gregory.

For as Warren and Philippa had understood from the photographs in the newspaper and on Sylvia Thorbinson's mantelpiece, Paula Gregory and Gavin Burridge were one and the same person: Paula, scrunched in a wheelchair under a blanket, concealing extra height and masculine build, a pretty kaftan covering her shape and adding femininity, skilfully applied make-up completing the illusion; a harmless disabled woman, unable to walk unaided, let alone run up and down two steep, narrow flights of stairs between the Theatre Royal's stage door and the stage; and Gavin, now desperate and at bay, a homicidal psychopath capable of smashing Philippa's windpipe and snapping her neck in seconds, as he had Sir Roger Nutley's.

Peter Baxter shouted at him: "Jesus Christ, you stupid bastard."

"She came upstairs," shrieked Burridge. His voice was uncannily high-pitched for a man. It was the voice of Paula Gregory; the product of a congenital vocal disorder which had helped him fool everyone at the Theatre Royal into believing he was a woman. "I couldn't get away round the front, there's two big coppers out there by my car. Now shut up, the lot of you."

"Don't be a fool," said Warren, calmly.

"I'll break her neck if you piss about."

"Like you did Roger Nutley's?"

"Shut up and listen."

"Have you any idea what happens to cop killers in jail?"

"I'm not going to jail. I want a car out of here, now. She stays with me."

Everybody listening was astonished by Burridge's voice; he sounded like one of those cathedral singers whom the Church used to have castrated to enable them to keep their beautiful singing voices after they stopped being children.

"All right," said Warren. He could see that Philippa's breathing was constrained and unnaturally rapid. "I'll drive you myself, if you want, wherever you want to go. You're in charge. But please loosen your grip a little, she can hardly breathe."

"She can breathe enough. I know what I'm doing. I was trained to restrain Taliban terrorists."

Warren mentally willed Marion not to emerge from the cattery and startle Burridge. He was aware that the man had lost all contact with rationality and might kill Philippa if he were surprised.

Facing Burridge and Philippa at a distance of five to six yards were Warren, standing in the centre and in front of the others; behind Warren, on the cattery side, stood PC Robin Merryweather and Peter Baxter; to Warren's left, Faith Goodwin with Toby on the leash, the dog sitting placidly, staring at Burridge; and to their left Sergeant Waldron. It was a motionless tableau, a freeze-frame, silent but for the quiet panting of the Doberman.

"Where do you want me to take you?" asked Warren.

"Lowestoft."

"And then? What, you think you can get away in a boat?"

"I'll sort that out when we get there. I'm a trained commando. I'll get a boat all right."

The man had flipped. He was no longer living in the real world. He had to be humoured at all costs.

"Very well. That's absolutely fine. I've got a nearly full tank in the car, we can be in Lowestoft in, what, two and a quarter hours. Now how do you want to do this? Shall I walk out to my car in front of you or..."

From that moment everything went out of control and seemed to snap into fast-forward.

Carol Baxter appeared through the garden gate, shouting, "Gavin, for God's sake, stop it." She ran forward and began tugging at Burridge's arms from behind. Burridge tried to shake her off and consequently loosened his grip on Philippa's neck enough for her to drop rapidly, vertically and hurl herself to the left, as she had been trained to do in self-defence classes. Carol Baxter was now on Burridge's right, beating at his side with her tiny fists, and he grabbed her by an arm with his powerful left hand. She screamed, and he drew back his right arm, the massive hand flattened in preparation for a deadly karate chop to her throat.

On his left, Warren heard Faith say a crisp, loud command: "Toby, bad man!" as she let go of the leash restraining the Doberman.

The huge, powerful dog flew forwards and upwards like a snarling missile of muscle and claws, and plunged snarling on to Burridge's head, neck and shoulders. He sank his teeth into the side of the killer's neck while pushing his arms backwards with his weight over his mighty front legs. The ex-commando turned psychopathic murderer crashed down on to the concrete, screaming hysterically in pain and terror. Merryweather and Waldron rushed forward. Warren turned to Faith and snapped, "Call the dog off!"

"Toby, here," commanded Faith. The Doberman obediently withdrew from the prostrate, convulsing Burridge. Trembling herself, she clipped him back on to the leash, said, "Sit", and he obeyed meekly, panting.

"I thought you said that dog wasn't dangerous," said Merryweather.

"He isn't," said Waldron. "He's well-trained to defend his owner from attack, totally obedient, and he's just saved Mrs Baxter's life."

Carol Baxter herself was now lying on the ground whimpering. Warren wondered how many times this out-of-control lunatic had reduced Iraqi and Afghan prisoners to that state. The man should clearly never have been allowed into the armed forces. He made a mental note to check into the true circumstances of his retirement from the army. Marion appeared from the cattery and said, "I've called for an ambulance, sir."

Warren approached Burridge, who was lying on his side, being restrained by Waldron and Merryweather, although the dog had taken all the fight out of him.

"Can you hear me?" he asked.

A faint, high-pitched whisper: "Yes."

"Gavin Burridge, I am arresting you for the murder of Sir Roger Nutley. You do not have to say anything, but it may harm your defence if you do not mention when questioned something which you later rely on in court. Anything you do say may be given in evidence. Do you understand?"

Burridge's reply came out in a squeak: "Yes."

"Jesus, my constable was in the house, too," exclaimed Waldron. "What's happened to him?"

"I decked him," breathed Burridge. "He'll be all right, I didn't hit him hard."

Faith was kneeling beside Toby, stroking him and weeping. "Will he have to be put to sleep for this?" she asked through tears.

Warren put a comforting hand on her shoulder. "If I have my way," he said, "he'll get a medal."

*

Less than fifteen minutes after the arrest of Gavin Burridge at the Blue Shingles Kennels, a police car drew up outside the Theatre Royal North London. Sergeant Neville Quigley and PC Andy Jasper strode grim-faced up the steps and into the foyer, where Rebecca Bunting was in the box office selling tickets for the current visiting production, a comedy by Alan Ayckbourn, which was selling well. A couple in their sixties looked around.

"Sorry to interrupt," said Andy Jasper, "but we need to see Mr Strange. Is he here?"

"I saw him come in at about ten o'clock," said Rebecca Bunting. "He's probably in his office."

"Just tell us which way to go and we'll find him," said Quigley.

"It's all right," interrupted Andy, "I remember. I stood in there taking notes of the interviews last Saturday."

"Bit of real-life drama, for a change, by the look of it," said the elderly male customer to his wife.

"Probably just a routine check on our security arrangements," said Rebecca, who had, however, discerned in the eyes of the policemen that it was anything but.

Ivan Strange was alone in his office, seated behind his desk, typing into a laptop, when Quigley and Jasper entered without knocking. Trying and failing to appear calm, he looked up and asked, "What can I do for you, officers?"

"Ivan Strange?" asked Quigley.

"Yes. How can I help you?"

"I have to ask you to accompany us to Norton Hill Police Station, sir."

"What, now? I'm incredibly busy. Can't you tell me what it's about here?"

"Inspector Warren will tell you at the station, sir. Now, if you wouldn't mind."

Ivan Strange's expression changed to one of realisation. He said no more, but switched off the laptop, closed its lid, stood up and walked out of the theatre to the police car between the two constables. A wave of nausea swept over him as he realised that his freedom was almost certainly about to be taken away from him, possibly for a long time.

As the car drew away, he remarked pointlessly, "This Ayckbourn comedy's supposed to be very funny. I'd go and see it if I were you."

3

Abigail Taverner walked into Norton Hill Police Station wearing a knee-length Hobbs summer dress in gold, maroon and black chevrons. She was crowned by an expensive Toni & Guy wavy hairstyle with highlights of subtly contrasting shades of light brown down to just below the shoulders. She wafted a haze of Givenchy's fragrance for older women, Ysatis. It was as if a pampered Afghan Hound had blundered into a room full of mongrels. Ignoring the half-dozen less enticingly fragrant representatives of north London's lumpenproletariat waiting in slumped poses of resignation on uncomfortable benches around the foyer, she marched up to the counter where the civilian Station Reception Officer on duty, Janet Read, looked somewhat taken aback by this apparition from the other side of the tracks.

"Can I help you, madam?" she asked in a manner unconsciously more deferential than she would ever have dreamed of using on Norton Hill's regular clientele.

"I'm Abigail Taverner. Your Detective Sergeant Myers left a message at my home saying she wanted to see me as soon as I returned from Venezuela. Well, here I am."

Upon hearing the name of the actress they were accustomed to watching on television as the landlady of the Queen's Head in Docklanders, the slouched forms sat up, stared and paid attention.

"I'll see if I can find her," said Janet. "May I ask what it's concerning?"

"Sir Roger Nutley."

"Right, if you could just hang on a few moments," and she phoned up to the CID room.

Three minutes later, Warren appeared in the foyer. "I'm Detective Inspector Warren," he explained, "I'm the Senior Investigating Officer in the Nutley case. If you'd like to come through..."

"Gracious, an Inspector no less. Show me the way, DI Warren."

"Thank you, Janet," said Warren.

In his office, Warren explained to Abigail Taverner that Gavin Burridge had been arrested for the murder of Sir Roger Nutley and that Helen Burridge and Ivan Strange were under arrest as his accomplices, but that he was puzzled as to how the link had been established between Burridge and Strange that had allowed them to put it into practice.

"Well, you need puzzle no more," said Abigail Taverner. "I can tell you that."

"Would you mind explaining first why it has taken you so long to come forward?"

"Not my fault. I was persuaded against my better judgment to take part in one of those ghastly celebrity so-called reality programmes. Well, I say against my better judgment, but the ridiculous money they're paying for it will come in handy. It's to be called Stars Up the Creek, and if you can think of a less appealing title, I'll buy you a drink. They flew ten of us out to Caracas, it was all supposed to be done in secret, then we were put on board a small aircraft to some God-forsaken little town with an airstrip beside the Orinoco Delta. I have to say it's all mind-blowingly beautiful, and the wildlife takes your breath away: thousands of red parrots wheeling around the sky at dusk before roosting in the forest; the roar of hundreds of howler monkeys from across the river at dawn, like rolling thunder. So, every day for the past month, except on Sundays, we were given tasks to compete at, while we travelled in small motor-boats with canvas covers around various arms of the delta and then further up the river itself, staying overnight in disused oil drilling stations that have been converted into groups of huts and little canteens for the more adventurous kind of tourist. To give you an idea, I won the competition to catch the biggest piranha fish with a hook on a string attached to a branch, which we all ate for dinner barbecued on a camp fire.

"Enough – you want to know why I didn't get in touch with you before; for the simple reason that I had no idea that you wanted to talk to me, because the production crew in Venezuela were under strict instructions not to allow any of us any kind of contact whatsoever with civilisation, because that's how it's going to be marketed, and in this day and age it has to be true or the TV companies are in big trouble with the authorities."

"I see. Very well, I accept that. Now, I gather you have something to tell me that will shed some light."

"Your problem being?"

Warren explained to her about Burridge disguising himself as Paula Gregory and working as stage doorkeeper for several weeks with what now appeared to be the connivance of the Manager of the Theatre Royal, Ivan Strange, since he was the only person who knew that Warren and Philippa had identified Paula as being Burridge, and therefore the only person who could have tipped him off to do a runner from the flat he had been using on the Hollingdown Estate.

"The problem is, there appears to be no connection between Burridge and Strange prior to the existence of Paula Gregory. They both deny ever having met beforehand. Helen Burridge flatly denies knowing anything about any of it."

"Inspector, you must realise that I also had every reason to hate Roger Nutley. Perhaps not as much as Sylvia, whom he went so far as to rape, but enough."

"I hope that isn't going to make you withhold evidence, Mrs Taverner."

"Mrs Dennison, actually. Taverner's my maiden name and stage name. My husband died several years ago, but I've kept my married name for everything except work. And no, it isn't. As I said, I hated Nutley, not just for his behaviour towards me, but even more for what he did to younger and more vulnerable girls that you probably haven't even heard about because they've never come forward."

"When you say younger..."

"I mean under-age, Inspector; but let that pass for now. The man's dead, and there's no more can be done about it; but I can't condone murder, even of a monster like Roger Nutley, and I certainly cannot be a party to enabling those who may have committed this crime to escape from justice."

"So what are you going to tell me?"

"This is how it must have happened. As you know, I live in Highgate, which is not a million miles from the Theatre Royal North London. Well, about a year ago, my agent phoned me and told me they were going to do an in-house pantomime for the first time in donkey's years, and it was going to be Cinderella. I've always wanted to play the Fairy Godmother, and believe it or not I never had before. Okay, it's not one of the country's greatest venues, but I could travel to work in twenty minutes, and it would be lots of fun, and a heck of a change from Docklanders."

Abigail Taverner then told Warren of the extraordinary chain of coincidences, stretching back over 50 years, that had led, through her becoming Cinderella's Fairy Godmother, to a convoluted plot to commit murder at the Theatre Royal.

*

Three-quarters of an hour after Abigail Taverner had made her formal statement and left, Superintendent James Astbury summoned Warren to his office. The surveillance of Cyrus Gordon had so far turned up nothing.

"I have my doubts about the manpower we're committing to this obo," said Astbury. "Chances are the bags are already sold and the gang have split up. You're going to need to convince me it's worth keeping up over the weekend, Bunny."

"I've just got a horrible feeling it would be like waiting an hour at the bus stop at night, and five minutes after you give up and walk round the corner, a bus comes by and you don't even know you missed it," said Warren.

"Run by me what he does with his time."

Warren read from the summary he'd printed out and brought with him: "Yesterday he left his flat at seven-thirty sharp, drove to Cudmore's offices, parked up his own car in the car park round the back and went inside shortly before eight. He re-emerged driving Cudmore in his Jag, they went to a cafe together for breakfast, and headed off on Cudmore's errands all over London; mostly visiting flats in central districts where we presume Cudmore has his tarts working; no rough areas, no signs of any aggro. They went for lunch in a nice pub, returned to the office for a bit, then off to Cloisters night club in Mile End in the evening, where Cudmore has a financial interest, and stayed there till late evening, then Gordon drove Cudmore home, dropped off the Jag at the office and off home in his own car just after ten. Today he seems to have the morning off, because he's been playing golf with three other men all morning."

"No women?"

"No, sir."

"Do we have photos of the three men at the golf club?"

"They've been emailed in and it's being worked on now, sir."

"It's not exactly value for money, is it?"

"He was in possession of one of the stolen bags, sir. If we don't hold on to this lead we're all at sea."

Astbury looked down at his desk and considered. "I'll give it till Monday. Then it's over."

"Thank you, sir."

Warren spent the rest of the afternoon writing up his report on the arrest of Gavin Burridge, but at twenty-past-five he answered a call from forensics.

"You got five minutes to come and look at this wheelchair?" asked Tristan Hadaway.

"Sure. Now be all right?" replied Warren.

"Absolutely."

"On my way down."

"Any way we can link it to Burridge?"

"Somebody wiped any dabs off; thoroughly, a professional job."

"What you'd expect, I suppose."

"Nil desperandum."

"Why?"

"It's not an electric one. So the user had to be constantly pushing on the tops of the big wheels to propel it along; wearing minute particles of skin off their hands all the time, some of which get ingrained into the rubber. It's called touch DNA."

"Can you get a match from that?"

"We're trying. No promises. But it's possible. It's been done before on other objects."

"Such as?"

"Gun grips, steering wheels, suitcase handles, that sort of thing."

"Jesus. It's getting tough being a criminal."

"You catch 'em, we'll pin 'em to it. But I have to warn you, it's not as easy as it is with bloodstains and other body fluids, the amounts can be so tiny, might be just a few microscopic cells. We can use either the swabbing method or the cutting method. It's a question of..."

"Whoa, enough, no need to blind me with science. You're telling me we could get a match, that's enough for me."

"Don't get too excited. Wait and see."

SATURDAY 21 JUNE

At ten-past-eight on Saturday morning a grey Ford Galaxy seven-seater cruised slowly past Cy Gordon's house. The driver reversed into the nearest parking space on that side, about sixty yards to the east, and 150 yards from where DC Mark Quinn was observing from a fake telecoms van on the opposite side of the road, west of the house. Three powerfully-built men with shaven heads emerged. They removed four large, plain, grey suitcases made of a heavy plastic material from the rear hatch and two from on the rear seats, and carried them to Gordon's house, where the leading man rang the doorbell. Quinn judged from the ease with which the visitors swung the cases that they were empty. "This could be something," he murmured to DC Paul Wigfield, beside him in the rear of the van. Wigfield called in a report, giving the registration number of the Galaxy.

While he was waiting for a response, one of the men came back out carrying two of the cases, which now looked heavier, took them to the Galaxy, stowed them in the rear hatch and got into the middle line of seats.

Down the line came a voice: "I'm trying to get hold of DI Warren. Whatever happens, don't show yourselves. If they leave, try to follow them, but don't blow your cover. If they are the gang, they were armed when they robbed the first shop, so don't take any chances. Hang on, I've got Warren here for you."

A second man carried two more cases to the Galaxy, stowed them and joined his mate on the middle seats.

"You reckon they're moving the handbags?" asked Warren's voice.

"Must be sir," said Wigfield. "Six suitcases going into a Ford Galaxy."

"Follow them discreetly as far as you can but don't get caught, I'll set an unmarked pursuit to take over asap. I'm also alerting armed response." Wigfield moved into the driving seat of the van and started the engine while Quinn took up position in the passenger seat beside him.

The third visitor to the house emerged with Cy

Gordon. They were carrying a suitcase each. Gordon locked the Chubb on his front door and they stowed the last two cases on top of the rear seats of the Galaxy. The visitor got into the driving seat, Gordon into the passenger seat beside him, the Galaxy moved off, the telecoms van following at a discreet distance. Three minutes later they were cruising northwards on Great Cambridge Road.

"Heading north on the A10," Quinn called in. "Could be they're making for the M25 and the motorways, or if we go straight over it's towards Hertford and Cambridge. Hang on, sir, we're just coming to a crossroads, we may have to jump the lights."

"If you must." Warren stopped talking to allow Wigfield to get across the junction.

A few seconds of silence, then: "It's okay sir, we got across on the amber. There's a steady queue up the dual carriageway and the target's in no hurry, there's four cars between them and me so there's no problem so far."

"There may be a rendezvous and a cash payoff somewhere. I'd like to net the buyers as well, but I'll settle for these four if it's getting tricky. Hold on a tick." A minute's silence, then: "You'll see an Esso filling station on your left. Watch out for a black BMW 5 Series coming out. That's us, then you can hang back and let them take over the visual pursuit."

"Yes, sir. I'll let you know."

"Roger. I'll shut up now and let you get on with it. And well done."

Three minutes later, DCs Gareth Wainwright and Anand Patel, based at Enfield Police Station, swung their black BMW out of the petrol station as the telecoms van slowed down to let them out. Wainwright and Patel took over the pursuit and got put through to Warren. Wigfield slowed down and allowed traffic to overtake and widen the gap between the van and the Galaxy until it was well out of sight. When the Galaxy reached the roundabout over the M25 it swung right down the slip road.

"They're going clockwise on the M25," Patel reported. "Could be heading almost anywhere, Hertfordshire or Essex or over the bridge to Kent."

"I'll hang fire on calling in reinforcements until we know which," said Warren. "For God's sake, stay on their tails."

Warren ordered Quinn and Wigfield to head home with the telecoms van. A tense twenty minutes passed before the next call came in from the BMW: "Off the M25, sir, heading up the A12 towards Chelmsford."

"I'll get Essex to take over," said Warren. "Don't want them clocking you."

"Just let me know."

Ten minutes passed.

"Just passed Margaretting, they're staying on the A12, not repeat not entering Chelmsford. We're on the bypass."

"Roger."

Three minutes passed. Warren spoke to the Enfield car.

"An Essex car will come up behind you at Junction 19; a navy blue Ford Focus. Fall back and let them pass you, then stay with them half-a-mile back."

"Roger. Approaching Junction 17. Road looks clear ahead."

The Essex car overtook the BMW as they passed a sign reading Colchester 17 miles, Clacton 33, Harwich 36, Felixstowe 47.

"They could be going for a ferry," said Warren to both cars. "If it's Felixstowe I'll have to get Suffolk involved. Okay, I'm alerting Ipswich in case."

"Roger," said DC Scott Heneghan, sitting beside DC Malcolm Bain who was driving the Focus.

Warren came on again twelve minutes later: "Colchester are sending a beige Volvo to take over at Junction 28."

"Roger."

"By the way, there's an Essex armed response team behind you now, they've just left Boreham."

On the north side of Colchester the Volvo swooped down the slip road of the quiet country intersection, passed the Focus and fell in behind the Galaxy. Moments later, the

Galaxy left the A12 on a slip road.

DC Roger Crabb in the Volvo called in: "They've taken the A120. It's Harwich or Clacton unless they stop on the way."

"Right," said Warren.

Five minutes later: "It's Harwich," Crabb called in. "We'll be there in under ten minutes. Better alert the port people, sir."

"Roger, will do."

The traffic was reduced to a crawl past road works at the village of Wix, so it was a quarter of an hour before Crabb called in again: "We've just come into Harwich but they've turned off."

"Which way?"

"To the right, at the roundabout by the Premier Inn."

"Does that lead to the ferry port?"

"No, it looks like they're heading for Dovercourt."

"What's at Dovercourt?"

"It's just a little seaside resort, joined on to Harwich. Oldie worldy bucket-and-spade place."

The Galaxy hung a right and then a left. The Essex Focus kept behind it.

"I'm having to stay to close, I'm afraid they're gonna rumble me. Where's our other car?"

"About a quarter of a mile behind you."

"Tell him to put his foot down, pass me and take over."

The Galaxy headed down a long, straight stretch called Fronks Road towards Marine Parade. Crabb saw the navy Focus race up behind him and pulled over to park so that it could pass. DC Heneghan resumed the commentary to Warren.

"We're heading towards the sea front, no, hang on, they're turning off, up a residential street, it's called Highfield Avenue, big semi-detached houses, quiet, they're pulling up on the left, I can't stop, they'll clock me, hold on, they're outside a guest house, it's called Marine View, I've gone past, I'll try going round the block, I can see in the mirror two of them are getting out. Stopping further up the street on the other side to pretend to look at a map. How far away are armed response?"

"Wait a minute and I'll find out," said Warren.

"Two of them are going into the B&B. The driver and the man next to him are staying in the Galaxy. I'm going round the block, this is too obvious."

DC Bain turned left at the top of the street into Main Road, which despite the name proved also to be residential.

Warren came back on. "Armed response are just turning off at the Premier Inn roundabout. Less than five minutes."

Three minutes later the Focus pulled up on the left-hand side of Fronks Road just short of the turn into Highfield Avenue.

"Where's our Volvo? Can you get them to cruise by and see what's happening?"

Warren came back on: "Our own BMW's just going to pass you. I'll send them by for variety."

"Nice one."

Wainwright turned the black BMW into Highfield Avenue. There was no movement around the Galaxy, but the two men were still sitting in the front seats. They ignored the police vehicle.

"They haven't clocked us, sir, I'm parking a bit further up on the right-hand side."

"Any public around?"

"No, sir, it's very quiet."

"Thank God. I'm not sure what this could be about. When they went for Harwich I thought they'd be heading straight for the ferry."

"Just a minute, they're getting out. Yep, they're going in the guest house. Maybe they need a slash. They're all inside now, sir. I suggest both our other vehicles come and park up smartish while they're not looking."

"Roger that, I'll send them round."

Thirty seconds later the Focus turned into Highfield Avenue. Bain drove to the far end and parked on the same side as the Galaxy, screened from it by a line of half-a-dozen other parked cars. After another two minutes the Volvo swung in and halted just inside Highfield Avenue on the other side.

Heneghan said to Bain, "There's a four-wheel drive with foreign plates parked up here. Hardly unusual in a ferry port but I'll go and take a look anyway." He got out of the Focus, walked to the corner of the street without looking directly at the foreign Honda CR-V, and came back. "Lithuania," he said, and called the information in.

"Which is right on Russia's doorstep," said Warren. "Ten to one that's where our bags are going."

At that moment six men emerged from the front door of the guest house. They were the four who had driven from London, and two others, shaven headed, burly, wearing ill-fitting lightweight grey suits that hung so badly they could have been tailored for east European secret policemen in a low-budget 1960s cold war thriller movie. Cy Gordon was carrying a large, hard, black briefcase. The two other men headed for the Honda.

With perfect if fortuitous timing, a Mitsubishi Pajero with silver, yellow and blue police markings swooped around the corner from Fronks Road. It raced up to just short of the Galaxy and squealed to a halt in the middle of the road. Six officers wearing black flak jackets and gloves disembarked and spread out rapidly with their automatic weapons raised. Their commander shouted, "Armed police, step away from your vehicles, lie face down on the ground; now!" In the face of the overwhelming firepower, the six men did exactly as they were told.

"We're unarmed," called Cy Gordon.

"*Yob tvoyu mats, nam predavali!*" shouted one of the Russians.

"Shut up in whatever language that is," snapped the commander.

The firearms officers moved in close and kept their weapons trained on the suspects. The four officers from Essex and two from the Met got out of their cars and searched a man each for weapons. They found none, and handcuffed the gang. DC Heneghan opened the briefcase and peered inside. It was crammed with hundred-dollar banknotes. He snapped it shut again, then went to open the rear hatch of the Galaxy, pulled out one of the suitcases and opened it. The nearest firearms officer watched out of the corner of his eye. It was full of what they were looking for.

"Handbags?" gasped the firearms bloke. "All this for some ladies accessories? You lot are having a laugh, ain't you?"

"Apparently they're worth half a million quid," said Patel.

"Now you really have got to be joking."

"Amazing how the other half live, innit?" grinned Patel.

"The other one percent, more like," said Heneghan.

*

Warren phoned Zev Mendelsohn and the owner of Sacs-à-Porter to give them the good news that their merchandise had been recovered. He also told them that all four robbers been arrested along with two couriers from a Russian Mafia gang which had bought and paid for the handbags. Zev Mendelson was full of effusive thanks and congratulations. A woman called Julia Marshall-Bradbury, who owned the shop that had been ram-raided, could only manage to say in a plummy sneer: "Well, that's what we pay our taxes for, isn't it?"

No sooner had Warren disconnected than his phone rang. It was Tristan Hadaway.

"Any luck?" asked Warren.

"Yep. We got a perfect match. Gavin Burridge definitely used that wheelchair."

"I'll tell you what," said Warren.

"What?"

"This Saturday's turning out a lot better than last Saturday. Now if England could just beat Costa Rica on Tuesday..."

"Course they will," said Hadaway. "Piece of cake."

SUNDAY 22 JUNE

"None of this would have happened if Abigail Taverner hadn't taken a fancy to being in a pantomime," said Warren.

It was another hot, sunny afternoon. Warren, Philippa, Astbury and Daniel Spiller were awaiting Sunday roast at a table with a big sunshade in the beer garden of the Norton Arms in Norton Green. The murder had impacted traumatically on Spiller's professional and personal lives, so he had driven up from Brighton to hear the explanation at first-hand from the detective who had finally assembled all the pieces of the jigsaw.

"Not my idea of joy," said the Super. "Sticking on a red nose and standing in front of hundreds of kids shouting 'It's behind you' twice a day."

"Nevertheless it seems to be something these theatrical types like doing," said Warren, looking at Spiller, who smiled and nodded. "Anyway, last July the agent phoned the company that was going to be putting on Cinderella at our local Theatre Royal, and they'd already auditioned a lot of actors for it..."

"What, in June?" interrupted Philippa, amazed.

"A lot of companies audition even earlier than that," said Spiller. "They have to start advertising the show by the time the school holidays are over in September, so they need photos of the actors who are going to be in it, in the costumes they're going to be wearing, even before that."

"Anyway," continued Warren, "she was just in time, because although they had some names pencilled in, they hadn't sent out the contracts, and they jumped at the chance of getting a massive celebrity from a TV soap. They immediately offered her the role of the Fairy Godmother. So, she started rehearsing in mid-November, and having kept up a casual connection with Sylvia Thorbinson and Carol Baxter since they'd met at the trial, invited them and their close family members to the Preview Night. Carol Baxter came with her husband, Peter; and Sylvia, who was divorced, came with her daughter, Helen. And that's where, over the drinks and canapés after the show, Sylvia Thorbinson found herself shaking hands with Ivan Strange."

"So what?" asked Philippa.

"Fifty years previously, at drama school, where they were students together, Ivan Strange and Sylvia Thorbinson, whose name was then Sylvia Goddard, had fallen in love, and during their final year became engaged to be married. Then Roger Nutley, who was a visiting lecturer, forced himself on Sylvia. She complained to the college principal, who not only called her a liar, but even threatened her with expulsion if she repeated the accusation to the police or in public, because Nutley, despite being only 27 years old, was a very valuable asset because of his TV stardom, and his patronage meant high fees and a plentiful supply of students with families able to pay them. After the rape, Sylvia found that she couldn't bear to let a man touch her, not even her beloved Ivan, and told him it would be better if they broke off the engagement. Sylvia left the college with just over a term left to go, failed to graduate, and never realised her dream of becoming an actress. She did in fact get over her aversion to being touched by a man, but it was too late for Ivan, with whom she had lost contact; and two years later she married a man who was, by all accounts, very kind, gentle and understanding. He was seventeen years older than her, widowed without children, his first wife having died very young from cancer. His name was Eric Thorbinson, and he had built up a thriving independent estate agency in Chingford. In 1968 they had a daughter, Helen, and when Eric Thorbinson retired in 1992 it was Helen who mainly took over the running of the agency. Helen met and married Gavin Burridge, who was then in the army, in 1994. Ivan Strange completed his studies, but his heart was broken, and he never managed to break into any serious acting jobs, messing about in unpaid fringe productions before giving it up, taking a one-year course in management, and going into theatre administration. He spent the next half-century nursing a powerful grudge against Nutley. The trial brought back the pain, but he stayed away from the court. Helen's ex-husband, Gavin Burridge, also stayed away, except on the day of the verdict, when he couldn't resist turning up outside the court to shout abuse at Nutley, and his face got into the background of a press photo. If he hadn't done that, we might be none the wiser now. Anyhow, over the drinks after the panto, Ivan and Sylvia agreed to meet up for lunch and have a proper chinwag about old times; and it was on the very day of their nostalgic rendezvous that the news came out that Daniel Spiller had cast Nutley in his touring production of Hamlet that was already booked to come to Strange's own theatre in June. Strange said he wouldn't be responsible for his actions if he was forced to entertain Nutley in his theatre."

"Why didn't he just cancel the booking?" asked Astbury.

"He was only the manager, not the owner," explained Spiller. "The theatre belongs to the Council."

"Still, not quite a motive for murder," said Philippa. "Nasty, but no more."

"No, but that's when a fatal chain of coincidences started to close in around Nutley. In January, during rehearsals for the Hamlet tour at Mr Spiller's home base in Brighton, unbelievably for a man in his seventies, he tried it on again with a 22-year-old actress called Libby Lennox, only fortunately he was interrupted by another young actress before things had gone too far. Young Libby was too scared to report it to Mr Spiller because she knew how valuable Nutley was to the show and didn't think he would take her word against Nutley's; but at the same time she was desperately scared that Nutley might assault her again. So she made a feeble excuse to justify walking out of the production, thereby quite possibly ruining her future career, because these things get around in the theatrical world."

"You're right," said Spiller. "I was furious."

"What an evil bastard," said Philippa. "But if she didn't tell anybody about Nutley attacking her, what difference does it make?"

"The only people she did tell were her friend in Brighton and her mother; which brings us to the subject of stage names and real names. Libby Lennox adopted that name because her real name had already been registered with Equity by another actress."

"That's quite common," said Spiller.

"So what is her real name?" asked Astbury.

"Elizabeth Burridge."

Warren paused to let it sink in.

"You're bloody joking," said the Super. "So she's, what, Gavin and Helen Burridge's daughter?"

"Adopted, yes. And therefore Sylvia Thorbinson's grand-daughter. History was repeating itself. Nutley had ruined one young actress by raping her fifty years earlier, and somehow got away with it at his trial, and now he'd had a damn good crack at doing the same thing to her grand-daughter, although of course he had no idea who she was. The family could see it all starting again, and the lecherous old bastard possibly getting away with abusing more vulnerable young actresses. Helen phoned her ex-husband Gavin Burridge, who had indeed been living in the north for the past six years, in Bolton in fact, and arranged a meeting on neutral territory where they wouldn't be recognised together or overheard."

"But she hadn't had any contact with him for six years," said Astbury. "She had no idea where he was."

"A lie. With hindsight, what divorced woman with a teenage daughter to support would allow all contact with her ex-husband to be broken off?"

Philippa asked, "Do we know where they met up?"

"They weren't taking any chances. They travelled separately to Hampstead Heath and held their conversation walking in an isolated area. They all agreed they wanted Nutley killed. Helen was the brains of the conspiracy. She saw how the operation could be stitched together. Ivan Strange would in theory have the opportunity, with Nutley having to be in various dark corners in his theatre for a week, but in practice he wouldn't have the balls or strength to do it. Gavin Burridge had the commando training to kill a man swiftly and silently with his bare hands if he could get access; and Strange could give him that access. So in the following weeks, the three of them hatched and executed a plan to eliminate this man whom they regarded as a monster."

"Helen Burridge provided her ex-husband with a place to go and take on the identity of Paula Gregory for a few months. You see, her estate agency has a sideline in managing run-down ex-council flats for housing benefit lets. They've always got some empty, so all she had to do was look one up on the computer that was on the ground floor, nip down and make sure it could be wheelchair accessible, and give Burridge the keys until the job was done."

"The Council runs the Theatre Royal partly on volunteers because there's not enough revenue these days to pay staff to do jobs such as ushers. Only the technical staff are paid professionals. One of those volunteer jobs is stage doorkeeper, so he moved the woman who'd been doing it round the front to be an usher, which she liked because you're stuck on your own all the time out the back; had a wheelchair ramp built on to the stage door, and brought in a disabled woman called Paula Gregory to do it. The only people who knew that Paula Gregory was actually Gavin Burridge were Ivan Strange and Helen Burridge."

"The plan was to kill Nutley in a spectacular fashion that would put the murder on the front page of every newspaper in the country and get the gossip columnists asking questions about why his killer had chosen to do it that way. Meanwhile, the person everyone knew as Paula Gregory had no motive to kill Nutley, she was physically incapable of going up and down the back stairs to do it, and was soon going to give up the job and vanish into thin air."

"How did Burridge manage to talk in a high voice like a woman for all that time?" asked Astbury.

"He didn't have to try. That was part of what gave them the idea. You see, Gavin Burridge suffered from a rare genetic condition called Kallman's Syndrome. It shows up as a hormone deficiency in late childhood, one of the consequences of which is that, when a boy reaches puberty, he doesn't generate the testosterone which slackens the vocal chords and causes what we call the voice breaking. The most famous case in recent history was the American jazz singer Jimmy Scott, who, by a strange coincidence, died two days before the murder of Sir Roger Nutley. The condition also makes it virtually impossible for the sufferer to have children, which is why Burridge and his wife adopted Libby."

"Sylvia Thorbinson put it more crudely," interrupted

Philippa, "saying, as I recall, the poor bugger was firing blanks."

"How did he get a wheelchair big enough to make a man of his size look like a disabled woman?" asked Spiller.

"When he came out of the army he had a leg wound and he was given a custom-made chair. It healed eventually, after a couple of operations, and he could walk normally after a few years, but the family never got around to disposing of the chair. It remained in Helen Burridge's garden shed, sealed up in a plastic cover to prevent it from rusting."

"When did the Baxters get involved?" asked Astbury.

"Not until Burridge needed a bolthole after we identified him as the killer. Strange phoned Burridge and tipped him off as soon as we'd left the theatre after demanding Paula Gregory's address, so Burridge rang his ex-wife in a panic and she called the Baxters and asked them for a favour. She doesn't appear to have told them what he had done, just that he needed to lie low from some people that were looking for him. He might have got away with it if it hadn't been for Baxter's involvement in the dognapping and if Philippa hadn't recognised their van from an earlier visit."

"I still can't understand how Nutley got off on the rape and sexual assault charges," said Spiller.

"There's nothing we'll ever be able to prove, but he had powerful friends in low places. One of his very few real friends was Ralph Tennyson de Clare; such a good friend, in fact, that he was apparently prepared to wait until kingdom come if need be for Nutley to pay off a debt of nearly forty thousand pounds he owed him for drugs, a sum of money that no ordinary mortal would have been allowed to get away with; but it's very important to Ralph Tennyson de Clare's ego that he be seen mixing in public with celebrities, and Roger Nutley had always been his entry permit to that kind of society. If Tennyson's people were able to get at any of the jurors, they could have left them in no doubt whatsoever that they would have to choose between bringing in a verdict of not guilty, and reaping a substantial financial reward, or voting to convict Tennyson's bosom pal Nutley and suffering some very unpleasant consequences, either to themselves or their families. It's what the cartels in Colombia call *plata o plomo,* which is Spanish for silver or lead, in other words, you've got a choice between accepting a bribe or being shot, but there's no middle way. Like I said, we'll never be able to prove it, unfortunately."

"So Tennyson gets away with it," said Philippa.

"Not really. By getting his old friend Roger Nutley off going inside for a few years, he got him murdered. In any case..." Warren hesitated.

"What, sir?" asked Philippa.

"I'll bring that smug, supercilious northern bastard down one of these days, if it's the last thing I ever do as a copper."

MONDAY 11 AUGUST

At 11.15am, Marion Everitt was writing up her interrogation of a photographer accused of assaulting models in his studio when her phone rang.

"There's a man on the phone asking for you by name," said Kevin Foster. "Says it's very urgent."

"Any name?"

"Dennis Griffiths. Sounds old."

"Doesn't ring any bells. Put him on, though."

The voice sounded as if its owner had been born within the sound of Bow Bells at least seventy years ago.

"Hello, is that Detective Constable Everitt?"

"Speaking."

"I've seen him again. He's here, now."

"I'm sorry, Mr Griffiths, who's where?"

"The geezer. You told me to ring you straight off if I saw him again."

"What geezer is that, Mr Griffiths?"

"The one I saw walking up and down Roedale Avenue. You know, when them burglars broke in and they only took the dog."

"I remember; but that must have been, what, two months ago. Are you saying he's back there now?"

"Not in Roedale Avenue, I'm in Bedford, visiting my son, we come out for a walk, and I seen him sitting on a bench. Got two other geezers with him, another big bloke and a younger feller."

"Bedford?" It's a bit unlikely, thought Marion. "Is the young one tall and skinny, about 19 or 20?"

"That's him."

Jesus, thought Marion. This was either a stroke of incredible luck or the old bloke's got it wrong. But Bedford. What were the chances?

"How far away from you are they?"

"About 150 yards ahead. Just walking casually around Priory Lake."

"Is that a park, or what?"

"Yes, there's a lot of other people out walking dogs."

A favourite dog-walking spot. It could be them, then.

"Mr Griffiths, do not approach those men, they are dangerous, they have a record of unprovoked knife attacks. Tell me what they're wearing."

"One older geezer, black jumper, baggy black trousers. The other one, dark green anorak, scruffy brown corduroys. Young tall one, blue jeans, grey hoodie. No hats."

"Thank you, Mr Griffiths. Now, I'm going to call Bedford police to get someone down there. Do not, I repeat not, become involved, but please phone me again in half-an-hour's time. Is that clear?"

"Absolutely. Hope it helps."

When four of Bedfordshire Constabulary's finest hurtled into the Priory Lake car park ten minutes later, it was to find two big, muscular men in their forties, Samuel and Dukey Crutcher, loading a cage containing a white pedigree standard poodle into the back of a recently repainted but old green van, while a tall, skinny man of around twenty, Nelson Ducket, waited in the front passenger seat.

At 11.55am, Dennis Griffiths phoned Marion again. She thanked him profusely for being so observant.

"Only too pleased to do me duty, sweetheart," he said. It was an occasion to let the word sweetheart pass.

At 2.30pm, Marion set off from London with Robin Merryweather and Faith Goodwin for Greyfriars Police Station, just around the corner from Bedford Prison.

At 3.45pm, Marion, Robin and Faith identified Crutcher and Duckett, who were charged by Bedfordshire Constabulary with stealing the poodle, worth £900, prior to being driven down to Norton Hill to face the more serious charges associated with the stabbings and assaults on police officers.

At 9.30pm, Marion met Nick Boyd in The Old Guinea pub restaurant in the village of Ridge, roughly half-way between Hatfield and the northern edge of London. He gave her his usual light peck on the cheek before they sat down and ordered their favourite bottle of Chianti and set about the important business of the day: deciding whether to choose pizza or pasta.

MONDAY 3 NOVEMBER

It had been a remarkably mild autumn so far, and, indeed, there had been many days in September and October which felt as warm as a good English summer's day; but as Elizabeth Burridge, wearing her navy blue duffle-coat for the first time since the previous winter, walked briskly from Kennington Underground Station to begin her day-shift behind the bar at the recently refurbished White Bear theatre pub in south London, she definitely felt the first trace of a wintry bite in the air. The gloomy weather did nothing to improve her mood. Her career as an actress, if she had one, which was doubtful, was going nowhere fast, and she had been seriously considering alternatives such as training to become an accountant. Once inside, she hung up her coat and headed towards the ladies' loo to tidy herself up a bit, when the mobile phone in her bag emitted the tinkling fairy-dust tone of an incoming text. She didn't recognise the sender's number. The text simply said: "Call me asap. DS." She cast around in her memory for the names of friends with the initials DS, and couldn't think of one. Probably a nuisance call or a wrong number, she thought. Still, what the heck. She slipped into the little ante-room to the theatre at the back of the pub for privacy, and dialled the number.

"Hello Libby," said a vaguely familiar, mature, male voice. "How are you?"

"Er, who is this, please?"

"Daniel Spiller. Is this a good time to talk?"

"Er, yes, of course, Mr Spiller. Look, I'm sorry about what happened..."

"Forget it," Spiller interrupted. "I'm fully aware of what happened, and I'm not blaming you in any way. What have you been doing since then?"

"Just a couple of fringe plays, The Shoemakers' Holiday and Three Sisters, and a student film, and some classes at the Actors' Centre."

"What have you got coming up?"

"Nothing."

"Look ... I'm going to be producing Twelfth Night

starting in February. More or less the same tour as Hamlet was this year. I'll be casting the leading roles with people I know, and I'll be posting a casting call for some of the lesser roles through Spotlight next week."

Libby hesitated: "Are you saying I could apply for one of the lesser roles, despite what happened?"

"No, I'm not. I think you'd be a wonderful Viola. So, do you want the part? It's a lead and it'll be paid well above the Equity rate."

Libby felt tears welling up.

"Libby, are you there? Do you want to do it?"

"Yes," said Libby. "Yes, yes, yes!"

"Good. Who's your agent now?"

Oh, shit, she thought.

"I haven't got one."

"No problem. I'll email you the details directly. Rehearsals start in Brighton on January the twelfth. You'll need to book some digs for three weeks."

THE END

- -

Dear Reader

I hope you have enjoyed 'Murder at the Theatre Royal'. That was the 1st Inspector Warren Mystery.

On the next pages you can read the opening of the 2nd book in the series, 'Murder of a British Patriot', which I hope will tempt you to purchase it from Amazon.

Thank you for buying and reading my work.

Albert Clack

MURDER OF A BRITISH PATRIOT

An Inspector Warren Mystery

Copyright © 2016 by Albert Clack

- -

TUESDAY 21 JUNE 2016

You never know when you might need to start up a vehicle without its ignition key, do you? You might be stuck in the desert, or trying to escape from a hoodie gang, or you might just have lost the key while you were out shopping.

Or you might want to steal one to go and kill a man.

So you have a lock-picking kit put aside, just in case, for whatever eventuality. You keep it tucked away from prying eyes in a drawer. It's not illegal to own one, but if the law caught you wandering the streets with it at two o'clock in the morning they'd do you for 'going equipped for theft'. So you only take it out with you when it's absolutely necessary, and preferably during the hours when you won't attract the attention of the guardians of our liberty. Like now. Half-past-ten in the morning on a Tuesday.

You have one that's in a nice, innocent-looking little black pouch with a zip around three sides, a bit like a pipe-smoker's tobacco pouch, only made of canvas, not leather. Mind you, the contents wouldn't seem so innocent to anybody who knew what they were looking at: a range of little rakes and tension wrenches in various sizes. They'd get you into almost anywhere you wanted to go, or enable you to fire up the ignition on all but the most modern vehicles.

And then, if you didn't want anybody to recognise you, especially if there were CCTV cameras about, which is everywhere these days, you'd go and buy an old-fashioned motorcycle helmet and goggles from a junk-shop in Camden, which is a nice long way from where you live.

You drive your car to somewhere a safe distance from where you're going to do it, a mile or so, and park in a nice, quiet, respectable street, and you walk from there carrying the helmet, with the goggles tucked inside it along with that scarf you bought for a souvenir on that holiday in Sharm el Sheikh a few years ago, the one you only wore once when you got it home and never liked because it made you look like an Arab.

You need a place where there's always lots of motorbikes parked. Outside Drummond University would be a good spot. Most of the students can't afford much so there's always a lot of old bikes there, and they're the ones that are dead easy to nick.

You spot a Honda CB250 that looks in good shape, V-registration, 1999 or 2000, so it shouldn't break down, and it's got black trim, so it won't stand out. You look around, there's nobody much about, just a couple of blokes in suits, probably teachers, walking across the other side of the car park, and they ain't interested.

Put on the helmet, goggles, scarf over your nose and mouth. Normal people are programmed to ignore and forget anyone wearing a motorcycle helmet; climb on board, pull the ignition cover off, locate the starter wires, strip the ends off and cross the brown and red ones together, taking care not to touch the bare ends or you might get an electric shock. There's a tiny spark, and the engine roars into life. Separate those live wires now and cover the bare ends with a little bit of insulation tape. Health and safety. Even thieves have to be professional about that. You ride away, casually.

You saw him on the telly; showing his face to the whole world, bold as brass. So last night you made a telephone call to the BPP office. Some woman took it. You put on a foreign accent and said you're a member of the Norwegian Fatherland Party and you're over here on holiday and you'd like to help with the campaigning to get Britain out of Europe. You said you're a big fan of Mr Marshall and you want to shake his hand and wish him luck. They told you he'll be knocking on doors on the Hollingdown Estate this morning, but they couldn't tell you exactly where. That's no problem, they'll stick out like sore thumbs on the run-down estate with their suits and red-white-and-blue rosettes.

But it's nearly all tower-blocks and you're going to have to figure out which one he's in, so you pootle around a bit on the motorbike until you see three of the idiots troop out of Simmons House: two men in suits and a woman in a trouser-suit. They walk across to Macauley House and buzz the intercom to ask somebody to let them in.

The flats are tatty-looking grey blocks bordering a car park occupied by old bangers, the only sort of motors people can afford around here. The bins stink, and there are three, no four, mangy mongrel dogs scavenging around them. The walls of Simmons House are decorated with fading graffiti like, 'Jesus loves you,' 'Taylor Jenkins is a slag,' and 'Keep Britain White.' The slogans on Macauley House are a bit cleverer, but not much: 'If you're reading this you've arrived in hell, ' and 'You don't have to be mad to live here, but it helps'.

Once the group with their rosettes have gone inside you set about gaining entry for yourself. The bell-pushes on the rectangular metal plate beside the door number from one to 64. You've always imagined your lucky number's seven, so you press it. A female Indian voice asks, "Who is it?" You say, "Delivering leaflets, can I come in please?" She mumbles and buzzes the door open.

No sign of the canvassers. You push the bike inside the ground-floor lobby, lean it up against the wall, and leave it quietly ticking over. That's the riskiest bit. In a sink like this, some bit of pond-life might nick it. Better be quick.

You take the lift to the top floor, get out, wait, and listen. There's nothing but a mysterious humming noise and an intermittent clunking. Must be lovely to live here, you think.

Refocus. Quietly work your way downstairs, flight-by-flight, floor-by-floor.

They must have started at the bottom and be working their way up. Morons, they want to run the country yet they can't work out that it's easier to take the lift to the top and walk down. Any teenage paper-boy knows that. It smells of dried-up urine and stale cheese in here. The urine you can understand, but what's the cheese about?

From somewhere down below you can hear a woman talking. You walk down as far as the fourth-floor landing, stop, and pretend to look at your phone. She's talking to an old white man who's holding his front door wide open.

Having satisfied yourself that Marshall isn't on this level, you carry on quietly down to the floor below.

And there he is, having a lot less luck than his colleague upstairs. A large middle-aged black woman has half-opened her door. She's saying, "We don't need racists like you round here. Get out of my face." And she slams the door.

You slide the weapon out from the jacket's inside pocket and point it at him. You hope he'll recognise you just before he dies, so he'll know why this is happening, even though it's only going to be a momentary flash of understanding before his lights go out for ever. He turns around and you see his face.

To be up this close is amazing.

"Long time, no see," you say. "Know who I am?"

He doesn't. You push up the goggles and pull down the scarf so he can see your face, and now he recognises you and you savour his fear, you just hold him there, frozen like a statue.

He's terrified, and you're loving it.

You steady your aim at his chest, wait five seconds to enjoy the feeling, squeeze the trigger, just a single round, down he goes, his eyes not believing what's happening. The bang is deafening in the enclosed space. You take the time to step forward and put another one in his head, just to make sure.

You pull the goggles back over your eyes, pull the scarf back up, scuttle down the stairs, brandishing the gun so the bloke with a rosette who gets in your way steps back a bit sharpish, puts his hands up.

You roar out of that nasty, smelly, dog-infested quadrangle before they have a chance to recover from the shock and start trying to remember anything about you.

Four minutes later you pull up in a residential street of little bungalows the way you'd worked it out early this morning, next to a skip with a load of junk in it that you'd spotted on the little driveway of an empty bungalow with an overgrown garden; no curtains at the windows, a 'sold' sign outside.

Nobody about, unzip the jacket, transfer the firearm to your jeans pocket, toss the helmet, goggles, jacket and scarf in the skip. Three doors along an old man reverses his little blue Skoda out on to the road, but after a few seconds he drives off the other way. No problem.

Push the bike into the bungalow's jungle of a garden where it'll be hidden by the skip, stroll the half-mile to where you parked your car; drive home, being very careful and polite to other drivers, taking care not to exceed the speed limit, because you've got a smoking gun in your pocket.

By the time you're brewing a pot of tea in your own kitchen, the top story on the radio news is the assassination of George Marshall, Leader of the British Patriotic Party, by a mystery gunman.

You've got a huge grin on your face, because Marshall got what was coming to him, and it all went like clockwork, and there's nothing, absolutely nothing at all, that could connect you with the murder.

What could possibly go wrong?

FRIDAY 3 JUNE 2016

Barry Grout was proud to be a racist. Today, he reckoned, was going to be a good day for Paki-bashing.

The insistent beeping of the alarm clock had woken him at five-to-six. His wife, Cathy, moaned quietly and buried her face in the pillow. Barry gently kissed her hair. He pulled on his tracksuit, blue with narrow red-and-white stripes down the sleeves and trousers and a small St George's Cross logo on the breast, trotted downstairs, and put on his trainers.

Moments later the self-appointed leader of the British Patriotic League was crossing the hard standing which had replaced the small garden at the front of his semi-detached house, to jog to Norton Common for his daily five-mile run. At the age of 56, he could still turn in a good time.

He had concreted two tall flagpoles into the rear corners of the paved-over area where magnificent hydrangeas had once flourished. He occasionally changed the flags, but they were always patriotic.

Nobody else was on the move yet. He was enjoying the birdsong, the fresh morning air, the swoosh of a light breeze through the roadside plane trees. The month of June had begun unseasonably cloudy, damp and chilly in London, but this suited Barry for his exercise run.

At this time of the morning, he felt as if he had north London all to himself. He drank in the fresh air so that the oxygen would flood into his bloodstream and his brain, making him alert and starting him thinking.

It was the aim of the BPL, which he considered a mass movement even though it had fewer than 5,000 members, to restore the might of Britannia, to reclaim Britain's rightful place as the foremost nation in the world, and to send home all the immigrants who had infiltrated it over the past half-century.

When that traitor George Marshall had gone off with the League's funds two years ago to set up his own organisation, the British Patriotic Party, in the hope of getting himself elected to parliament, there hadn't been enough left in the bank to organise any more demos. But today they would show the world they were back in the game with a vengeance. This was to be the BPL's first major show of strength since Marshall's treachery had left it penniless.

He quickened his pace as he crossed Birch Lane and jogged on to Norton Common, readying body and mind for a long, hard morning. He loved the change in the feel of the ground under his feet as the thwack, thwack, thwack of running on paving-stones gave way to the squidge, squidge, squidge of treading on dewy grass. The scent of the air became earthy, woody, leafy; the smell of the real England, almost like the countryside.

He was back at home well before seven o'clock, towelling himself down after a shave and a hot shower. In front of the full-length bedroom mirror he practised a Nazi salute, something he made sure he was never seen doing in public; at least, for the time being.

There was a big new mosque opening today, right in the centre of Norton. There would be hundreds, maybe thousands of Muslims, converging on it for Friday prayers. The BPL would be out in force to spoil their day.

- -

Now read on by buying

MURDER OF A BRITISH PATRIOT

from Amazon

Printed in Great Britain
by Amazon